KT-220-385

'Good-bye, till we meet again!' she said as cheerfully as she could.

'I shouldn't know you again if we did meet,' Humpty Dumpty replied in a discontented tone, giving her one of his fingers to shake: 'you're so exactly like other people.'

Alice in Wonderland, Lewis Carroll

1

Laura

I OPEN MY EYES ONE AT A TIME, WINCING, NERVOUS OF what I might find, muddled images from last night making me curl my body into a tight ball under the covers. Beside me, he is fast asleep, an unfamiliar and worrying hump in the darkness, his face to the wall, his back and shoulders covered by the duvet. Teeth gritted, I tentatively reach out before snatching my hand away.

Oh God, Laura. You are an idiot.

There are things I could have done, people I could have found some way of asking, but I didn't. I was caught up in the moment, euphoric and pissed. Then it occurs to me that he'll have a wallet in one of his pockets. If I can find that before he wakes up, there's my problem solved. I'll know his name. I am disproportionately pleased with myself for thinking of that.

I slide on to the floor, toes first and then hands. He rolls over and mumbles while I crouch frozen beside the bed. When I'm certain he's deeply asleep I pull myself up and stumble along the corridor, my palm pressed against the wall. In my bathroom, I find painkillers in the cabinet above the basin and swallow two of them.

The woman in the mirror is me, that much is clear. She looks terrible; make-up smudged, lips puffy, hair tangled. I splash my face and clean my teeth. I remember that I liked him and that he seemed to like me. I wonder if he still will. I wonder if he's even single. I suppose he must be if he's stayed the night here without a qualm. Mostly I wonder who he is. I probably shouldn't have done it, but there's no point pretending that it didn't happen. And it was so good; so hot and sweaty and downright steamy. I grimace and cringe. It's such a surprise to know that I can do that, be the woman who gets off her face and goes home with a . . . not a stranger, no, but a man of whose identity she is ignorant. Explain that to your mother.

My mind drifts. Maybe we can spend the morning together. I could cook him a fry-up. I have eggs in the fridge and half a loaf of bread. I have coffee and milk. I could nip down to my local Tesco for bacon and fresh orange juice. It opens at seven. We could curl up and watch a movie, or we could go for a walk on the Heath. I assess the sick pain in my head and groan. If he wakes up feeling anything like I do, that is not going to happen.

Last night I knew him by his pink shirt. This morning his nakedness renders him anonymous.

I should explain what it is about me that got me into this situation in the first place.

My name is Laura Maguire, I am twenty-eight years old and I am face-blind. I do not have a terrible memory for faces, I am not so uninterested in other people that I don't remember them from one day to the next, I do care about my friends, my family and colleagues and I do not have a mental health issue. Face-blindness has nothing to do with poor memory but everything to do with the way the brain receives visual information. Imagine your eye sending light to the back of the retina where the resulting image is interpreted as a face, checked against any information you already have and filed away for future reference. In my case, my brain picks it up, but instead of filing it, chucks it straight into Trash. It doesn't even stay in Trash. I could be talking to someone, turn away, and next time I looked it would be as though I'd never met them before. In and out in a millisecond. But only with faces. Bizarrely, the part of my brain that processes data about a million other objects works fine.

The scientific term is prosopagnosia. Deriving from the Greek: *prosopon* for face, *agnosia* for ignorance. Pronounce it how you like. Personally, I put the emphasis on the first syllable.

A surprising number of people experience some level of face-blindness – two in every fifty – but mine is the most profound case Professor Deborah Robinson, who runs the Centre for Face-Processing Disorders at Southampton University, has ever seen. Which is why she adores me.

I suppose I can best describe living with the condition by asking people to imagine walking through a field of sheep. I see faces, not a confusion of features, but I don't perceive any difference between them. I rely on hair, ears, gait, clothes and, most importantly, context. If a colleague is sitting behind her desk and has the attributes I know are hers – shoulder-length brown hair or whatever – then I can make a safe assumption that she is who I think she is, but I won't spot her standing near me on a tube platform. She might wish me a good morning, and then I'll know that I ought to know her, but I still won't have a clue. I'll begin to feel anxious; my palms will sweat, my fingers start to itch.

Imagine not being able to recognize your husband, your child, your neighbour. Imagine seeing a stranger walking towards you and then realizing that you are walking towards a mirror. Imagine introducing yourself to a close friend at a party or being expected to introduce people, especially when both assume you know them. Wriggle out of that one. Imagine ending up in Lost Children at a ski resort or a theme park so often that your parents are taken aside and given a stern talking to. Imagine going into a nursery to pick up your toddler and attempting to take the wrong one.

When I open the bathroom door I leave the light on so that it shines into the corridor, on to the pale laminate floorboards. I smile at our clothes strewn along them and I'm about to reach for his coat when something stops my breath. I stand, transfixed, as the Vent-Axia fan whirrs. I pick his shirt up, let it flop across my hands, then drop it as if it has suddenly wriggled into life.

The shirt is blue.

I blink, frowning, then pick it up again. I turn it around, bring it to my nose and smell it, pull the sleeves through my hand from shoulder to cuff. Whichever way I look at it, this is a different shirt. I arrange it exactly as I found it, slip back into the bathroom and close the door.

Who is the man in my bed? I realize my fingers have formed fists, my knuckles whitening as scraps of last night penetrate my hangover. Do I confront him? Or do I act like I haven't noticed that there's something wrong? I close my eyes and search my dulled memories.

Imagine waking up to discover the man lying beside you is not the man you thought you invited into your bed last night. Pink shirt. Blue shirt. What happened?

What happened to me?

2

Laura

The Day Before

AS I PUSH MY BIKE INTO THE LARGE, LIGHT-FILLED reception of the Gunner Munro Advertising Agency, angling my back against the door and trying not to hit my shins with a pedal, someone brings his bike up behind mine. He leans over, stretches out an arm and helps me through. I cross the shiny floor and press the button for the hospital-sized lift. David Gunner, who is a bit of a genius, famous for making stay-at-home dads sexy and selling a million tubes of toothpaste into the bargain, had the old goods lift from when the building was a clothing factory extended to the roof and designed a state-of-the-art bike shelter with lockers and a row of shower cubicles. They are eccentric and Scandi in style; a witty juxtaposition against the jagged London skyline. I cycle too sedately to need the showers, but I like coming up here, sniffing the wind, taking in the panoramic views before I start work.

I have no choice but to get into the lift with this man, shuffling my bike to the side and taking off my helmet. I run my fingers through the kinks in my hair. His forehead shimmers with beaded sweat and there are dark patches under the sleeves of his high-vis jacket.

'One more day,' he says to me. 'What're you doing for Christmas?'

'Going to stay with my mother. My brother and sister and their families are coming, so it's going to be a full house.' I jabber on, trying to keep up a flow of general conversation as the lift doors close and we jerk into motion. 'What about you?'

He grumbles about having to drive down to the West Country with his cousin. I don't know who he is, but as I listen my mind works, triangulating his face, looking for clues. Blokes in body-hugging Lycra are a problem, as hard to tell apart as insects.

'You are coming to the party tonight, aren't you?' he says, as the lift clunks to a stop and the doors slide open.

'I can't, I'm afraid.'

We wheel our bikes across the flat roof, still puddled from yesterday's rain, and clip them into the stands. No one bothers with locks up here. I look out over the leaden sky, listen to the sounds beyond Percy Row; traffic and drills, mainly, with the occasional blast of a siren.

I should have had an excuse up my sleeve, but, stupidly, I've failed to prepare.

He goes to the showers. I get back in the lift.

Most of the first floor, where I work, is open plan with rows of back-to-back desks running from one end to the other. Eddie and I have the luxury of an office because we need to be able to shut out the chatter. The other creative team, Guy and Jamie – or Jay, as I secretly refer to them since I can't tell them apart – have to be content with screens. But then they've only been with the company for three months.

On the other side of the building there is a large terrace, accessed from our floor, furnished with wooden picnic tables and benches. It means that workers from all parts of the agency pass through from time to time and it makes the media floor the most sociable area of the building.

We don't wear suits at Gunner Munro but there is a uniform all the same and amongst the men it's black jeans and a casual shirt. A lot of them have beards and tattoos – the tattoos are great as far as I'm concerned, but whoever invented beards has made my life hell. Women show a more helpful flair for individuality, but they are apt to change on a whim. I cope by not making assumptions. If someone turns up with a brand-new bob and a fringe, I don't panic. I wait and see where they go.

People think I'm a dreamer, that my thoughts are elsewhere, focused on the product, ideas crowding out real life. I come up with the goods, so I'm forgiven my social inadequacy.

Eddie hasn't arrived when Rebecca Munro walks into our office on a waft of the expensive perfume that is her signature scent. I know what make it is, because she keeps a bottle in her bag and I've seen her spray it. Joy by Jean Patou. Not that I need help recognizing her. My boss is fabulous; she has style and pizazz, an unmissable presence and a head for business. She is highly successful and in demand as a speaker. Her TED Talk on Women in Advertising has had over ten thousand hits and is well worth a listen.

She gives me a look, part sympathetic, part speculative. 'Do you have a minute, Laura?'

'Of course I do.'

I try to read her tone and feel that familiar, unwelcome tension in my diaphragm that precedes anxiety.

'Apparently, you're not coming to the Christmas party this evening.' Rebecca rubs her temple.

'You know parties are hell for me.' I say it with a grimace, brushing it off as though it doesn't matter at all. I wonder who dropped me in it.

Rebecca rolls Eddie's chair out from behind his desk and sits down. She folds her arms across her ample breasts, crosses one slender leg over the other and studies my face.

The problem for me is that I've chosen a career in which mixing with people is part and parcel of the job. Being an Art Director isn't just about the ideas, it's about enthusing the client, getting your passion for their product across. It's vital to be able to engage with others, and for me that means working harder than my colleagues.

'Laura,' Rebecca says, 'I understand that it's tough for you, but this business doesn't make allowances. If you're going to cut it, you'll have to make more of an effort.'

I nod, but I'm hurt. It isn't about effort with me, and she does know that, she just doesn't seem to see why it can't be overcome. Rebecca is the only person outside my family that I've told about my face-blindness. I felt I had to when she took me on. She understood, as a woman, why it makes me feel vulnerable, why I would insist on keeping it quiet, even though telling people would surely make my life easier. She promised that I could trust her to keep it confidential. It doesn't mean I get special treatment though.

'I don't want to upset you,' she says, 'but we're about to enter a brand-new year. It's a good time to check in on staff, pick up on any little things that need tweaking. I know you have your difficulty. But you're an adult, you'll just have to deal with it.'

I can feel the heat rising up my neck to tinge my cheeks. 'I always go to the campaign launch parties.' I often have a hand in their organization. It gives me a degree of control over what happens on the night and where to expect to find particular people. It's the other stuff; the drinks after work, the matey games of ping pong in the basement, the endless opportunities to make mistakes and cause offence that give me problems.

She runs her fingers through her long dark hair and sweeps it behind her shoulders. She's wearing diamond studs. Although, at a glance, one person's earlobes look very similar to another's, they actually differ a lot. I watch her mouth as she speaks.

'But you don't come to staff socials and these things matter. I understand we can't all be party animals, and between you and me I can't think of anything worse. But despite that I will be there tonight, and I will be seen to enjoy myself, because I am part of the team and I value my teammates. You can't let your face-blindness affect your ability to do what this company needs you to do. You know that.' She glances at her watch. This is almost over. She takes a deep breath and sits forward.

'I hate to say this to you, but if you don't come, what the rest of the team might take from that is that you don't see yourself as an integral part of Gunner Munro. And if that is the case, then maybe you should think about how much you really want to work here.'

My jaw drops at the unfairness of it. I am fiercely loyal to the company and incredibly grateful, but the idea of walking into a bar full of people I'm meant to know makes me feel physically sick.

'I love my job. I just don't enjoy parties. I get into a panic because I don't know who's talking to me.'

'Laura, you told me that you created your own strategies as a child and got by. Maybe you need to create some more, to deal with your adult life.'

As if I don't already.

She stands up and pats me on the shoulder. 'Come on. Cheer up. It'll be fine. You'll wing it. And you can always come to me if you're stuck.'

I nod because I can't think of anything to say. She's right. If I'm going to survive and prosper in a job I love, I have to make it work. It's my problem, no one else's.

'Of course. I'm sorry. I'll be there.'

'Good, I am glad. Because if you're happy then I am happy, and Gunner Munro is happy.'

As she opens the door Eddie comes in. He looks from her face to mine and raises his eyebrows. Eddie is no problem. Although I don't recognize him either, this is his office and I know that he has a beard, wears a wedding ring and most usefully has the Arabic for *love* tattooed on his right wrist. I thought it was a sledge.

'Morning,' he says. He pulls a tissue out of his pocket and blows his nose. 'Sorry, filthy cold.'

'Poor you.' Rebecca edges away from him. She leaves the room and he drops down on to his chair.

'Ugh. Warmed by the boss's illustrious derrière. Everything OK?'

3

Laura

I SIT OUT ON THE TERRACE, SHIVERING WITH COLD, MY mobile pressed to my ear, hunched over my body, my booted feet aligned on the grey decking. In the background, my nephews are having an argument in French.

My sister married Eric Larebie ten years ago, after meeting him at university. They moved to France when my nephew Dominic was born, so the boys are fluent in both languages and my sister could pass for a Frenchwoman. They live in Paris, in a baroque apartment in the ninth arrondissement. Eric works for Banque de Paris and Isabel teaches at her local *école maternelle*. I miss her. When things go wrong, I find it so much easier to tell her than I do Mum.

Dad, on the increasingly rare occasions that we speak, doesn't listen anyway. Or actually he does, he listens for pauses so that he can turn the conversation back to him. And his wife is often in the background, gabbling away in Spanish.

Mum is a worrier, so I let her assume that it's all easy now, that my coping strategies are so firmly rooted I barely notice my condition. Even so, she always wears the ruby ring she inherited from her grandmother. My sister has a tiny tattoo on her left wrist. A swallow. She did it for me when I was eighteen, the year we found out that I wasn't extremely forgetful, there was something wrong with me.

'Calm down,' Isabel says. 'It's only a party. Everyone will be so pissed they won't notice if you make a mistake, or if they do they won't remember. Your boss is right, *chérie*. If you don't muck in, people will think you're standoffish and you'll never get on.'

I love it when she calls me *chérie*. 'They already do,' I say. 'And perhaps I don't want to get on.'

'Don't be pathetic,' she says with a laugh.

I stare at the grooves in the decking. My fingers and toes are getting cold.

'Who's going? Is it the whole company?' Isabel asks, then interrupts herself. '*Dominic, tais-toi! Milo, arrête d'énerver ton frère, s'il te plaît!*'

'Yeah. But we've hired the bar, so at least I won't molest any strangers.'

Isabel laughs. 'But you are intending to molest someone?'

'Chance would be a fine thing. When's your flight?'

'Four o'clock. So, I'll see you tomorrow evening. Try and relax tonight, OK, and be open if someone chats you up. You are a beautiful woman and you should be in a relationship. You spend much too much time on your own.'

'That doesn't help.'

But she's right. If I wasn't going this evening, I'd only mope. I'd watch a film – preferably one with only two characters – then drag my feet into the bathroom where I'd greet the stranger in the mirror before cleaning my teeth. I'd think about the fun the rest of them were having as I slid into bed, imagining the thump of the music, the flushed faces, the pumping arms. Perhaps I'd even sing a Christmas anthem to myself.

'You've gone quiet,' Isabel says.

Someone comes out and lights a cigarette. Two scavenging pigeons fly up on to a ledge, feathers ruffling in the breeze. I move towards the door. 'Please stop worrying about me.'

'You can tell me all about it tomorrow,' Isabel says.

I smile at the smoker and murmur a greeting before ending the call. He nods. I do not have a clue who he is.

The mood in the building is buoyant, Christmas songs playing from someone's computer. We've all crowded into the top-floor conference room to hear David give his pep talk. He is dressed in a diabolical Father Christmas onesie and hat. I'm standing with Eddie, watching.

David Gunner is in his element, loving his audience and feeling our love for him. With his boundless enthusiasm and his constant reiteration that we are the best, it's impossible not to absorb some of his magic and feel bigger and better than we really are. It's his enthusiasm and his often-voiced gratitude to even the lowliest member of staff that ensures our loyalty. At a time in my life when I was nervous and unsure, he made me feel that my input was valuable. That's his skill: he talks to people as though he thinks he can learn something from them.

'Gunner Munro has had a phenomenal year and we are in terrific shape. Now I'm not going to give you a load of stats – for one thing, Bettina has neglected to provide me with a whiteboard . . .'

'Thank Christ for that,' Eddie mutters.

'But suffice to say, with a little help from our big brands, we are nudging upwards and competing more than well with the market leaders. We are young and dynamic and, frankly, those dinosaurs can learn from us. You have all worked incredibly hard, and I could not have hoped for a more loyal, good-humoured and talented bunch of people. I'm going to shut up now, because Secret Santa is ready and waiting, but before I let you go, I have an announcement to make.'

Eddie nudges me, and I turn and wrinkle my nose.

'We're on the shortlist for the GZ contract. For those of you who have been living at the bottom of a well for the last three months, this is huge. Bettina, could you do the honours?'

Bettina moves amongst us carrying a tray laden with shot glasses two-thirds filled with a sunset orange liquid. I've already tried it, but I enjoy watching my colleagues sipping gingerly and raising their eyebrows. It's too sweet for me and tastes like something that should be kept in the bathroom cupboard for medicinal emergencies, but American kids love it and it certainly packs a punch.

'Zee pronounced the American way, guys. I don't want to hear anyone saying Zed and I don't care if your

English teacher turns in her grave. It's GZ to you and when you're at the bar it's "A GZ, please, guv," not "A glass of your finest fucking Generation-Zed." The guys in social media will give you the hashtag so you can get a conversation going online the instant we get the green light.'

The client wants something anarchic, something that will appeal to British youth; something that will go viral.

'Delicious,' he finishes, raising his glass. 'To GZ. This should get you in the mood for tonight. I want you all to be peeing amber tomorrow.'

This is met with appreciative laughter and some covert grimaces.

'We're up against the big boys on this one, but we're on that shortlist for a reason. They've looked at our campaigns, so they know we're not scared to be disrespectful or give a toss about deviating from the norm. Our strength is that we might not always take the traditional route, but we keep it simple, we get it noticed. They fucking love all that shit. Eddie and Laura, obviously, I don't expect you to work through Christmas . . .'

I glance at Eddie and raise my eyebrows.

'. . . but I want to see something on the first day back.'

'Here you go.'

Bettina plonks a cardboard box down on the floor and kneels beside it. Bettina is an intern who is desperate to get taken on in any capacity, but her long-term aim is to be a copywriter, so she makes herself especially useful to me and Eddie. She came to us through Graham Ludgrove. Graham has been here as long as me; in fact, we initially met at the interview for the Art Director job. I got it, but they offered him the company website, which he redesigned, rebuilt and now manages, working closely with Finn, the social media expert and one-time YouTuber who sits beside him.

Bettina pulls out a sparkly plastic headband with star antennae and loops it over my outstretched hand. The blokes are all wearing antlers. I asked Bettina to order them, because it was expected – part of the fun – but they're not going to make my life any easier.

'Thanks.' I dutifully arrange it in my hair and flick the stars so that they bounce from side to side.

At six I leave the building with everyone else from my floor, sticking to Eddie's side. I know the man behind us is Guy because he was still working and Eddie had to drag him away from his desk. He's wearing a green and maroon scarf.

Guy comes up beside me at the traffic lights and grins. 'You've done well to get that brief.' He sighs. 'Cat food is a bastard. Ever since "nine out of ten owners . . . " Nothing has come close to following it.'

I know what he means. That campaign wormed its way into the public consciousness. It's unforgettable, and it's nothing, just a set of ordinary words. And that's pure chance, alchemy.

'You'll come up with something.'

He looks perfectly cheerful. I doubt he's losing sleep over it.

'Got to earn my stripes,' he says. 'I'm glad you're here this evening. Jamie said you weren't coming.'

Jamie? Was that him in the lift then? 'Oh. Well I was, and I am.'

My colleagues are surprised to see me, but no one is complaining. They're a friendly bunch. We set off towards Curtain Road in high spirits, scarves and gloves protecting us from the biting cold. At Hoxton 101, we negotiate the crowded bar and file downstairs to the basement where our coats are whisked away. We wander into a darkened room, low-ceilinged to the point of claustrophobia and throbbing with sound. There are already a dozen people there – accounts and IT, I'd guess, because they're the ones who tend to leave work dead on five o'clock whereas the rest of us have to be more flexible with our hours.

The bar has been provided with a generous subsidy of £1,000, so after knocking back a compulsory shot from the tray of GZ, I fortify myself with a double vodka tonic, downing it quickly to get rid of the lingering taste of the product. I stand at the bar for a few minutes, looking round for someone I can recognize, and the barman passes me another glass with a sympathetic smile. I sip it quickly, feeling uncomfortable, until I spot Bettina's glorious, tumbling black curls and join her on the dance floor. My plastic headband feels tight, but I'm determined to keep it on; to show Rebecca that I can be one of the team. Bettina grins at me. The music pulses through my muscles. Under the revolving disco lights people move in and out of my vision, a blur of indistinguishable faces.

But there is no need to worry. It's far too noisy for conversation and with two double vodka tonics already downed, not to mention the GZ, on top of an empty stomach, my natural reserve is starting to go. I'm doing my thing, not caring who with. I move to the rhythm, singing along with the others, my arms in the air, my hands curled into fists, egged on by my friends, whoever they may be. I feel freed, ecstatic, my body escaping, the alcohol and the music fuzzing the sharp edges. And if that wasn't enough to fill my cup to overflowing, I'm being pursued in the nicest possible way. I don't know who he is, but he keeps getting in front of me, edging other men out, copying my moves. It's as if he's desperate for me to notice him. And it's working.

'Laura!' he bellows.

I look at his face, scanning hair and shape, trying to ignore the ridiculous antlers, hoping to find something that identifies him. Even his voice is unrecognizable; slurred by booze and drowned in noise. In any case, voices have never been all that helpful to me, not unless there's a distinctive accent.

He holds out his hand and I take it. He whirls me into him and away and I giggle hysterically as I twirl under his arm. He's wearing a pale pink shirt, with the sleeves rolled up; the only pink shirt in the room as far as I can see. Its colour changes with the flashing lights, but it's still recognizable from its white collar. Once I realize this, I relax. He is Pink-Shirt from now on, and I stop trying to study the precise curve of his ear or the size of his Adam's apple. I'm enjoying myself.

We dance, behaving like kids, uninhibited and a little

bit stupid. Occasionally Pink-Shirt pulls me into his arms and murmurs flattering nonsense, most of which I can't hear. It's extraordinary how close you can feel to someone within such a short space of time. I'm drunk and all over the place but the unexpected is happening. I want to touch him, and he wants to touch me, and soon we're sneaking away from the dance floor and into a dark corner and he's holding me, and his cheek is pressed against my head. He is sweaty all over, his shirt glued to his back, but I don't care. It's me and him and lips and hands and damp tendrils of hair plastered to foreheads. It's giggly and sweet and I am happy and out of control.

'I need to take a piss,' he says. 'Don't go away.'

When he leaves my side, I lose confidence, unanchored in a sea of strangers. I move to the bar and order another vodka. Bettina is beside me, her arm pressing against mine.

'Having fun?' she shouts.

'Yes!'

'Hurrah for that!' She dances off into the crowd.

That pierces my good mood. Is that the impression I give? That I don't normally have a good time? The vodka goes down even quicker than the first two. Someone squeezes into the space beside me and orders a drink, then he puts his mouth close to my ear and says:

'Dark horse.'

He touches my waist and the hot dampness of his palm soaks through to my skin. I don't know who it is, but I know instantly that I don't like him.

I detach his fingers, leave the bar and weave across the floor, in search of Pink-Shirt.

'Thought I'd lost you,' he says when I find him.

I remember, years ago. I must have been fourteen, because it was the first house party I'd been invited to; the first at least that involved boys, illicit alcohol smuggled in under bomber jackets, disco lights and dance music, much like this one, with people, particularly the boys, going way over the top. Like tonight the music was loud, making it impossible to talk, like tonight I drank to get rid of my nerves. I exploded out of my bubble, unfurled my wings and shed my inhibitions. And, again like tonight, a boy made a play for me. I knew his name because some girl squealed it as she threw her arms around him, but by the end of the evening he was paralytic and barely able to string a sentence together, let alone ask me for my phone number. Back at school on Monday, faced with a hundred lookie-likies in their frayed uniform trousers, mucky-collared white shirts and blazers, I couldn't find him without asking someone, and I wasn't going to do that. I hoped he would find me and, if he was shy, make some excuse to bump into me by-mistake-on-purpose. We had made out after all. When that didn't happen, I made myself available, hanging out where I could easily be seen at breaks and lunch and at the end of the day. But to no avail. He never approached me and none of the girls came to whisper in my ear that he fancied me. And then I heard he was having a party – a gathering really – at his house. Only a select few invited, but not me. I pity my fourteen-year-old self. It's tough enough being an adolescent when you can recognize your fellow man. I couldn't slip out of the way whenever I saw him coming, because I never saw him coming. I moved through those days in a permanent state of alarm.

I am bursting for the loo, so even though I don't want to leave Pink-Shirt's side again, I sway through the crowd, turning more than once, checking where he is, like Hansel trying to remind himself of the way back through the woods.

4

Rebecca

THE MUSIC FEELS AS THOUGH IT'S INSIDE REBECCA'S head, its pulse sandwiched between her brain and her skull. She cannot take much more of this. She stands beside the bar, her smile feeling as though it's been stitched in place, making her jaw muscles ache and the metallic pain in the right-hand side of her face even worse.

She's happy to see Laura is enjoying herself. She's thrown herself in with an abandon that Rebecca would find funny, if she didn't feel so awful. Laura is shaking her stuff, hands combing through her hair, like a sex kitten. She is the last person Rebecca would have described as a sex kitten so it's touching to see her letting go like this. At least she doesn't need to feel guilty about insisting she come. Laura's difficulties are irrelevant here. No one could possibly notice.

Unable to tolerate alcohol, she sips from a glass of fizzy water, dreaming of her bed, her cool sheets and plump pillows. She wants to curl up and let the paracetamol do its work. She has already let her boyfriend know that tonight is off. She'd only be cranky. He certainly wouldn't get any sex.

Not that he would mind. They have been together for seven years and have known each other for nine and he's seen her at her worst; revolting with flu, lying in a sea of snotty tissues, her nose raw from being blown too often. He's seen her angry and he's seen her heartbroken. He's seen her snappish and irritable.

Why does she do this to herself? Sometimes she thinks she will break in two. She remembers lying beside his wife on a sunlounger at their house in the South of France, him and their children splashing around in the pool, and noticing the curve of her friend's belly. She knows that if he was going to leave his family, he would have done so already, but she's not giving up. They are meant to be together.

She flinches at a wave of pain. Her head is pounding, and she feels sick. She discreetly checks the time on her phone. It's only twenty past nine. The strobing lights are too much, they confuse and half blind her. She breaks out in a cold sweat and rushes into the poorly lit atrium, locates the door to the Ladies, bangs into a cubicle and throws up.

When she comes out, Laura is pulling back her hair and swallowing water from the tap. Her face is flushed, her eyes bright.

Rebecca studies her own reflection in the mirror. It would be hard for her to look ugly, but the downlights don't do her any favours.

Laura hands her a couple of sheets of paper towel from the dispenser. 'Are you all right? You're as white as a sheet.'

'Migraine. I'm going home.'

'You poor thing. I'll get your coat for you, if you like.'

Laura is slurring her words and Rebecca's coat is cashmere. She doesn't want it handled clumsily or dropped on the sticky floor.

'That's sweet of you, but I can manage.' She takes the little fold-up brush she keeps in her clutch, runs it through her hair and gives Laura a wan smile. 'I was meant to be seeing someone tonight. Best-laid plans, eh?'

She takes a deep breath and heads for the door. Graham is just outside, his coat hanging over his arm, a guilty look on his face. She's sure she had a question for him earlier, about the website, but for the life of her . . . Anyway, this is not the place.

'I need to be somewhere,' he says.

'OK,' Rebecca shrugs.

She is way past caring who sneaks off and who stays, but she doesn't want him to know she's going in case he suggests sharing a taxi, so she walks back into the party. The lights feel as though they are out to get her.

David is talking to Guy, shouting in his ear and gesticulating. Rebecca makes her way over and taps David on the shoulder. He turns and smiles, his eyebrows raised.

'I'm off,' she says. 'Sorry to leave you playing dad to this lot, but I've got a horrible migraine.' She decides not to mention the puking. It's not a good look.

He nods and kisses her cheek. 'Look after yourself and have a lovely Christmas.'

'You too,' she responds. 'See you both in the New Year.'

It's too noisy to say anything else, so she leaves them. She finds Laura standing by the door, scanning the crowd.

'You OK? No problems?'

She can see why Laura hates this sort of thing. It must be so confusing for her. She feels a twinge of guilt but absolves herself. She made her come for the sake of the company as a whole, because the team is more important than the individual.

'Just catching my breath.'

'Well, I'd better . . .' She indicates the stairway that Laura is blocking, and the girl moves and stumbles.

'Oops.'

'Laura, perhaps you should slow down a little. The night is young.'

'I will. Don't worry about me.'

Rebecca pauses, then decides to leave it. She is not her mother. But when she gets to the top of the stairs and looks back, Laura is still standing there. Fight or flight, Rebecca thinks instinctively. Poor thing.

Upstairs in the public bar, there's another Christmas party in full swing, this one possibly even more raucous than theirs. The revellers make room for her, holding their glasses out of the way, wishing her a cheery farewell. 'Fairytale of New York' is playing, the crowd bellowing the words.

Someone shouts, so close to her ear that she jumps, 'Stay with us, gorgeous!'

Rebecca pushes through to the doors and bursts outside with a sigh of relief, the cold temporarily easing her headache. Her taxi is waiting, the ticking of its engine cutting through Kirsty MacColl's voice. She gets in, tucks herself into the corner and closes her eyes.

5

Laura

AT THE END OF THE NIGHT, WE FETCH OUR COATS. Mine is the lightweight down jacket I use for winter cycling. My bike is still on the roof. I think that's a good thing. I can't stand straight, and I don't want to land in the gutter. That would be bad. I have a feeling there's more vodka in my veins than blood. I wish I hadn't drunk the GZ as well.

The cold air on the street is great after the stuffy basement. Really great. I press my hands against my cheeks. This is red-nose weather. I hope I don't have one. I touch the end of my nose and Pink-Shirt laughs and kisses my mouth.

'Damn. Forgot my scarf,' he says. 'Don't move, I'll be thirty seconds.'

He's gone. I stand on my own, feeling like an idiot, surrounded by loads of people I don't recognize puffing out fog and bellowing, 'Happy Christmas!' at each other. It's like I've walked into my worst nightmare. I edge away from the kerb, steadying myself against a bollard. Fortunately, no one expects me to say their name, they're all too drunk.

'See you in the new year, you jammy bastard!'

'Has anyone seen Kerry?'

'Got to run, I'm going to miss the last tube!'

'Someone check on Guy, he's absolutely hammered. He shouldn't be cycling.'

Eddie appears in front of me and gives me a huge hug. 'Aren't you glad you came tonight?'

'Yes.' I kiss his bearded cheek. 'How're you getting home?'

'I'm not. I'm staying the night with my brother. What about you? I'm going in the opposite direction, or I'd share a cab. You're not getting on your bike, are you?'

'Uh . . . no. I don't think so,' I laugh, gripping his arm to steady myself. 'I'm practically seeing double.'

This is major for me, this human contact, the hugs and smiles. Someone else speaks to me, grips my shoulder, her mouth pulling into a wide grin. I don't know who, but it doesn't matter. I wish her a happy Christmas.

Pink-Shirt should be back, but I can't find him amongst the other men in their overcoats. I start to panic, my gaze darting from face to face, frantic, thinking I've been abandoned, that I read the signals all wrong. It's only seconds but it feels like minutes before he takes hold of my hand.

'Come on,' he says. 'I've got us a cab.'

I grin with relief and hold on tight. He steers me along the kerb and around the corner, where the minicab is waiting. He opens the door and I get in and collapse into the seats, my eyes closing as my cheek comes to rest against the window. There's a slight delay and I think I may even have nodded off in the few seconds before he asks me for my address. Figuring out where the hell I live wakes me up. The driver pulls out and moves off, braking with a curse as a man sways across the road into his path. Pink-Shirt automatically throws his arm across me. I allow him to leave it there for a while, and then to curl it around my shoulders. I lean on his shoulder, snuggling into the warmth of his coat, and breathe in the mixture of wool and frost. When he turns and tips my head up and kisses me I don't protest. My mind is blurry, but I do know what's happening, what I want. I'm fed up with my life; fed up with being careful all the time. I want to cut loose, misbehave for once, and I'm in no fit state to argue myself out of it. I let my lips part on a sigh. I am really, really hammered.

He makes a funny noise in his throat, then drags me against him. I don't care what the cab driver thinks. We kiss all the way back to Kentish Town, his hands exploring under my jacket, warm and firm against my ribcage, my hands curved round his neck and jaw.

Outside my flat, he presses me against the wall at the top of the stairs while I fumble for my keys and drop them. He scoops them up and unlocks the door without letting me go. It flies open and we collapse inside. I reach for the light switch, but he grabs my wrist and stops me, and then it's like in the movies as we strip off each other's clothes with clumsy hands and leave them in a trail that snakes along the corridor to my bedroom. He moves me backwards, step by unsteady step, kissing my neck, barely managing to keep us both upright. I kneel on my bed and twitch the curtains closed as he undoes my bra and removes my knickers.

'Do you have anything?' he whispers.

I reach into the pine drawer beside the bed and riffle through hair elastics, pens, packets of Nurofen and other miscellany until my fingers touch a small square of metallic wrap. He rips open the condom packet with his teeth and rolls it on while I watch, grinning. This is the first sensible thing I've done all evening.

We tumble on to the mattress, an ungainly tangle of legs and arms, and make love like animals. He's strong and a little aggressive, but I like it. I have never had sex like this before, never had anyone do to me what he is doing to me, never been so brazen in my life.

Later, I pass out with my head on his chest and his arms around me, my world revolving.

6

Laura

The Present

WHO IS THE MAN IN MY BED?

The man I thought I brought home was wearing a pink shirt. I know that for a fact. It's the only fact I can rely on.

Under the white glare of the halogen spots, I stare down at my naked flesh, at the invisible tracks of his lips. There have been times when my face-blindness has caused excruciating embarrassment on my side and resentful confusion on someone else's. There have been farcical mix-ups; dates when I've met one man, thinking I'm going to meet someone entirely different, our conversation at cross purposes until he realizes that it wasn't him I wanted. There have been family functions, weddings and funerals when I've had to feign a sudden and intense headache to avoid the risk of introducing an aunt to a cousin, my brother-in-law to a friend of long standing. There have been countless times when I have wanted the ground to swallow me whole. But never in my wildest imaginings could I have come up with this.

The fan is even louder and more erratic than usual, then I realize that what I am hearing is my own breath. I look around me, trying to wake up properly, to bring some order to my mind. Am I the victim of a crime? At that thought, tears suddenly well and spill down my cheeks. Whatever has happened isn't good, it's wrong. I smear the tears away with the back of my hand and blow my nose. I'm confused. Is this something I should report? But what would be the point, when I don't know what *it* is? An echo of last night suddenly ricochets through me, an erotic charge that I cannot stop, that sends a hot flush into my cheeks. I see us writhing on the bed, and I see myself kissing his jaw, licking the salty sweat from his skin. What will it prove? Someone is going to look like a liar, and in all likelihood that someone will be me. And there are those uncomfortable truths: I consented. I participated. I enjoyed it.

If I do tell the police, I can imagine how the conversation will go.

So, what makes you so sure this is not the man you spent the evening with?

The man in Hoxton 101 was wearing a pink shirt. The man in my bed stripped off a blue shirt.

Are you telling me that he changed his shirt?

No. It was two different men. One in a pink shirt and one in a blue shirt. I liked the man in the pink shirt, I did not like or encourage the man in the blue shirt. He tricked me.

Are you sure you didn't get it wrong? Are you sure

the disco lights didn't affect the colour of his shirt? It can happen.

I did not make a mistake. His shirt was pink.

Did you or did you not consent to have sex?

I did, but I didn't know it was a different man.

I imagine the policeman leaning back and scratching his head. He will study me for a few seconds and then he will say something like, *Let me get this straight. You were under the impression that the man you invited into your home was the same man who had been paying you attention all night. You had drunk at least five vodka tonics, if not more; not to mention the glass of GZ you forced down to please your bosses. You were, by your own admission, out of your skull. You wake up the next morning and discover the man you slept with had been wearing a different shirt to the one you remembered him wearing. Despite enjoying your sexual encounter, you would be willing to destroy a man's reputation based on the colour of his shirt and a drunken memory?*

Yes. No. I don't know!

I think that deliberately concealing your identity from the person you have persuaded to sleep with you could be a criminal offence. I'll have to look it up. But even if it is, can I prove that he did that? He could just as easily swear that I knew who he was, that he told me. I run my fingers over my body, pressing at the tender areas. We were rough with each other, me as much as him. He is all over me; his saliva, his skin cells and traces of semen. If I get in the shower and wash those traces away, then they're gone for ever, along with my credibility. I sit on the side of the bath and make myself work through last night, examining what I can remember about the man I danced with. It isn't much. I need to go through his coat pockets.

I slide the bolt across, careful not to let it click, but as soon as I cross the threshold my stomach heaves. I slap my hand over my mouth and throw up into the loo. When the retching stops, I hear something and the hairs on the back of my neck stand on end.

A dull click. The familiar sound of my front door closing. He's left the flat. I burst out on to the landing, but I'm naked, so I scoot back in and run to the front window, wrap the heavy curtain around me, clutching it together over my breasts, release the bolts and shove it up, shouting, 'Hey!' at the figure sprinting down the road. He doesn't hesitate, doesn't look back.

In the hallway, my shirt and my black jeans sprawl like a deflated version of me. My tasselled ankle boots are leaning against the skirting.

I wander back into my bedroom, stand over my bed looking down at the rumpled sheet and duvet, the pillow with the imprint of his head in it. I pick it up and bring it to my nose and inhale the scent of my own shampoo. I press my face into bedding that smells of sex.

He's been busy. The condom is nowhere to be found. I pull back the duvet and search for evidence that he has been here, but there is nothing, not even a stray hair or a scrunched-up tissue. He must have woken up when I did and realized the trouble he would be in if he didn't run. Coward.

I open the curtains. In the time that I have been shut in the bathroom, a grey, hung-over dawn has broken. It's raining, not frozen like yesterday, and the clouds hang low and dark. The street feels dead, shut down for Christmas, the families packed up and gone to grandparents with houses in the countryside, the flat-sharers back to family homes. I glance at the digital clock. Was it only twenty minutes ago that I thought I might be spending the whole morning with him? I drag the duvet off the bed and take it into the sitting room, where I spread it on the sofa, crawl underneath it and curl up in a ball as tears spring to my eyes. I don't know what this means. My head aches, and when I try and work through the muddle I get a wave of anxiety, an urge to push it away, to shovel it under the carpet.

I fall asleep and when I wake it's almost eleven. I get up and wander into the bathroom, lean over the basin and stare into the mirror. Why is my brain this way? Why do I not recognize this woman? I know her hair, so why don't I know her eyes? Why the hell do I not know who I slept with last night?

I pull aside the shower curtain and reach to turn it on, watch the steam rise and fill the room. I climb into the bath and stand back from the water so that it only hits my ankles and feet, hold out my hands and let it beat on my palms and cascade through my fingers. Then I release my breath and step under the shower. I won't go to the police. I am not prepared to be ridiculed, dragged through the gutter by the press and humiliated. It doesn't mean his actions will go unpunished; although precisely how I'm going to make him pay is unclear. I'll get there though; I'll find out who did this to me and think of something.

I head out to the station, pulling my wheelie case, striding along the pavement, trying to think about GZ and not let the flashbacks interrupt, because when they do, they throw me so badly that my vision mists. I'm proud of myself for making it to Waterloo without breaking down, for getting on my train and stashing my case without visibly trembling, for smiling at the child sitting opposite me with her father and not bursting into tears.

And then my mobile rings.

7

Rebecca

IN THE MORNING REBECCA'S MIGRAINE HAS DISSIPATED, as it does if she's lucky, leaving no trace. Her head is clear, her body relaxed. Christ, she's tired though; it's been a tough few weeks, chasing that contract. It's age. Thirty-nine; that Plimsoll line between floating and sinking. Thank God for the Christmas break.

Rebecca sits up, drops her feet to the floor and stands, stretching her arms above her head and arching her neck backwards, feeling the feathered ends of her hair tickle between her shoulder blades. Yawning, she pads into the en-suite and splashes her face with cold water, then leans forward and stares at her reflection, homing in on details like a scientist peering through her microscope at a collection of amoebas. She has no idea why she does this. Her boyfriend hates it, frowning when he catches her transfixed by a tiny clogged pore below the corner of his eye. But, mostly, she looks at herself, her eyes scanning for signs of deterioration, for loss of elasticity, for the deepening of the lines at the corners of her eyes or between her brows.

She has been thinking about Botox. She works in an industry where she regularly has meetings with people theoretically young enough to be her children and every year brings more of them. Advertising values youth over experience, but maybe that's the same everywhere. She wonders what she's doing; she could be married by now; she could have had children and been back at work for the last five years. She presses her hands to her flat stomach and imagines it swelling, her smooth skin riven with spiralling crescents of puckered scars, like her mother's.

After she brushes her teeth, she unrolls her yoga mat in the drawing room in front of the French windows, and lights candles. They cast their glow into the hazy darkness of the December morning. She does her Surya Namaskar, her Downward Dog, her Warrior and the rest. She allows herself five minutes of relaxation afterwards, lying on her back listening to the radio, staring up at the elaborate coving that borders the high ceiling, a Kelly Hoppen cashmere rug shrouding her body.

The French windows overlook communal gardens iced with frost, the denuded trees fuzzy in the washed-out dawn. The houses on the other side are far enough away that anybody wanting to watch and giggle would need a pair of binoculars. She doesn't care what anyone thinks anyway.

Or maybe she does. Sometimes she doesn't know who or what she is. She has lied to colleagues, friends and family for so long that it's as though her personality has had to contort itself to stay inside the box. She suspects her parents think she's a lesbian.

She is Rebecca Munro; the youngest daughter of a surgeon and a stay-at-home mother, although they're divorced now, the baby of the family; petted and spoiled. She is the princess for whom only a prince will do. Well, her two siblings are happily married with seven children between them and the princess is sitting in her ivory tower waiting for a married man to get a move on and decide.

Breakfast is porridge and fruit. She has trouble getting the claggy mess down, but it stops her snacking and sees her through till lunch. Rebecca Munro does not do flab. She eats, wrinkling her nose like her five-year-old nephew faced with the pale green flesh of an avocado, drinks the coffee, then brushes her teeth and rinses with mouthwash to stop her teeth from staining.

Make-up is a necessity these days, whereas before it was an optional enhancement. She applies it, smoothing in a tinted moisturizer, obliterating the shadows from her eyes with concealer and using blusher to contour an already contoured face, lipstick on her full lips. She swipes lines of black kohl, wing-tipped at the ends, above her eyelashes and blinks.

She could have been a model if she hadn't had such big tits, but tragically, she does. She has correspondingly big feet. Not that she's ever had complaints about either.

She sprays a puff of perfume into the air and walks through it. Then she packs swiftly, expertly, into her Louis Vuitton case, knowing exactly what she will need for four days in the depths of the country, which is basically her normal clothes with Wellington boots and this season's Barbour. She double-checks she has her keys, MacBook, phone and reading glasses in the gratifyingly expensive Anya Hindmarch bag he gave her for an early Christmas present, then lets herself out. She can't help it, she runs an advertising agency; she tends to think in labels. Her sister will quirk an expressive eyebrow but would only be disappointed if Rebecca rolled up without make-up and in jeans and a jumper. Her driver is waiting to take her to Paddington station.

And then she remembers and darts back inside. She takes the package of contraceptive pills from the cupboard in the bathroom, pops one out of its tiny blister, takes it between her finger and thumb and drops it ceremonially into the plughole. Rebecca has been doing this for five months. It started off randomly, missing the odd day or two here and there, but she realized she would have no idea whether her period was due or not, so she stopped taking it altogether, just kept up the pretence. She needs to think about herself and what she wants in the long term. To be honest, she isn't particularly interested in the whole baby thing; what she would like is the adult her baby will become. She picks up her keys, closes the door behind her and presses the button for the lift. It may never happen anyway.

If she gets pregnant and he finishes with her – she forces herself to entertain the scenario even though it goes against everything she believes of him, of herself – at the very least the baby will have alpha-male genes. Rebecca is a pragmatist, always has been, always will be, but she's a fighter too, and doesn't give up easily. She has no intention of letting go.

As they cut through Primrose Hill her phone rings. She sees it's David and picks up.

'Sorry I had to vanish last night,' she says. 'Did you get home OK?'

'Rebecca,' David says, his voice catching. 'Something's happened.'

8

Laura

I ALMOST DON'T TAKE THE CALL, BECAUSE FOR ONE horrible, illogical moment, I thought it must be him, but it's Rebecca.

'Hey,' I say. 'Everything all right?'

'Laura,' she says, throwing my name at me, 'David and I . . .' Her voice falters, which worries me. Rebecca Munro is forthright and never shirks bad news.

'We're emailing the whole company but we're calling a few of you, those who . . .' She pauses again, and this time my throat constricts. The last time we received an emergency communication it was because of a terrorist threat in the area. 'It's Guy,' she says finally. 'He was knocked off his bike on his way home from the party last night.'

'Oh my God. Is he OK?'

'No, I'm afraid he isn't. He's dead.'

'Shit. That's awful.' Disbelief and surprise quickly curdle into a kind of sick horror. This is real.

She sighs. 'I'm on my way down to Somerset, but I've spoken to his parents.'

'What about the driver?'

'It was a hit-and-run.'

'That's terrible.'

The train pulls into Clapham Junction and two elderly women take the vacated seats in front of me. I can feel their curious glances, even as I stare down at my knees.

'Laura?'

'I can't believe . . .' I sniff and dash the back of my hand under my nose. 'It's not fair. Poor Guy.'

'I have to ring Eddie now, Laura. Are you going to be OK?'

'Yes,' I say, trying to pull myself together.

'I'll be in touch when I know more,' Rebecca says, then disconnects.

I struggle not to cry. I can picture it as clearly as if I had been there. Guy is lying in the road, broken and bleeding, tangled in the bicycle frame. The back wheel is still spinning, the front wheel buckled. His eyes are open, staring up at the street light. He's hoping someone will stop, that they will call his parents or his partner, that he won't die alone. I put my hand to my mouth, stifling an involuntary moan of shock. One of the old ladies leans forward and offers me a tissue. I take it, with a muttered 'Thanks', blow my nose and wipe away the tears. I fix my gaze on my knees until the wave of agony passes.

Mum is waiting in her car in the station car park, too used to me walking straight past her to risk a busy platform. I endure her chatter for the ten-minute journey, doing my best to respond cheerfully, but when we pull on to the drive, I apologize gruffly and dash inside. I shout a greeting at my sister, which is echoed from somewhere deep in the house, and run straight up to my old bedroom. There is too much in my head. Guy's death; what happened to me last night. My instinct is to hide, but barely a minute passes before someone follows me up.

'What's happened, darling?'

It's Mum. Isabel would have called me *chérie*. Not being able to recognize your mother goes against the laws of nature. One of my earliest memories is of Mum arriving at the church hall where my nursery school was. I picked up the finger-painting I wanted to show her, but instead of coming to me, she went up to another little girl, took her in her arms, kissed her cheek and hugged her. I burst into tears, howling with fury, jealous and hurt, pointing at them and yelling, 'My mum! My mum!' My teacher picked me up, a sodden, irate, red-faced bundle, and told me that my mummy would be here any minute. Then the door opened, and another lady walked in, and the teacher said, 'There you are, Laura. Mummy's here. All better now?' I remember being embarrassed but going with the story – that I had got it into my head that she wasn't coming – even at that age wanting to protect my mother from the dreadful fact that I had confused her with someone else.

'I'll be down later, Mum. I need to close my eyes for an hour. Too much to drink last night.'

'Oh. OK.' She sounds faintly disapproving, as if I should have grown out of such behaviour by now. 'Do you want me to call you when supper's ready?'

'No. I just want to sleep. Sorry.'

I can feel her struggling with her maternal urge, but I don't want to be hugged. I don't think I can bear to be held. I don't want to be touched at all.

'You're scratching your hands again.'

I look down. I hadn't even realized I was doing it.

'Do you have any of your cream with you? There's some in the bathroom cupboard. It's probably out of date, but it'll help.'

She hurries out of the room and comes back with a twisted tube of hydrocortisone.

'Thank you.' I unscrew the cap, squeeze some out and rub it into the reddened skin. I can feel tiny bumps where the rash is developing.

'I'll nip out and get some more. Is there anything else you'd like? Some hot Ribena?'

I harden myself. I have to protect my mother; she worries enough already.

'Mum, I'm OK.'

Once she's gone, I shut the curtains and then pull off my jeans and jumper and get into bed. It's such a relief that I start to cry, stifling the noise with the pillow pressed to my mouth.

Later I tell them about Guy and I hate myself for using his tragedy to allow myself the luxury of breaking down. It's for him as well, of course it is, but I can feel my skin burning where that man touched me. My lips are sensitive and feel swollen from kissing and the tears camouflage that too.

'His poor parents,' Mum says. 'They must be feeling destroyed. I don't think I would cope if anything happened to one of you three.'

'It's unbearable,' Isabel says, reaching over.

She's always been more physically affectionate than me and it's usually nice to be touched by her. Her hands are cool, her fingers slim and delicate. But this time I slip my hand out of hers. The action feels more portentous than it is.

'Will you go to the funeral?' she asks.

'Yes, I expect so.'

I get a call from the police that evening. All they want to know is if I own a car and how I got home that night. They are asking everyone who was at Hoxton 101, including the party from the upstairs bar.

'I don't drive,' I told them. 'I went home in a cab.'

'Did you share the cab?'

A cold stream trickles through my veins. 'Why do you need to know that?'

'We're trying to ascertain who was out on the street last night, Miss Maguire. We're not being nosy.'

'Oh. Sorry. I was alone.' I can hardly tell them I don't have a clue who I shared my taxi with.

The steadiness of my voice when I tell the lie surprises me. I put the phone down and curl into the corner of the sofa. My nephews are watching a superhero movie, and I close my eyes, listening to the *Kapows!* and the *Aaarghs!* and the supersonic booms and finally dozing. At some point I feel a hand on my leg and jolt with shock. Isabel is sitting there, her head cocked, her mouth smiling. The television screen is dark and blank.

'Bedtime, *chérie*.'

Christmas Eve passes in a blur. Still hung-over, miserable and uncommunicative, I curl up on Mum's battered old sofa and watch TV or read. Isabel soon lets me know how underwhelmed she is. On Christmas morning, I emerge having slept for another twelve hours, determined to make more of an effort. I feel better physically, in that my headache has lifted at least, but I still find it hard to talk, hard to think of anything to say. It's easier with my nephews, so I join in with them, admiring the contents of their stockings and instigating a game of Cluedo.

After a brunch of scrambled eggs and smoked salmon on crusty granary bread, we go for a walk along the River Mole, Dominic and Milo grumbling and dragging their feet and generally behaving as though they are being tortured. My brother Mark is due at two with his new wife, three daughters and two stepdaughters. I'm looking forward to the mayhem.

Isabel's boys are indistinguishable to me; their skin honey-toned and their brown hair floppy. Milo, the eldest at eight, is half an inch taller than Dominic but as they are almost always on the move or slouched on the sofa with their smartphones, this is not much help. My sister lets me know who is wearing what in the morning, but sometimes they mess with my head, swapping shirts for fun. They know I can't tell them apart, but don't know that it's caused by anything other than their aunt's rank stupidity.

My other point of reference is that Dominic has a habit of stuffing his hands into his pockets when he's talking to an adult, whereas Milo hooks his thumbs into his waistband; a real cool dude. Eric, my brother-in-law, is a dream. Not only does he have an accent as thick and stretchy as a Salvador Dalí clock, but he is half Ghanaian, half French and bald.

'How're you doing?' Isabel asks. She's been casting me worried looks all day.

We're prepping vegetables for this evening's feast. I peel another potato, slice it into quarters and drop it into the big pan where it bobs amongst its fellows. Isabel strips the outer leaves from Brussels sprouts and cuts crosses into the green flesh of their stumps. She has lost the argument with Mum about slicing them in half and steaming them. The kitchen smells of roasting turkey, stuffing and the cloves that Mum insists on adding to the bread sauce even though neither Isabel's boys nor my brother's girls like them. There are other aromas: mulled wine, mince pie filling, the log fire in the sitting room.

'Better than when I got here.'

'You've had a shock.'

For a moment I think she means what happened to me, then I realize she's talking about Guy. That makes me feel even more guilty.

Isabel puts an arm around me and I flinch. She notices and withdraws. 'You haven't told me about the party yet. I suppose if you got that drunk, it wasn't as bad as you expected?'

I tease a blemish from a potato with the tip of my knife and so avoid looking at her. 'No, not really. It was fun.'

'And?'

I eye her warily.

She sighs. 'Did anything happen? Did you meet someone? Is that why you're so tired? You were up all night shagging. Come on. Give me some gossip, for Christ's sake. I spend my life with small children, I need to live vicariously through my little sister.'

I am trying hard not to react, but I can feel him on me, feel his fingers inside me, his mouth all over me. I have to force myself to be the girl that Isabel knows; not the new Laura, the broken and shrivelled creature I've become overnight.

'Then you're doomed to disappointment. I went home alone.'

She looks at me a while longer and then gives up and goes back to her sprouts. I finish peeling the potatoes and carry them in the heavy saucepan to the stove to be parboiled before they are roasted. Mum's trick is to simmer them for seven minutes precisely, drain the water – keeping some by for the gravy – throw in a dessertspoonful of Colman's mustard powder, put the lid back on and give the whole thing a good shake. When they cook, the outsides become golden and crusty, the mustard disappears and can't be tasted. I focus on this, to take my mind off the images from that night that keep flashing through my brain. He was circumcised.

The memory springs out of nowhere. The information isn't going to be much use to me, but I file it away all the same.

I put the pan on to boil and stand watching it. Isabel switches the radio on, but I don't listen. I am locked inside my head; desperate. He is stroking me, my breasts, the inside of my thighs. Who is he? My breathing becomes irregular and my hands tighten into fists.

There is something else, something unpleasant that I've tried not to think about because it's bad enough already. When I bundled up my clothes that morning, to put them in the wash, my knickers were missing. They were nothing special – I hadn't been expecting to go out partying that night, after all – they were standard black cotton Marks & Spencer, faded by countless washings. I checked down between the bed and the wall, amongst the tumbled heap of bedding that I had ripped off, and under the bed; they were gone. I almost gagged as I imagined him fingering them in his pocket, bringing them to his nose.

There's a tap as Isabel puts her knife down on the kitchen table and the screech of chair legs against tiles. The noise snaps me out of it and I realize that the potatoes are boiling over. She nudges me to one side with her hip and takes them off the heat, removes the lid and pokes them with a fork then puts them back with the gas turned right down.

I move away from her, take a chocolate-chip cookie out of the tin and lean against the counter nibbling it. My relationship with my sister has never been straightforward. When we were younger I felt removed from her because there was Mark between us. There never seemed to be a time when all three kids got along. It was only when I entered my twenties that we became close and now it feels as though I may lose her again because this looming horror has come to sit between us and I can't tell her. I don't want her to know that I put myself at risk or that something ugly has happened to me.

'You don't look happy,' she says. 'You've got shadows under your eyes.'

'I'm OK. Just a bit stressed at work.'

Isabel waits, her eyes on my face. I envy her being able to read it so accurately.

'Something's wrong,' she says. 'Why don't you get it over with and tell me? You never know, I might be able to help.'

'There's nothing to tell.' That came out harder than I meant it to. I rinse a cloth out under the hot tap and start wiping the table, moving aside newspapers and keys, Nintendos and spectacles.

'Fine.' She stalks out of the room.

I go for a run on my own, and no one says anything, although I can imagine they didn't hold back once the door closed behind me. I pound up the hill and dog-leg through the genteel residential streets. Brown, water-logged leaves attach themselves to the soles of my trainers and rain creeps under my zip-up jacket and tickles my forehead. Christmas trees stand in bay windows, draped in fairy lights and baubles. I feel a world away from reality. In eight days' time Gunner Munro will be open for business and I will have to deal with what comes next; I will have to breathe the same air as the man who assaulted me.

And there's the question of Pink-Shirt. In my endless, looping post-mortem of that evening, I accept that I could have discovered his name one way or another. It wouldn't have been impossible. The truth is I didn't want to break the mood because I so rarely have a connection with a man. I didn't want to say something stupid and lose him. But now I have because how can I be with him after what has happened?

And what about him? The man. There are things I need to say to him; things I hope his inner voice is telling him already.

You should be ashamed of yourself.

Why did you do it, you inadequate piece of shit?

I am coming for you.

I've come out without keys, so I ring the doorbell. Eric opens the door. He gives me a worried smile.

'Where's Isabel?' I ask.

'In here,' she calls from the sitting room. She meets me halfway. 'Sorry.'

'No, I'm sorry,' I say, making myself hug her. 'I was out of order.' I lower my voice so that Mum, who is in the sitting room with the new arrivals, can't hear. 'I'll tell you all about it; but not yet. It's too raw.'

There is a pause while she digests this. I can read her thoughts. *What does she mean by raw?* Raw is not a positive word; raw is bloody and it stings when you touch it. And will the time ever be right to tell her? At this point in my life, I can't imagine it.

9

Laura

BACK TO WORK TODAY. I SHOWER IN THE DARK, BECAUSE one of the bathroom walls is mirrored and I don't want to look at my naked body. I drink coffee and eat toast and marmalade standing up, while I check messages on my phone. I clean my teeth, rub soothing cream into my flaring skin and make the bed.

Will I know him if I see him? Will I sense him? Will he seek me out and let me know who he is? Or will he take a perverse pleasure in my discomfort?

Some days I bump into my neighbour on my way out, in the hall with her baby, waving goodbye to her husband, but not this morning, and I don't realize until my shoulders relax how much I've been dreading that contact. The calm of the morning leaves me in a rush. If I can't face seeing the neighbour I barely know, how will I face my colleagues? It takes a supreme effort of will to get me out on to the street. I wish I had my bicycle, but it's still in Percy Row, on the roof.

At Kentish Town, I step on to the crowded platform.

Once I'm on the train, I huddle against the glass panel by the door, fixing my eyes on the adverts running along the curve of the ceiling. I don't look at anybody. I barely even breathe as the train shrieks into Old Street. I walk blindly to work and when I get to Percy Row, I stop and pretend to be messaging someone, steeling myself. But I'm left alone. People's memories of that night are about Guy, not me making a fool of myself on the dance floor.

I want to go in, but my feet won't move. I wonder if he's there already, waiting for me; if he's terrified too. How much does he know about me? If he doesn't know about my face-blindness and he's relying on me having been paralytic to keep him safe, then he'll be nervous. I look up at the windows. If he's in there, I will find him. I can't imagine being near him without my skin prickling. The only problem is, how do I get to him and what can I do that will hurt him without making my own life worse? There's always the Internet; I could stalk and troll him, but somehow that seems weak and unfulfilling. Once I know, once I'm sure, then something will happen. My mind swirls with half-formed plans and possibilities: confront him publicly, learn his secrets and unravel his life, start the whispers that will ruin his reputation. Get him fired.

I hate myself for obsessing about this when every single person in the building is still reeling, when Guy's desk is empty, his mug unused in the cupboard. There was a big piece in the press – Last London Cyclist Killed This Year. A gorgeous young man in the prime of his life. Devastated parents and bereft girlfriend and a plea for the driver to do the decent thing and come forward.

But there wasn't much after that. We've grown used to these tragedies in London.

As I walk across the media floor towards the door to my office, all I can hear is my own breathing, magnified a hundred times. Everything else: the phones ringing, computers humming, people catching up – all that is wallpaper. I study each of them, but I feel like a goldfish peering out of the tank, trying to remember who fed me yesterday. These humans all look the same. We are much of a type here: young, attractive, trendy, fit.

The mood is understandably sombre, less banter, more moving around with frozen expressions. Coming back to work to find one less person, even when you've been warned what to expect, is pretty harrowing. Guy hadn't been with the company long, but he was well-liked. And for the regular cyclists amongst us, it's another case of *it could have been me.* It could so easily have been me.

Eddie is unpacking his laptop as I walk in and he greets me with a sad smile. We don't need to say anything. I sit down and switch my computer on. It feels strange being here, and yet it's so familiar. In the light of what's happened, both to me and to Guy, everything that was solid seems insubstantial. It's as if the walls, the windows, the floor, could all fold in on themselves in a moment. Although it's me that's changed, not the space.

Eddie isn't showing it, at least not yet, but he's annoyed. My head hasn't been where it ought to have been; in sync with his, playing with ideas, reacting to his snatches of copy; but I'm not going to use Guy as an excuse. My hands are shaking, and I keep them below my desk. The ideas I sent Eddie last night were better than decent, but I should have had more, and thought them through, not treated it like a piece of homework, dashed off at the last minute.

Eddie is one of the few people I count as a friend even though we don't see as much of each other as we used to. He and Esther moved to Sussex when she got pregnant. Before, we would have a quick half in the pub after work once or twice a week and I relied on him for company. I miss that.

'Did you manage to have a look at the pictures I sent you?'

'Yes,' he says. 'But it feels like you didn't look at it until last night and . . .' He sighs.

'And what?'

'Well, you didn't make me want to grab a bottle off the shelf. We can both do better than this. I know GZ is rank, but that's what we love, isn't it? The challenge.'

It was what I used to love. Now I just don't care. My shoulders droop. I owe it to Eddie and my own sanity to make more of an effort.

I organized the Christmas party – not that it needed much organizing – but I found and booked the venue and I have the email I sent out to all the staff, so I have a list of everyone who works in this building. What I don't have is a list of who actually came. I'm not even sure if such a thing exists. There was pressure to attend, but no one was ticking names off at the door. I find the original Excel spreadsheet I took the emails from, save a copy from which I remove all the women. And Guy. I highlight his name, pause, and then click delete.

Eddie is sitting opposite me, his coat-hanger shoulders hunched, his brow furrowed as he stares into his monitor. I can't start checking off the names with him sitting there. I'm meant to be working.

He senses me watching him, raises his head with a grin. I smile back.

'Sorry I was grumpy,' he says.

'You had every right to be.'

'So, what happened between you and Jamie at the Christmas party?'

I dart a look at him. Jamie. Is that who it was? 'Nothing much.'

'You were all over each other. There's no need to be embarrassed about it. It was nice to see you having a good time.'

'We were both drunk. It was a mistake.'

'He likes you. And he's a nice guy. He couldn't take his eyes off you. Why don't you give him a chance?'

'He's not my type.'

Eddie gazes at me, the corners of his lips twitching. 'You must like him a little bit.'

'Not really.' I pick up my pencil and tap it on the desk. 'He's a lovely bloke but . . .'

'But what? Surely if you know for a fact that a man fancies you, you'd explore that, unless there was something wrong with him. You'd give him a chance, see if you connect.'

I frown, unable to tell him why he's wrong, to explain that I feel violated and that the thought of being in a relationship, putting my trust in someone, would be like asking me to swim a piranha-infested river. Restless suddenly, I stand up and glance through the window in our door.

'He's not here,' Eddie says, correctly interpreting my thoughts. 'He's down with the flu.'

'Oh dear. Poor Jamie.' I try not to look relieved. 'You'd make a fantastic agony aunt,' I say instead, keeping it light. 'And you're probably right, but now is not the time. I have some other issues I need to straighten out before I can think about that.'

'Time stops for no one.'

'I know. I'll be twenty-nine next month, and my mother is starting to twitch.' I remove my glasses and give them a wipe. 'We should crack on, or we're not going to be ready for the meeting.'

I smile to set his mind at ease, but I've already decided that my situation here is untenable. I knew that as soon as I walked in and felt the fear descend. The feeling that I'm being watched, examined for every expression and reaction by someone who has abused his power in the most unspeakable way, is eventually going to warp me beyond recognition. I will become someone else.

I glance at Eddie. If I have to go, I'd want him to come with me, to apply with me as the other half of a winning creative team, but why should he do that? He has a great future with Gunner Munro and loves it here. He has an excellent relationship with the senior editors and account managers and the more junior teams love him. I'm the one who has failed to develop the relationships. Rebecca was right: if I don't join in more, I won't cut it, and it's only going to get harder.

On the other hand, why should I be the one to leave, while that man keeps his job and his reputation?

I try and work, but my mind won't let it go. Abused doesn't feel like the right word for what he did. If he knew I was face-blind and deliberately tricked me, then it was something else, something much worse. But how could he know? – I haven't told anyone except Rebecca about my condition – or is he just an idiot who got too drunk at a Christmas party to exercise his judgement? Was it my fault as much as his? I still think about going to the police, but if I'm not clear about what happened or what to call it, then how can I possibly expect anyone to believe me?

At lunchtime, I slip out of the building unnoticed. I walk through Hoxton and beyond into Hackney, to one of the cafés less frequented by Gunner Munro employees. I buy a wrap and a cup of tea and sit down at the back. I take the sheet of names out of my bag and carefully, diligently, rule out some of the men through familiarity with their individual characteristics, their build or race, and see who's left. It could be any of them. I need pictures.

It's time to go back. I fold up the list and clasp my hands in front of me. I'm going to have to learn to compartmentalize if I'm going to survive this. I close my eyes and make myself picture two people in a bed, all the things we did. I go hot, so hot that I think I'm going to faint, but I make myself see the images and imagine placing them in a box, closing the lid and sticking packaging tape all over it, then hiding it away at the back of a deep, dark cupboard.

It turns out Bettina has uploaded the photographs she took on her smartphone of the party on to her Facebook page. And I don't even have to ask; she insists on showing me. Some of the pictures have tags. The first is of Guy with his Father Christmas hat on and a glass raised to the camera. She's written something about him and there are lots of messages responding and commiserating. I scroll through, haunted by his face. There are several pictures that include me and Jamie together. Thanks to Eddie, I can put a name to him now. It makes me feel both better and worse. I know who he is, and can rule him out, but I'm also excruciatingly embarrassed. Thank God he's away.

Jamie in his pink shirt. I am flooded with the memory of music, the heavy dancefloor pulse, the cacophony of people trying to be heard above it, the clink and clatter of the bar. I have physical recall of his proprietorial hand on the small of my back, his breath on my neck. I see myself laughing and breaking out of his grasp, twirling away and then turning back in alarm, not wanting to let him out of my sight in case I can't find him amongst the sea of sweaty, gurning faces. How much of that was worry, how much of it attraction? I was enjoying myself, feeling my freedom and an unfamiliar power. Most of all I was alive in a way I haven't been for a long time, if ever. Even as a child I was rarely unrestrained. I hope he didn't see me leave with that other man. I hope he does believe my version of events.

I frown as another memory surfaces, dissipates then melds. Someone, a man, put his hand on me and I didn't like it. He said something creepy. What was it? Dark horse. I shudder.

I keep looking. Oddly enough, I don't see any blue shirts, even allowing for the effect of the disco lighting. Not a single one. Could he have changed for some reason? It seems unlikely, but he must have. Perhaps he spilt his drink and happened to have a spare shirt in his bag. Perhaps he had cleaned out his locker for the holidays. Even if this was the case, I still can't find anyone who fits my memory. Some of the men are the wrong race, others have the wrong hair or build. I zoom in on a tattoo under a cuff, or a sprout of dark hair at a collar. I make a list of those I'm not sure of, and then seek them out discreetly. I associate my colleagues with their desks. It's a memory game to me, like covering a random collection of objects on a tray. I used to play it as a child and would always win. My excuse for wandering into my colleagues' line of sight is that someone left a pair of gloves behind at Hoxton 101. This is true. Bettina collected a large carrier bag of lost property, including a pair of glasses and some wonky festive headbands. She left it with Chris at reception, but I took the gloves, saying I knew who they belonged to.

After I've dismissed all the beards and visible distinguishing marks, there are five men in the running; John Cormack, Graham Ludgrove and Lucas Bradley, Finn Broadbent and David Gunner. John barely uses Facebook and hasn't posted since November but the pictures I find show a happy man. He got married to Hannah in

July and they are expecting their first baby in March. I don't think it's him; his build is all wrong for a start, his shoulders sloping. I close my eyes and I picture myself running my fingers down the man's neck, discovering him inch by inch. I can still feel the shape of his shoulders. They didn't slope; I can swear to it.

Lucas uses Facebook a lot more, documenting his life with gusto. He is a kick-boxer and keen climber and there are pictures of him clambering up rock faces trussed in a harness, giving a grinning thumbs up. He also enjoys rugby and likes to take selfies with his girlfriend, Sian. I don't discount him at first. For all I know, she was out that night, perhaps already on her way to spend Christmas with her family. A deeper scrutiny, and I discover Sian and Lucas flew to Dublin on the morning after the party, making it extremely unlikely, if not impossible, for him to have accompanied me home. Scrolling back to their summer holiday, I find several of him in his swimming trunks, sporting a tattoo on his stomach. Lucas is out. I can only find one picture that Graham is featured in, and I have to ask Bettina, couching it as gossip.

'Did Graham pull at the Christmas party? Only, I thought I saw him get into a taxi with one of the girls. I didn't see her face.'

'Graham pulled?' She smirks. 'I don't think so. Anyway, he left early. I saw him sneak out about the same time as Rebecca and he didn't have anyone with him, unless they were hiding under his coat.'

Which leaves Finn and David.

It feels too easy, as though he wants to be found.

David is a married man and a father of three; surely he wouldn't risk his family and reputation on what amounts to a throw of the dice. On the other hand, successful men do this from time to time, self-destructing while in the grip of a primitive urge. I need to know if David's family went away for Christmas, and if they left before him. I now regret not accepting Felicity Gunner's offer of a lift back from the funeral later this week. I could have used that time to find out.

Agnes keeps David's diary on management software these days. She, Rebecca and Paul Digby, the senior account manager, all have access. His holiday arrangements will be on it; it's just a question of getting into one or other of their offices while they're still logged on.

Over Christmas, our mail is held in the post room, then distributed by the interns or whoever isn't mad busy. Someone has been in with ours. Eddie's pile is bigger than mine, which he doesn't hesitate to mention. I make a face and sit down, flicking quickly through the letters. Apart from a couple of Christmas cards that missed the last post, most of it is junk or industry contractors selling their services. There are one or two parcels; most of us get our online shopping delivered to work these days.

As I reach for the pile, a jiffy bag slides on to the floor. I pick it up. Whatever is in there is soft and I try to remember if I've ordered any clothes recently. I open it and peer inside. There's no dispatch form, just a piece of dark fabric folded up. I put my hand in and feel it and I go cold.

'Any idea what's eating Bettina?' Eddie asks. He doesn't look up from his laptop, for which I'm grateful.

I push the packet into my bag. 'I haven't noticed anything. She seems the same as usual.'

'Maybe I'm imagining it.' Eddie glances up when I don't respond, and frowns. 'What's up? You've gone as white as a sheet.'

I shake my head. 'Nothing.' I pause. 'Actually, I have to go. I feel dreadful.'

'What kind of dreadful? Can't you wait until after the meeting?'

'No, I don't think I can. I had a chicken sandwich for lunch and I think there might have been something wrong with it.'

To make my point I push my chair back and race out of the room, colliding with a colleague. I apologize, but before I can even start trying to work out who it is another question pops into my head. *Was it you?*

'Sorry.'

He's blocking my path. There is something challenging about him. He's standing close enough for me to see the pores in his skin. He takes my elbow to steady me.

'Finn, do you have a minute?' someone says, and he turns away, letting me go, but it feels as though his hand is still there, his fingers lightly pressing into the dips around the joint.

I run into the Ladies, slam the door of the cubicle. I can't breathe, my brain feels wild, unable to focus on anything. I know what's in the envelope, I don't have to take it out and inspect it. It's a pair of black knickers, the ones I wore to the Christmas party, the ones he peeled off me. I am fragmenting, coming apart at the seams. I can't do this. I cannot keep walking past those rows of desks, knowing that someone here has seen me naked.

My mind goes back a few minutes, to the man who was about to speak to me. Finn Broadbent. Thinking about it, I realize that he fits better than anyone else. He works alongside Eddie and me, picking up our campaigns when they need a boost on social media. In my situation, I can't know anyone well – even those I should. They don't have a face to show me, so I rely on gut instinct. I close my eyes and try to remember something about that night and the man in my bed, anything that could tie his body or his mannerisms to Finn, but I can't. I can taste my own frustration.

10

Rebecca

CONSIGNED TO THE BACK SEAT OF FELICITY GUNNER'S car while David talks to Paige Adler in New York, by turns charming, voluble and cajoling, Rebecca sits with one hand clasped over the other. The interior smells of dog and old fruit – there is a desiccated apple core rolling around the footwell – and Daisy's car seat could do with being hoovered out. Every so often Felicity flicks a glance at her in the rear-view mirror, smiling conspiratorially as if they are both in on the fond joke: that David is a snake-charmer, shamelessly flattering producers and clients into offering their business, better rates, an introduction to someone important.

'We're good.' David wraps things up. 'Let's talk about it some more when you come over. You're going to love Eddie and Laura. This is going to be a fantastic working partnership. My guys are the best . . . Fuck,' he says, barely waiting for the connection to break. 'That woman is a pain in the arse.'

'Prickly?'

'A porcupine. Are we nearly there?'

He taps his fingertips on his thighs. It's a sign of stress when he becomes hyper like that. She wonders, with a flash of jealousy, whether he and Felicity will have sex tonight. He's told her that they don't do it, but she doesn't believe him; it's a lie they both buy into. Small children make it harder to find time and easier to make excuses, but they must do it occasionally, or Felicity would have left him, surely.

She looks out at the bustling thirties suburb. She has never been to this part of London and isn't even convinced it counts as London.

'Ten minutes,' Felicity says.

David grunts. He is tired; they all are. It's been a difficult first week back. They haven't spoken much, partly out of respect for the occasion, partly because David and Rebecca, like doctors, are never off duty, always focused on the job. She feels sorry for Felicity, who after all didn't know Guy and is basically acting as their chauffeur.

She slips her phone into her bag and leans forward. 'So how was your Christmas?'

They have pulled up at traffic lights, and Felicity turns to her with a grimace. 'Mixed. Sad, of course, but we made an effort for the children. It was going well, until we had to drop everything and shoot over to Buckinghamshire.'

'Oh dear. What happened?'

'Georgie managed to offend the latest carer, so they were on their own. Honestly, Rebecca, I was so shocked. Tony was covered in bruises. He says he fell, but it's more like Georgie's been taking out her frustration on him.'

'Don't go on,' David says impatiently. 'She can't help it.'

In the mirror, Rebecca sees Felicity frown, hurt. She knows all this, because David has told her. Dementia has made David's grandfather sweet and docile, but it's made Georgie filthy-tempered and borderline violent. He is devoted to the grandparents who brought him up after the death of his parents, but he isn't coping brilliantly with their decline.

There's something about David, something different. He seems entirely unconcerned that his wife and mistress are in the same car at the same time. It's happened before, of course; Felicity and Rebecca are old friends. She's accompanied them to the theatre, she's been to openings at art galleries, exhibitions by artists whose work Felicity collects, she's even been on holiday with them, so what's different?

She hadn't expected a frisson; they are too used to this to let anything like that happen, and they are at a funeral, after all; but she had anticipated a glance from him at least, something that acknowledged the unusualness of the situation. It makes her feel insecure.

They crawl up Ruislip high street, spot the church and the car park beyond it.

'Are we late, do you think?' Felicity asks.

'No, look, there's Agnes.' David lowers the window as their PA hurries over and ducks down.

'Oh good,' she says. 'You're here. I didn't fancy going in on my own. This is so awful. Poor Guy. And what his parents must be going through.' She presses her hand to her bosom.

Felicity finds a space. They wait while David bangs off a quick email, reluctant to get out of the warm car. As they walk across the road, Rebecca studies Felicity. She is wearing a belted suede coat over her dress, an extravagantly long woolly scarf, a bobble hat and brown leather boots. Rebecca gave her the hat and scarf several years ago and is pleased she's still wearing them. Felicity reaches for David's hand, but he lifts it, sweeping his fingers through his hair.

'I still can't believe this has happened,' he says. 'Poor sod.'

'Dreadful,' Agnes says, hurrying along beside them.

The church has a pretty lychgate and a path leading up to the porch. There are snowdrops in the grass. They remind Rebecca of her grandmother and make her feel sad and think about renewal and that makes her think about babies. Once inside she scans the heads. Laura looks at her blankly, then smiles. Jamie has come, although he doesn't look well. She's pleased that he's made it, but sincerely hopes he's sensible enough to avoid physical contact with anyone.

There's only room for three more on their pew, so Agnes slides into a space behind them. David reaches over Felicity and Rebecca to shake a couple of hands, his mouth pulled down at the corners.

Rebecca likes churches, likes their smell of wax polish and flowers. Because it's winter the displays are dominated by sludgy, mossy greens and calming shades of white; colours she is particularly fond of. She feels a sense of peace descend as the vicar begins his eulogy, the sound of muffled weeping, of noses blown and the occasional explosion of a suppressed cough, bringing tears to her eyes. Beside her, Felicity leans her blonde head against David's shoulder. Rebecca glances down at their linked hands and then away, quickly, back to the vicar.

As they file out to a choir singing a version of Mozart's *Lacrimosa* that moves Rebecca more than she could ever express, she checks who is with them from Gunner Munro. She counts thirteen, the colleagues who were closest to Guy. Everyone apart from his immediate family looks so young. How bleak it is.

She spots Laura and Eddie amongst a group who have moved out of the way, on to the grass. Laura is as white as a sheet, looking stunned and not altogether present. Lack of animation makes her appear like a character in a painting, someone in the deep background, her features not properly realized. Come to think of it, she's been a bit off all week. Jamie looks miserable. She and David have talked about him, trying to figure out the best way forward.

She catches up with Felicity, understanding that her friend is feeling surplus. 'How's David coping?'

Felicity shrugs. 'You know what he's like. He's been up and down. He spent Christmas either in tears or behaving like some sort of manic puppy.'

They both glance at him. He is standing with Guy's ashen-faced mother, holding her hands clasped between his own. Under the warm glow of his attention the colour is slowly returning to her face. Felicity gives a wan smile.

'It's a horrible, shocking thing to have happened,' Rebecca says. 'Guy is going to be tough to replace. But we'll deal with it. Gunner Munro is healthy. We're a family.'

'I wish I worked,' Felicity says suddenly. 'I wish I was part of that side of David's life and could help him more.'

'You help him by being his wife, by giving him a happy and stable home. Men like David need that normality and you do a fantastic job and, from what he tells me, you're an enormous help with Georgie and Tony.'

'Jesus, Rebecca. Do you have to be so bloody patronizing?'

She apologizes. 'All I mean is, he needs you.'

Felicity pauses, assessing her for sincerity. 'I don't have any choice.' She rests her hand against the bark of a tree, then takes it away and brushes the damp from her fingertips. 'He just assumes that I'll look after them, drop everything to drive forty miles every time there's an emergency. It disrupts Daisy's routine. And frankly, they're not my grandparents.' She pauses. 'Sorry. That sounds mean, doesn't it? At any rate, it's lovely to see you; we don't see enough of each other. We should make a date.'

'Darling, of course,' Rebecca says smoothly. 'Let me get back on track at work and I'll give you a call.'

Felicity rummages through the junk in her bag for her phone. 'No. Let's do it now, or another three months will go by. We'll do something on my birthday. Just the two of us, like the old days.'

'Won't David want to take you out for supper?'

'We can do something during the day, a spa break. David will pay. You can give yourself one day off, can't you?'

Rebecca grimaces. 'I'm not sure. Let me see how things go.'

She tells herself it's work, that without her, the place will fall apart, but really, it's the idea of a day spent in Felicity's company, wondering if there's something more behind her friend's request than a birthday treat; a day spent reading between the lines of everything Felicity says and watching her own words carefully. It doesn't appeal.

Rebecca was the one who introduced Felicity to David, having met him when they were both working for the agency goliath, S&C. They left to start their own agency, taking with them, to their tiny Soho workspace, one of their former employer's largest customers. It was ugly, but both she and David had thick skins and ruthless ambition. Back then, Rebecca had encouraged Felicity to go out with him even though his record with girlfriends was terrible. Why had she done that? She was seeing someone else at the time, but he hadn't been important. Stupidly she hadn't recognized her own feelings until it was too late.

Beside her, Felicity shivers. 'I can do without going to the wake.'

'We'll just show our faces,' Rebecca says. 'Then we can go home.'

She tucks her arm through Felicity's and leads her back to David, handing her over like she's returning someone's child. She looks into his eyes and something moves in their depths. A darkness she only ever sees when they're by themselves. She's relieved. It's what she's been waiting for; the glimpse beneath the façade he shows the world; the reminder that the truth of him is for her alone.

11

Laura

A MAN STOPS TO TALK TO ME. HIS HANDS ARE IN HIS trouser pockets, his feet set apart. He has a thick scarf wrapped around his neck. He wants to look casual, but his body language is all wrong. He's shy. That's my assessment anyway.

'Laura,' he says. 'How are you?'

'Not great. What about you?'

He pulls a hanky out of his pocket, blows his reddened nose and apologizes.

I don't know his face; his black suit looks like it might belong to his father or a taller brother. Is this someone I should know well? Or someone who works on a different floor? The fact that he's here, at the funeral, means that he must have been good friends with Guy. It could be Jamie, but I never assume anything.

'I spent most of Christmas in bed with flu.'

I breathe. OK. That's one problem out of the way. On the other hand, I'm not ready for this. 'So I heard. Poor you.' Perhaps he won't mention the Christmas party.

There are people milling around and his voice drops to a whisper. 'Where did you disappear to? I went to get my scarf and when I came out of the club you had gone.'

I feel the flush creep up my neck. How weird to think I spent the evening with this man, that we kissed in dark corners, that we connected. If he had come home with me, how would we react to each other now? Probably with the same, toe-curling embarrassment.

'Sorry. I was so drunk I could barely stand, and the cab was there and I kind of fell in.'

'It was my fault for leaving you stranded. I didn't have your number, otherwise I'd have sent you a text. I was worried about you.'

'Sorry.' I grimace. I'm apologizing too much. 'I was out of it.'

He laughs. 'No, I understand. I was only hurt for a moment. I was too far gone to worry about it.' He hesitates. 'I don't suppose you fancy a meal? Or coffee or lunch? We could talk to each other without seeing double.'

I don't say anything, and the silence expands into a bubble that won't pop. I can't say what I want to say, that I don't recognize him now and will not recognize him next time he speaks to me. That I'm bruised and angry and no good to anyone. That there is only one thing I need, and that's to know the truth.

'I'm sorry,' he says. 'I just thought . . .'

'There are things . . . I can't . . .' I start again. 'I'm in a situation. I can't get involved with anyone at the moment. I'm flattered that you asked me though.'

Then a woman appears, and my brain kicks in,

clocking her grey hair and short stature, the shawl draped around her coat. It's Agnes. Like a sheepdog herding its flock, she propels us towards the door.

'I wish it could be different,' I say to Jamie as I unwind my scarf and take off my coat.

He shrugs. 'Don't worry about it.' Then he walks away from me.

I wish I could do the same, but there are so many people here, so many old school friends, uni friends and colleagues of Guy's, so many aunts and uncles and cousins, that it's impossible. The room is buzzing with conversation. I stand against the wall, nursing a glass of wine, a sandwich on a paper plate balanced precariously on the arm of the sofa beside me. I'm not certain which of the women is Guy's mother and which of the men his father. I want to find them and offer my condolences, but even Jamie has melted into the crowd. I feel rude and inadequate. When someone catches my eye, I smile regretfully. But it's not real. Everything about me feels false. I must seem cold.

While I'm contemplating leaving and trying to work out how I'm going to get from this pretty suburban house back to Ruislip station, a woman bears down on me. She's blonde and slim, and she's smiling. She's obviously a relative, scooping up fragile-looking guests.

'I'm Laura,' I say. 'I worked with Guy.'

'We've met before.' Her tone is clipped. 'More than once. I'm Felicity Gunner. David's wife?'

I blush, shaking my head at my stupidity. She had been wearing a woolly hat with a faux fur bobble in the church. 'Of course you are. I'm so sorry. I should have worn my glasses.'

'We're going to make a move. Rebecca said you might like a lift? You live near us, don't you? I've seen you running on the Heath. There's room for one more body, if you don't mind being squashed in the middle.'

It's kind of her, but I turn the offer down. It would feel weird, driving off with my two bosses and leaving the others to make their way back on the Piccadilly line. Instead I tag along with my colleagues, managing somehow not to sit next to Jamie Buchanan, but not to look like I'm avoiding him either. That's quite a feat when all the men are in black suits and overcoats. An echo of the immediate aftermath of the party makes me wince. I chat to Bettina and Agnes for most of the way. The journey takes for ever.

Back in my flat I sit down at the table in the window of my sitting-room-cum-kitchen and force my brain to think about GZ, but I can't help wondering if one of the men who came today was him. David, Jamie, Eddie, Graham, Finn and Mike were all there. I log into Facebook and track them, but Bettina hasn't tagged every face on every picture. None of them are a perfect fit, not when I stop to think. Both Eddie and Mike have beards. David, well I'm sure I'd have recognized him because of his energy, but I can't rule him out. Jamie is well and truly out of the picture. Graham and Finn are young, brown-haired and similar in build, but that proves nothing.

In the cold light of day, I realize that there are things about all of them that could have signalled their identity; the way Graham rounds his shoulders and pokes his head forward, like a turtle; Finn with his public-school confidence and bred-in-the-bone assumption that people are always delighted to see him; David because of his Tiggerishness. That night, I wasn't looking and anyway, pressed up against each other in the cab, it would have been even harder to run my usual checklist: the hair and the ears, the presence or lack of a ring. The truth is, I was way too drunk by then to even think of it.

He is not important. I will get over this and move on.

Once I've found him, that is.

I flip open my sketchbook and start to draw. As soon as I focus, as soon as my pencil touches the paper and whisks that first line across it, I feel better. I have the ability to shut out the things I don't like. It began as a way of shutting others out when I was too scared of slipping up to engage, but it's second nature now. I sketch and think, rubbing out and starting again, googling images and chewing my bottom lip.

When I go to bed, my brain refuses to quieten. It goes off like a firework display; words and phrases, images and memories, zapping on synapses that seem supercharged. It's as though I've drunk two cans of Red Bull. I don't fall asleep until the small hours and I wake before my alarm, clawing at my fingers.

12

Laura

I PRESS SHARE ON THE FILE CONTAINING THE DRAWINGS I've uploaded and lob a piece of screwed-up paper at Eddie.

'Look at the folder,' I say.

'I'm already there.'

I open my emails and scroll through them, but I'm not really looking; I feel itchy with impatience. Rebecca and David are in a meeting upstairs with the senior account manager, and I need to use the opportunity to get into their shared diary. Eventually I swivel my chair and get up.

Eddie looks up from his screen. 'Tea, if you're making it.'

I roll my eyes, pick up a bunch of papers and leave the room, close the door behind me and wander casually past the desks, past Finn and Graham, past Bettina. I can see Agnes through the window in David's door. There is no one in Rebecca's office. I decide to brazen it out and go in. I put the papers on her desk, then nip round the other side and click her mouse. The screen lights up with a picture of a woman and three teenagers, carefully posed; outdoorsy, hair windblown, huge toothy smiles. *Password.* Abort.

I sigh and get up, check the coast is clear and see David and Rebecca coming in. My heart almost bolts out of my mouth. There is nothing I can do. I sit down on her leather sofa and take out my phone, then look up from my messages as she comes in. She stops short and lifts her eyebrows.

'What are you doing in here?'

'I'm so sorry,' I say, jumping up. 'I needed to make a private call.'

I have a feeling about Finn. He's in and out of our office all the time, poring over the briefs and advising on how we can tweak to give an ad the best chance of being shared online, but he hasn't been in as much since the New Year. For him not to show his face is unusual.

Was it him? And if it was, why would he do that to me?

Finn's desk is on the end row, next to Graham. I imagine myself confronting him, but I don't move. I need to slow down. Be sure.

Finn Broadbent shares a flat with friends from university. This is information gleaned from Bettina, who knows something about everyone. She talks to people, finding out about their roles; the perfect intern, always interested, always keen to learn. Finn doesn't have a girlfriend currently.

Unfortunately, my oblique queries had the wrong effect and her eyes narrowed.

'Why are you so interested in Finn?'

'No reason. Just gossiping.'

'Well, I wouldn't touch him if I was you. He's bad news.'

There was a look on her face I didn't like; part arch, part hostile. 'I have no intention of touching him, Bettina.'

I lean back in my chair, tapping my fingers on the surface of my desk. Eddie glances at me.

'What's up with you?' he says.

I shrug and carry on drawing. 'I'm fine.'

'I've known you for three years, so don't tell me there's nothing wrong.'

I don't respond. The tension in my shoulders grows, I put my pencil down and massage the painful muscles. My fingers start to itch like crazy.

'Normally you'd be on this,' he says. 'You'd be messaging me all hours of the night with daft ideas, but you haven't been doing that and it feels like you've backed off. I want this job, Laura. Don't mess it up.'

'I'm sorry. I've had a lot on my mind but it's not fair on you. And I do have an idea, as it happens.'

He waits, possibly wondering what I've had on my mind, since my life is outwardly so uneventful.

'Fire away.'

I crumple up the sheet of paper I've been doodling on and aim it at the wastepaper basket. I miss.

'OK, listen. The client wants to attract British youth, but British youth comes in all sorts of shapes and sizes; you've got Street; there's Essex and Chelsea; there's the underprivileged and the privileged, the disabled, the content and the angry and the kids in between. You have Jews and Muslims, Christians; dog lovers and cat lovers. LGBTQ. Some non-stereotypes thrown in for good measure. There is no umbrella that's going to cover them all, but that's where the inspiration is. You give them something to unite them.'

He raises his eyebrows. 'And what better than an over-sweetened alcoholic beverage?'

'Don't be cynical.'

'Only in this room,' he quips. 'Actually, I think you may have something there. We just need an original take on an old story.'

I grin at him. 'Now you need to find the words, my friend. Or we're buggered.'

We are meeting the American clients tomorrow. Before we've taken their measure, before they've outlined their vision, it's hard to pull ideas out of thin air. I like to watch a client's body language. I can learn as much from that as Eddie can from a face. We can both tell if they really mean it; if they have real passion for what they are selling or if it's merely about the money.

I have the slender bottle of GZ in front of me and the January sun that streams through our blinds makes it look like maple syrup. I run my finger down the smooth glass. Since the assault, I'm afraid that I'm losing it. One of the few advantages of being face-blind is that your powers of concentration are ludicrously high. I spend my life terrified of missing clues and screwing up, hence, I focus. Or I used to.

‘OK.’ Eddie stands up and grabs his coat. ‘I’m going out on the terrace for a think. Want to come?’

When he says a think, he means a fag. Esther thinks he’s given up. I shake my head. ‘It’s too cold. I’ll keep drawing and see what comes out of this. Let me know if you have a brainwave.’

As soon as he’s gone I start to scratch my fingers and the relief is so intense I groan.

I log back on to Facebook. There’s one picture I keep revisiting. It’s of Finn. He is standing at the edge of the dance floor, his eyes glued to one person. Me. I’m beckoning to him, in an embarrassingly overt come-hither way.

Is he the one who called me a dark horse?

Jamie is behind me, leaning to shout something in someone’s ear. I have no memory of this, and at the time would have had no idea who it was I was encouraging. Only now do I realize what a dangerous game I was playing.

Was it Finn? My body is trembling. I try to block out the mental image of him in my bed. I examine his picture and then stand up and peer through the window in my door. He’s hunched forward, staring at his monitor, but then he clasps his hands behind his neck, forces his shoulders back and turns his head and there’s something about his body language, the way he stretches, his shirt coming untucked to show a triangle of flat stomach, that makes my own stomach clench. I leap backwards, my thigh connecting painfully with the corner of my desk. Tears spring to my eyes and I dash them away.

13

Laura

THAT EVENING MY RIDE HOME TAKES ME NORTH ALONG Fortress Road, past the grocer's, the barber's, the boarded-up shops and then right, to dog-leg through the residential streets. The area is edgy, expensive renovations butting up against deprivation. When I get home, my street is empty, no one lying in wait, no one watching, but I imagine danger in every shadow. I take my bag out of the basket, but while I'm rummaging for my keys I sense a movement. I spin round as a man crosses the road towards me, moving with purpose. My hands tighten around the handlebars; I'm ready to jump back on if I need to, but he only nods his thanks as I pull my bike out of his way.

There's something about him, something familiar, but I'm not sure. It may just be paranoia. I'm good on body language, and that nod was impersonal. It didn't signal that we knew each other. Disconcerted, I push the bike through the wrought-iron gate and over the cracked tessellated tiles. The Hills are in; the light is on in the downstairs flat, the blue flicker of the television set glowing behind lacy net curtains.

I shove the key into the lock and accidentally throw the door open so violently that it bounces against the wall and leaves a nick in the paint. I wince and wait for my neighbour to appear, but nothing happens. There is one letter lying on the little table, addressed to me, and the first thing I notice about it is that it has been hand-delivered. Unsettled, I lean my bike against the wall and open the door again. The cold air kisses my cheek as I look up and down the road, scrutinizing shadows. There's no one there, but I can't help thinking about the man who passed me just now. Did he really need to cross the road at that precise point? Did he have to come so close? Chilled, I shut the door and take the stairs two at a time.

Once safely in my flat, with the door double-locked and bolted, I check behind the sitting-room curtains before closing them. They are heavy, inter-lined brocade, and ten inches too long. I bought them from a second-hand curtain shop and didn't bother to raise the hem. I like the way they pool on the floor. I move to the bedroom and throw open the wardrobe. Nothing. It's cold and I shiver as I remove my coat and pull my grandfather's enormous old sweater on over my thin merino V-neck then change into sweatpants and sheepskin slippers.

Curled up on the sofa under a woollen throw, the TV control in one hand, the letter resting against the hill of my thighs, I settle on a repeat of a property programme so many years out of date that it has no relevance. I lift the envelope to my nose, but it only smells of the glue that keeps it closed. I open it and pull out a sheet of A4 white copy paper, folded in three. The words have been typed. I put my glasses on.

Dear Laura

This is a weird situation, don't you think? I expect you want me to feel guilty, but I don't see why I should. You made it clear you were up for it and didn't care who I was. I knew you wouldn't recognize me – I know all about your little problem

My hand drops to my thigh, the letter slipping to the floor. The only person I've told is Rebecca. Unless they've worked it out for themselves, no one else has a clue. But someone obviously does. I feel twitchy, hunted, even here, in my flat. This changes everything, because if he knows the truth about me, then that means what he did wasn't a stupid mistake, but something thought about, planned, fantasized over. Malicious. I reach for the letter and smooth it on to my knee.

– but no decent woman would behave like you did. The only thing I'll apologize for is leaving without saying anything, but if I hadn't, you would have accused me of something I didn't do and that would have been wrong – I know what women are like. If you think about it properly, you'll know it's true. Just because you felt shit in the morning, doesn't make me a bad human being. No one likes a tease.

I jump up, rip it in half and drop it into the kitchen bin, then I sit with my hands clamped between my legs, trembling with anger and disgust. He wants me to believe it was my fault; my fault I got drunk; my fault I invited him back into my flat; my fault I had sex with him. And part of me did believe it. But it's not my fault that I feel violated; not my fault that he chose to trick me; not my fault that he ran away rather than face me. My eyes sting as I swallow back the bile.

I'm not hungry, but I force down a few mouthfuls of a microwave tagliatelle. When I open the bin to throw away the remains, the letter is lying there, bright and white amongst the teabags and packaging. I carefully take the two halves out, lay them on the work surface and read what else the prick has to say.

> *I'm guessing you haven't figured out who I am. I'll tell you when I know that I can trust you not to make a fuss, but if you go to the police about this, I promise you, they are going to hear things you might want kept quiet. It was a great night. Epic. I still think about your hair draped over my face, about winding it round my hand and pulling you against me. You look nice with it up too but wear it down tomorrow. I like it like that.*
>
> *By the way, I didn't steal your pants. I picked them up with my stuff by mistake.*
>
> *x*

My body seems to know where to go and what to do. In my kitchen, there's a drawer and in that drawer, there is a pair of scissors. I take them into the bathroom, pull the light cord and face the woman in the mirror. I grab a hank of hair and cut through it. Then another and another, until my feet are covered with silky strands of dirty gold. I stare at myself. Short hair, chopped clumsily round a stranger's face. I touch it tentatively, feeling the ends. I try and even them out, but my efforts only make it worse.

I put the scissors down slowly and turn away, feeling less calm now, more inclined to break something. In the kitchen, I take a mug from the cupboard and drop it on the floor, but it bounces on the linoleum and doesn't shatter. A second one does. It makes a loud noise and the handle breaks off, but it is still inadequate, still not enough to pop my bubble. I pick up my wine glass and fling it at the tiles with a yell. This time it smashes, the pieces landing in the sink and skittering across the white work surface, shards bouncing off the edge, drops of red wine, like blood, spattered amongst them. Glass crunches under my slippered feet.

A sharp rap startles me. My immediate thought is that it's him. But how would he open the street door? Did he ring the downstairs bell? Would the Hills be stupid enough to let a stranger in?

Maybe, if I keep quiet, he'll leave.

Someone shouts. 'It's Phoebe, Laura. Is everything OK in there?'

Dizzy with relief, I lean against the door and slide down.

'Laura? I'm worried about you. Could you let me in?'

She pauses, listening. 'If you don't open up, I'll call the police.'

'I'm all right.'

'I can't be sure until I see you. Open up. I've got my phone in my hand. I'm pressing 999.'

I get to my feet reluctantly and pull the bolt.

She has her baby in her arms, and he twists round and stares at me. Phoebe is tall and slender and wears figure-hugging clothes. I don't know her well; just to say hello. They only moved in last August.

'Oh. My. God,' she says. She looks horrified and upset. As if I've committed a sacrilegious offence.

I bring my finger and thumb to the tips of my hair and test it gently, rubbing it between them. She reaches towards me and I wince, but she smiles and gently peels a long strand off my shoulder. I don't know what to say but fortunately Phoebe isn't the type to be bothered by an awkward situation. She bustles into my flat and I follow her, closing the door behind me.

'Sorry about the mess,' I mumble. 'Give me a second while I sweep this lot up.'

She takes the dustpan and brush out of my hand and puts them down. 'You're coming downstairs with me. Where are your keys?'

'I can't.'

'Yes, you can. It's just me and Noah and I'm about to put him down for the night.'

I feel irresolute, embarrassed and miserable. She stretches out a hand.

'Come on.'

I nod and pick up my keys. I don't want to be alone.

'Where's your husband?' I ask as Phoebe joins me, proffering a glass of wine, Noah having gone off with barely a murmur. She sits down beside me, watching me intently, searching my face, sympathetic. Her calm begins to steal over me, soothing my nerves.

'Elliot's at his book club. There's a group of blokes from work. I don't think they actually read the books though. He doesn't anyway – I read them for him.'

There are specific things that my brain has tagged about Phoebe. She has two earrings in each ear. She has a birthmark in the dip where her right shoulder meets her neck. When she stands her left foot points slightly inwards.

Phoebe nips out of the room and returns with a workman-like black bag. It turns out that she cuts hair for a living. I am so drained I don't argue when she offers to tidy up the mess I've created. I sit quietly while she snips and chatters, and I learn several things about her. She is the eldest of three but is closest to Harriet. She wants another baby. She is besotted with her husband. I feel guilty that I give so little of myself, but she's too polite to probe.

And now I am even more of a stranger to myself than ever; the owner of a feathery bob that starts high at the back of my head and flows into peaks at my jaw. The fringe changes the shape of my face. I try to flick it aside, with mixed results.

'Use heavier eyeliner and mascara,' Phoebe suggests. 'To balance things out.'

The main thing is, it looks deliberate, not the pitiful result of a moment's lunacy.

We hear the key in the latch and Phoebe immediately stands up. I follow suit, it's getting late and I don't want to be in the way. Elliot comes in, smiling as she embraces him. He sees me, and his surprise shows in the way he unwraps his wife's arms.

'Hi,' he says. 'I didn't recognize you.' He indicates my hair.

I nod, and because I can't think of anything else to do, I walk up to him and hold out my hand. 'We haven't met properly yet,' I say. 'I'm Laura Maguire.'

'Elliot Hill.' He takes my hand then looks from me to Phoebe. 'So, what have I missed?'

'Nothing,' Phoebe shrugs. 'Girl talk. I thought it was time Laura and I got to know each other, so I knocked on her door.'

'I'm off,' I say, as a silence develops. It's obvious Elliot wants his wife to himself. I edge past them to the door. 'Thanks so much for the haircut, Phoebe. Thanks for everything.'

'De nada,' she says. 'Anytime. Sleep well.'

When I get in I see I have several messages from Eddie. I scroll through them, feeling guilty that I haven't done any work for the meeting tomorrow. I bang out a reply, reassuring him that I'm on it; love his ideas; will get in early and we'll have a treatment done by nine. He doesn't reply, so I hope he's getting an early night like a sensible new dad.

I tidy up the flat, sweeping up the breakages in the kitchen and the hair from the bathroom, where it's got into the sink and the tub as well as all over the floor. There's so much of it.

I slide the torn-up letter between Patricia Cornwell and Val McDermid on the shelf to the left of the chimneypiece. My one piece of evidence. Then I fall into bed and I sleep.

14

Laura

IT'S POURING WITH RAIN, BUT MY BODY REFUSES TO move. It won't allow me to cross the threshold into work, even though my umbrella is embarrassingly inadequate with its broken spoke and tendency to suddenly invert. The wind is cold on my newly bared neck, a reminder of last night's madness.

I wonder if he already knows that I'm out here, barely able to breathe, or if he slept any better than I did last night, anticipating the day ahead. Did he picture me finding his letter, examining the envelope, opening it, reading the words he agonized over? I can guess. In his wildest imaginings, I will walk in with my hair up and then pull out the pins, toss my head and let it tumble around my shoulders. His words will catch in his throat as he rises to greet me . . . The picture dissipates. Reality intervenes.

How will he interpret my deliberate act of sabotage? I'm beginning to regret what I've done. It's going to send out the message that he's got to me, not that I don't give a toss what he thinks of my hair. People like him don't rationalize normally. They interpret every act to fit their own narrative.

Miserable little prick. I refuse to let this ruin my life. Whoever he is, he is going to find out that he is not in control.

People are looking at me, wondering what I'm doing. I'm not even pretending to be on the phone; just standing on the pavement getting wet, staring at the building. Someone, a woman, hesitates at the door with its sloping, intertwined G & M, then turns and asks me if I'm OK.

'I'm fine,' I say. 'I had an idea on the way in and I'm trying to pin it down before I forget it.'

'Like your hair, by the way.'

'Thanks.' I want to believe her.

Discouraged, she leaves me to it with an apology for breaking my train of thought.

I meant to be early, to be at my desk by half seven, so that I could fulfil my promise to Eddie and also to avoid making an entrance with my new look, but even though I fell asleep straight away last night, I woke at three and didn't drop off again until nearly five, then I overslept.

Years ago, when I was studying *Macbeth* in sixth form, I came across a line that stuck with me. The quote is Duncan's: '*There's no art to find the mind's construction in the face; He was a gentleman on whom I built an absolute trust.*'

I read the quote so often that I learned it by heart. It struck me that I had never experienced what he described,

I never truly felt that I understood or trusted anyone. How could I, when I found it so hard to recognize my friends? A face is a catalyst to action; it launches a thousand ships, it affects behaviour and outcomes. We are judged and judge by its symmetry, the pleasure or dislike it engenders. It is life's greatest lottery.

Without that, how am I supposed to know?

Finn didn't have a girlfriend waiting for him at home that night. So, what did he do when the evening ended? Did he seize his opportunity and get into the taxi with me? I've rechecked the lists several times over. There is no one else except David. I need to find out where he was, as a matter of urgency, but, so far, I haven't been able to access his diary.

The stairwell is so quiet I can hear the internal workings of the building, the heating system, the hum of the server. My senses are overactive, the cold touch of the brass banister stinging my fingers, the lingering smell of pine cleaning fluid sickening me. I open the doors to the first floor and the buzz of conversation dies as people take in what I've done. I cross to my office and close the door behind me and the noise starts up again. I glance through the window, but everyone is studiously gazing at their monitors. Everyone except one man. He is standing, his head slightly tilted, watching. I turn away.

When I look again he's gone, and I could kick myself. If that was him, I should have watched to see where he went. Even so, I remember the essentials, his figure is burnt on my retinas; dark jeans, white shirt with the sleeves rolled up.

I dump the now-defunct umbrella in the bin, hang my coat on the hook and boot up my computer. I follow my normal routines. My hands are trembling, as they have been since Christmas. There's a click and my stomach does a somersault. I turn around and release my breath on a sigh. It's Agnes. The only grey-haired, middle-aged woman in the building.

'You look gorgeous, Laura. Like a 1920s starlet.'

'Thank you.' I should be smiling, but my lips won't move. 'It feels unnatural.'

'Well, it suits you.'

Her kindness is soothing, like Phoebe's was last night. But it's not enough. The anticipation of what this day will bring is so great that I can barely focus.

'I wanted to let you know that I've bought a book of condolences for everyone to sign. It's on my desk. Can I make you a coffee? Tea?' She smiles. 'Eddie's just come in.'

'Oh good.' I wince inwardly. I'm in trouble.

Eddie's reaction is classic delayed shock. He doesn't mention the glaringly obvious for several minutes. Then he asks me why I did it.

'I felt like a change,' I say.

'Bit drastic, wasn't it?'

'Do you hate it?'

'No, of course I don't hate it. It'll take some getting used to, that's all. At least I won't find any more long hairs in my tea.'

I poke out my tongue and touch my hair for the millionth time.

I open my emails and scroll through them, deleting the junk, thinking things through. It takes someone particularly small to make a victim of a vulnerable woman. The man who did it, did it for two reasons: malice and the need to feel powerful. Finn is on his way up in an industry that values his gregarious nature and charm. David Gunner is already there. This company is successful, and he has respect throughout the industry. If it was him, then he has a weakness, something he's ashamed of.

Men like them think they are untouchable.

She enjoyed it. Where's the harm?

Deep inside I shrivel a little bit more.

'Show me what you've done?' Eddie says.

I grimace. 'Give me half an hour.'

He stares at me. 'I don't believe it. Christ, Laura. This is important.'

'I know, I know. And I'm sorry I've let you down. Something happened last night, and I was upset.'

'Well, now I'm upset. I thought we were a team.'

'I said I was sorry.' I drag my sketchbook over and flip it open on a clean page. My movements are sharp.

His tone softens. 'Is it the haircut? Because it's fine, you know. It's cool.'

'Yes,' I say, not looking at him. 'But it wasn't what I wanted.'

'It's not the end of the world. It'll grow out.'

He's trying to be sensitive, but I know what he's thinking. I'm turning out to be the sort of girl who lets a bad haircut get in the way of her job. He's disappointed and so am I.

I look at him and try to smile.

He sighs and puts his hands on my shoulders. 'Guy's death has affected us all.'

I haven't thought about Guy, not for hours. Eddie's hands begin to feel like weights on my shoulders. I move, so that he does too, and turn away.

15

Laura

BETTINA IS ARRANGING BOTTLES OF GZ ON THE GLASS shelves either side of the giant GM badge. With the lights trained on them, they glow neon against the deep blue wall. They are the first thing your eye is drawn to when you walk in. Bettina is grappling with David's instructions that there should be exactly four centimetres between each bottle. Since, according to Bettina at least, she is numerically dyslexic, the task is proving a good deal more challenging than it ought to be. Her struggle doesn't go unnoticed, and she has the odd facetious comment thrown her way.

I'm standing, hands on hips, resisting the urge to help, when someone moves into my personal space. My nerves jangle.

'It looks great, Bettina,' I say, glancing round to see who isn't at their desk. I release a breath. It's only Graham. 'I think you can stop fiddling now.' The labels are all perfectly aligned, the bottles running along the centre of the shelf; nothing out of place by so much as a millimetre. I look at my watch. 'The cab should be picking them up from the airport round about now.'

'What?' She sounds surprised. 'No. Not for half an hour.'

My stomach does a sickening flop. 'The pick-up was at ten fifteen.'

'Shit.' The colour drains from her face. 'I told them ten forty-five. Oh my God, Laura. What am I going to do? They'll kill me.'

I press my fingertips against my forehead with a grimace. 'Get on the phone, get hold of the cab company. And don't panic,' I add, because her mouth is hanging open, her eyes brimming with tears. 'Just deal with it.'

'Idiot,' Graham says, shrugging as he turns away.

Bettina races back to her desk and grabs the phone. I hope she can resolve this quickly. If there's a car in the area, it won't be more than five minutes late and with any luck Paige Adler will be none the wiser.

That hope dwindles when David throws open the door to his office and strides over to Bettina's desk. As she finishes the call, he says something to her and she looks up. Instinctively, I move towards them. She looks terrified. And then he lets rip, in full view of the rest of us. I watch in dismay as she dissolves.

'You fucking cretin,' he explodes. 'Do you know how important this woman is? Do you even appreciate the lengths I've been to, to get her business? Do you have a single fucking brain cell under that mop of yours? There are people who would kill to be in your shoes. Where did you come from anyway? I assume you're somebody's daughter. Christ! Why do I get lumbered with the morons?'

Tears roll down Bettina's cheeks. Around the room, her colleagues have paused, hands hovering over keyboards, conversations cut off.

'I'm sorry,' she sobs. 'I'm really sorry.'

'Fucking fix it and then pack up your belongings and get lost.'

'You . . . you mean I've got to go?'

'What do *you* think?' he snarls. 'You're a liability.'

He turns on his heel and slams back into his office. There's a moment's silence before the normal clatter of the room starts again. I follow him, but Rebecca is there before me, standing in front of his door as if she's guarding it. I'm not on my own. Someone else, a man, has joined us.

'He can't speak to her like that,' he says.

'I know, Finn,' she soothes. 'I know, and I'll talk to him.'

'He humiliated her in front of everyone,' I say. 'We can't . . .' I hesitate, thrown off track; David is wearing black jeans and a white shirt with the sleeves rolled up. It was him watching me earlier. I realize Finn and Rebecca are waiting. 'We can't let him get away with it. It was horrible.'

'Laura . . . Finn, please. You both need to stay out of this. David has been under a lot of pressure recently. We need to give him a chance to calm down. I guarantee he already knows he was wrong. I promise you. I know David. The best way to take the heat out of his anger is to ignore him.'

She's like a bird protecting its chicks from predators. I'm sure that's the way my sister used to deal with

Dominic and Milo's tantrums. I have a memory of her stepping over one of them, blithely getting on with whatever it was she was doing, while he pounded the floor with his fists and howled. Now my boss has just thrown a paddy and is being treated like a toddler by his business partner.

'Ignore him?' I say.

'Try and see it his way. He doesn't like being made to look bad, or the company coming across as inefficient or unprofessional. He is quite literally rolling out the red carpet for Paige Adler, and if anything goes wrong it reflects badly on him.'

'Unbelievable,' Finn says.

I stare at him, not realizing I'm frowning until he raises his eyebrows at me.

Bettina has run out of the room and up to the Ladies. I go after her and knock on the door, then knock harder because she's sobbing so loudly that she can't hear me. I give her a minute to pull herself together before I speak. Finally, she blows her nose.

'Rebecca's going to talk to him,' I say. 'Don't leave yet.'

I worry that the moment she steps outside the building, that will be it. Even if David relents, she won't return. Better to keep her here on the off chance. God, what a dick.

'But he's right. I am stupid. And everyone heard me make a fool of myself.'

'No one's going to remember it was you. What's going to stick in their minds is David Gunner kicking off like a spoilt brat. So, don't worry. You have their sympathy. Finn stuck up for you.' It physically hurts to say that.

'Did he?'

'Yes, he did. You made a mistake, that's all. Fortunately, you work for an advertising agency, not a hospital. You haven't killed anyone.'

She laughs. 'You're so funny.'

'Did you have a chance to book a new car?'

'Yes. There was one dropping a passenger off. They said it'd be two minutes.'

'There you go then. It's going to be fine.'

She comes out and splashes her face with cold water. I stand beside her, looking at our reflection in the mirror. That's Bettina, and that's me, Laura Maguire. We are different in so many ways. And yet. Cover our hair, take away this building, show me again. I would not know. I feel a wave of frustration and despair. I almost tell her, I so badly want to take the burden off my shoulders, but this is Bettina, I remind myself, so I can't risk it.

She blows her nose again, sighs deeply and smiles at me. 'You're a good friend, Laura.'

On impulse I give her a hug; something I only ever do with my family. She's surprisingly strong as she hugs me back.

'I've never heard him yell like that before,' she says as she pulls away. She combs her fingers through her hair and pushes it behind her shoulders. 'That was *so* not OK.'

Fifteen minutes later, while I'm running some colour photocopies of my drawings, David saunters out of his office and over to Bettina, who, at mine and Rebecca's urging, has valiantly stayed put.

'I apologize,' he says. 'I was out of order. I've spoken to Paige Adler and she wasn't kept waiting long.'

'I really am sorry.'

'I know you are, sweetheart. And so am I. My life is mad crazy right now. I need to know I can rely on my staff one hundred per cent. So, no more fuck-ups.'

'No more fuck-ups.'

He smiles warmly at her. 'I'll have a latte if you've nothing better to do.'

I roll my eyes. We're all good then? David, it strikes me as I make my way back to my office, is the type of man who gets away with murder. I wonder what his childhood was like. I'd guess he's the only boy amongst doting sisters. Either that or he's an only child and his parents think the sun shines out of his arse.

'Fifteen minutes, Laura,' he calls over. 'You two ready?'

'Yup,' I say.

I think, if you're the one, David, then you'll be thinking you're safe. Things don't go wrong for men like you. Until they do.

16

Laura

THE MEETING ROOM SMELLS OF FRESH COFFEE AND pastries bought from a trendy local bakery where they use spelt flour, and price accordingly. The clients, Paige Adler and her assistant Charlie Adams, take their coffee black. David fusses, giving them his 'five-star treatment'. There is no sign of his earlier outburst. It's as if it never happened.

Paige Adler has dark hair and a curvaceous figure, and, like Rebecca, she knows how to make the best of her assets. She doesn't wear earrings and has a pair of glasses hanging on a chain around her neck that draws attention to her bust. Charlie has a ponytail and a silver hoop in his left ear.

I pour myself a coffee and when I look round there is someone beside me. White shirt, sleeves rolled up. He is standing too close, so that I can feel the electricity from the hairs on his forearm. I look down at his shoes and recognize David's pointed brogues.

'You cut your hair,' he says.

'I fancied a change.'

David frowns and takes a closer look. And then he touches it, and I recoil.

'Is it a statement?' he asks.

I stiffen, and the cup almost slips from my hand, coffee spilling on to the polished cherry-wood cabinet. 'What do you mean?'

'Isn't it the sort of thing women do when they want to send a message to a bloke?'

'It's not all about men, you know,' I say. 'Sometimes we women do things just because we want to.'

'I humbly apologize,' he says, sounding neither humble nor apologetic. He sounds amused.

While I'm wiping up the coffee, the door opens, and a woman walks in. From her confidence and, frankly, the shape of her figure, I can tell it's Rebecca Munro.

'Ah, Rebecca,' David says. 'Now we can start.'

I force away the idea of David in my bed because if I allow myself to think about it now, I'll fall apart. Instead I do what I always do at these meetings and spend a few moments orientating myself and putting names to each figure. The Americans are easy because of their abrasive New York accents and because they are the guests of honour and David, who always takes the same seat at the head of the table, has been laying on the charm. Eddie sits next to me, like he always does. Bettina, who has stayed because she asked to observe, I have no problem with, and our senior account manager, the one who gets the big brands, Paul Digby – grey hair, glasses, short neck – is sitting to the left of the client.

I can't help stealing glances at David's mouth and hands, and Christ, when at one point he stands up, my eyes drop to his crotch. I am so aware of him, so tuned into everything he says, to every movement, every gesture, that I barely listen while he eulogizes the product. I look at his lips and his ears, at his hairline, hoping for a spark of recognition, and take a mental picture of his hand and place it on my skin.

If it was him and not Finn, has he got the message that I'm not interested in forgiveness or understanding? Or maybe he thinks he's won. I could have made things worse for myself. There's nothing I can do about that, though. The damage is done.

I'm stressed and angry and anxious and it's not a helpful way to be. I try harder, grounding myself, thinking about where I am, not who I'm with, and the job I am here to do.

'Over to you, Laura and Eddie. Let's see what you've got.'

Eddie stands up and I follow suit. I prefer to work on a sketchbook than a MacBook, at least in the early stages, so we have a flip chart. I explain, not brilliantly, the core elements of our ideas and then Eddie takes over and, with his boyish enthusiasm, brings my pictures to life. Finally, he hits them with his strapline.

'We are one when we are many.'

'Uh huh,' Paige says. 'That's it?'

'Yes,' Eddie says, his puppyish enthusiasm still in evidence despite the underwhelming response. 'It's supposed to imply embracing our differences and being stronger; connected yet retaining our individuality.'

'I get that. So, this is what you're going with? The Coca-Cola moment. Perfect harmony.'

'Oh no,' I say. 'Let me explain my thinking. Your problem with the product is, how do we get people to choose GZ when there are thousands of alcoholic drinks? We need to go back a step, not try and reel them in with the label, colour or even the taste, but to find a human truth. What do we fear, deep down?' I look at Rebecca and her lips twitch into a small smile. 'We fear missing out; we fear loneliness; we fear not being respected, not being part of the zeitgeist, of falling behind. We are all scrabbling to keep up, when there's only one thing that is important, and that is communication. You are not alone if you talk to each other. We've grown away from the ideals of the 1970s and we know that there will never be perfect harmony. If we can accept that and accept each other, we can be stronger together. It rests on the idea that we've matured, and that we rise above the things that cause friction between different cultures, even within our own societies, and hold on to each other because we're human beings. The message is simple and powerful: Give people a chance. But we don't sermonize, we make them laugh.'

'Bravo,' Rebecca says too brightly. 'Well done, you two. So, Paige? Charlie? What do you think?'

There's a silence.

First meetings are more about getting an idea of what is in the client's head than having the perfect words and drawings to show them, but even so it feels like we have disappointed. Sometimes, during a meeting, magic happens. It's like a successful dinner party:

there's chemistry between the guests, there's a kind of delight in each other; conversation sparkles between suits and creatives and no one is silent. Sometimes that doesn't happen, the match strikes again and again, but doesn't light. At times like that there's an unnerving solidity about the proceedings and it can feel like a double chemistry lesson.

'Laugh?' Paige says. 'I'm not sure I understand.'

'I don't mean split your sides hilarious,' I say. 'I just mean inject some dry humour. It's very British.'

'Let me think about that and get back to you.'

David has his hands steepled in front of his mouth. He is quieter than normal, allowing Rebecca to lead.

Paige and Charlie tilt their heads, like birds contemplating a worm. 'Yeah,' Paige says. 'Needs fleshing out, but I think we have a germ here. Let's talk next week.'

'What do you think?' I hear Rebecca say, after Paige and Charlie have left.

David twitches his brows. 'What do I think? I think the American trollop's bought it.'

Rebecca laughs. 'Don't let her hear you call her that. Do you want to go and get some lunch?'

'Laura?' David says, spotting me lurking. 'What were you on?'

I flush. 'I don't know what you mean.'

'You appear to have cut off your pizzazz with your hair.'

I stand there stupidly, just looking at him.

'Off you go.'

* * *

When I come out, some of my more curious colleagues turn their heads. I give them an embarrassed smile but inside I freeze. It's as though I'm on a stage in front of a thousand people and have forgotten what I'm going to say.

Which one are you? Which one? Which one?

I need to get out of here.

'Budge yourself, Laura. You're causing a bottleneck,' Eddie says.

I walk straight to our room and grab my bag and coat. I don't even shut down my computer. Eddie comes after me as I hurry through the stairwell doors and clatter down the stairs.

'Where're you going?' He takes my arm, but I shake him off.

'Out.'

'Hey, come on. Is this to do with what I said earlier? I'm sorry if you thought I was getting at you. Don't go off in a huff.'

I can feel the heat in my face and the sheen of tears across my eyes. Eddie studies me, concerned and bewildered. I rush out of the building into the driving rain. He comes after me, but I turn and shriek at him.

'Eddie, leave me alone!'

He holds his hands up and backs off. 'OK. Calm down. Go for a walk, Laura. Get your head straight and come back.'

I look up at the building. A shadow moves behind David's Gunner's blinds.

'I'll call you,' I say. 'Go in, Eddie. You're getting soaked to the skin.'

'But—'

But I've gone, half running to the corner, desperate for space to breathe, my legs so wobbly that I clutch hold of a railing. The main road is a blur of traffic and people, rain and sound. A bell rings and I jerk back, realizing I've stepped into the road without looking. A cyclist skids, stops a yard or so further on, glares at me over his shoulder and calls me something disgusting before speeding off.

It doesn't last long. I have only to catch sight of the dishevelled creature in the window of a solicitor's office to wonder what on earth I'm doing, allowing this situation to literally drive me crazy. I retrace my steps, working out in my head what I'm going to say to Eddie. Outside the door, I glance across the road at David's car parked in its little wedge and something occurs to me. I remember that it was there when we left the office to walk to the club that night. I scan the walls of the buildings to either side of it. There is a camera trained on the space. I chew my lip, thinking, then I push open the doors and go up to the desk.

Chris, one of two security guys employed at the agency, looks up from his newspaper. He wears his long, greying hair tied back in a ponytail at the nape of his neck. The other, Jason, is a lot rounder.

'The security camera pointed at David's car? Is it working?'

'Yup. Why? Is he worried about it?'

'No. He's fine. I was wondering how long you keep the recordings for.'

'They get wiped every couple of months.'

It's the tenth of January. Getting on for three weeks since that night. Chances are the footage is still there. If I can find out whether David's car stayed in the car park, then I'll have some confirmation, if not proof. If the car park was empty, then it wasn't him. I thank Chris and run upstairs. Now I need to think up a convincing excuse to review the recordings.

'Sorry,' I say, as Eddie pushes his chair back and stands up.

Mollified, he puts his arms around me and I stand, stiff as a board, my nose pressed into his shoulder.

'Do you want to talk about it?'

I pull away. 'No, it's OK. I'm fine now.'

I'm not, but at least I have a sense of purpose. I don't know if it was Finn or David, but I do know it was one of them. I'm going to smoke him out, and I know how I'm going to do it.

17

Rebecca

'I KNOW YOU THINK YOU HAVE PAIGE WRAPPED AROUND your little finger,' Rebecca says when the waiter has left their food; her seared tuna on a bed of celeriac mash; David's rare steak and hand-cut, twice-cooked chips. She likes the air of hushed intimacy here, the darkness produced by a paint colour that blurs the distinction between blue and black. The art posters tacked to the walls are funky and current. 'But she's a businesswoman. She didn't look particularly fired up.'

'It'll be fine.' He dismisses her concerns with an impatient flick of his hand, which she reads as defensive.

'In what way will it be fine? You should have been backing Eddie and Laura up, throwing a little David Gunner stardust their way, but you sat there with a face like a wet weekend. If we lose out because you couldn't be bothered to pitch in . . . And what the hell was all that about with Bettina?' She feels buoyed by righteous anger. On this issue at least, she is in the right.

'She fucked up.'

'She did, but you went way over the top, in front of everyone. What were you thinking?'

'I apologized. It's over.'

He leans forward and looks straight into her eyes. 'You don't have to be jealous of Paige, you know.'

'I'm not! That is not what this is about.'

He ignores her. 'I was only trying to keep her sweet. I know what women like her want.'

Rebecca groans. 'That is a ridiculous thing to say. Do you even know what I want?'

'I think I do. At least, I haven't had any complaints.'

'I don't mean that, David. I mean the years are going by and here we are, in the same place. You have everything, and I have nothing.'

His face closes. He carves into his steak and pops a bloody morsel into his mouth.

'You have me,' he says eventually. 'And you have half of Gunner Munro. I wouldn't call that nothing.'

'Lucky me. Perhaps I should find someone to marry. If I get on with it, my first baby will be able to play with Daisy.' She laughs dryly and drinks some water, wishing it was wine, suffering for the sake of a probably non-existent foetus. This is a ridiculous argument, manufactured by her, that they shouldn't be having. She's got to calm down.

To her surprise, he nods. 'Actually, that's not such a duff idea. You could get married and we could carry on as we are. There are plenty of single directors out there. You could take your pick.'

She isn't flattered. 'Yeah. Single for a good reason. I was joking, David.'

'Look, I do know what you're talking about. I understand, but there is nothing I can do, short of leaving my wife and children and losing everything I've worked for. Lissy would stick me in the fucking washing machine and wring me out with her bare hands.'

The analogy makes her smile. 'Are you saying it's about the money? Because I have money. You don't need hers.'

He looks sympathetic and that makes her tense. 'You know it's not that simple. Lissy is my home. She is where I go for peace and comfort. She's normality, boring but necessary. I don't need any more pressure right now.'

She laughs. She can't help herself, it's such a ridiculous concept. 'You thrive on pressure.'

He glares at her, and she can feel his hostility. She's not sure what she's done, apart from state the obvious. Then it's gone, the suspicion that he resents her for some reason has dissolved and his brown eyes are full of love.

'Will you relax, Becs. GZ is in the bag.'

She picks at her tuna, refusing to melt. 'You'd better be right.'

'Don't be cross with me,' he wheedles. 'Come on, smile.'

She tries not to, but he keeps looking at her and eventually she caves, her lips pulling up at the corners.

'That's better. Friends?'

'I suppose so,' she grumbles. 'You drive me nuts, David. You know that, don't you?'

'Of course I do. And you drive me wild with desire.'

'Will you stop it.'

'You're laughing,' he says, grinning at her.

'I am not.'

'Yes, you are.'

'For God's sake.' She presses her lips together. 'Seriously, David.'

'Sweetheart, let's not get serious.'

She doesn't say anything; she eats and allows the silence to open out and flow, winding between the other tables, cooling to condensation on the windows. After a while she tells him about her sister's latest bee in her bonnet. It's better to stick to safe subjects.

'I don't know,' David mutters.

She's not sure if he's speaking to her, but he sounds sad and somehow far away, as if he isn't sitting here, but in another place. She reaches for his hand, bringing him back to the now, to her.

'Is this about Guy?' she asks.

He shrugs. 'He worked for me, and he's gone. Of course I feel crap about it. Who doesn't? Let's get out of here. I need a fag.'

'Since when did you start smoking again?'

'If you'd had the Christmas I had, you'd understand. Look, I'm sorry if I've seemed disengaged lately. I'm stressing about Tony and Georgie. I don't know what's best for them, or for me for that matter. I feel guilty because I want them to be gone even though I love them, and I couldn't be more grateful for everything they've done for me. But honestly? I can't cope with them much longer.'

He weaves his fingers through hers and squeezes. His hand is warm and dry, reassuring.

Rebecca has met Tony and Georgie many times over the years. In fact, she has a feeling she met them before Felicity did. She's been at the christenings of all their great-grandchildren. At Spike's, the changes were barely noticeable but by the time it got to Daisy's it was obvious that the roles had been reversed. She feels compassion, but they're old. They need to be guided into a safe space and looked after with understanding and kindness. They should be in a home. God knows, David can afford it. But even so, he'll still feel responsible, like he does for his wife and kids. Out of the trio of pressures, there is only one that would be easily jettisoned, that it would be morally right for him to jettison. Her.

'I don't know what I would do without you,' he says, gazing into her eyes.

'You don't have to do without me, ever.'

'Rebecca,' David says.

She feels it in his tone, he's realized that the door has opened a crack. She needs to close it fast.

'Let's talk later, shall we?' she says. 'Come to mine tonight.'

She needs to know what's going on with him. Did Christmas in the bosom of his family remind him of what he stands to lose? Is he still feeling the residual warmth of his sister-in-law's fireside, of basking in their approval? It'll wear off eventually, she supposes. In the meantime, she's expected to keep her mouth shut, to be uncomplaining and patient.

David gestures at the waitress for the bill and slaps his company credit card on to the tray.

'Thank you, that was delicious,' he tells her. 'I love this place.'

'Fucking daylight robbery,' he says, when she's out of earshot. 'Just because they've stuck a load of twatty art posters on the walls and whipped the floorboards with chains. Pretentious wankers.'

Rebecca winces, knowing the bearded, tweed-jacketed maître d' with the skinny jeans and pointed boots has heard. When she looks at the floor though, she concedes he's right. No way have these boards come by their dents and dark patina naturally. She grins at him and as she picks up her bag, scratches her fingernail down his black jeans.

They shrug into their coats and David winds the moss-green cashmere scarf that Felicity gave him for Christmas around his neck. Rebecca does up her buttons and turns up her faux fur collar and together they step out into the bitter cold. David buys a packet of cigarettes from the newsagent and lights up. She takes the cigarette from him and takes a long drag, then realizes what she's doing and blows the smoke out without inhaling.

18

Laura

LATER ON THAT DAY I TYPE THE WORDS, *I KNOW IT WAS you* on two halves of a sheet of A4, print it out and cut it in two. I fold one of them into four and put the other in an envelope. I close the document without saving it. Little in my world is cut and dried, little of it black and white. When faces merge, so do all lines of separation. There is what I want and what I know and what I believe, and somewhere in those three are other people's truths and the truth of what happened that night. I don't know whether it was Finn Broadbent or David Gunner who got into the taxi with me, and I can't ask them. And to accuse the wrong person would be to destroy my working relationship with him and possibly my career.

My solution is to hide in an emptying building and leave my messages, like the Easter bunny hiding chocolate eggs, hoping to cause no more than confusion in one man, and something else, something I can taste, in another.

Finn leaves with a group of men that includes Eddie

at around six forty-five, the rest drift away over the next half hour, Rebecca at half seven, to catch an exhibition of photographic works by a hot commercial director. She pokes her head around my door and tells me not to stay too late. David is still here and, just when I'm getting jittery, he's joined by Paul Digby and they leave together. While the cleaners bang round the desks and chairs, dragging their red Henry Hoovers behind them, I discreetly put the door to the terrace on the latch, wedging it with a folded Christmas card that I found in the recycle bin, so that it won't fly open.

'You off?' Chris says, when I finally emerge and come downstairs.

'Yup. It's been a long day. How's Carl doing?'

His eldest son started at Edinburgh University last October and as the first in the family to go to uni, let alone do A levels, Chris is bursting with pride.

'He's loving it. Got himself a posh girlfriend too.'

I open my bag and pretend to be looking for something, working up the courage to say what I need to. 'Chris. Would it be possible to take a look at the security tapes for the twenty-second of December? It's just that I thought I saw something weird when I came back to get my bike. A man loitering. It's been preying on my mind. If it's a pain, don't worry. It doesn't matter.' Chris wouldn't know or care that I didn't come back for my bike.

He considers my question, then puts down the paper. 'What time?'

'Oh, let me think. I didn't look at the time. Start at midnight, through to two a.m. That should cover it.'

'Jason would have been on then.' He taps, and frowns. Taps again and his frown deepens. 'Sorry. It's gone. Maybe it was something to do with it being the end of the year, but there's nothing here.'

'Are you sure?'

'Do you want me to take another look?'

The disappointment is crushing. 'Do they get wiped automatically?'

'No. I do it every few months. I don't remember doing this one though, but I wouldn't put it past me. Start of a brand-new year and all that. I expect I was being over-efficient.'

Or someone else was.

'Sorry about that,' Chris says.

When I leave, David's car is still parked opposite. Maybe he and Paul have gone for a drink.

Instead of turning left towards Old Street, I walk round the block to the alleyway at the back of the buildings and stand in the shadow of the terrace, concealed by the industrial wastepaper bins, and wait. To distract myself I think through my storyboard, frame by frame, working out how many shots it'll need, what sort of backgrounds. Everything I draw has to reflect Eddie's words and move the message on.

Once the lights go out upstairs, I climb the metal steps and quietly let myself in. I've planned every detail, so that I won't have to stop and think. A few of the monitors are still live, giving off a ghostly glow. A phone rings, the sound echoing through the empty room before it stops.

I tuck one of the notes under Finn's keyboard so that only a tiny corner shows, then I go into Agnes's office and sit down at her desk. I type the name of her cat into the password box. Ignatius. Incorrect. I try it again, this time substituting '1's for the 'i's. It works, and I say a silent thank you to the God of Obvious Passwords then open the shared diary and click on December. On the twenty-second it says *staff party.* On the twenty-third it says *David Somerset.* But on the twenty-first Agnes has written: *Felicity Somerset*, so there was no wife waiting for him to come home that night. He had as much opportunity as Finn did. I close my eyes and breathe out.

Remembering to click back into January in case it doesn't do it automatically, I close the diary, move to David's office and place the envelope on his desk. I shift it this way and that, first propping it against his phone, then laying it flat on top of his closed laptop. Finally, I prop it up again. It feels more sinister that way. As I turn, the strip lights flicker into life, the fluorescent strips marching across the room. Startled, I don't move for a second, and then I hear voices. David calling down to Chris.

'Give me two minutes!'

19

Laura

I SPIN ROUND, MY HAND TO MY THROAT, LOOKING FOR somewhere to hide. I have no reason to be in David's office, no excuse up my sleeve. The room is oblong, with a window, a desk, and a sofa and two chairs arranged around a coffee table. There is no helpful cupboard to slip into, no adjoining door into Rebecca's office. My palms are sweating as I duck down behind the sofa.

The door opens and closes behind him. He lifts the lid of his laptop and it illuminates the room. His fingers tap the keys. He swears to himself. The room goes still and my nerves tingle. I can feel him looking at the envelope, feel his curiosity. The radiator I'm pressed against is going off but is still warm enough to make me sweat under my coat, and the dust on the fabric of the chair tickles my nose. I hang on to every nerve, every fibre, willing my body to control itself. In the silence the seal rips, he pulls the paper out and unfolds it. I imagine his initial bewilderment as he reads my words.

'What the fuck?'

There's a noise that sounds like a stifled groan and a thump that could be the side of his fist hitting the wall. I wince and screw up my face.

'Christ.'

He walks to the door, opens it and looks out. Then he goes to the window and parts the blinds.

Time stands still. His shoes shuffle and his chair castors rotate against the hard floor as he sits down. A drawer opens and slams, and then, finally, he snaps his laptop shut and gets up. His phone beeps. He swears again, tapping out a reply as he crosses the room to the window. He leans against it. If he looked to the side he would see something, a section of shoulder, the heel of my boot, a part of me at least, crouched and trembling like a petrified dog.

And then he's gone. As soon as the lights go out, I crawl from my hiding place and watch him through the blind. His car lights flash and he gets in and reverses with a shriek of tyres. My breathing is ragged, my fingernails have dug so hard into my palms that they have left small indentations like elongated dashes: like Morse code. He's gone, but there is still a light on in the stairwell and I hear lumbering steps. I dash across the room to the terrace and let myself out then crouch in the shadows under the fire escape until I'm certain Chris is back behind his desk. Finally, I go home.

20

Rebecca

DAVID LIES ON HIS FRONT ON HER BED IN THE DARKNESS, his face turned towards her. He is naked, and his arms are stretched across the pillows as he drowses. Rebecca is on her side, her elbow crooked under her head, lazily observing him. After a while he opens his eyes and smiles.

He arrived later than she anticipated, leaving her twiddling her thumbs for an hour. In order to have a convincing alibi for Felicity, he had gone for a drink with Paul, but he stayed longer than he meant to. Paul's fault, he said, but the truth is, he doesn't want to have that talk. And, so far, they haven't, and she's not going to. Why waste their precious hour? She said her piece the other night and has since cooled off, and now she's showing him that there's no pressure, that everything's fine. She was just having a moment. Probably PMT. David believes it, and the question of their relationship has, yet again, been brushed under the carpet.

'Time?'

She glances at her bedside clock, although she doesn't need to. She has been watching it for the last half hour, the minutes turning over too fast, while she silently urges his sperm on. If she could have managed it without the worry that David might wake up and want to know what she was doing, she would have stood on her head. 'Just gone ten.'

He groans and rolls on to his back, scratches his balls through the sheet and then pulls her hand to his lips and kisses it. Rebecca takes his hands, placing them on her breasts. He caresses her nipples and she sighs.

'Gotta go.' He extracts himself, disappearing into the bathroom.

She listens to him shower while she slips into her cashmere pyjamas. Her relationship with what she's doing goes through its ups and downs and guilt is never far beneath the surface. When she gets pregnant, nothing will ever be the same for any of them.

She takes the glasses into the kitchen and potters around, wiping the surfaces, disposing of the remains of their Deliveroo supper and filling the dishwasher.

David is shouting. She stops what she's doing and listens. He shouts to himself in the shower when he's under stress. Felicity laughs about it, but then she doesn't work with him. He shouts things like 'Bastard!' and 'You little shit!' When he is tense, so is she, particularly if it has anything to do with the business.

He comes out of the bathroom, smelling clean. He keeps the same soap and shampoo here as he does at home, the same toothpaste and antiperspirant, but Rebecca sometimes wonders if Felicity doesn't suspect. She knows she would.

'Do you think I'm a good person?' he says suddenly. His eyes are cast down, his long lashes curling away from his cheek.

'In what way?'

'Thanks for the overwhelming vote of confidence.'

'Don't be childish. What do you mean by good? Being nice to the elderly? You get points for that. But being unfaithful to your wife loses you a few. I don't think you are particularly nice. I think you're self-serving and attention-seeking. But I also think you are extremely sexy, I love being with you, you're great in bed and you make me laugh.'

'But do you think other people like me, or just want to please me? What do they say about me behind my back?'

'Bloody hell, you're a needy bastard sometimes. I don't know what they say, but I do know that you're respected, and your staff are loyal. What more do you want?'

She wants to embrace him, but he drops his keys, takes hold of her wrists and holds her at a safe distance. She pouts, but she backs off. He looks as though he's about to say something, his expression mellowing, but then he changes his mind and lifts his hand in farewell.

Rebecca puts on some music. Vaughan Williams. Perfect. She rolls back the soft white rug from the sitting-room floor. The candles are already lit, but she relocates them to the side of the room, out of the way, and then she dances, letting her body flow, stretching and arching, pirouetting so that her hair fans out. She uses her hips and her breasts, her hands and fingers. Every bit of her.

She doesn't close the curtains. She likes the idea that the people over the gardens can see her. Maybe there are some for whom this is a regular source of entertainment. Maybe they get their friends round to watch the mad woman dancing out her despair. Maybe there's a guy who masturbates. Let him.

21

Laura

THE FOLLOWING MORNING, I GET IN EARLY. I AM NUMB with fear, wishing I hadn't done it, not quite believing that I was brave enough, thinking that perhaps it was stupidity, not courage. If David hadn't already read his message, I might well have removed them both. I am tempted to put my coat back on and never darken the Gunner Munro doorstep again, but I can't leave like this, throwing everything in the air and not caring where it lands. My exit needs to be managed in a way that will help me, not put the kibosh on my career. I won't allow him to do that to me.

I start work, but I can't sit still, and every time I hear someone come in, I tense. How will David and Finn behave this morning? Shame makes people defensive and angry; it doesn't necessarily lead them to put things right. Nowadays people are constantly shamed on social media; for infidelity, for putting on weight, for not recycling, for being different. So much of it goes on that it feels as though its currency has been devalued. So, will he care? Does he even believe he's done anything to be ashamed of? Oh God, I hope so. I hope he fears for his job.

Am I over-thinking this? If I had talked to Isabel about it at Christmas, what would her advice have been? To go straight to the police? Well, it's too late for that now.

I'm making coffee, feeling unpleasantly on edge, starting every time the door opens, when Bettina arrives.

'Do you want anything?' I ask, rummaging through the variety of capsules.

'Tea, thanks.'

Something's wrong. Even I, in my current state, can see that. She barely acknowledges me until I set her drink down on the desk, then she presses the edge of her sleeve to her eyes. Behind me the door to the stairwell opens and someone shouts a good morning. He takes off his coat and boots up his computer. We both ignore him.

'Do you want to come into my office? Eddie isn't in yet.' Frankly, I'm glad of the distraction.

Bettina nods, and follows me. She goes to the window and peers out. Like she's waiting for someone to arrive.

'What's happened?' I ask.

She shrugs and blows her nose again. 'I've been so stupid, and now I think I might have to leave.'

'Oh, Bettina. Are you still worried about getting the time mixed up? They've already forgotten about it. You apologized and put it right; no one's going to hold it against you.'

She hangs her head and fiddles with the neckline of her dress. 'It's not about that.'

'What is it about then?'

'I slept with Finn after the Christmas party.' Her hair has fallen forward, and she peers at me through her curls. 'And now he doesn't want to know and it's really awkward. He won't even look at me, let alone talk to me.'

I stop breathing; my head is roaring. I put my hand on the back of my chair to support myself, but it rolls away, and I almost go with it. Bettina is too wrapped up in herself to notice.

'Before Christmas, Rebecca was hinting that I might get a permanent job. I really want it, but now David thinks I'm useless and Finn won't even look at me.'

At this she bursts into tears, but all I can do is twitch. If I stand at a certain angle, I can see the door to the stairs opening and closing. I have to get that note back and I have to do it quickly, but I don't want to look heartless, leaving a tearful woman alone in my office.

'You won't tell anyone, will you?'

The gaze she throws at me is beseeching and I shake my head.

'Of course not.'

'Could you do me a huge favour? Could you get my bag? It's got my make-up in it. I can repair the damage in here . . .' She hesitates. 'If you don't mind.'

I breathe out. 'I don't mind.'

The main room has filled up, and although there's no

one sitting at Finn's desk, his jacket is hanging over the back of his chair and there's a takeaway coffee touching the edge of the note. I glance round nervously. He could be the man chatting to Agnes outside David's office. I just don't know.

I walk up to his desk and linger. Graham drags his eyes off his screen to look at me. I have no idea what to do but I don't have long; maybe only a few seconds.

'Can I borrow that pen?' I say, leaning across the desk and knocking my hand against Finn's coffee. The effect is more dramatic than I had expected. It gets everywhere.

'Jesus!' Graham jerks his chair backwards.

'Oh God, I'm so sorry. I don't know how that happened.'

'Well, look what you're bloody doing next time.'

He starts dabbing at the coffee with a screen wipe. I pick up the cup and take the note while he's distracted.

'I'll find something to mop it up,' I say, making my escape.

I grab a J-cloth from the cleaners' cupboard but by the time I've got back, Agnes, ever efficient and unflappable, has the situation and a roll of kitchen towel in hand. There's a man in a stripy shirt standing behind the chair and, at a guess, it's Finn. I back away, and he frowns. I mouth an apology and hurry back to Bettina, grabbing her bag on the way.

She looks up with wounded eyes as I hand her the bag.

'I don't want to leave,' she says.

I sit on the corner of my desk and make her look at me. 'Bettina, listen. You've done nothing wrong. He's an arsehole, but that does not mean you leave. It means the opposite. Don't let a man dictate what you do. You are brilliant, and beautiful, and you have a career ahead of you. So, hold your head up high, ignore Finn Broadbent, and dig your heels in.'

Only after she's gone do I allow myself to accept what has seemed so improbable. If it wasn't Finn, it was David. My boss. The man I've looked up to for three years. He's the man who makes things happen, the genie who creates the magic. He has charisma and he's generous. I've seen him in the evening, talking to the cleaners, a hand patting an arm, a sympathetic smile as they tell him about their problems. He knows all their names and family circumstances. He is the last person I would have thought . . . but you never know with people, do you? David has the confidence to take a risk and the arrogance to think he'd be safe; maybe even to convince himself he'd done nothing wrong.

He knows who sent that note. He knows it's me. What will he do? Maybe he'll call my bluff and do nothing at all.

Someone comes into the office and I jump. Eddie says, 'Hi, mate,' which isn't much use to me. And then he gets up and walks out, mumbling something about needing to talk to Finn. I watch him go in horror, wondering what he's doing, who he's leaving me with.

'Just touching base,' he says unhelpfully.

I look at his mouth. He's smiling. I search for other clues. His hair is brown. He's holding a sheaf of papers in his hand.

'What do you need?'

This is my reliable fallback question. If it goes beyond this, it becomes farcical and my only tactic is a sudden, bursting need to use the loo, or see Rebecca. To leave the room at any rate.

Encouraged, he steps forward. 'I've been going through CVs and it's doing my head in. I'm sure they're great, but no one can replace Guy. How will I know if they share my sense of humour, or if I can be in the same space as them for more than five minutes? What if I get it wrong?'

It's Jamie. I take a reading of my response to him. I am happy that he is in the room with me. I feel warmth towards him. I remember being in his arms, pressed against the bar, kissing. I ask myself if I would do that again. I don't know. Certainly not now.

'Would you like me to look through them?'

'Would you? That would be fantastic. But only if you have time.'

I don't, but I'm grateful that the awkwardness is officially over. I suspect that leaving the room was Eddie's idea of tact. I hold out my hand and he passes over the CVs and hovers.

I smile. 'I'll come and find you when I've read them.'

He blushes. 'Oh. OK. Well, thanks.'

I feel a depressing sense of lethargy this afternoon. I know that it's my own fault; I haven't exercised since the incident. Normally I run on the Heath at the weekend, and, during the week, because it doesn't feel safe after dark, I go to the sports centre and do a class. There's a

Spanish woman there who I've been slowly getting to know. She has a fringe and wears her hair in a thick plait that falls to her coccyx. It isn't a friendship, as such, but it is a connection. Now the thought of connecting with anyone makes me want to hide under the covers. My routine has been broken.

David did this to me.

I'm trying to concentrate but the lines of my drawings keep blurring until, out of frustration, I push them away and lean back in my chair, yawning. My bones and muscles feel heavy and achy; perhaps I've caught Jamie's bug.

Behind me the door opens, and three men crowd into our little room. One of them is Eddie, one is Finn, because I recognize his stripy shirt. Having misjudged him so badly, I am nervous around him, terrified that he knows what's going on in my head. Even though it doesn't matter, because he didn't find out, I still feel embarrassed. I've pictured myself in bed with him, after all. I tried to find things that tied him neatly to that person. I studied his hair and ears, his neck and hands. I stared at him whenever I thought he wouldn't notice. He must have been aware of my scrutiny at times. It makes me feel hot and clammy just wondering what he thinks of me.

The other, I'm not sure. I glance up at them, then pull my sketchpad back and hunch over it. They are kidding about and I'm not in the mood.

Eddie sits down. Finn leans against the windowsill and folds his arms. The third guy inspects our shelves. I think it's Graham. All that manly banter grates on my nerves, and I wish they would go. Their presence, the smell of them and their sheer physicality, is making me claustrophobic.

I blink, to clear my vision, then tear the sheet off and start again. Self-conscious, I curl my arm round my sketch. Nothing is going right today. My throat begins to ache. I look up at Eddie, who has his hands steepled over his stomach. He appears to be finding Graham's lame story about his landlord hilarious.

The banter is still going on. I make an effort to put a smile into my voice. 'I'm trying to work, guys. Could you find somewhere else for your party?'

Finn moves round and leans over my shoulder to see what I'm doing. I want to jab back with my elbow, but instead I wait, stiffening every muscle, for him to move away. He picks up the drawing I've discarded, and I twist round and yell at him.

'Give me that!'

'Whoa.' He drops it and holds up his hands. 'Calm down.'

I turn away and grip the edge of my desk. Something is very wrong. I feel as though I'm lurching, like the floor is rippling under my feet, my chair swaying. Am I having a stroke? Faces gurn, pink relief maps formed of bumps and dips that mean nothing. My shoulders, throat and neck are so tight they hurt. I try to speak but the words won't come.

'Is she all right?' someone says.

'Laura? Laura!'

Every breath I take is painful and barely fills my lungs, and I start to panic in earnest, convinced I'm going to die. I thump the side of my chair with my fist.

Someone is kneeling beside me, her face a pale oval, her hair a dark and shining mass. She tells me it's OK, she's here now. She takes hold of my hands. Her voice is like warm honey, smothering the spikes.

'It's all right, Laura, you're having an anxiety attack, but you're safe. I'm not going to leave you. Breathe deeply. That's right. You're doing so well.'

David. David did this.

22

Laura

I AM IN MY FLAT, BUT I BARELY REMEMBER COMING home; or even leaving work. The last thing I remember clearly, Rebecca and Eddie were leading me out of the building. People turned to look at me and it felt like one of those dreams in which you're naked, and your body starts shattering, and little pieces of you are all over the floor. The rest is a blur.

Eddie propels me gently on to the sofa. He sits, one knee on the seat, facing me.

'Talk to me.'

I bury my head in my hands and rock my body. I don't know where to start; words cluster then burst upwards like a flock of starlings disturbed in the treetops. Fragile threads of meaning, of feeling and knowledge, float away. My eyes well with tears which overflow, running down my cheeks and catching in the corners of my mouth.

'Laura, look at me.'

I raise my eyes to his face and almost laugh. How can I confide in someone I don't recognize? The loneliness pools at my feet and starts to rise.

'Give me the number of your GP.'

'I don't need a doctor.'

'Maybe you don't, or maybe you do. It wouldn't hurt to talk to someone.'

Because I can't and won't tell him what happened to me, I don't have any other words to fill the silence. My life has jumped on to a track that I don't like; I'm losing my way. I stare at my knees for a while and Eddie says nothing, just waits.

'It's on the board.' It's a relief when the words finally come. It helps to be told what to do.

'Good girl.'

I get my hopes up when it seems every doctor is fully booked, but Eddie perseveres, and they manage to squeeze me in.

'Five ten. We should leave soon,' he says.

'I can't go out. I just want to sleep.'

I hug myself and curl away from him into the corner of the sofa. He puts a warm hand on my shoulder.

'You can sleep later.'

I shake my head.

'I'm coming with you. You don't have to do this on your own.'

He treats me like a child, bundling me outside and holding my arm as we walk to the surgery. The doctor is calming and sympathetic. He prescribes rest and recuperation and prints out a letter signing me off work for ten days. Then he promises to refer me to a psychiatrist; but that, he explains, could take up to three months, maybe more.

I tear up the letter as soon as we are out in the street and shove the pieces in my pocket.

'What're you doing?' Eddie asks.

'I'll be back in a day or two. I'd have to be dying to take off more than that. You know what it's like.'

He looks at me sceptically, although he understands. 'Don't worry. Rebecca said she'd tell David you had a virus. And listen, I called your mum. I got her number from your phone. She's on her way.'

'Seriously?'

'Seriously. I'm not leaving you on your own, and I don't think Esther would appreciate me spending the weekend in your flat.'

'Fine.'

Cutting through London, because Mum hates the M25, I fall in and out of sleep. She keeps the radio on and doesn't try to talk to me, for which I am grateful. I doze with my cheek pressed against the stretch of seat belt at my shoulder, blinking my eyes open occasionally at the tick of the indicator. I feel both childlike and ancient.

What happens now? Do I shut down or do I let people in? I don't know what to do or who to talk to; I want to bury myself and not think for a while. I want to stop hurting, to stop feeling this way, to rid myself of the horrible voice in my head; the one that says, you could have stopped it happening. It was your fault. You got drunk. You made yourself available. You didn't use your brain.

I press my nails into the back of my hand. I must stop this. Whatever I did, he had no right to take advantage. In his letter he admitted he knew about me, so he also knows that he should have seen me safely through the door, then gone on his way.

23

Laura

I ONLY WANTED TO STAY UNTIL SUNDAY, BUT I END UP spending over a week in Dorking in the little semi that's been home since Mum and Dad split up. I overestimated myself or underestimated this thing that has me in its grip. It feels like an illness, but there's nothing physically wrong. I just sleep a lot, retreating to the bedroom I've had since I was eight although it now boasts a king-size double bed. My mother isn't one of those women who keep their children's rooms sacred. After we moved out, she redecorated and repurposed. Isabel's room is where Mum sews the beautiful ragdolls she sells at the craft shop on the high street. Mine is the spare and Mark's has been converted into an en-suite for guests. The loft is where all her grandchildren sleep.

Days go by and the moment at which I might have told the truth passes without a word. Instead I tell her that I've been under a lot of pressure at work. I need to explain the hair, especially as Phoebe has already put her tuppence-worth in. They met when Mum picked me up.

Mum believes it must be man trouble and I don't deny it. Technically, it's true. I have one session with a private psychotherapist, but I don't get much out of it, or I don't feel like I do. It doesn't help that I don't tell her the truth either.

During the day, when I'm not drowsing, I work on the kitchen table to the comforting hum of Mum's sewing machine above me. I stay in touch with Eddie, developing the storyboards while he plays with the scripts. In the evenings, Mum and I cook together, eat at the kitchen table and move into the sitting room to watch something comforting on the television. We choose programmes like *Death in Paradise* and *Midsomer Murders* and avoid anything where the pain goes deeper than the surface.

'You made it! Fantastic.'

Professor Deborah Robinson kisses my cheek. She's a tall woman in her mid-forties with black hair sprinkled with grey. I originally found her through an article in the Sunday papers. A woman was explaining why she couldn't recognize friends and family, and everything she said chimed with me. Prosopagnosia. The word sounded important and medically glamorous. The article mentioned Deborah and said that she was looking for people who suspected they might be face-blind, to help with her research. Mum came with me, and I'll always remember how she glowed with pride when Deborah told us how amazing I was to have coped for so long.

I used to take part in her cognitive training programme, which basically means practising at home, distinguishing tiny variations in a selection of faces on a computer, but I gave that up because it was no good to me. It's all very well staring at someone's nose trying to remember if so-and-so has a kink or a flat bridge or particularly large nostrils, but it makes them self-conscious and makes you feel like you're encroaching on their personal space. I stick to what I do best and employ a structural process of elimination to recall defining features. The face is my last port of call.

Working with Deborah has made me more aware of the subtle differences between humans and of the way our brains work. It's made me less impatient with other people and less inclined to resent them for being lucky enough to be normal. I use strategies without having to think about them, just through being born like this, but Deborah has helped me add to and refine them.

At half past one we stroll across the campus to get some lunch. Southampton University was built in the fifties and consists of dramatic, brutalist concrete structures nestling in sloping, serene landscape gardens. It's one of those odd places that manages to be both ugly and beautiful at the same time.

We lay claim to a table near the window in the Terrace Restaurant and join the queue for food. I choose the chicken soup with bread and butter and carry it over to the table with a glass of water. Deborah has a sandwich.

'You said you're having a tough time,' she says, as we take off our coats and sit down.

'Yeah. It's not been a great year so far.' I lean on my elbows and press my fingers to my forehead, massaging my temples. Staring at a screen for two and a half hours has left me with the beginnings of a tension headache.

The steam from my soup floats up my nose. 'I did something stupid. I got absolutely plastered at the staff party and got myself into a situation.'

Deborah pauses and asks, 'What kind of situation?'

I look up at her. Her face gives me nothing. 'I think I was raped,' I whisper. It is shockingly hard to say that word.

'My God, you poor darling. Did you go to the police?'

I shake my head and a tear rolls down my cheek. 'It wasn't like that. Nobody dragged me into an alleyway and assaulted me. I invited him back to my flat and had sex with him willingly. Only he wasn't the guy I thought he was. He knew about me and realized he could take advantage.' I pick up my napkin, dab it against my eyes and blow my nose and then explain about the shirts. 'How could I have been so stupid?'

'You were not stupid,' Deborah says firmly. 'Whoever did that to you is evil. You should have reported him.'

I pinch my lips together to stop myself crying. 'I did think about going to the police, but in the end, I decided not to because I didn't think they would believe me or take it seriously, since I'd consented. I don't even know for sure if it was rape.'

'What do you mean? Of course it was. If somebody exploits your vulnerability and tricks his way into your bed, then it's rape and you should report it. It doesn't matter how long ago it happened.'

Despite myself, I smile. It's the relief, the confirmation by someone other than myself that I have been raped, that I can call it that without feeling the need to explain or convince, without feeling ashamed somehow.

'Do you know how he found out about you?' Deborah asks.

'I've no idea. He could have read about it, or maybe he knows someone with the same condition and recognized it.'

'Do you know who he is?'

'Yes.'

'Who?'

'I can't tell you.'

'Because you're not sure?'

I look out of the window, unable to face her pity. 'Unless I can prove it, it's my word against his.'

'Have you spoken to your mother, or a counsellor?'

'No. I don't want Mum hearing about this. She worries enough as it is.'

Deborah is agitated, and I'm sorry that I told her. At least when it was just me who knew I only had my own pain to worry about.

'I'm so sorry,' Deborah says.

'It's not your fault.'

'What are you going to do about it?'

'I'm playing it by ear. I wrote him a note.'

'Oh my God, you didn't?' Deborah is so horrified she forgets to whisper. I wince, and she reacts instantly, leaning closer and dropping her voice. 'For heaven's sake, that's crazy. You should have left it to the police.'

I shrug. 'Maybe it was a mistake, but it made me feel better at the time. There's not much I can do to him, but at the very least I want him to feel threatened.'

'Yes, but it's harassment, Laura. And what if you're wrong?'

'I'm not. I know it's him.'

'What about motive?'

'Do you need a motive to rape someone? I was drunk, and he saw an opportunity. He was drunk too, so maybe he lost control and his moral judgement went out the window.'

For the first time I wonder if he was drunk. Everyone else was; but David? I have no proof of that either. I suppose it depended on whether he had originally been intending to drive home.

Deborah takes a bite of her sandwich and I drink my soup. She sits back and studies me.

'Promise me you won't write any more notes. And at least think about reporting him.'

'All I want is to forget about it and get my life back on track. I hate him, and I want him to pay, but I don't want to go through a court case and have some pissy defence lawyer pick apart everything I say.'

'Even with me as an expert witness?' she says.

'You'd do that for me?'

'Absolutely. What he did to you was wicked and cruel.'

'But then everyone would know about me.' There is a plaintive note in my voice and I blush. I don't like sounding like a wimp.

'In your note, did you threaten him with the police?'

I grimace. 'No. He has no idea what I might do. But one thing I do know, from recent experience, is that we fear most what we know least about. As long as he doesn't know what to expect, I can keep him in a state of fear for as long as I like.'

'He may be too arrogant to be scared,' Deborah says. 'He probably thinks he's got away with it.'

She's right about the arrogance, but not about the rest. 'No, he doesn't. I promise you, Deborah. He doesn't think that at all.'

Eddie calls when I'm on the train. I can feel the excitement in his voice.

'We've just heard,' he says. 'GZ have confirmed. We pulled it off.'

'That's fantastic.' I look out of the window at the fields whipping by, at the pylons in the distance. I trace my finger through the patch of mist left by my breath. An upside-down face. One of the ways of explaining the experience of face-blindness to others is to show them familiar faces upside down and ask them to identify the person. It's surprisingly hard. 'I'm sorry I wasn't there.' Why didn't Rebecca or David call me as soon as they knew? Have they forgotten about me already?

'Me too. You missed out on David's big moment. I expect he or Rebecca will call you later, fill you in. But this is down to you, Laura. It was your idea. When're you back?'

'Monday,' I say firmly. It's Friday afternoon now; ready or not, I need to be there. I've missed out on too much already.

As soon as Eddie hangs up, my phone rings again: Rebecca.

I fold my things into my case and carry it down to the front hall. Mum is sorting out scraps of fabric on the kitchen table and when she turns I experience that nanosecond of confusion. The part of my brain that ignores context and the obvious, thinks, What is that woman doing in my mother's kitchen?

Then I hug her like I haven't done since I was a child.

'You're going,' she says. It's a statement of fact.

These last few days have convinced me that I'm not mad or incapable. It's vital that I get well quickly. I can't allow David Gunner space to breathe. He may be hoping I'll leave the company, and I might one day. But not yet.

'Please don't worry about me. I know the signs now and, if it happens again, I'll get help long before it gets that bad.'

She cups my face with her hands and looks straight into my eyes. 'Promise?'

'Promise.'

When I fell apart last week, I was close to resigning and turning my back on the whole miserable mess, even if it meant letting him get away with it. The pressure bearing down on me was too intense, the task too unpleasant. But talking to Deborah has hardened my resolve. It's my life he's turned upside down, my job that's at risk, and it was my body, my privacy and my sense of self he violated. I am taking them back.

24

Laura

AS SOON AS I GET HOME I GO OUT AGAIN, UP TO THE Heath. I run past the ponds and up the hill where there are children flying kites and people taking in the views of the city, enjoying their weekend. I run down the other side, through the trees and up towards Kenwood House, through the woods and round the lakes. Two swans lift their heads and then plunge them back into the water. I pick paths at random, relaxed and beginning to enjoy myself, up and down the hills, feeling alive and almost normal. Better for spending time with my mother, better for the space it gave me.

As I jog round a bend, I see a group of teenagers up ahead. Five of them, wearing hoodies, one of them pulling a dog on a leash. They look like they're between fourteen and sixteen years old, pumped with testosterone and full of attitude. The dog's a Staffie and is wearing a spiked collar and its eyes are as dark as its coat. It strains towards me and barks twice, before being yanked back. As I catch up, they turn to watch me but don't move out of the way, forcing me to veer off the path on to the muddy verge. One of them says something obscene and I have to physically restrain myself from whirling round and laying into them. Another chases me but gives up after a few metres.

'Only messing with you,' he shouts. 'Don't you like me, lady?'

This parry is greeted with hilarity by his friends and another abrupt bark from the dog. They are kids, I tell myself. All they are looking for is a reaction. After what happened, I refuse to be scared by bullies. They can't touch me.

I've run far enough and I'm strolling home, past the café, when someone calls my name. I don't recognize either of the women sitting at an outside table, but I do recognize Phoebe's baby Noah from his purple snowsuit and Caterpillar boots. I wander over to say hello and Phoebe introduces me to the heavily pregnant woman sitting with her as Harriet, her sister.

'Come and sit with us,' Phoebe says, patting the metal chair beside her. 'Get yourself a cup of tea.'

I pause, unsure, but both women are beaming at me and the baby reaches for my hand. I take his sticky fingers in mine and smile. 'OK. Just for a minute.'

Harriet is nice. She sits enfolded in an enormous wool coat, her gloved hands crossed over her bulge. More than a bulge, though. A hill. She has thick, mousy hair cut to her shoulders and keeps one side tucked behind her ear. We talk about when Phoebe used to work in films and TV as a make-up artist and find places where our paths might have crossed. Harriet is an accountant.

'The sensible sister,' Phoebe says.

'Well you're the pretty one,' Harriet says with a satisfied smile.

I look from one to the other. I can't tell which of them is more attractive. They're both open and friendly, and that's all that matters.

It's sunny, but the chill creeps through my running gear. I cup my hands around my mug to warm them. I probably should go, but the sisters talk so much that it's hard to find the moment to butt in. Then a little boy runs up to Harriet and tries to scramble on to her knee.

'Careful, darling,' she says. 'Don't squash the baby.'

'Daddy got me a truck!'

'That's so cool, Liam,' says Phoebe.

I turn to see two men approaching. For a few seconds I can't work out which is Elliot, both of them are wearing jeans and dark Puffa jackets. Then Noah stretches out his hands to one of them, and I settle.

'Hey,' Elliot says, taking the baby off Phoebe's knee and kissing him on the head.

'Hi.'

Harriet's husband has sat down beside his wife. I look round to see if there's another chair free, realizing that I've pinched Elliot's rightful place, but the ones outside are all taken. I expect him to see if he can find another, but he doesn't, he just stands there as though he's waiting for me to relinquish mine.

I get the message and stand up.

'Oh, don't go yet,' Phoebe says. 'Stay for a few minutes. Gavin, this is my lovely upstairs neighbour, Laura.'

I smile at Gavin, who nods at me. 'Heard about you.'

I dart a glance at Phoebe, but she shakes her head. 'I haven't told him any of your secrets. Just that it's nice to have someone my age upstairs, not some grumpy old man complaining about Noah crying, like we had in the last place. You never complain.'

'It doesn't bother me.'

It does a little, but only on weekend mornings when his six a.m. cries interrupt my dreams. I won't mention it. The last thing I want to do is alienate them. Also, there is something about Elliot that makes me think he already isn't hugely keen on me.

Elliot puts his shopping bag down on the floor and takes the chair I've vacated with an unembarrassed thanks. It's like I've pushed myself into his little world and he doesn't want me there. But I haven't. Phoebe insisted I join them.

'I'm freezing anyway,' I say.

When I leave, I don't look back. I don't need to. I imagine Gavin and Elliot regaling the women with tales of their shopping trip, Liam showing off his new truck, Noah excitedly clutching at whatever anyone foolishly leaves near his outstretched hands, and Harriet and Phoebe picking up where they left off when I arrived. I know that they are happy in their closeness. Elliot obviously has a problem with me; maybe I've ignored him on Kentish High Street. Still, there was no need to make me feel about as welcome as a parent at a teen disco. The thought jogs a memory. Years ago, when Isabel was ten or eleven, she had a problem with this boy at school, who kept picking on her. Mum said, 'That's what boys do when they like you too much.' I replay my few dealings with Elliot, wondering if he has a secret crush on me, but I decide it's unlikely. I suspect he's clocked that I don't have friends round, thinks I'm weird and doesn't want me latching on to his kind and caring wife. It wouldn't be unreasonable.

25

Laura

A TAXI PULLS OVER AS I ARRIVE AT THE OFFICE ON Monday morning. I smile as Rebecca gets out.

'Ready for the American trollop?' I say, echoing David's nickname for Paige, but really trying to forestall enquiries about my mental health. I take my helmet off and hook the strap over my wrist.

Then another head appears out of the taxi's dark interior, crowned with the same glossy dark hair. The first woman glares at me and I look from one to the other and little details start to jump out. The blood drains from my face as I realize my mistake.

'Laura, right?' Paige drawls.

'Nice to have you back,' Rebecca says with a frosty smile.

I nod, trying to find the words to apologize, but Paige doesn't want to hear them. How could I have been so stupid?

Rebecca holds open the door just as someone comes running down the stairs. I let it close in my face and watch them through the glass. I realize it's David when he leans in to kiss Paige on both cheeks and catches sight of me. His body language changes; like a cat raising its hairs, it becomes subtly hostile. It occurs to me that Rebecca, who I texted yesterday, might not have told him I would be in. He won't like it. I'm a threat to him now. He replies to something Paige says and the corners of his mouth turn down in disgust and irritation, before he leads both women upstairs.

When I skulk miserably into the office, everything feels unbearably bright and loud. From his desk, Finn lifts a hand in greeting, but everyone else is seemingly too busy to pay me any attention.

I'm not blind or stupid. People are averting their gaze. I try not to ignore the stab of hurt. I have more important things to think about, like Eddie and me presenting our polished-up ideas to the client this morning. Finn will be joining us, outlining his plans for the all-important social media push, and the director and producer from Messenger Films will be in later to go over the wish list for the TV and cinema adverts. For me and Eddie and our creative partnership, this is a big deal. It could make our name in the industry. It will mean being head-hunted by rival agencies. My one anxiety is that I've been away too long and that, despite all the effort I've put in, in my absence things will have moved on.

Eddie looks up as I walk in. I take off my coat and hang it over the back of my chair.

'Hey,' I say. 'I'm back.'

'About time,' he jokes. But his tone is odd; too upbeat.

'So, are we all set for the meeting?' I won't tell him

what happened in the street just now. Least said, soonest mended. And how would I explain it anyway?

'Laura . . .'

I'm leaning over my chair, my hand on the mouse, clicking on my emails. 'Uh huh.'

'I don't know how to say this.'

I look up at him. 'What?'

'Jamie's been working with me, you know, picking up the slack? David wants him at the meeting as well. He'll be doing the presentation with me.'

I roll my chair round and sit down with a thump. 'What do you mean? I've sent over drawings. We don't need Jamie.'

'I'm sorry. We've used your ideas, and Jamie has tweaked them, but without you here, it's made it easier having someone . . .' His voice tails off as he runs his hands through his hair. He grimaces. 'You don't need to be in there at all. To be honest, it might be better if you're not.'

I give him a look, my eyebrows raised. 'That's how it is, is it?'

'Laura . . .'

'Don't worry.'

I should never have taken the time off; all it's done is prove I'm dispensable and given Eddie and Jamie a chance to show how well they work together. With Jamie without a partner and me now perceived as the weak link, this could be the outcome everyone wants. It's humiliating.

Five minutes later, Eddie gets up, picks up his phone, puts his hand on my shoulder and squeezes it. 'Sorry.'

The meeting starts without me, and there is nothing I can do except pretend I don't care. And not one soul here is going to believe that.

After the clients have gone, Agnes pops her head round our door and asks me to go and see David. I brace myself against a wave of anxiety, expecting him to shove the note in my face and demand answers. To my relief, Rebecca is there, sitting to one side, long legs crossed. I take a seat on the sofa, and immediately feel small and inadequate.

'There's no nice way of putting this,' David says. 'So, I'll come straight to the point. Paige wants you off GZ. She's not going to drop Gunner Munro, but only on condition we lose you.'

'Lose me? Do you mean fire me?'

'No. I mean you're off the job.'

'I am so sorry.' I direct my apology to Rebecca. 'I'd just got off my bike and I didn't have my glasses on. It's the hair. I mixed you up.'

David knows I'm face-blind, but he can't say it. He knows I've guessed it's him. The awareness ties us together in a dangerous, toxic dance. He is watching me, wanting to know what my next step will be. It's a wonder that Rebecca doesn't sense the static between us.

She sighs deeply, her bosom rising and falling under her cream silk shirt. 'You bring a lot to this company, Laura, and I'm sorry this has happened. I stuck up for you, but Paige couldn't have been clearer. They'll go with someone else if we don't do what she asks.'

I am trying so hard to be professional, to separate

what David did to me from what I need to do to function, but I'm failing. I'm letting the horror of it trip me up. My mouth dries as I realize that there is no way I can win. I can take revenge, but I cannot get back what I had.

'We all make mistakes,' Rebecca says, her voice softening. 'But you're going to have to take a back seat for a while. I've got something else in mind for you.'

'A different campaign? But what about Eddie? We work together. He needs me.'

Those last three words ring hollow. It's been made patently obvious that he doesn't.

'He'll have to do without you. You've done the groundwork, but I'm going to look at reshuffling.'

'Reshuffling? Do you mean giving Jamie my job?'

She pauses. 'We haven't discussed it yet.' She blushes. She knows how unlikely that sounds. Her gaze shifts to David, and then back to me. 'We're launching the GZ campaign with an event in three weeks' time. I want you to organize everything. I know it's short notice, but you're so good at that sort of thing.'

I don't comment but a thin stream of cold coils through my veins.

'We can rely on you, can't we?' David says.

'You're demoting me?'

'Not demoting. Putting you on the benches for a few weeks. Don't take it personally, Laura. Surely it's better than getting fired? Come on, sweetheart. I need you to do this for me. Nobody else would do it as well as you.'

I glare at him. How can he speak to me like that? Call me sweetheart? Pretend he values me? Is he so certain I'm going that he can afford to beg me to stay?

I shrug. 'I'll do it. But what about Paige?'

'I mentioned it to her, and she had no objection. She sees it as a come-down for you.'

I press my fingers against my forehead. 'I bet she loves that.'

'It's that attitude that got you into trouble in the first place,' David suddenly roars. 'If you can't respect our clients, maybe you need to think about whether this is the job for you.'

I feel it like a blast from a volcano. To me it's way over the top, as though he's using this unhelpful situation to funnel his fury. Even Rebecca looks shocked. I'm glad he's letting his anger show. It shifts the balance of power up a notch in my favour.

'David . . .' Rebecca says. 'They can hear you in the next street.'

'I don't give a flying fuck who hears me.'

She lifts her palms. 'OK.'

'I apologize,' I say stiffly. 'Is that everything?'

'Put on a fantastic party, Laura,' she says, as she begins to see me out, 'and it'll all be forgotten. You'll be back behind your desk before you know it.'

'I have to move out of my office?' The words come out in a shriek. I am so horrified, I stammer. 'But where am I going to go. I can't . . .'

'There's a spare desk next to Graham. You'll be fine there for a few weeks.'

They don't suggest Guy's desk. That speaks for itself. I look down at the floor, then up at the two creative directors. My heart is racing. I am furious but powerless. I don't think before I speak.

'I'm giving notice as of today.'

'Oh no,' Rebecca says. 'Please, Laura. Give yourself time to cool down. We don't want that at all. Do we, David?'

'Laura knows what's best for her,' he says. 'She'll make her own decision.'

'Don't be silly. She's upset. Laura, don't do anything hasty. Organize the party for me, and then decide whether you still want to go. But please, give it some thought.'

I look straight at David Gunner, challenging him. A tiny muscle twitches at his temple. 'I don't need to think. Things have happened that have made my life impossible here, but this is the final straw.' I take a deep breath and pull back from the brink. I have to be practical; I'll need a reference from them. 'Thank you for the opportunities you've given me. I'll take on the party and go when it's over.'

Several heads turn as I leave the room, no doubt curious to know what I've done to incur David's wrath. I glance back at his office. This is his fault, not mine. I don't want to be the only one to suffer.

I spend the afternoon moving out of the office I've shared with Eddie for three years. Eddie hugs me like I'm about to go on a trek across the Sahara, not moving fifteen feet away. He is furious but what can he do? He can't wreck his career out of loyalty to me; he has his family to consider.

26

Rebecca

FELICITY OPENS THE DOOR, HOLDING ON TO PEBBLES'S collar as she yaps and dances on her hind legs.

Rebecca embraces her. 'Happy birthday, darling.'

She holds out a small box, gift-wrapped in silver and tied with a pale pink ribbon.

'Thanks, Becs.' Felicity takes it and closes the door, shutting out the dismal morning. 'Take off your coat and pour yourself a coffee. The taxi won't be here for ten minutes and the boys are dying to see you.'

On cue Spike and Buzz come thundering down the stairs, clamouring for attention. Buzz, the younger one, although she can't remember how old either of them is – somewhere in that zone between six and eight, she reckons – is so like his father he makes her want to giggle.

'What did you get?' Buzz asks.

'I don't know yet. I haven't opened it.'

'Daddy gave Mummy *jewlly*,' Spike says importantly, and Felicity holds out her hand to reveal an impressive-looking diamond-and-emerald ring.

'How gorgeous.'

Rebecca ignores a stab of displeasure, smiles above the boys' heads and follows Felicity into the kitchen, the boys dragging on her hands.

'All ready for your ladies day out?' The nanny scrapes mashed banana from under Daisy's bottom lip with the edge of a buttercup-yellow plastic spoon. Daisy twists her head away, staring at Rebecca and breaking into a wide, gummy grin. Rebecca grins back.

'David assumed I'd invite one of the other mums,' Felicity says. 'But you know what, I do too much of that already.'

Rebecca nods, feeling twitchy. She doesn't take days off, not even at the weekend unless she can't get out of it. If she isn't at Gunner Munro, she's networking, if she isn't networking she's exercising and if she isn't exercising she's meditating. If she did take a day off, she wouldn't choose to spend it with the woman she's been lying to for years. The thought of the test of endurance ahead has been causing her agonies all week. Normally she avoids soul-searching, but things have been ramped up recently and it feels as though the pieces of string tying everything down are about to snap.

Her phone pings, and she checks it, aware of Felicity pausing, hand on hip, eyebrows raised. Rebecca sighs and switches it on to silent.

In the taxi on their way to the Sanctuary they talk about the children and about Felicity's sister and David's grandparents, and Rebecca endeavours to appear interested. Usually, there's a crowd when they see each other, and hours can go by without Rebecca realizing they've barely spoken, at least not directly. Now she can't think of anything to say. The fact is, she finds Felicity dull, her life shrunk to her family and her home. When they were living together, Felicity had been full of plans. She had talked about setting up her own interiors business, but she never got round to it. And then she had married David and had his children and that was that. Plans 'temporarily' on hold, and no sign of a career. She realizes how revoltingly judgemental that sounds. Everyone is entitled to their choices. And just how great have hers been?

They are handed white waffle robes and their programme for the day, kicking off with a breakfast of fruit, yoghurt and mint tea.

When they strip off for the sauna, Rebecca can't resist a covert glance. It's the first time in many years that she's seen Felicity naked. Her stomach and breasts are soft and stretched, and there are scars, snail-like trails on the tops of her thighs, spiralling round her belly button and radiating from her nipples. It's painfully easy to tell which woman has given birth and which has not. She has a feeling Felicity thinks she's envious. She is, in a way, but also curious. If it happens to her, how will she cope with the damage to her beauty? How will David cope? Felicity doesn't seem bothered about her scars, or if she is, she would dismiss it as vanity, with a content little smile. To her it's a badge of sorts. God, Rebecca thinks, today is going to screw with her head.

* * *

'Does David talk to you?' Felicity asks. They are having lunch: soup and salad, healthy and delicious, with glasses of organic juice.

Rebecca dabs her lips with a snowy napkin and holds her gaze. 'What do you mean, talk to me? We talk all the time.'

'I don't mean about work, I mean about personal stuff, about life.'

'Oh. Not much. To be frank, the company sucks up everything. We don't sit in his office putting the world to rights.' She smiles. 'We used to, of course, but he has you for that now.'

Felicity falls silent. Rebecca breathes lightly, trying to ignore the flutter under her ribcage. Was that patronizing? Yes, it was, disgustingly so. This time, however, Felicity doesn't pull her up on it.

'Is everything OK at home?' she asks.

Felicity's eyes swim with tears. 'I haven't told anyone this.'

Rebecca waits.

'We haven't had sex since I found out I was pregnant with Daisy. It's been eighteen months.'

'Ah. Have you talked to him about it?'

Felicity shakes her head.

'Oh, come on, don't worry. I'm sure it's perfectly normal. You have three children and a busy life. That stuff can get set aside. Or so I've heard. Are you still sleeping in the same bedroom?'

'Yes, but he comes to bed so late. And even if I attempt anything he just kisses me and rolls over. It's awful. I think he might be having an affair.'

Rebecca laughs. She hopes it doesn't sound as false to Felicity as it does to her. 'David does nothing but work. When on earth would he have time?'

Felicity plays with her food, pushing it around the plate with her fork. 'You know what he's like. If there was someone he wanted, he would make the time. Is there . . . do you know anyone at Gunner Munro that might be . . .'

'No,' Rebecca says. Her voice is firm, confident, betraying nothing. 'Absolutely not.'

'Only, I was watching Laura Maguire at Guy's funeral. I thought maybe . . .' She bites her lip. 'I even asked her if she wanted a lift back with us, so that I could see how they were together.'

'Well, that's nuts. Of course he isn't having an affair with Laura. She's given her notice anyway.'

'Really? David hasn't said anything.'

'I expect that's because he hasn't given her a second thought. Felicity, he loves you. You've gone off track because you've had three babies in quick succession. Maybe he needs to be reminded that you're a woman, not just a mother.'

Felicity wipes her eyes with her napkin. 'I shouldn't have allowed him into the delivery room. He's so squeamish. It was probably that, that put him off.'

'If you saw something bloody being ripped out of your husband's arse, wouldn't you be put off for a while?'

Felicity stares at her, appalled, then dissolves into laughter, giggling so hard that she starts hiccuping. Rebecca laughs with her, signalling the waitress over and asking for a glass of water.

'That's better,' she says.

Seven years is a long time to keep a secret. She feels as though things are beginning to bubble to the surface and it's taking more energy and resources to keep the lid from blowing off the pan. This is so difficult. She can dehumanize Felicity when she doesn't see her, but this laughing, moist-eyed woman reminds her so much of their younger, naughtier days, it makes her feel a complete bitch.

She brushes her hair and coils it up. It feels oily from the massage. Felicity does the same, smiling at her in the mirror. It's time to go. She is relieved it's over. Close contact with Felicity has to be rationed. A day of lying through her teeth has left her emotionally wrung out.

'What are you doing tomorrow?' Felicity asks.

Her heart drops. 'Catching up with today.'

'Could you do me a huge favour and come with us to Tony and Georgie's?'

It's the last thing she expected. 'Why would you want me there?'

'Because it would help to have someone who hasn't seen them in months; to see the difference. To see what they're like and back me up. David wants me to help out, but I can't. It's just too much with everything I've got on. It's not that I don't care, it's just that I've got the kids, and the dog and God knows what else.'

Rebecca decides not to point out that she has a part-time nanny, a cleaner and a gardener. 'I don't think . . .'

'Please. It would be fun to have you along. David would like it.'

She laughs. 'David sees me every day.'

'At work. This'll be different. It'll be like old times.'

What makes her agree, isn't altruism, it's the idea of seeing for herself the stresses on David. She's curious about his home life, about his relationship with Felicity. Being at the same dinner parties or formal events gives her frustratingly little insight.

Rebecca doesn't want to come back to Constable Lane, but Felicity insists that the boys will be disappointed. Spike and Buzz aren't bothered in the slightest; they are cosily ensconced in front of *Despicable Me* with their father. David lifts a hand and waves without looking round, then peels the boys' arms from around his neck, their fluffy-socked feet from his lap, and joins them in the hall. To Rebecca it feels as though he doesn't want her to come in any further.

Their gazes clash and Rebecca feels an atmospheric shift, experiencing the sensation a little like the Northern Lights, swirling currents of colour between them. The colours are dark this evening, with wisps of yellow and white. She marvels that Felicity is so unaware. This is the woman who thought she could work out whether Laura and David were involved by sitting in the car with them for an hour.

'You got away early,' Felicity says.

'I wanted to see you two gorgeous ladies after your day out, so I brought my work home. Daisy's in bed. Colleen left half an hour ago. Everyone's been fed and bathed.'

'Well, I'm not stopping. I've got a ton of messages to deal with.'

'Have a glass of wine first,' Felicity says. 'What time is our reservation, darling?'

'Not till eight. I thought you might want a bath after all your exertions.' He kisses her cheek. 'You're both glowing.'

Felicity winds her arm around David's waist and smiles at Rebecca. It's a smile of conspiracy. A smile that says that, despite her revelation, she wants her friend to know that there is still love between them.

'To be honest, all I want to do is fall asleep,' Rebecca responds. 'The therapies have left me feeling like warm mud. You two have fun tonight. I'll see you in the morning.'

David flicks her a look of surprise.

'Rebecca's coming with us tomorrow, darling,' Felicity says. 'She said she needed some country air.'

He looks even more surprised, but he doesn't argue, and she leaves them and walks back to Belsize Park. She often thinks she ought to move further away, maybe into Kensington. She can sometimes feel like a limpet, glued to David's hull, and that is not an ideal way to live.

She re-examines the day, particularly the conversation about David. That had come a little too close to the bone. Of course, David had told her he and Felicity weren't having sex any more but hearing it from Felicity's lips and seeing her eyes redden and shimmer with tears, hadn't made her happy. It had made her feel guilty and grubby. And who did Felicity really suspect? Was the mention of Laura disingenuous after all? Had it been an oblique warning? Had she been saying, I know it's you, I'm giving you a chance to back off? Has she asked her tomorrow so that she can watch how they behave together?

Would Felicity talk to him? Would she have the courage to sit him down and ask him point-blank why he didn't want to touch her? And what would he say if she did? She imagines the conversation.

Because I am sexually fixated on another woman. Because you can't even begin to imagine what I want, and I don't want to have to explain it to you.

She laughs out loud, imagining Felicity walking into a sex shop, perhaps passing it several times first, and asking tentatively, blushingly, for a pair of handcuffs and some crotchless knickers, and speaking so quietly that she has to be asked to repeat her request. Then standing in front of David, looking a little pathetic. She winces. What a mean-spirited thought to have. She isn't a bad person; not really. It gets to her sometimes, that's all.

She presses her hand to her belly. Another month, another agonizing stretch of acute anticipation. She has never liked leaving things to chance. It's a ridiculous way to live your life.

27

Rebecca

'HELLO, GEORGIE-PORGIE,' DAVID SAYS, PICKING HIS frail grandmother up off her feet and turning a half-circle before putting her down. 'You are looking utterly adorable.'

Georgie Gunner is eighty-seven and far from adorable in Rebecca's book. Rebecca sees herself as compassionate, but she has never liked Georgie. Tony is easy, a charmer like David and, even at ninety-two, one for the ladies. Georgie grumbles at David and then walks off down the garden to join Tony without acknowledging either her or Felicity.

'Shall I make us all some tea?' Rebecca offers, because she needs something to do. She wrinkles her nose at the sticky surfaces, the stained mugs. She doesn't like to touch anything, let alone eat off the china.

Felicity takes a cake out of a Tupperware box and sets it on to a plate. The boys are in the garden with their great-grandparents, wrapped up like Eskimos and trampling Tony's vegetable patch, looking for signs of growth and, she suspects, worms. Felicity has left Daisy sound asleep in her car seat in the front room. Rebecca wonders what the baby will think when she wakes up and sees all those china figurines staring down at her.

'I don't know what the hell the cleaner does when she's here,' Felicity says, opening the fridge and inspecting the contents, taking out mouldy cheese, jars of furry jam and a pair of underpants wrapped round something hard and round. It turns out to be a potato.

Rebecca laughs. 'Something to do with Tony's veg patch?'

'Perhaps he's nurturing a new variety.'

'Royal Pants?'

Felicity smiles and pops the eggs one by one into a bowl of cold water. Every single one of them floats to the top. She throws them away, pushing them down into the bin with a wooden spoon and covering the evidence with an old carrier bag.

Rebecca fills the kettle, switches it on then walks outside through the conservatory, clapping her arms around her body to keep herself warm, puffing out great breaths of mist.

She tries to spare her boots by keeping to the trodden path, but the toes are dark with wet by the time she gets to the veg patch.

'Who are you?' Georgie asks suspiciously.

'It's Rebecca,' she says. 'Felicity's friend.'

Georgie peers at her as she brushes earth from her gloved hands. 'I get muddled these days. Felicity's the wife, isn't she? The tricky one.'

'Yes.' Rebecca bends to pet the dog, hiding her

response. 'Tea and cake in a minute, boys. Do you want to go and wash your hands?'

'Cake!' Spike yells, dropping the trowel and springing up, Pebbles scampering after him.

Buzz carefully pats down the mound he's made around a leafless twig and wipes his hands on his jeans.

'What are you planting?'

He blasts her with David's smile, knowing he'll be forgiven for getting filthy. 'It's not for planting. It's where I put the dead beetle. One of his legs camed off. It wasn't me. Grandpa said it was probably a bird.'

The boys take Georgie's hands, touchingly protective around her, while Tony gives Rebecca his arm as they walk back up the garden to the house. Felicity brings the tea into the conservatory, setting it down on the wicker and glass table, and then perches on the edge of one of the uncomfortable matching chairs. David brings the baby in in her car seat, still sound asleep, slumped in a position that looks acutely uncomfortable to Rebecca, her cheek on her shoulder, her chubby fingers splayed over the buckle. The boys take ancient puzzles out of the toy cupboard and scatter the pieces on to the floor. Spike has chosen Animals of the Rainforest, Buzz, a map of a long-ago Europe in which Yugoslavia and the Berlin Wall still exist.

Rebecca studies this Victorian picture of family life with detachment. As Felicity turns her back on her to pour the tea, she catches David's eye and he winks. She imagines him sitting on the floor with the same puzzles, a lost boy growing up with a missing generation. Tony and Georgie did well by him, but they were in their fifties when their daughter and her husband died, leaving them in charge of a hyperactive little boy. It can't have been easy.

David's gaze sharpens as he holds hers. He was as much bemused by Felicity's insistence that she come as she was.

'So, Felicity,' Georgie says, with a malicious gleam in her eye. 'What's this?' She holds out her hand and uncurls her fingers. An egg quivers on her palm.

Felicity reddens. 'It's off, Georgie. I tested it.'

'It's perfectly good. I had one of them this morning.'

'Georgie,' Felicity says gently. 'I don't think you did. Maybe it was last week.'

'Lissy sweetheart,' David says. 'I don't think it's worth making a big deal out of. Georgie, why don't you give me the egg? We brought some groceries with us, so you've got plenty of fresh food.'

Georgie glowers at him. Tony says, 'Now, my dear,' and his wife lobs the egg straight at the fireplace, where it smashes against the surround and dribbles, wetly, on to the brown-tiled hearth. Tony bursts out laughing, then stops abruptly.

Spike and Buzz sit frozen over their puzzles, Daisy's arms jerk upwards and she bursts into tears.

'Cake, anyone?' Felicity asks, arching an eyebrow at Rebecca, a *What did I tell you?* expression on her face.

'Bitch,' Georgie says.

'Now dear, that's enough,' Tony says, planting his hands on the armrests of his chair and elevating himself a little, as if he might have to leap between the two of them. 'Rebecca didn't deserve that.'

'Felicity,' Felicity says through her teeth.

'Rebecca is Daddy's friend, Grandpa,' Spike says. 'Rebecca has black hair and Mummy has yellow hair.'

Felicity hands round slices of Victoria sponge and they sit with their plates on their knees trying to make conversation. Rebecca watches David. She has to admire his patience, but he treats Georgie and Tony like children. And not like his own kids, but as though he is the grandparent and can hand them back at six p.m. and put his feet up. But it isn't like that. From the state of the house, it's clear that systems are breaking down. Buzz has already demanded to know who the nappies in the bathroom are for and Felicity had to explain that they weren't nappies, they were incontinence pads and that when you got old sometimes things stopped working as they ought. Buzz had wrinkled his freckled nose.

When Rebecca first met David's grandparents, Georgie had been in her late seventies and sharp as a tack, Tony eighty-three and as fit and spry as a fifty-year-old. Georgie was the jealous type and they had never hit it off. Same with her relationship with her long-suffering granddaughter-in-law. Georgie thought David could have done better. And not only that; in her view, Felicity had stolen him away from her. Felicity had told her all this on their wedding day and it was a favourite topic of conversation between them; the undermining that went on, the words whispered in David's ear, the comments to her boys. The passive-aggressive behaviour. Rebecca doubted Georgie would have the slightest idea what passive-aggressive meant, but, according to Felicity, she had fulfilled the ten thousand hours that supposedly made you an expert in your chosen field. Mind you, Felicity should know.

Before they leave, David has a quick look around the house, taking Daisy with him, kissing her pink cheeks and tickling her.

'Who's my oochy-coochy girl?' he says and blows a raspberry on his daughter's flesh. She squeals with laughter.

'I would like him to be home more, obviously, but at least he tries to be a good father when he is,' Felicity says, as she packs up the puzzles. She straightens up and looks Rebecca in the eye. 'You know, what I said about an affair, I was just having a moment.'

'That's so you, though, isn't it? Always searching for the means to hurt yourself and rustling up your own weapons when you can't find any to hand.'

'Oh,' Felicity says, surprised.

Rebecca comes out of the bathroom and stands at the top of the stairs. She had been holding on, because she didn't fancy using the loo, but in the end, they were taking so long that she had to submit to need. It wasn't too bad in the end, probably because the cleaner uses it herself. She shouldn't be angry with David, but she is. He has enjoyed having both women with him, showing off because he craves female adulation, grubbing round his hen house for proof of love.

David and Felicity come in from putting the children and the dog in the car. She is about to run down when David speaks.

'Perhaps you could pop in once or twice during the week,' he says.

'No, I could not,' Felicity says. 'You'll have to talk to the carers again, David.'

'I only meant this week.'

'Yes, and that would lead to two weeks, and then three, and before you know it, I'll be made to feel terrible if I don't go. And why should I come here and be insulted by Georgie and called Rebecca by Tony? I'm not doing it. And that's that.'

'I'm working, sweetheart. I thought we were a team.'

'Yup. With you as the captain calling the shots. Sorry. I'm not playing.'

'Georgie doesn't mean to be rude. She's confused.'

'Uh-uh. There are some things your grandmother is not in the slightest bit confused about, and top of the list is me. I didn't tell you, because I didn't want to upset you, but last time I came down, she spat at me.'

Rebecca flinches. How awful.

'Spat,' David says. 'Jesus. That's not on. I'll have a word with her.'

'It'll go in one ear and out the other. What pisses me off is that when I inconvenience myself and the children and dash all the way over here without you, she accuses me of keeping you from her, as though you're ten years old and it's a custody battle.'

'Maybe there's something in that. Maybe you being here reminds her of when they had to fight my father's parents for me.'

'You are joking, aren't you?'

'Of course I am, Lissy darling. Help me out here. They aren't going to be around for ever. Come twice a week, that way we can support the carers and make them feel appreciated. Then maybe they won't keep walking out.'

'No. Sorry,' Felicity responds. 'Your grandmother might be losing her marbles, but she's physically healthy. She could go on for years. I spend my life thinking about you and the kids, and them. I want to think about myself for a change.'

'I do understand, but it's putting me under a shedload of pressure. I'm asking for your help here.'

'What do you want, David? A wife or a PA?'

'A wife who supports me, of course.'

'Hm. Well, I'd like a husband who fucks me. Of course. But we don't always get what we want.'

Rebecca lifts her hand to her mouth to hide her smile, her eyes widening. Good on her. She waits, then when Felicity calls to the boys, she judges it safe to descend.

David looks up, his brow knitting. They lock eyes and she gives a little shrug. He deserved that, and he knows it. She is perfectly willing to back Felicity up. He is a frustrating man. Other people's problems don't matter to him. He lives in the bubble that is David Gunner's charmed life and refuses to acknowledge the impact that that has on his family, crashing blithely through other people's concerns, other people's distress, as if by not stopping, he renders his behaviour harmless.

He touches her hand as she passes him, the tips of their fingers glancing, sending an electric current through her skin.

28

Laura

'I NEED TO TELL YOU SOMETHING.'

It's Jamie and he's holding the CVs with my Post-it notes, covered in scrawls, still attached. I'm zipping up my coat, ready to cycle home. It's only five, but I have no reason to stay late any more.

What had started out as a search for Guy's replacement has become a search for mine. There are two candidates who have potential, in my view, but nothing will happen. HR are merely going through the motions because, legally, they have to advertise the role beyond the company. Jamie has got the job already and he knows it. It doesn't make me feel particularly charitable towards him.

I frown. 'What?'

He takes a deep breath and puts the pages down, resting his hand on them. 'Rebecca and David have asked me to carry on working with Eddie on the GZ account.' He pauses. 'And then to become his partner.'

'Congratulations.'

'I'm sorry.' Jamie scratches his head. 'It's been difficult without Guy. I've felt like I'm floating around. It's hard to explain.'

'You don't have to. I understand.' I pull myself together. He isn't taking any pleasure in this. He's found himself in a difficult position through no fault of his own. 'I already assumed you would be filling my shoes. They would have been mad not to offer it to you.'

He looks at me for a moment. 'Thanks. That's kind of you but I don't deserve it. Guy was my friend and now he's gone, and I'm moving on without him, doing the stuff he would love to be doing, having a career, having fun. I can't lie: when they suggested I take over from you, see how Eddie and I got along, I said yes immediately. I didn't need to think about it. But I swear to God, I wish you hadn't resigned.'

'Who told you I resigned?' The speed news travels round this place is brutal.

'Sorry, wasn't I meant to know? Eddie said something. He's really cut up about it.'

He means I've let him down. It's true, but I can't work in this building any more. Being here makes me feel as though I'm stuck in a small room with a spider. And the spider is watching me, stripping me and knowing me. David. It makes me feel sick.

'He'll get over it.'

I'm still standing in front of his desk, and he's sitting, with his chair pushed back and his arms folded across his chest.

'OK,' I add, when he doesn't speak. 'Well, I guess you won't be needing those.' I point at the CVs.

'Sorry. I wasted your time.' He sits up and shuffles them together and pushes them into a drawer. 'That is, if you won't change your mind.'

'I won't.'

'Will you come out for a drink with me?'

'I don't think . . . Look, I'm sorry, Jamie, but I can't.'

The offer sounded half-hearted; part of his apology, a no-hard-feelings kind of invitation. On the other hand, it could just as easily have been fear of rejection. I look at him, try to recognize what I found so attractive when I was drunk, but all I see is a collection of features that spark no response. I need to get to know someone before I can recognize the intangible in them, the quirks and the fleeting gestures and expressions, and even then . . .

I went out with a bloke a couple of years ago. I knew him because his hair was incredibly curly, so much so that it bounced off his head. I could see him at a distance, pick him out in a crowd. That made me feel happy and safe. Then he came back from a weekend away and he had cut his hair, a buzz-cut that took it down to his skull. I didn't recognize him amongst the group of friends at the bar where we had agreed to meet, even though we had been inseparable for six months. We split up. Perhaps before Christmas I would have made the effort with Jamie, but I can't now. I can't undo what has been done or take away the self-disgust and the hurt. I don't know who I can trust any more.

'See you tomorrow then,' he says.

'Yeah. See you.'

29

Laura

Police are still appealing for witnesses to the hit-and-run that took the life of a twenty-seven-year-old man at the end of last year. Guy Holt was cycling back to his home in Chalk Farm after attending a party in Hackney when he was knocked down and left for dead by an unknown driver. If you were in the Hawley Road area between one and two a.m. on the morning of the twenty-third of December, and think you saw or heard anything, Thames Valley Police would like to hear from you. Guy worked for advertising agency Gunner Munro. His devastated parents described him as a cheerful, generous young man with everything to live for.

Poor Guy, and his poor family. The police have talked to everyone at work and cleared us all. I hope they find the bastard who did it. Some idiot drunk, driving home from their own Christmas party, no doubt. What a waste.

I switch off the television and rub my face, tired after

a long day of trying to look as though I don't mind sitting between Graham and the wall. I get up and pace to the window. The night is crisp; windscreens already frosting over. In the sky, the brighter stars battle through London's light pollution to twinkle at me. I'll be twenty-nine this Saturday. That's in two days' time. I have nothing arranged and my heart sinks at the thought of my mother's birthday card flopping on to the scruffy welcome mat, along with the glossy flyers for pizzas and estate agents.

Downstairs, Phoebe's little boy has been crying for a while. He always does at this time of the evening. When he finally quietens down, I imagine him and Phoebe snuggled up on a nursing chair with a blanket enveloping them both, Phoebe turning the pages of a picture book or quietly singing to him as his eyes grow heavy. The Hills won't be here for ever. They'll want their own front door, a little house to grow their family in. But I hope they stay a while longer because I like knowing they're there.

I switch the television back on but there's nothing to tempt me. The big productions are daunting. I can't watch *Game of Thrones* because I haven't the slightest idea who anyone is, except of course the dwarf, my favourite character. In fact, anything with dirty faces, leather outfits and swords and shields is impossible. I prefer limited casts, using actors who have different hairstyles and ethnicity. Dramas involving police in uniform are out.

I get a message from Phoebe. *Glass of wine, neighbour? On my own till 8* ☹

I start to type, *Sorry, I've got loads of work to catch up on.* Then I delete one letter at a time and start again. *See you in a minute.*

Before Phoebe switches the television off I catch a repeat of the feature about Guy. She's like Bettina, in that she has an over-developed interest in other people's lives and, discovering I worked with Guy, she's taken an interest.

'How well did you know him?' she asks as she pours me a glass of white wine. She empties a packet of salt-and-vinegar crisps into a bowl and puts it on the table.

'Reasonably. He'd only been with us a short time, but he was lovely. Everyone liked him.'

'Only takes one piss artist to put his foot down on the accelerator . . . You can bet it was a young bloke. I read something online.' She lowers her voice to an unnecessary whisper. 'They're saying the driver shifted him to the side of the road before driving on. If he had called an ambulance straight away, he would have had a chance.'

To my horror, my eyes well over. I dash away my tears with the back of my hand.

Phoebe jumps up and runs out of the room, coming back with a box of tissues. I give her a watery smile as I blow my nose and dab at my eyes.

'Sorry. I didn't mean to start blubbing all over you. It's been a rubbish day.' I take a deep breath, crumple the hanky and push it under my sleeve. 'I miss my hair.'

She pulls on her bottom lip with her teeth as she looks at me. 'It's already grown out a little.'

I laugh, touching it automatically. 'You know what's

weird? When I go to bed, I can't bear the feeling of cold air on my ears, so I've been wearing a woolly hat pulled down over them. It's a good thing I don't have a boyfriend.' The tears and snot start threatening again. I drink some wine and eat a handful of crisps.

'I don't know what to say. I wish I could make it better.'

I don't want her to feel guilty for being happy. 'Don't be silly. You've made it better by inviting me over. I don't want you to think I'm sitting up there like Miss Havisham, destined to be alone all my life. It's just that things have happened that have tripped me up and I haven't coped as well as I should have.'

'Do you want to talk about it?'

'I can't. I'm sorry.'

'Someone hurt you,' she says.

'In a way. But it's over now.' I smile to reassure her. 'I might go home this weekend. It's my birthday on Saturday and I don't want to spend it gazing at my navel.'

'Come to us,' she says eagerly. 'We're having a few friends round for supper. Very casual.'

'Oh no. Don't worry. I don't want to impose.'

'You wouldn't be imposing. I promise we won't talk about babies all night. Joe works in advertising as well, so you'll have something in common. Say yes. Go on.'

'On one condition.'

She raises her eyebrows.

'You let me babysit Noah once in a while, so the two of you can get out.'

Phoebe grins and raises her hand in a high-five. 'Done.'

* * *

We hear a key in the lock and Phoebe and I both scrape our chairs back and jump up. I take my wine glass to the sink and tip out the dregs. Elliot comes in, wind-blown and smiling. He greets me and kisses his wife. I leave, because that's the unspoken rule. This is their precious time together.

As I close the door behind me, I wait in the chilly hallway long enough to overhear him say, 'Thank God she left. I thought I was going to have to make conversation with her.'

I don't wait for Phoebe's response. She's going to have to tell him that, far from distancing herself from her proven-to-be-unhinged neighbour, she's asked her over for supper on Saturday evening.

30

Laura

DAVID GUNNER IS STANDING IN THE DOORWAY OF HIS office watching us, his gaze sweeping the media floor. I'm watching him too, whenever I can. And I don't care if he knows it.

Bettina and I have had a busy morning identifying venues that can pencil us in for three possible dates, then we get going on caterers and ticking off boring details like the Temporary Alcohol Licence. Graham is out, so Bettina is sitting at his desk.

I need to get hold of a good set designer, someone who'll do me a deal because they want to get on. A lighting designer as well. Once I've pinned down a date where everything aligns, I start on Bettina's list of potential invitees. I'm keen to get representatives from the trendiest bars in the country along. Not just the London pubs and clubs, but from some of the major cities: Manchester, Liverpool and Birmingham. These are the men and women who are going to make this campaign fly.

Their recommendations to customers will count for more than any poster.

I'm doing my best to appear enthusiastic. I've loved working with Eddie, I've relished the pace at which everything moves and enjoyed those moments when I've presented my drawings and seen faces light up, because I've understood what's in their minds and transferred it to paper. But that's all gone. Even so, for my own sake and for Rebecca's, I'm determined to leave on a positive note.

'God,' Bettina tuts. 'This desk is sticky.'

'Umm,' I respond, distracted. David is still there, leaning on his door frame, talking to one of the blokes now. I try not to scratch but the urge festers, like a little imp in my mind. I discreetly rub the backs of my hands against the rough nap of my black jeans. It feels like David is under my skin. Maybe that's the point. He's reminding me of his physicality, gloating, exalting. Thinking he's unassailable.

Bettina picks at the elbow of her sleeve, wrinkling her nose. 'I don't know what he's been doing.'

'If you're that bothered about it, go and get a cloth.'

'I'm not cleaning up his mess.'

'I thought he was a friend of yours. Didn't he get you the job?'

She clicks on the Internet and types something in then scrolls down and picks a website. 'Yeah, he did. But I'm friends with his stepsister, not him. I've known her since nursery and our mums are mates. I don't like Graham. Oh, this place looks great.'

I lean over. 'The Studio. Yeah, looks interesting. Do

you want to take a look? We could go later if you like. Give them a ring.'

'Bettina!'

Rebecca is standing in the doorway to her office, scanning the room.

Bettina pushes the chair back with her feet and spins round. 'Here we go. What do you think she wants?'

I'm on the phone when, minutes later, she reaches for her bag. I put my hand over the speaker and mouth, 'Where are you going?'

'Rebecca left a USB stick at home. There's a taxi waiting downstairs. I won't be long, I'm only going to run in and out.'

When she's gone, David wanders over and stands behind me. He puts his hand on my shoulder and leans forward, peering at the screen. I tense from the top of my head to the tips of my toes. I can smell the coffee on his breath. He taps the screen.

'This guy.'

'Adam Powell? What about him.' Adam used to work for Gunner Munro, until he left a year ago, and started his own agency. It was no worse than David and Rebecca had done.

'I can't stand the little shit but pull out all the stops to make sure he comes.'

In my head, a tight voice is saying, *Take. Your. Hand. Off. Me.*

At lunch, despite the cold, I go out on to the terrace. I'm not hungry and haven't bought myself a sandwich or made a packed lunch, but I've taken some chocolate from the enormous old-fashioned jar that David keeps filled. He's always done that, and I used to think it was sweet, him trying to endear himself to his workers.

Bettina joins me, and we sit on the bench, huddled in our coats.

'You'll never guess what I found out this morning.'

I'm in no mood for office gossip, but Bettina doesn't need encouragement. She's like a squirrel, finding her nuts and burying them everywhere. Little treasures for her to guzzle later.

'You won't believe it.'

'No, I probably won't.'

'David and Rebecca are having an affair.'

My chocolate goes down the wrong way. Bettina pats me firmly on the back and I flap my hand, signalling her to stop.

'What are you talking about? They can't be.'

I would have known. There is no way they could have hidden something like that.

'No, they are. I swear.'

I shuffle round on the wooden bench and stare at her. 'Are you sure it's not Chinese whispers?'

I shuffle to shake her. Her face falls. She doesn't like my expression. I'm taking what she sees as a bit of fun far too seriously.

'It's true.' Her voice is sulky.

I smile to try and get her back. She starts to stand up, but I hang on to her jacket. 'How do you know?'

She sighs and sits down again, glancing at the door to check no one's coming. Her voice drops to a conspiratorial whisper. 'When I went to her flat this morning, I found something.'

'I thought you were just running in and out.'

She makes a face: part guilty, part mischievous. 'Well, I was. The USB was on the little table in her hall. But I'd only just finished my coffee and Rebecca didn't even give me a chance to go to the loo. I was absolutely bursting by the time I got there. So, anyway, I was having a pee, my eyes possibly wandering around the room. Her bathroom is gorgeous by the way. She has one of those roll-top baths . . .'

'I don't need a description of her interiors.' I am on tenterhooks, my mind racing, trying to gauge what this means.

'I saw a man's wash bag and I had a peek inside. There was a set of toiletries in there. Razor, shampoo, underarm stuff.'

I release a long breath and stand up, stepping awkwardly over the bench. 'That's hardly proof it's David. She's probably got a boyfriend.'

'No,' she hisses. She looks up, grimacing. 'There's more. There was a packet of pills with his name on it.'

I look back through the windows. Beyond the desks and their hive of activity, I can see the closed doors to David and Rebecca's offices. My mouth gapes.

'When you think about it, it's not that surprising,' she says. 'They practically live in each other's pockets.'

'You mustn't tell anyone else, Bettina.' I don't have time to think this through, and it's only an instinctive reaction, but it might be more useful to me if it doesn't become public knowledge. It will eventually, but I'm hoping Bettina will resist the temptation at least until I've gone. 'If it gets back to either of them that you've been spreading rumours, you'll be out.'

She looks hurt and we walk back to our desks in silence. I turn and say, so that the others can hear, 'Which bands did you have in mind?'

'Milo are possible,' she says grudgingly. 'If you want that lived-in sound. Or maybe Red Wing. They're upbeat and fun. There's a couple of others I want to try.'

I came in on the tube because my back tyre was flat and, that evening, I squeeze on to a packed train. I have nothing to hold on to as the doors close and, as the train moves, I stumble. Someone puts a steadying hand on my arm and I whip my head round to find a man smiling at me.

'Fancy meeting you here,' he says.

He is holding on to the bar, his arm outstretched across the curve of my shoulder. I have nothing to hold on to and keep my balance by standing with my feet apart. I break into a sweat, scanning his hair, checking his ears and his neck, his clothes, but I don't have a clue.

'Sorry, I was miles away.'

'No worries. How's your day been?'

'I've had better. What about you?'

This is hideous. I start to pray that he'll get out before it becomes obvious that I have no idea who I'm talking to. I rack my brains for something to say, but he saves me the trouble.

'I'm shattered, to be honest. I didn't have five minutes to walk away from my desk, so my brain is fried.' His mouth pulls into a smile as we shriek into King's Cross.

'I know what you mean. I have to get some air at lunchtime or I start feeling sick.'

IT? One of the Media guys? I try and fix on something, but my eyes skitter around his face.

'So, I hear you're coming to ours tomorrow night.'

Jesus. It's Elliot. I hope my relief doesn't show on my face. Thank Christ I didn't start blathering on about colleagues or campaigns.

'It's nice of you both to have me.'

'It's a pleasure,' he says.

If I believe that, I'll believe anything, but full marks for trying. I hope Phoebe hasn't told him it's my birthday tomorrow. I don't want to look pathetic.

'So, where do you work?' I say.

'You won't have heard of it. It's a company called IdTech Solutions. A couple of minutes from the station. What about you?'

'An advertising agency, just off Curtain Road. Hoxton really.'

'Very trendy.' He smiles. 'We'll have to keep an eye out for each other.'

'Yes,' I say, thinking the exact opposite.

The train breaks and I almost topple, and, once again, Elliot puts a hand out to steady me. It's an involuntary action, but I don't like it. This new piece of knowledge, that I work a few hundred yards from him, is acutely disconcerting. How many times have I ignored him in the street, on the tube, or in one of the local sandwich bars? I steer the subject towards Noah, knowing, from spending time with my siblings, that it's the easiest way to distract them from a topic that's making me anxious. I start to dread the walk from Kentish Town to the flat, but he lets me off the hook, stopping outside our local, the Spanish Arms, for a quick half because he needs to wind down so that he doesn't inflict his stress on Phoebe.

Great excuse, I think, liking him a little bit less.

It's been a day of surprises, mainly nasty ones. As I walk, I picture David and Rebecca. I turn their affair over in my mind and wonder how it impacts on me. This is a successful man with a wife and children and a mistress. Why would he put all that at risk for a night of passion with a woman who thought he was someone else? It's hardly flattering to his ego.

All I can think is that it was arrogance, that he knew about me and thought he'd see how far he could take it. He may not have expected it to go as far as it did, but he should have stopped as soon as he realized how drunk I was. And that's it. It makes a horrible kind of sense. David Gunner thinks what happened was my fault. Sometimes I weaken and think the same. Things would be so much easier if I just accepted that, and let it go. I lift my hand to my hair and feel the cropped ends and my eyes film over. Unfortunately for David, I can't. I hurry up to the door, and throw myself in, stopping only to pick up the neat pile of post that Phoebe has left me, before running up to the safety of my flat.

I have two cards. One is from Isabel; there's a French stamp and the address is handwritten. The other has a printed label which makes me immediately suspicious. I open it first. It has a picture of a silhouetted couple entwined on the front and inside there's a folded piece of paper.

Be careful.
x

I refold the note and replace it in the card, in its envelope, and tuck it in beside the torn letter on my bookshelves. I'm not going to let this upset me.

31

Laura

SATURDAY. MY BIRTHDAY. I MEET MUM OUTSIDE FOYLES at Waterloo station and we walk along Southbank to the Tate Modern. Over lunch in the restaurant she gives me a card with fifty quid tucked inside.

'Spend it on something fun,' she says.

The last time I had fun was at the work Christmas party. Life has not been fun since. I thank her with a kiss and a hug.

'So how have you been?' she asks. 'No relapse?'

'No. I'm fine. Well, perhaps not fine. I've chucked in the job.'

Mum's reaction to unsettling news from her children is always the same. She silently processes it, looking at it from all angles, searching for the positive. This time she doesn't find one.

'Was that a good idea? I thought you loved it there.'

I shrug, picking at a bit of salad. 'I did.'

'So?' She waits, her head tilted. 'Was it the people? The work?'

'The people. A person. I don't want to talk about it.'

'But, you should—'

I interrupt. 'I spoke to Dad this morning.'

'Oh good. I'm glad he remembered his daughter's birthday. How is he?'

'Fine. No dramas.'

Mum waits, and then leans back in her chair and looks out of the window. I follow her gaze to the dome of St Paul's. 'I'm worried about you, Laura.'

'You needn't be. I'm OK.'

'Are you getting out at all? Seeing anyone? What are you doing tonight?'

'Yes. Not at the moment. And I'm going to my neighbours' for supper.'

She isn't reassured. 'I just want you to be happy.'

I smile. 'That's because you're my mum. I'm happy sometimes, and sometimes I'm not, like most people. I'd like to be happier, and maybe once I've left Gunner Munro, that will happen.'

'Do you meet any men?'

'Yes! Well, not in the way you'd like.' I decide to give her something to make her feel better, something to take home. I hate the thought of her picturing me alone in my flat, snacking on cereal, glued to the telly. It's too accurate. 'There's a bloke at work who keeps asking me out, but I haven't said yes yet.'

She looks so hopeful, it hurts. 'You're going to though, aren't you? You should give him a chance. Unless he's really horrible. Is he?'

'You sound like Eddie. There's nothing wrong with him. He's nice. It's just that I don't have the energy right now.'

'Oh, Laura, for heaven's sake. You'd better find some, otherwise someone else will get her mitts on him.'

We talk about other things for a while; about Mark and Isabel and her grandchildren mostly, but, being Mum, she can't contain herself for long and, as we stand up and gather our belongings, she asks in a laughably nonchalant way:

'So, what's his name?'

If I tell her, she'll keep asking about him, and something that is nothing will gather strength and meaning. When I think his name, something happens, something that tells me he has got under my skin.

'You'll be the first to know.'

Phoebe and Elliot have extended the table that sits in the window of their front room and pushed the sofa and armchair back. There are candles on the mantelpiece and dotted around the room; a row of tea lights on the mahogany coffee table. We squash on to the sofa and armchair for pre-supper drinks, with Elliot perched on the arm of the sofa and Phoebe arranged on a cushion on the floor, from which she uncurls every few minutes to check on the food. The only other light is from a standard lamp in the corner. It makes the place feel less like a rental and more grown-up. There is no sign of baby paraphernalia; not a single book or toy.

I hold back, as I always do in these situations, waiting until I'm comfortable with who everyone is, until their hair and clothes become linked in my mind with their names. There are seven of us; our hosts, two couples and me. The couples are called Cathy and Rob, and Louisa and Joe. The three women are dissimilar enough for it to be easy. There's Phoebe with her straightened brown hair, Cathy wearing hers in a loose chignon from which strands artfully escape, and Louisa wears glasses and has a fringe. Joe has brown hair, brushed back from his face, Elliot is wearing his stripy shirt, and Rob is greying.

'So, what do you do, Laura?' Cathy asks.

The talk round the table has been about houses so far; who is buying, who is renting and what their prospects are. I've admitted to owning the flat above, with a large mortgage, having been helped with a deposit by my grandmother.

'I work in advertising. I'm an art director.'

Joe, who is sitting diagonally opposite me, leans forward, holding his glass. 'We've met before,' he says.

I rapidly scan his hair and clothes, but, as far as I can tell, I've never seen him before in my life. Not that that means anything. I only hope that if we have met, it was so long ago that I can be forgiven for forgetting. A blush creeps up my neck and I give silent thanks to Phoebe for dimming the lights.

'You do seem familiar,' I say, as my heart sinks. I thought I would be safe tonight. 'Where did we meet?'

'At Gunner Munro. I work in advertising too.'

'Oh. Right. Yes, Phoebe mentioned that.' Under the table I scratch my fingers.

'We met when I came for an interview. About four months ago?'

That would have been the same time Guy and Jamie were applying. But I don't say that.

'David Gunner brought me into your office to meet you and your partner. Eddie isn't it?'

If David likes a job applicant, he'll give them a tour of the building. It's a way of drawing them out. People often say things they haven't planned to when they're released from the interview environment, especially when David is piling on the charm. I cover up an involuntary grimace by coughing into my napkin.

Joe persists. 'We talked about coffee. You were doing drawings for Mocca Smooth.'

It rings a bell, but I shrug and shake my head. I'm beginning to feel uncomfortable; cornered into becoming defensive. Everyone is watching me.

'You had long hair and you were wearing glasses – that's why I didn't recognize you straight away. I didn't get the job – probably because I'm unmemorable.'

He laughs to show that he doesn't mean it, but it leaves an unpleasant taste in the atmosphere. I feel resentful; even without my condition I would be justified in forgetting one job applicant out of the many that pass through our doors.

'Of course you aren't, darling,' his wife says, giving me a dirty look.

'We met outside,' he says. 'We sat on the tube and talked.'

Ah. I do remember. It was summer, and he was wearing a paisley shirt, so that when he spoke to me I had no trouble connecting him with the young man David had introduced to me and Eddie.

'I'm with you now,' I say. 'Where did you find a job in the end?'

He name-checks one of the big beasts.

'I'm impressed.'

He preens at that, and I feel forgiven. And relieved when he turns to talk to Phoebe.

Phoebe clears the plates and brings out the main course: chicken Kiev and mash. We drink and talk, but as the evening wears on and people relax, they slip into the habit of talking about what they have in common. Their babies. They compare photographs on their phones and I play with the idea of telling them that all their babies look exactly the same to me, and that their parents do too. If I cut out their hair and the clothes they're wearing, those oval spaces with the eyes, noses and mouths have little to distinguish them. Humans without identifying characteristics are like rabbits in a field, fish in the sea. I try to join in but, bar the odd anecdote about my nephews and nieces, I don't know much about babies. I can't stop thinking about the card. Yesterday evening, alone in my flat, it scared me. David's terse message reeked of suppressed anger. In the cold light of day, I told myself not to worry. That if that is how he chooses to lash out, I'm in no danger. Tonight though, right now, the bad feelings are coming back.

I look round the table, at the flushed faces and sparkling eyes. The wine and conversation flows. Louisa recounts an incident in the playground when her daughter proposed marriage to a little boy with the biggest brown eyes she has ever seen. He burst into tears and ran to his mum.

'The thing is,' Rob says. 'Cathy proposed to me, so it's obviously genetic.'

'I'm sure Darwin said something about that,' Elliot says. 'Females want to mate with the alpha male and cut out their rivals.'

He leans towards me and murmurs, 'We must be boring the pants off you.'

I smile although his choice of words couldn't have been worse. 'Don't be silly. I don't mind at all.'

'Liar. So, how's work?'

'I've resigned.'

He looks wrong-footed. 'Is that a good or a bad thing?'

'Ask me in three months' time and I'll tell you.'

'Resigned?' Phoebe must have sharp hearing. 'Why've you done that?'

'I felt it was time for a change,' I say. 'I've started applying to other agencies. I'll be fine.' I glance at Joe. 'You never know, I might be coming to you for a job.'

Phoebe opens her eyes wide, as though she's trying to signal to me that she cares. She just looks pissed.

'My last project is to organize a launch party for a big campaign. It's going to be my swansong.'

'Well, that sounds positive,' Joe says. 'I'm sure you'll be snapped up.'

This sentiment is echoed by the others, then they resume their conversations. Only Elliot looks concerned. Perhaps I imagined that he had a problem with me. Maybe I caught him on a bad day. I don't want to talk about what happened, so I tell him that I've booked a band from round here: Red Wing.

'Really? Fantastic!'

'Have you heard of them then?'

'Yeah. They've played at the Fiddler's Elbow a couple of times. I like their mix of American folk and Street.' He waves to get Phoebe's attention. 'Hey, babes. Laura's got Red Wing playing at her do.'

'Oh wow. I love them. God, I so miss live music. That's one of the hardest things about babies. You can't go out on a whim. It costs fifty quid before we've even left the flat. When did we last see a live band?'

'You know I'll babysit anytime,' I say, delighted to be able to repay Phoebe in some measure. 'You only have to ask. I'd love to do it. And, listen, why don't you come to the party?'

'Wouldn't people think it was odd?' Phoebe says.

'It'll be packed out, so no one will even notice. And anyway, I'm leaving, so I don't give a shit.'

'Way to go, Laura,' Elliot whoops.

I blush.

'Harriet could have Noah for the night,' Phoebe says, appealing to Elliot. She turns to me. 'I'm the designated babysitter for when my sister goes into labour, so I reckon she owes me.' She chews her bottom lip. 'It's tempting.'

'I'll put you on the invitation list, then you can make your minds up. And if anyone wants to know who you are, you are an in-demand hair-and-make-up artist to the stars and Elliot . . .' I turn to him. 'Who shall I say you are?'

'An expert in digital marketing. Which is true.' He gives me an almost imperceptible nod. 'This is really good of you, Laura. I had you down wrong.'

'Did you? What did you have me down as?'

'You got me there. I don't know, maybe a little aloof.'

'Aloof?'

'Good word isn't it. A-Loof. Not easy to approach.'

'Ah. Well, you know how it is? You have to check the neighbour isn't a nutter before you get to know them.'

'Touché.'

I smile. 'Look, I know that you think I'm off my trolley.' I realize I'm fingering the ends of my hair and drop my hand to my lap. 'You're worried I'm going to be clingy with Phoebe . . .'

He cocks his head. 'What gave you that impression?'

'Come on. It's obvious. I've had a crap couple of months, and your wife has been incredibly kind to me. She is one of the sweetest people I've ever met.' I hate that there's a tremor in my voice. I take a sip of wine and start again. 'I really like Phoebe and I'd love to be friends with both of you. I meant what I said about the babysitting.'

'What are you two plotting down there?' Cathy asks, immediately drawing everyone's attention to the fact that we have our heads together.

At a discreet signal from Phoebe, Elliot scrapes his chair back and picks up the empty wine bottles. He ducks his head as he rises and says in my ear, 'The haircut suits you, by the way.'

Then he glances over my shoulder, stands up and leans over the table and blows out the tea lights one by one. The room is cast into darkness and Phoebe comes in bearing a plate with a chocolate tart on it and one, flickering candle.

'Happy birthday to you . . .'

* * *

As soon as I close my eyes something clicks, like a cog finding its place in the wheel. If Rebecca and David are lovers, then that is where David got his information. I can imagine Rebecca telling him: *Strictly between you and me, darling – and for God's sake, don't let on that you know – Laura is face-blind.*

Sunday goes by, slow as a stopping train. I sleep in then go for a run. I clean the bathroom and kitchen, phone Isabel for a chat and shop for the following week. I don't look at the card again, but I know it's there, I'm keenly aware of it. I watch five back-to-back episodes of a Netflix drama in the evening, then switch it off and fetch the card and pull my laptop on to my knee. My fingers fly across the keyboard, barely keeping up with my thoughts. I delete some, rewrite parts. The result is emotional and threatening; absolutely true to the way I feel.

> *I don't understand why you aren't weighed down by guilt. You seem not to care about what you did. How can you carry on as though nothing has happened? Your behaviour is so unbelievably arrogant. There are things I can do, people I can talk to. It might be too late for proof, but it's not too late to damage your reputation.*

My pen hovers as I debate signing my name. I don't. I know it's cowardly, but Deborah warned me against harassment, and I don't want to give him ammunition to take to a lawyer. I fold the sheet of paper and put it in a white envelope that I've printed with his name and the words *Private & Confidential.* I don't want Felicity opening it. I have no problem locating David's address. I have it in my contacts because I've had stuff biked to his home often enough.

Two a.m. It's the dead hour and no one is out, the restaurants closed and the street eerie. I head up Willow Road and when I reach the corner of Constable Lane, I stop. The Gunners live about halfway along, in a graceful black-bricked Georgian house. I walk along the opposite side of the road. The curtains are open downstairs, caught back to frame a towering flower arrangement so perfect that I suspect it might be fake. The lights are out and there is no sign of life.

Rain splashes on the windowsills and on to the pavement. I run across the road, push open the letterbox and slide the envelope in. I hear it hit the mat as I ease the flap back down. From deep inside, a dog yaps, its nails clicking on the stone floor as it comes to investigate. I start to jog and don't stop until I'm back at the shops. The heat from my body turns the dampness from the driving rain to steam. I'm sweating and cold and wet at the same time, but it's done. I picture David catching sight of the envelope lying on the doormat when he comes down in the morning, picking it up and frowning as he reads the address, puzzling over a letter delivered by hand in the night, and finally opening it and reading my words.

I imagine Felicity following him downstairs, the baby on her hip, pausing to ask what it is. He won't look at her as he folds it and stuffs it into his pocket. He'll say something like, *Just one of those irritating estate agent letters. Mr & Mrs X are keen to buy a house in this street*. He'll shrug it off with a distracted smile, but later, he will get it out, read those words again and understand their implication.

This isn't over yet.

I am exhilarated, elated, surging with energy.

32

Rebecca

'THANK GOD YOU'RE HERE.'

Felicity opens the door, wide-eyed and frazzled, her hair tied back with what looks suspiciously like a pair of underpants, Daisy wailing in her arms. The boys are yelling at each other, still in their pyjamas, Buzz stamping his foot and Spike howling, 'Mum! Mum!'

It's pandemonium and Felicity seems incapable of action, concerning herself solely with her daughter. From the depths of the house there's a crash. Rebecca pushes past her. In the kitchen, it looks as though David has swept everything from the island counter: bowls of cereal lie broken, their contents spreading across the limestone, the iPad has a crack across the corner of the screen, a mug has come to rest some way from its handle. The *Today* programme is playing on the radio, a female presenter interviewing a member of the Shadow Cabinet. Rebecca crosses the room and switches it off. Only then does David appear to notice she's there.

She glances from his red face to the clock on the wall. If they are going to make their breakfast meeting, then they need to go, but it doesn't seem to her that David is going anywhere this morning. She quashes a spurt of panic. She knows from watching her father deal with her mother's periodic histrionics that a show of anxiety on her part will only make matters worse. It's better to absorb his raging energy like a sponge and step in once he's worn himself out. He paces the room, stopping every so often to stare out of the wall of glass doors that stretches from one side of the house to the other. Eventually he presses his palms and forehead to the cold glass and groans.

'David,' she says. 'What's going on?'

He drops his hands and turns and is about to speak, but Felicity comes in, followed hard on her heels by the two boys, her gaze darting between her husband and Rebecca.

'Dad!' Spike is furious, tears welling. 'Buzz took my Skeletor.'

'Will you shut up about your fucking Skeletor,' David roars.

Spike stares at his father, the colour draining from his face, and throws himself at his mother.

'You can't take it to school anyway,' Felicity says, stroking his head and scowling furiously at David. She mouths, 'You bastard,' at him, and starts to pull her children towards the door. Daisy's cries grow louder, more tragic.

'Why don't you go up and get dressed, boys?' Rebecca says, striving for calm. She feels like a ship's captain in the middle of a squall. 'Mummy will come and find you in a minute. Go on,' she adds, surprised not to be instantly obeyed. 'Clothes on.'

Shutting the door to the kitchen, she finds Felicity sitting on the stairs, steepled hands against her brow. 'Would you mind taking them to school for me?'

'Felicity! I can't look after your children.'

'Buzz is your godchild.'

'Right. Yes, I know but I'm not really equipped. Sorry.' The apology is for her flippancy, for her betrayal, for possibly driving her friend's husband to this. She nods in David's direction. 'What happened?'

'I don't know! Everything was fine, and then Daisy got her fingers caught in the door, poor darling, and started screaming blue murder and Buzz and Spike started squabbling and he just lost it.' Her voice rises. 'I don't know what to do.'

Rebecca opens the door a crack and peers through. David is sitting on the floor with his back to the glass, his eyes closed. 'Why don't you take them to school while I get him out of here?'

'It's too early.'

She sighs with exasperation. 'Well, what were you expecting *me* to do with them then?'

'Take them to the playground for half an hour?' Felicity says hopefully.

'Felicity, you know I can't do that. We have a meeting, and, anyway, I'd probably lose them. I'll talk to him. You get yourself and the kids out of the house. Is there anywhere you can go?'

'I suppose I could give Harriet a call,' Felicity says. 'I

don't expect she'll mind if we land on her. Can you take Daisy for a minute while I finish dressing?'

Rebecca cradles a wet-faced Daisy in her arms, the child giving little sniffs just in case anyone should forget she's upset. Daisy is warm and heavy, and Rebecca holds her close and breathes her in. There's a school sweatshirt hanging over the back of the sofa and she uses it to protect her coat, then snuggles the baby's head into her neck. It's an amazing feeling, so ordinary and yet so precious. She's reluctant to hand her over when Felicity reappears with Spike and Buzz. Rebecca is grateful to see she has released her hair from the underpants.

Once she's hustled all four of them out of the house she calls Agnes and tells her they won't be at the meeting, and that Agnes has to make something up. Agnes doesn't ask questions. Rebecca hangs her coat over the banister and goes back to David.

She stands in the doorway, regarding him wordlessly. He holds her eyes for a moment, then his gaze drops. Rain batters the windows. A fat pigeon roosts on the bare branches of the cherry tree that dominates the end of the garden. In the spring it will be heavy with pink blossom. She walks round the room, picking things up; a rabbit soft toy with elongated limbs and ears, a black-and-white photograph of David flanked by his sons, taken before Daisy was born. She puts them down on the table and starts to clear up the mess, dealing with the broken china, wrapping it in yesterday's newspaper and depositing it in the bin. She wipes up the puddle of milk and cornflakes and rinses the rag out under the tap, checks the iPad is working. There is no sign that this is bothering David, or that he's wondering why he isn't the centre of attention. Finally, she approaches him, making a tutting sound in her mouth with a click of her tongue against her palate, positioning herself at his feet, in the invisible arc between them.

David stares straight ahead. Every so often he twitches, once or twice he raises his hand and rubs his jaw. He needs a shave. She pulls over a chair, sits down, and presses his head against her knee. She strokes his hair, then weaves her fingers through it, twists her hand and tugs his head back.

'What's the matter with you?' she asks. She keeps her voice even, doesn't allow emphasis on any of the words.

He begins to count out loud. 'One two three four . . .' When he reaches twelve, she tightens her grip and he stops. 'What the fuck?' He takes hold of her wrist and tries to prise apart her fingers.

'I assume Felicity has tried love and sympathy,' she says, releasing him. She takes his hand and slides it between her legs, clamping it halfway between her knees and her crotch. 'What's brought this on?'

He releases a long breath.

'Nothing. I just flipped out. I didn't sleep last night, and the kids started kicking off and it was like someone had flicked a switch. All the shit came tumbling in.'

'Perhaps you should see a doctor . . . if it's depression, or a breakdown of some sort.'

'It's not.'

He raises his voice and she flinches. Ignoring her reaction, he jumps up and goes upstairs. She follows him into the en-suite and watches him face his reflection in the mirror and rub his hand across his stubble.

'I look like fuck.'

She raises her eyebrows.

'Did they go out?'

She nods. 'They went round to Harriet's.'

'Good. She's not one of the harpies. How're we doing for time?'

'We're fine. I cancelled.'

He stops what he's doing. 'You did what?'

'I cancelled the meeting, David,' she says slowly. 'You're in no fit state.'

He takes a long time to answer. 'OK. Great. We'll have to fit them in before the end of the week.'

He seems to have recovered, but she's worried that it's only a temporary respite; that this will happen again. As the car takes them through London, she thinks about Felicity dressed any-old-how with her sobbing baby in her arms, two boys demanding her attention and an equally needy man-child having a life-crisis in the kitchen. Is that what she wants? Kids and chaos instead of her ordered and beautiful existence with the spikes of excitement that being with David brings? David is working, checking his messages, the last hour apparently forgotten. She should forget it too. She touches his knee and he covers her hand with his. If she could guarantee their relationship would not end, she could go without the baby. But there is no guarantee. Worse, after this morning she can't hide from the fact that he won't only let her down, he might let their child down too.

33

Laura

DAVID WALKS BRISKLY ACROSS THE MEDIA FLOOR. I'M working on my plans for the party, tweaking the drawings that have come back from Good Sets and keeping my head down. He doesn't speak to anyone. David is one of those people who change the atmosphere of an entire building according to their moods; and today he's in a weird one. People have noticed.

Graham turns and says, 'What's got up his arse?'

'Christ knows,' Finn responds.

'He looks like shit.'

We go silent when he stops at the door to the stairwell, pulls it open and then seems to change his mind. He retraces his footsteps, comes round to where we three are sitting, and places his hands firmly on the back of my chair. My neck is on fire. Graham and Finn turn their attention to their screens, pretending not to notice.

'How're the preparations going?' he says, leaning over me to see what I've been doing.

There's an Excel spreadsheet on my screen with a list

of invitees and a note on who they are, and where they are in the pecking order. He reaches past me and taps the screen. I can feel his heat on my back, hear his breath and smell his lunch. This is becoming intolerable.

'Why have you invited that knob?'

He means Adam. 'Because you told me to.'

'I did no such thing.'

'Actually, you did, David. And he's a good person to have at a party. He's fun.'

Graham stops what he's doing and turns his head to look at me. Finn is on the phone, but his last sentence misses a beat.

'I don't care if he can stand on his head stark bollock naked. He's the fucking competition.'

'OK. I must have misheard.' I didn't. 'It's a launch party,' I point out. 'We are about to tell the world about GZ.' I'm leaving, so I don't have to be humble, and what's more I hate him. 'We need people like him there.'

'I need him like a fucking hole in my head. Uninvite him.'

He lets go of my chair and steps back, and I swivel round and glare at his departing form. 'Just because he left and went to work for someone else? How petty can you get?'

David stops in his tracks and turns slowly. 'You'll do what I fucking tell you or you are leaving here without a reference. And not only that, I'll make sure you don't work in this industry again. Do you understand me?'

'I understand you.' I stare straight into his eyes and hold them there. Locked with mine.

Beside me, Graham types, then pauses to blow his nose on a screwed-up hanky. David walks off.

'Jesus,' Finn says, when he's out of earshot. 'Easy, Tiger.'

'He's got a point,' Graham says. 'Adam was disloyal.'

'Adam was doing what anyone else his age would have done: advancing his career,' I say.

I have no intention of uninviting him. There won't be a thing David can do about it on the night and, given his recent form, he probably won't remember what he said anyway. All that was about me and a night in December, not Adam.

'He was underhand about it,' Graham says. 'He didn't tell anyone what he was up to. David would have been supportive if he had been honest.'

I roll my eyes. Not at him but at my screen. He notices and gives me a hostile glare.

'You don't give a shit about anyone, do you? No wonder no one round here likes you.'

'Hey,' Finn says. 'That was below the belt, mate.'

Graham leaps up and I sit, frozen, staring at the names on my monitor. I didn't realize, until I moved to this desk, how much Graham resents me; he still hasn't got over me getting the job he wanted.

Thursday. I've been crazy busy all week, trying to pull the party together, worrying whether I can find this or that in time, keeping the budget down with the added challenge of Paige's grandiose expectations. A product launch is like producing a commercial – a short but intense activity, when nothing matters but the job. Then everything ends up in a skip.

Finn is on the phone and hasn't stopped talking for the last ten minutes, making me wonder if the person on the receiving end has fallen asleep. I find it hard out here, what with the buzz of conversation, the unrelenting energy, and the assumption that anyone is open for a chat at any time, no matter how hard they are trying to concentrate.

I'm not alone for more than half a minute before someone plants himself in the vacated chair. I don't look round because I know it isn't Graham. The trousers are different. I keep my eyes on my spreadsheet and my hand on the mouse. I am so tired of this; so weary of the effort it takes to be constantly ready. I can feel his eyes on my profile and my body becomes as tense as a violin string. Perhaps for my next job, I'll retrain as a shepherdess. Finn's phone rings, he picks it up and lounges back, crossing one leg over the other, cupping his neck with his free hand.

'Are you busy?' the man says.

I keep scrolling through my list of invitees to see who I have yet to have an answer from, and don't look round when I reply. 'Sorry. What?'

He lowers his voice to a whisper. 'I haven't made a very good case for myself.'

It must be Jamie. I swiftly scan his clothes and hair, his air of anxious expectation. It is him. I feel the tension flow from me and a warmth in my smile. A real smile for once.

'You don't need to.'

'Yes, I do.'

He leans an elbow on Graham's desk and scratches his thumbnail across his forehead. 'Whatever I did at the Christmas party, if I came on too strong or I crossed a line, I apologize. I should have apologized weeks ago.'

'We were as bad as each other. I should apologize for leaving you looking like a plonker.'

Jamie laughs. 'Yeah, you did. So, what I want to ask is, will you give me another chance? Will you let me take you out for that drink?'

I don't say anything, because I'm not sure what to say.

'Do you know how long I was awake last night, thinking about how I would ask you? You don't make things easy.'

'Jamie, I . . .'

To my horror, I start to fall to pieces. It feels like a mild version of the last time. My hands are trembling. I want to explain that it isn't personal, that it's because I'm a mess, but I can't because I'm not ready for the rest of that conversation. His face falls, and he pushes the chair back, but I grab the armrest. He waits for me to speak, and I close my eyes and take a deep breath. I have this. I am under control. I remind myself that I have a choice; embrace life despite what happened, or let it go and accept that I'm on my own.

Then David Gunner will have won, and that is not going to happen.

I take a deep breath. 'OK. Yes. I'll go for a drink with you after work.'

He doesn't exactly punch the air, because that would be weird and uncool, but he does grin. He would hate me if he knew why I agreed.

Jamie and I go to a pub equidistant between our respective flats in Chalk Farm and Kentish Town. We cycle back from work together, me following him, and even though it's dark and damp, it feels like we're on a jaunt.

On the way, we cut through the back streets, a mix of council estates and shabby Georgian terraces. We are cycling past a row of houses being renovated when Jamie waves his right hand, slows into the kerb and brakes. He points. It's dark, so it's hard to make out what it is at first. Three yards before the turning on to the Chalk Farm Road, there is a railing. Tied to it are several cellophane-wrapped bunches of flowers, some wilting, some still vibrant.

'Poor Guy,' I say. 'What a shitty way to go.'

We find a table in a quiet corner of the pub and tuck our helmets underneath the bench. I insist on buying the first round and Jamie argues, but I want to set the subliminal ground rules. I don't want to feel as though I'm being bought, in the old-fashioned sense. Not that I tell him that; I just say that I owe him and leave it there. I bring our drinks over and place them on the table; Jamie puts down his phone and smiles.

'Do you come here often?' I say, because I can't think of anything else.

The first ten minutes are sluggish, but then the alcohol hits, loosening both of us. His awkwardness becomes less obvious, my reticence less rigid. We begin to discover the things we have in common. We love reading and have both used books to escape bad times. We both enjoy historical novels, which leads to a fierce debate on the relative merits of Bernard Cornwell and Conn Iggulden, whom I favour. Jamie describes a childhood spent moving from country to country with his Armed Forces father. He talks about the loneliness of arriving at different schools and having to start all over again and how tired he used to get of having to remember names and faces. Even now he can't recall the boys and girls who, for a few fleeting months at a time, he could call his best friends. I get that.

By now he's told me so much, been so open and funny about his mistakes and his growing up, it's become painfully obvious that I've been less generous. After I come back from a trip to the bar and look for the chair with my coat hanging over it, rather than for him, I realize that I have to make that leap of faith and tell the truth. It's that or lose him. I set the glasses down on the table, sit and chew my lip. I don't know where to start.

'What?' he says.

'Can I tell you something about me?'

'So, what you're saying,' Jamie says. 'Is that you can see that my eyes are brown, but you won't remember that?'

'Kind of.' I think about how I've heard Deborah explaining it to her students. 'Basically, it's the difference between vision, the actual seeing by the eye with its component parts, and perception, which is the part your brain plays. It's not something that you can pin down. An optician can't help you improve your perception, only your vision. The information your brain receives is interpreted using things that aren't quantifiable, like memory and emotional connection. My perception is fine for everything that isn't a human face. So, I can see each of your features, I can acknowledge the brownness of your eyes, but I can't see the Jamie-ness of it. If I was asked tomorrow what colour your eyes were, I'd probably remember, but if you approached me, like you did at Guy's wake, I wouldn't know who you were, despite that piece of knowledge. If I knew you well enough to know that you had a mole on your left ear, that would help me enormously. Bettina is easy because of her hair, but I could easily mistake a similar stranger in the street for her, so I don't look at people when I'm out and about, in case they wave at me or something. It's like a game I can never win.' When he nods encouragement, I hesitate. 'Are you falling asleep at the back of the lecture theatre?'

'No! You're doing brilliantly. So, you aren't forgetting me, you just haven't retained a memory of my face that makes any sense or distinguishes me from the next man. Just a bunch of features that have no associations attached to them. Brown-eyed male.'

'Yes,' I say, smiling. Apart from explaining it to Rebecca, I don't get the chance to marshal my thoughts like this and try to make a normal person understand what it is I have or lack. It's both hard work and a pleasure. 'When you think about the brain and how it reacts to a face, you can understand how much someone like me can miss. Your brain takes in a mountain of information and makes a judgement as to all sorts of things, both physical and emotional: whether it's been given this information before or whether it's new, whether it wants to trust it, engage with it or whether there are more negative thoughts and associations. Did you know that, during an interview, the interviewee will have got the job or been rejected within fifty-five seconds of walking into the room? Never mind what's on their CV. Am I making sense?'

'Yeah. I'm not struggling with it. So, let's say you were interviewing somebody, you'd be more interested in their achievements than their face. You'd make a great interviewer, because your focus would be what makes them tick, not the physical attributes they were born with. A bit like *The Voice*. That would be a plus, wouldn't it?'

'I've never thought about it that way.' I smile. 'Thanks, Jamie. It's nice to hear something positive for a change.'

He sits back and takes a long drink. 'I aim to please.'

'I can empathize with your experience of changing schools and having to get to know a new set of people. When I was at school, it felt like that every day.'

'It must have been hard.'

'Particularly since back then I had no idea there was anything wrong with the way my brain worked. Once,' I say, smiling now at the memory, 'I was swimming in the sea with Isabel and Mark – I think I must have been about seven because Dad was still around – and I got pulled under a wave and when I surfaced I couldn't see them anywhere, so I got out and sat down on a towel next to Mum and Dad.' I glance at Jamie's face. He's listening intently. 'Anyway, it wasn't until Dad started speaking French that I realized they weren't my family.'

Jamie laughs his head off and I protest that it wasn't funny, that I was incredibly embarrassed, but soon I'm laughing too, tears streaming.

'Laura.'

And there it is, in the way he says my name, as if he's caressing it, as if it's new to him and wonderful to say out loud, that takes me back to Hoxton 101, to that lovely, happy, drunken connection, to what it was that I found in him that night.

He cups my cheek with his hand and I tingle.

'After the Christmas party,' he says, 'I thought you might have gone off with someone else.'

My happiness drains. 'Why would you think that?' I say carefully.

'I saw the cab driving away. It looked like there were two people in it.'

'Then it wasn't mine. There were loads of people out there; loads of minicabs and Ubers.'

'Sorry. Forget I said anything. You confuse me.'

'So, it's my fault?'

'No. I don't mean that at all.'

He sounds so frustrated that I feel bad. We both pick up our glasses at the same time and there's an awkward silence. He shuffles, plays with his phone, checks his messages. I do pretty much the same. To anyone observing us, we must look like a date gone wrong.

'I've spoiled the evening,' he says, looking stricken.

He isn't to blame for any of this. I'm upset because I'm ashamed.

'Nothing's been spoiled.'

I reach over and touch his cheek, slide my hand around the back of his head and draw him to me. When we part, he looks both surprised and delighted. Once again, David is at the back of my mind. I meant the kiss, but I also needed to claw back some of the power he took from me. But I've told a lie and Jamie believed me. Or he wants to. Not the healthiest start to a relationship, if this is what it is.

'My sister says that I'm too nice,' he says. 'I should try and be more of a bastard if I want to get the girl.'

'That won't be necessary.'

We look at each other for a moment too long, then we get up at the same time, laughing as we scramble into our coats. I want so badly to salvage the evening.

'Coffee?' he asks as we go out into the night and the brightly lit street. A bus rumbles by, nondescript faces behind steamed-up windows.

'There's nowhere open.'

'I didn't mean that.'

'I know you didn't. And yes, I'd love one.' I surprise myself. 'I only mean . . . God, sorry.' What do I mean?

Jamie laughs. 'I'm not assuming anything, Laura. I just don't want the evening to end and it's too cold to be outside.'

'OK. Good. Thank you.' I unlock my bike, pull my gloves on and follow him on to the road.

34

Laura

I MIGHT SLEEP WITH HIM, I THINK, AS WE CUT THROUGH the residential streets to his flat. He has a racing bike, mine is a sit-up-and-beg, but he goes slowly, making sure I don't fall behind. I want to know that I am still capable of enjoying a man's company and his body; that I can lose myself. If I do, I'll be doing it in full possession of my faculties. It's a decision, not an impulse. My behaviour must seem calculating, but I calculate constantly: that is my problem and my salvation.

And I don't want to go back to my flat. Not yet.

He helps me get our bicycles into the narrow hall, giving a dry laugh when I offer to chain mine up outside. We squeeze past and I follow him into his tiny sitting room. I don't want to lose sight of his face, so I hover round him, like an irritating fly. He doesn't seem to mind.

Jamie's flat resembles any other cheap rental I've ever been in: magnolia walls, trunking round electrical cables, brown carpet, beige sofa, beige curtains. In the corner of the sitting room is a disproportionately large TV. There are French windows and I cup my hands against them, making out a small paved patio with a garden table, three chairs and a couple of sad-looking pots. Behind me, on the coffee table, there are several days' worth of *Evening Standard*s and a mug with the dried remnants of his morning coffee. A plate with crumbs. Jamie tidies all this away while the kettle is boiling. I sit down and watch him, my hands clasped round my knees. He is never more than eight foot from me, which is comforting.

He sits down at the other end of the sofa, and we hold our mugs, mirroring each other.

'So?' Jamie says. 'What do you think of the place?'

'It's functional.'

He grins. 'I had somewhere nicer – well, more interesting at least – when I shared with three other guys. I've only been living on my own since last September. I'm still adjusting.'

'I've lived on my own since leaving uni.'

'That must be lonely.'

I lean back into the cushions and stifle a yawn. 'I like it. I shared for three years and that was enough. I could get a handle on my flatmates, but their friends and lovers were a total nightmare. I need somewhere I'm not going to run into a stranger in my kitchen every time I come home.'

'Makes sense.' He's looking at me over his mug as he takes a sip, his lashes lowered. 'I was thinking . . .'

I twitch my eyebrows. 'You were, were you?'

'I'm not just a pretty face.'

'That's lucky because it would be lost on me.' He laughs. 'Anyway, I was thinking that if your brain won't accept information about faces that comes through your eyes, what about using your fingertips? Like blind people do?'

'Jamie, that is so creepy. I can't go up to people and start running my fingers all over their faces. Maybe if I was in a relationship. And I don't think it would work anyway.' I touch my own face, palping my fingertips over the ridge of my nose, the swell of my lips, brushing my eyelashes. 'It doesn't say anything to me. Just lumps and bumps.'

'Try on me.' He puts his coffee down, and I nod, feeling an odd tingle.

I close my eyes and try to relax as I touch his skin, moving my fingers firmly. His cheeks are slightly rough, his lips feel more generous than they are. His lashes tickle my thumb pads.

'You're right.' He laughs. 'It is a bit creepy.' He takes my hand and kisses my knuckles.

'Can I tell you something awful,' I say, because the tension is scaling up too fast for me.

'Yeah, go on.'

'When I was sixteen, I spent practically the whole end-of-term disco snogging this boy because I didn't know who he was and was too embarrassed to ask. As soon as the last slow dance was over, I said I was going to the loo, and I legged it out of there.'

Jamie laughs. 'Poor kid.'

'It was all right. At least I wasn't propping up the wall all night.'

'I meant the boy. Did you find out his name?' He leans forward to kiss me, but I put my finger against his lips.

'Yes, because he asked me out eventually. I said no.'

'That must have taken a lot of courage.'

'No. Cowardice really.'

'Again, I meant the boy.'

'You are so funny.' I don't often get teased and it feels nice.

'So, is that what happened at the staff party?' Jamie asks. 'It was easier to snog me than ask me?'

'Er . . . well, partly.' I make a face; a grimace to show him how mortified I am. 'I hadn't wanted to be there, and you being so persistent was such a surprise. I didn't want to spoil it.'

He folds his arms. 'Not sure how I should take that. If you had found out it was me, it would have broken the spell? Is that it?'

'No, it isn't! Not at all.'

'Then kiss me.'

I let him lead me into his bedroom. I block out the image of another man's naked body, of a blue shirt lying rumpled on my hallway floor. Even Guy tries to intrude, riding his bicycle along that dark street. Jamie crushes me into his arms and I sink against his chest. We stand with our bodies pressed together, and for a while this is all I need.

'I didn't change the sheets,' he admits, embarrassed. 'I thought it might look like I was making assumptions.'

'Are you saying this whole evening was premeditated?'

Two spots of colour appear on his cheeks. 'I didn't

ask you on impulse. Many sleepless nights went into planning.'

My top has no buttons and he pulls it up over my head and I notice that his hands are shaking too. I undo my bra myself as he steps out of his jeans and stands in his white boxers and maroon socks. I will myself to stay calm, not to let the fear creep under my skin. I put my hands on his shoulders to warm them and he holds my waist. He lowers me down and then collapses on to the bed beside me and it's all so clumsy and silly. Laughter catches in my throat as he kisses me again, sliding his hand down and round the curve of my waist and hip.

I try so hard to focus on him, on his caresses and the warmth of his body, the tension in his muscles, but the world darkens so that the night is inside my head as well as outside, and I experience a rush of horror.

It's as if a door has opened, even though I push against it with all my strength. Jamie's lips become his lips, Jamie's hands become his hands. I squirm at his touch, but he thinks it's pleasure. I begin to fight harder, frantic, jerking my head away from his kisses. I wedge my arms between us, curling my hands into fists to hit him with. He lets me go abruptly and I sit up and shove myself backwards against the headboard, wrap my arms around my breasts and drop my head. Tears trickle into the gap between my forearms and my knees. I can hear the rasp of Jamie's breath as he pulls himself together. When he tries to hold me, to give comfort, I shrink from his touch. The bedsprings move as he stands up and I think he's left the room but then he comes back and drapes his dressing gown over me. It smells of him.

'I'm sorry. I'm so, so sorry,' I mumble.

He sits down again, but this time he doesn't attempt to touch me. 'Do you want to talk about it?'

'No. I need to go. I . . . Can you leave the room while I get dressed?'

'Of course.' He pauses. 'Whatever it is, Laura, I want you to know that I would give anything to be able to help you.'

I wait until the door closes, then I unwrap myself carefully. I'm still crying, my throat aching from suppressing the howl of anguish that has built up inside me. I move like an elderly woman, dressing myself slowly, my hands clumsy, my bones rattling. When I'm ready I find Jamie in the kitchen, leaning against the cabinets, his brow furrowed with worry.

'Are you going to be OK?'

He's scared of touching me now.

'Yes,' I manage. 'I'll be fine. This isn't your fault. I've really enjoyed myself tonight. It's just that I don't think I'm ready.'

'Did someone hurt you?' he asks.

I draw in a deep breath. 'You could say that.'

'How?'

I shake my head. 'Please don't ask me.'

A tear dribbles down my cheek and I brush it away. He stands in front of me in a pair of pyjama trousers, not knowing what to do, confused and worried. Now that I'm dressed and feeling less exposed, I want him to hold me, to hug me tight against his bare chest, but that wouldn't be fair, so I don't ask it of him. If I don't tell him the truth, I can hardly expect him to understand that someone else has scraped me out.

Jamie disentangles my bike pedal from his spokes, then brings the bike outside and waits while I clip on my helmet. I still want him to touch me, even if it's only to nudge me fondly on the shoulder, like my brother does, just to know that it's not all gone. He would like some sign that it's going to be all right, but I can't give it to him. I don't want to make promises that I might not be able to keep.

35

Laura

DAVID IS STANDING INSIDE HIS OFFICE, HOLDING THE door open, talking to someone. I get up to make myself a coffee and he stops talking when I walk by. It feels like war. What happened with Jamie last night was his fault. I wouldn't have moved things along so fast if I hadn't been thinking about him. And now I'm running out of time. Just one more week until I leave.

I sit down and my internal line buzzes. David's name comes up on the display. I consider ignoring it then realize how stupid that would be. I don't need a public dressing-down from him.

'Can you come in, Laura?'

'OK,' I say.

I close my eyes for a second, resting my hands on my lap, and take a deep breath.

'Been summoned?' Graham says.

I don't answer him. I push my chair back and walk away. He mutters something to my back. I don't care. I need never see any of them again after next Friday.

Outside David's door, I hesitate. Is this it? Is this where we have the conversation? If it is, I'll call his bluff and threaten to go to the police. He isn't to know that I washed away all trace of him from my flat and my bed. I'll tell him that I've kept evidence.

He looks up from his paperwork as I push open the door, and points to a chair. I sit down, my back straight, scared but ready to unleash hell if he so much as mentions the note.

'I've written you a reference,' he says after a pause. His manner is stiff and unfriendly. 'Have a read and see if there's anything you'd like me to add.' He hands me a sheet of paper.

It takes me a second or two to recalibrate, then I read what he's written.

Much of it is composed of stock phrases, but there are parts that allude to things that are specific to me. It's complimentary and surprisingly generous. This is probably to make sure I go and stay gone. I've sent off applications to other advertising agencies, snatching precious spare moments to work on them. I'd forgotten how time-consuming and demoralizing the process can be. I have enough money to pay my mortgage for three months, if I'm careful. After that, if I haven't found a job, I'll be in serious trouble. I need this reference.

'Thank you. I appreciate it.' I squeeze the words out between my teeth.

'No more than you deserve.' His tone echoes mine. We are both acting parts. 'Don't forget that I know everyone in this business, and I will know the people you're applying to. Anyone who considers taking you on will want a conversation with me.'

'What does that mean?'

But he stands up and crosses the room to open the door for me. I open my mouth to speak, and then close it again. Someone comes in, nods at me and I nod back, wondering if it might be Jamie, who I've been avoiding all morning. You'd think I'd be able to tell after getting so close to him, but I can't. Jamie is another worry, another reason to spend the day in a cold sweat. Thank God organizing the campaign launch is taking up all my time.

'Why don't you come in? Phoebe'll be glad to see you.'

I've bumped into Elliot parking Noah's pram in the space under the stairs.

'Well . . .'

I'm torn, longing to collapse on to the sofa and put the strains of the day behind me, but not that keen to be on my own. The good thing about Phoebe is that she has nothing to do with the other side of my life.

It's nice to know that my company is desired. Elliot's manner has changed since the supper party and I get the sense that he's warmed to me. He probably still thinks I'm odd, but not in a way that threatens his family dynamic. That pleases me enormously.

Phoebe has been cooking and the kitchen smells of meat juices and fried onions. It makes my mouth water, especially since all I've got to look forward to is a shop-bought lasagne.

Elliot pours me a glass of wine then slopes off into the sitting room with a beer.

'Almost there,' she says, referring to my imminent departure from Gunner Munro. 'Are you going to have a leaving party?'

That would be funny if it wasn't so sad.

'No. The GZ launch will be enough. I don't want a fuss.'

'Your colleagues may feel differently.'

'Maybe.' I've been pleasantly surprised by the number of people who've told me that they're sad I'm leaving. But I won't kid myself; I haven't made lasting relationships. I would hope Eddie will keep in touch, maybe even Jamie and Rebecca, but the others will forget me as soon as I'm gone. 'I'm glad to go actually. The atmosphere isn't great. I've . . .' I'm about to tell her about Jamie, but I realize that I don't want to. Instead something else pops out of my mouth. 'My bosses are having an affair.'

'Really?' She raises her eyebrows. 'But why would that make any difference to you?'

'It doesn't, but it makes me less sad to leave. The atmosphere is so uncomfortable. He's married.' Now I sound like a prude and she's watching me. My excuse is no excuse, it's an embarrassing ramble. 'I'm not being judgemental, it's just that he's a complete and utter dick and she's . . . well, she's someone I admire.'

I used to respect him, not mind the arrogance, feel it was his due. Now I have an overwhelming desire to make other people see him for what he is. But I find I can't go further than this, I can't tell this kind woman what he's done to me.

'Does his wife know?' Phoebe asks.

'I don't think so. She and Rebecca are old friends, so it's all a bit tacky.' I change the subject, asking after her pregnant sister, but Phoebe is more interested in salacious gossip.

'How did you find out?'

'The intern has a nose for these things.'

She laughs and opens the oven, lifts out a casserole and places it on the hob. She takes off the lid, gives it a stir and then puts it back. It smells heavenly.

'Perhaps you should tell the wife.'

'It's none of my business.'

Do I really mean that?

I want David Gunner's marriage to implode; I want his wife to hate him as much as I do. The idea of David being brought down by the women he's screwed seems so right. But I can't tell Felicity: the idea makes me feel grubby.

36

Rebecca

REBECCA RISES FROM HER DRESSING TABLE, WANDERS over to the cheval mirror and takes a good long look at herself. She is almost two years older than David, but she's fit, lithe and attractive and she takes care of herself. Her hair is glossy, catching the light and bouncing when she moves. David will be here soon.

This is the first evening in she doesn't know how long that she has been home before eight p.m. and she should be happy, but she isn't. Her karma is all wrong. The bad atmosphere at work is affecting her. It used to be such a happy place, but first Guy's death and then that business with Laura . . . They've taken their toll. She blames David for the Laura situation. If anyone could have persuaded Paige Adler to change her mind, it was him, but he had point-blank refused to talk about it, and when Rebecca had offered, he had turned on her.

'Don't even think about it,' he had said. 'The decision's been made. She goes, and we move on. No one is indispensable.'

‘Fine.’ She walked out of his office and back into her own, pacing from door to window, furious. It was as if he was washing his hands of Laura. Job done. But these were people, not just staff, and Laura was her protégé, not his. She feels protective of her, invested in her. And now she’s going.

She has no complaints about Jamie. He’s good, excellent even, but it isn’t the same. The creative partnership between him and Eddie hasn’t had time to bed in, and Eddie naturally resents having someone thrust upon him. Eddie and Laura have a long-standing friendship and proven chemistry; a symbiotic relationship. They bicker like an old married couple, but they respect each other. She thinks they may lose Eddie and she told David that, only to have him shrug it off. Laura screwed up, but don’t they all, from time to time. Even David has had his moments. She remembers one client he pissed off so royally that lawyers became involved. She’d had to force him to grovel, which, to give him his due, he had done with a convincing amount of grace. Why can’t he grovel now?

After what happened at David’s house the other morning, her worries have taken on a new urgency. And there’s something else that’s been bothering her, the tension between him and Laura, that she can feel in the small knot tucked tight and hot under her breastbone. Has something happened? Has David made a pass at her, or has it gone further than that? That would explain the toxic atmosphere between them. The other evening, she left before both of them, when the building was almost empty . . . but she mustn't think that way, or she'll go mad. It hurts so much. It's as though all of the stuff that she's been keeping at a distance is gathering, pushing and shoving to get to her, clambering up her body.

She chooses some music; something to rebalance her mind. David likes Elgar, so she puts on the *Enigma Variations*. As soon as those haunting chords begin to rise and dip, she wants to stop time and dance. It's so romantic, so sorrowful and it makes her feel better, more open to receiving him. She restricts herself to stretching her muscles in front of the mirror. Her make-up is minimal: a light foundation to perk her up, eyeliner, mascara and blusher. Her dress is black, sleeveless and fitted on top with a low bust, and a flared skirt; she chose it because it flatters her curves. She puts on stockings and an ivory-lace suspender belt and is buckling the delicate diamanté straps of her shoes around her ankles when the doorbell rings.

David closes the curtains. Rebecca watches him closely. She's seen him at work every day, of course, but it's been so frenetic that she hasn't had time to itemize the physical changes in him. He's lost weight and, even in the soft light of her drawing room, his face looks gaunt. She passes him a glass of champagne. He moves away and sits down on the sofa. Rebecca tries to pretend that there's nothing wrong, but she's terrified. Is he here to tell her that she is the problem? He has been her friend, business partner and lover for so many years that the idea of an existence without him is hard to contemplate without panic. She will not give him back to Felicity.

Rebecca has booked supper to be delivered in half an hour. The minutes seem to stretch and hollow out like blown glass.

'Did you have trouble getting away?' she asks.

He brings himself back from wherever he's been. 'I could have stayed for another hour, but I thought, bollocks to that, I'm going. I left Eddie and Jamie there. Bettina stayed as well.'

'She's showing real commitment.'

She sinks into the armchair and crosses her legs, letting her dress fall back along her thigh. David gives no sign that he's noticed. The silence between them fills with piano music, as forlorn and lonely as the last autumn leaf.

After a moment, she moves across the room, arranging herself on his knee and caressing his face, smoothing the worry lines from his brow.

'David, relax.'

She tilts her head so that her hair flows to one side and kisses him. He pushes his hand into her scalp and, with the other, crumples the skirt of her dress. She laughs into the kiss, and he rolls her on to the sofa.

'Are you wearing anything under this?'

She puts her finger in his mouth. 'I can't remember. Why don't you check?'

The doorbell rings.

'Supper,' Rebecca says, reluctantly peeling herself off him.

David has started laying the table by the time she comes back with the delivery in her arms. It is as warm as a baby. She watches him before he sees her and imagines him, like she often does, living here, part of the furniture. She blinks the image away. If she wants it, she'll have to fight for it. She'll have to be ruthless.

They discuss work while they eat. This is perfectly normal; the company obsesses them both; it is their child in a way, but tonight it feels as though he's avoiding talking about anything personal. After supper, they clear up together then she pours them both a brandy and they take their glasses back to the drawing room.

They haven't discussed his meltdown at home even though she's tried. Being David, he's pretending it didn't happen, but she can't forget what she saw; how crushed he looked; how drained of his essential 'Davidness'. It frightened her.

'We need to talk.'

He looks up, his glass in his hand. 'About what?'

She gets off his knee and paces across the room, looks out beyond the pitch-dark gardens to the lit windows beyond. 'You know. I find you crashing round your kitchen, with Felicity and the children in pieces. If you can't talk to me or Felicity, at least see a psychiatrist.'

The brandy comes alive in the candlelight, the amber dancing because he is shaking. He looks so unhappy. She wishes she hadn't said anything.

'Would you still love me if I'd done something wrong?'

Her stomach turns over. She laughs it off. 'As long as it doesn't involve rape, murder or incest.'

Her flippancy is lost on him. She watches in horror as tears well in his eyes. He rubs them away angrily. This is worse than the last time.

'What is it, darling? You're scaring me. Is it Felicity? Have you done something to her? Is it Tony and Georgie?'

'It's nothing to do with any of them.'

'What then? Have you taken money from Gunner Munro?' That would be bad. If he was in debt, he should have told her, but she'll forgive him. She just needs honesty.

'No.' His tone is abrupt and impatient.

'Is it about Laura?'

His head snaps up. 'No. Why would it be?'

She raises her eyebrows. 'Are you having a thing with her?'

'Don't be so fucking ridiculous.'

He sets his mug down on the coffee table and leans back into the sofa. He closes his eyes and she waits and after a while she thinks he might have gone to sleep but then he suddenly opens them and looks straight at her. She feels a jolt of shock, desire too.

'I need you to punish me, Rebecca.'

This is a game that they often play, but after what's been said, there's added piquancy. Her body goes still. She is intensely aware of every part of her, of every atom. She has woken up. Her breath catches. She sits on the armchair, her back straight, and gathers the skirt of her dress in her fingers, until the tops of her stockings show. 'Say. Please.'

'Fuck you.'

'I'm not touching you unless you say please.'

He glares at her. 'Please.'

Rebecca uncrosses her legs. 'Come here.'

David slides off the couch and gets down on his hands and knees. He crawls over and sits back on his heels and Rebecca slaps him hard across the face. His head jerks to the side and she hits him again. Twin welts bloom on his cheeks. He reaches for her, tries to grab her thighs, but she catches his wrists and holds them, straining against his greater strength.

'What have you done, David?'

He breaks down, his face rumpling as his tears mingle with snot. It's unbearable; loud and ugly. Stricken, Rebecca throws herself down beside him. She can feel the tremors going through his body. She can't bear his torment, she can't bear to see him like this. Whatever has gone wrong for him, it feels like he's desperately trying to stop it getting out of hand. She wonders how it affects her.

She pulls her dress up over her head. Their lovemaking is angry and over too soon. It feels like they are fighting, not making love. Rebecca climbs on top, so that it's her who ends up with bruising on her knees. She keeps her eyes open throughout, watching his face and the expressions that move across it like the shadows of moths. Exhaustion, pain and fear all register, fleeting and shocking.

Afterwards, she strokes his hair and murmurs words of comfort and gradually his body stills, and he sighs.

'I'm sorry I worried you,' he says.

She reaches for the armchair and pulls herself up, trying to do it elegantly, but stumbling on her heels. David grasps her elbow. Even in this moment of emotion, as she feels the trickle of semen on the inside of her thighs, she wonders whether she has already conceived their child. She is three days late.

'It's the stress of work,' he adds. 'It's been getting to me lately.'

He's holding something back, if not actively lying. She feels better after the sex, but not triumphant. There's part of her that feels lost and alone. If she's going to keep him, it'll take more than that.

Rebecca forces herself to sound calm and reasonable, as if nothing out of the ordinary has occurred. 'Take a break after GZ.'

He laughs. 'You know it doesn't work like that.' He kisses her on the lips and pats her bottom. 'I should probably get off home. I told Lissy I'd be back by ten.' He kisses her slowly and she clings to him. 'I don't know what I'd do if I didn't have you. You keep me sane.'

She'll have to be content with that for now. While he showers, she gets down on the floor, rests her head on the carpet, her hands splayed either side of her shoulders, her knees to her chest. Then she slowly raises her legs and holds the pose. She counts two minutes and when she comes out of the position she touches her belly and says a silent prayer.

37

Laura

I'VE HIRED THE STUDIO IN DALSTON, A DEFUNCT THEATRE that has found a new identity as a fashionable party venue and location. The stage still exists, but the rows of seats have been replaced by a dance floor with seating areas around the side furnished with mismatched and distressed armchairs and sofas. Its mix of baroque and decayed urban chic is perfect for the profile we are trying to achieve for GZ. It's edgy, cool and not as expensive as hiring somewhere in central London. I arrive early, buying a banana at the station for breakfast. The lorry from Good Sets is parked behind the theatre and they have started unloading. I am soon joined by Eddie, Jamie, Finn and Bettina.

It's strange being with Eddie but not bouncing ideas off him. I miss the camaraderie and the banter. I even miss hearing about his baby. Instead I have to listen to him and Jamie, who already appear to have developed a working relationship, discussing the idea I came up with, and it feels horrible. I regret not taking the time to think before I resigned. I could have got through this; the campaign would have come and gone, and I would have been reinstated in my office without another word spoken. It's only because of David that I acted in the way I did. He provoked me. *He* should be the one with his career in tatters; not me.

'You should reconsider,' Eddie says. 'Rebecca would have you back like a shot.'

We are snatching a quick break, sitting on the uncarpeted stairs. The walls are stripped-back plaster, collaged with aged scraps of paint and wallpaper.

My eyebrows shoot up. 'But not David?'

'No, but he's a git. I miss working with you. Jamie's a top bloke, but it isn't the same. I might resign.'

'Don't.' My lips twitch into a smile of pleasure, even though I suspect he's only trying to make me feel better.

'Why not? We could apply for jobs as a team. With GZ behind me, and you taking the credit for developing the initial idea, we could get picked up by one of the big agencies, no problem.' He smiles. 'Or even start our own.'

'Not if you want to stay married.'

Visions of Felicity Gunner sitting at home on her own in the evenings, while David works late or snuggles up to Rebecca, make my facial muscles tighten.

'Cynic.' He sighs. 'Let's wait and see. Have you been to any recruitment agencies?'

'It's on my list,' I say.

The truth is, although I've made a mental note to do

it, I haven't had the time or the heart. I've put out feelers amongst my contacts and I've had a couple of responses from the online applications and an interview lined up for next week, but since I resigned I've had trouble accepting that it's real and I haven't thought beyond each day. I don't think it'll hit me until it's over. I have a vague idea that I might go to Mum's, but I haven't said anything to her about it. She doesn't need notice anyway.

Jamie is up a ladder, hanging the banners I've had made. He's wearing the same pink shirt he wore on the night of the Christmas party, and I've been wondering whether this is a cunning ploy to make sure I always know where he is. It's the way I would think, but would it occur to him? And to make me feel an even greater failure, Bettina, who appears to have recovered from her crush on Finn, has him firmly in her sights. Bettina is girl-next-door pretty in scruffy jeans and a gingham shirt knotted at her navel, her abundant hair wrapped in a scarf to keep it clean. I would be extremely surprised if he was immune. They've been thrown together a lot more since Jamie's been working in my old office.

I feel a pang, and wonder if it's jealousy, then push it aside. I had my chance.

'Come on,' I say to Eddie. 'Work to do.'

We are creating something energetic and yet intimate out of this echoing space. The theme is urban jungle, so I've hired a scenic artist, who I've met on the sets of various commercials, to graffiti fake walls. And I've added a twist. Six models are being body-painted, wearing jeans and tight vest-tops, camouflaged to disappear into the background. When the lights are dimmed, it's impossible to tell they're there. They've been rehearsing, and when they move in and out of position, the effect is mesmerizing. I've busted a gut making this happen and I am determined it's going to be a success.

The band, who have been setting up for the last half hour, launch into a spoken ballad. It's witty and rude and catchy and Bettina and I spontaneously stop what we're doing and give each other a congratulatory nod.

Jamie hefts pieces of MDF on to the stage and I watch as he sets them up, working out how the pieces fit to create a back-of-houses, trompe-l'œil, inner-city feel. A carpenter asks him a question and I watch him explain what needs doing. Eddie is peculiarly impractical, and can barely hang a picture, and I've noticed that people go to Jamie whenever they have a logistical problem, trusting him to have the answer. It's interesting. I like people who offer solutions rather than saying they haven't got a clue, like Eddie does. I sigh and turn away. He isn't ignoring me, but he is keeping his distance, understandably.

The number comes to an end and the band members huddle round and confer before starting again. The caterers arrive and need to know where to set up; time is disappearing fast. I get a message from Rebecca saying they'll be here in ten minutes and I run up on to the stage, waving to get everyone's attention.

'Get rid of the rubbish and straighten things out. Rebecca and David are bringing the client over for a look.'

Someone yells, 'Shitting hell!' and there's a burst of laughter.

I need to get changed. I brought everything with me, knowing there wouldn't be time to go home. I pick up my bag and run downstairs to the dressing rooms where I put on my dress. It's dove-grey chiffon, and off-the-shoulder with a tight bodice, full skirt and sleeves that finish under the elbows. I bought it in Paris with Isabel two years ago and it makes me feel like Audrey Hepburn. I refresh my make-up, slip my feet into a pair of high-heels and do what I can with my hair. It's still as much a surprise to me when I look in the mirror as my own face is.

I climb the stairs and push open the heavy double doors. David, Rebecca and Paige have their backs to me as they look up at the stage. I take a deep breath and walk over.

'It's awesome,' Paige gushes.

She directs her words at me, and I try not to show surprise. Perhaps she has a short memory. At any rate, I appear to be out of that particular doghouse. Rebecca is wearing her hair down and huge chunky platinum-and-diamond earrings gleam through her glossy tresses. Paige has her hair up.

'Fantastic, isn't it?' David says, without looking at me.

'Everyone's worked hard.' I don't look at him either.

David is wearing a white shirt with the top two buttons undone, under a suit, fashionably short in the leg to show a glimpse of orange socks. This is presumably in homage to the product, since there's an orange hanky tucked into the breast pocket too. Thank God for the quirky touches. The thought of the challenge ahead sends a wave of despair through me. I should have insisted on labels and not let myself be overridden by Rebecca, who said it would spoil the look of the thing, and that I would just have to cope.

'Laura,' Rebecca says warmly. 'It looks amazing. Clever you.'

'You did good,' Paige says, surprising me again. She checks her watch. 'One hour.' She turns to Rebecca. 'We'd better let these guys get on.'

And with that the three of them leave. They are going to have a quick, stomach-lining supper at a local Italian restaurant. That banana I ate on the way in seems a long time ago. My stomach rumbles. I catch Bettina's attention and wave her over.

'You couldn't be an angel and get me a sandwich, could you?'

'Of course I can. Any preferences?'

'Big, with meat. And a fizzy drink. Oh, and a Crunchie . . . no, make that a Mars Bar.'

She laughs, and I watch her walk across the room and speak to Jamie. He looks down at her, then turns and says something to Eddie before following her to the exit like an obedient hound. I watch them go with my mouth hanging open. How many people does it take to buy a sandwich?

38

Laura

IT'S AT TIMES LIKE THIS THAT I'M REMINDED FORCIBLY of why I don't like parties and I ache with envy for everyone who can recognize a face in the crowd, who knows their mother from their neighbour, their friend from their enemy. I despair of finding any equilibrium in my life.

I am standing in the doorway and the guests have arrived, most of them straight from work. There are mixologists and agency people, GZ employees and representatives from all the best outlets. We want the drink to be seen in places like Selfridges and Harrods, as well as behind the trendiest bars. The beautiful people are here; the models and actresses that Bettina and I have reeled in with promises of being snapped by photographer to the stars, Simon McAulay. Some of these faces brighten when they see me, lifting their hands in greeting as I swiftly move away.

Someone is heading towards me, and I break out in a cold sweat. Every sound is intensified; the music, the chatter and the clink of glasses making it harder to think.

'Laura! What a fantastic event. I hear it's all your doing.'

I smile. 'I can't take all the credit. I have a great team.'

Give me a clue. Say something to help me place you. Please.

Then someone else comes up, a man in a black shirt. In a moment of panic, I think I'm going to have to introduce them and brace myself for flight, but I'm spared that humiliation when he kisses the woman on both cheeks.

'Maxine! Where have you been hiding yourself?'

Maxine Lorimer. She's the producer at the production company we've chosen to make the commercial. The man though – do I know him or not? He has silver hair and broad shoulders.

'This is Laura Maguire,' Maxine says. 'She's the creative force behind all this.' She indicates the room, with a sweep of her hand.

'Nice to put a face to the voice.' He holds out his hand and I take it. 'I'm Colin Pask.'

I grin, relieved. We've never met but we have spoken on the phone. We talk for a minute or two and then politely sidle away from each other, me saying I need to keep an eye on things. Every so often guests stop and stare at the wall, frown then laugh. My actors glide in and out of vision, creating a surreal, unsettling effect. It'll be that extra touch that makes the party and the product memorable.

I weave amongst the crowd, greeting anyone who catches my eye with a promise to come and find them when I've done some made-up task, like checking on the drink situation. It works, but it isn't something I can keep up. I'll have to stop moving and have a conversation at some point.

Rebecca comes over. She raises her glass and I tap it with mine.

'Not drinking the product, Laura?' she says, eyebrows arched.

'Nope.' I take a long sip from my wine. 'I'm leaving, so I can drink what I like.'

Her eyes narrow for a second, but she lets it pass, as I knew she would. 'Do you see what I see?' she asks.

'What?' I look around.

'Can you see David? Next to the lady with the pink hair. Guess who he's talking to.'

I spot him. He's with a man, and they are chatting animatedly, David all back-thumping bonhomie.

'Who is it?' I ask.

'Adam Powell. So, there you go. A lot of fuss about nothing.'

'I didn't realize you knew about that.'

She shrugs. 'He was just blowing off steam. This is great, by the way. Are you enjoying yourself?'

'Yes,' I say firmly. 'It's all under control.'

She takes a deep breath. 'Listen, Laura. I don't think we behaved well by you. And I wanted you to know I'm sorry about that.'

'You've done nothing wrong.' I glance again at David. A woman has joined them, and he's in his element; animated by their fawning respect.

'You shouldn't take what he says to heart,' she says, following my gaze. 'His bark is worse than his bite. He just needs more people to stand up to him.'

'He's a bully, Rebecca.'

She doesn't need me to tell her anything else. She

certainly doesn't need me to tell her that her secret's out, or to make oblique and bitchy comments about how well she knows him. I'm angry, but not the kind of angry that would deliberately cause collateral damage.

As soon as she's left my side, someone touches my arm.

'Phoebe sends her apologies,' Elliot says. He reaches for my shoulder and we clumsily knock heads as we both go for the wrong cheek. 'Her sister's gone into labour.'

My phone rings and it's Phoebe's name on the caller display. I assume that she's phoning to apologize, so when I pick up I immediately tell her not to worry. I'm only sorry she can't make it. There's a slight hesitation before she speaks.

'It isn't about that. I should have called you earlier but what with Harriet's waters breaking and all that drama, I forgot. I think I might have put you in it.'

I cup my hand over my other ear so that I can hear better and make my way backstage. 'What do you mean? What's happened?'

'I told my sister about your bosses having an affair. It was idle gossip, you know. Not malicious or anything. But, the thing is, Laura . . .'

She pauses, and I can feel the difficulty she's having.

'Tell me.'

'She knows Felicity Gunner through the school. Apparently, they're old friends. I had no idea. But she told her, and Felicity went ballistic. That's when Harriet went into labour.'

I can feel a cold trickle down my spine. This is all I need.

'I thought I'd better warn you. I'm sorry if it causes you problems.'

'It's not ideal,' I say. It's a gross understatement, but I'm at work and need to maintain my professional front. Inside, I'm swearing. 'Listen, Phoebe, I've got to go, but thanks for the heads-up.'

I loiter backstage for a few minutes. I don't blame Phoebe. It's my own fault. I wonder whether David and Rebecca know yet, whether Felicity will wait till he's home before she lets rip. If it was me, I think I would wait, so hopefully nothing will happen this evening. If I can get through this, I can get through anything.

'You shouldn't have resigned, you silly thing,' Paige says. 'I didn't mean for that to happen, I was just mad at you.'

She's different when she's been drinking. Softer, almost puppyish; another big ego, like David, needing a constant supply of admiration and love. 'Well, I am sorry,' I say.

She must have been keenly attuned to my tone, because her mouth pulls down. 'Don't be like that, darling. I'm not out to wreck your career. You want me to talk to David?'

'That's kind of you, Paige, but there's no point. I've started looking for another job.'

'Now, that's a shame. If you change your mind, let me know.'

She teeters off and I watch her until she finds someone new to cling to, then I discreetly make my way to the door. The place is crammed, so Rebecca won't notice if I slip away for a while. I go downstairs to the dressing room where there's a threadbare couch and a basketful of magazines. I toe my shoes off and sink down with relief, resting my head against the cool wall and closing my eyes. I can hear the band and the hum of conversation, the clatter in the kitchen as the caterers plate up the canapés. I'm taking a step back from the human race and it's stupid and I shouldn't do it, but tonight I don't have the strength for the battle.

In the end it's the cold that gets me going again. I had pulled a tasselled throw over me and dozed for a while, but it's slipped off and I wake shivering. Reluctantly, I squash my aching feet back into my shoes and try to smooth out the creases in the skirt of my dress.

Back upstairs the bar has closed, and the staff are packing up. I've stayed away longer than I meant to, and I expect to be called up on it, but no one asks where I've been, which is somehow worse because it makes me think I'm already fading in people's minds. The guests have thinned out, going on to clubs and restaurants where they will hopefully discuss the product, although I don't think, from a quick glance at the boxes, much GZ was consumed. People drank, but they preferred beer or wine. Oh well. It's not my problem any more.

Eddie comes to find me, and we talk for a minute or two. I spot Bettina and Jamie deep in conversation in a corner. Bettina is wearing a little black dress and her hair looks amazing, dark curls tumbling over her bare shoulders. I look away.

Once the guests have gone, I help with the clear-up. I could just go. No one would care. The event was a roaring success, so there is an air of tipsy, adrenaline-fuelled bonhomie, a post-party atmosphere that I don't feel part of. I hear snatches of discussion about where to go on to.

I take a bag of rubbish downstairs to the bins in the alleyway. It's nippy and this is no place to linger. I open the lid and drop it in. When I turn, I yelp with fright. A man is standing in front of me, his arms crossed, his feet apart. Hostility pulses from him. I look over his shoulder, hoping someone else will come outside. There is plenty to bring down after all.

'A word,' he says.

I know it's David because of the orange hanky, but I think I would have known anyway. I push past him, but he catches my arm.

'Let go of me.'

'Not until you've told me what you're up to. I know it's you sending those malicious little notes, so don't pretend that it isn't.'

'I don't know what you're talking about.'

The lie slips out automatically but already feels futile. We've both known this conversation was coming.

He laughs. 'I don't sleep well these days. I saw you. Don't piss me around, Laura. You don't know who you're dealing with.'

'That's the whole point, isn't it? I do know. I'm dealing with a creep and a monster and a coward.' Just saying those words makes me braver. 'You've done a bad thing, but you're not man enough to admit it, so I'm going to do it for you. I'm going to say something tomorrow, David, and I don't care who believes me. People need to know what you're capable of.'

'Who the fuck do you think you are?'

The door swings open and Bettina comes out carrying a box of empties. She stops in her tracks.

David stares at me and whispers, 'I haven't finished with you yet.' Then he walks straight past her.

She shifts her gaze to me. 'What's going on?'

'Nothing. We had a difference of opinion.'

She is unsure whether to leave me or not. I force a smile and go back inside, tripping on an uneven step and crying out when I wrench my ankle. My elbow hurts like crazy and when I cup it with my hand, my fingers probing gingerly, I feel a tear and the wet stickiness of blood. My dress. Somehow this hits me harder than David's words. The perfect end to a shitty night.

Upstairs, I'm so shaky that I have to sit down on one of the leather sofas. There's a half-full glass on the floor – there have been several of those, discreetly left behind chairs and other objects. I knock back the dregs, not enjoying the tepid stickiness of it, my eyes watering. GZ is never going to take off here, however much they spend on it. It's disgusting. It was a mistake trying to make it cool. Shame Paige said no to making the ad funny. I can't help feeling pleased about that.

There aren't many people left. Eddie and Jamie are helping the chippie load the dismantled stage set, Bettina is holding a ladder while someone else unties the banners. The band have packed up with practised efficiency and are about to go. I slip my shoes off and get up to thank them, limping over to the stage, the soles of my tights snagging on the floorboards. Someone else is already talking to the lead singer.

'Fun evening,' he says, turning to me. 'Phoebe's gutted that she's missed out.'

Elliot.

I speak to the band members, complimenting them and promising to bear them in mind for other promotional events, not mentioning that anything else is now beyond my power. I feel desperately sad. This is it. I am no longer an employee of Gunner Munro.

'Is everything all right?' Bettina asks.

I surprise myself by replying honestly. 'No.'

'What was David having a go at you about?'

'Nothing important.'

I walk away, not wanting anyone to witness my reddening eyes, and hobble towards the door.

'You're bleeding,' she calls after me.

I hear footsteps and spin round, expecting Bettina hot on my heels, curious and persistent, but it's a man.

'Laura, what's the matter? What's happened?'

I glance at the hand he's holding out, with its platinum wedding ring. Elliot again. The relief is so huge that I struggle to hold back the tears.

'Talk to me,' he says, drawing me into a shadowed corner.

'I've got blood on your shirt.'

'It'll come out in the wash.'

I sniff and wipe my eyes. 'It's been a tough week, but I'm fine. Really. How're you getting home?'

'I'll get the tube. Are you ready to go?'

'I will be in ten minutes. Let me say goodbye to everyone.'

Either no one notices, or they're too polite to mention my smudged make-up and tear-stained face. David has gone already, and I'm so thankful I don't have to speak to him again. Tomorrow I'm just going to whizz in and out, collect my belongings and say my goodbyes. I feel a sense of failure; an anti-climax. I've been playing a silly, dangerous game, in which the only person to be made a fool of is me. For all my brave words this evening, David must know my threats are worthless, that I can do nothing, prove nothing, accomplish nothing. He's itching for me to be gone so that he can move on and put his nasty, grubby little secret behind him. And what can I do? I can't go to the police, because I won't be taken seriously, and I don't want to be made to feel any smaller. His wife knows about his affair, so that bubble has been popped. He'll just deal with it. I could ask everyone to gather round, then tell them what happened. A couple of people might believe I didn't know who I slept with; others will suspect I had an inkling; some will think it's sour grapes. Someone will mutter, 'She's finally lost it.'

Rebecca comes over to thank me for all my hard work, her coat already on. Her manner is odd. Maybe the message got through and she knows that her love affair isn't a secret any more.

'We'll see you in the morning, won't we?' she says.

I nod, and she wanders off. I look after her, bothered. My actions have hurt her.

'I am going to miss you so much,' Eddie says, hugging me. 'And listen, if someone wants to employ you with a partner, then give me a call. I'll jump ship.'

I try to laugh.

'You look depressed.'

'I'm fine.'

'Laura.' He touches my cheek. 'Just because you're leaving doesn't mean we aren't friends any more. We can meet up, have lunch, bitch about our bosses. Esther said to ask you to come and visit us as soon as you like.'

'I will,' I say.

Jamie and Bettina join us, and they're so kind and thoughtful, but I can't help wishing that they would go away. Bettina is leaning against him, almost as though she's telling me: *Look, this is what you turned down.*

'We're going on to Culebras,' she says. 'Loads of people have gone already. Are you coming with us?'

Eddie shakes his head mock-dolefully. 'Sorry, my nightclub days are over.'

'Ah, Dad,' she coos. 'What about you, Laura?'

'Oh, no. I'm completely done in.'

Neither Bettina nor Jamie try to persuade me.

'You will be in tomorrow morning, won't you?' she says.

I reassure her and see a look pass between her and Eddie. God knows what they're planning. But it pleases me, and I smile. Security is waiting to lock up. I slip my feet into my flats, wincing at my ankle, put on my coat, and by the time I'm ready to hobble to the station, Elliot has summoned an Uber.

'There's no way you're going on public transport in that state,' he says, opening the door for me.

'I'm not that bad, am I?' I look into the dark maw of the cab and falter, remembering the last time I did this. Then I get in and move right up into the corner. Elliot follows suit, leaving a decent, unthreatening space between us. If he hadn't done that, if he had sat right up next to me, I would have got out and run. As we pull away from the kerb we pass Bettina and Jamie, her arm through his.

Elliot doesn't say much, and I suppose it does feel odd, being thrown together like this, but when we reach Kentish Town, he suggests we have a quick drink in the pub and as I'm so tightly wound that the thought of closing the door to my flat makes me feel like a jack-in-the-box, I agree.

39

Laura

UNFORTUNATELY, ELLIOT PICKS THE SAME PUB I WENT to with Jamie, and the memory of that night troubles me.

'That looks sore,' he says, indicating my reddened fingers.

I quickly move my hands to my lap.

'It's stress,' I say, embarrassed. 'It'll clear up now that's all over.' I change the subject. 'Did you enjoy yourself? I'm sorry I ignored you for most of the evening.'

'Don't worry. I could see you were rushed off your feet. Red Wing were excellent. And there was free booze and food. What's not to like?'

It's easy to misread people, particularly in my peculiar situation, and I want to tell him that he's grown on me, but I hold back because I sense it might overstep the mark.

'GZ?' I suggest.

'Yeah, it wasn't great. But, honestly, I'm not complaining. I had a good time and it was interesting to watch you in action. You were a ball of energy, bouncing around the room.'

Only so that I didn't have to stop and talk to people.

'I appreciated you taking care of yourself,' I say, after a pause. 'And thanks for bringing me back. I didn't realize how knackered I was until I got in the cab.'

I don't think he's had as much to drink as I have, either that or he can hold it better. I check my elbow. There's a tear in the sleeve, not a huge one, but the dress is ruined. I carefully pick strands of chiffon out of the wound and pat it dry with a tissue.

'Phoebe could do something about that. She's amazing with a needle and thread. You've had quite a night, by the looks of it.'

'You could say that.'

'Why were you so upset? I got the feeling it was more than just because you were leaving.'

'Very perceptive. Someone . . . actually, do you mind? I'd rather not talk about it. It's over now and after tomorrow I need never see them again. I'm so glad I've made friends with you and Phoebe.' My words slide on my tongue; come out soft at the edges. The GZ effect. 'She's such a lovely person.'

'She is,' Elliot agrees.

'Where did you two meet?'

'In Covent Garden.'

He tells me the story and then he asks me where I met my boyfriend, and I frown. What boyfriend? Is he fishing?

'I'm currently single,' I say, jokingly.

'Oh,' he says. 'I thought . . . Well, I must be mistaken.'

'Not that it's beyond the bounds of possibility, of course.'

He smiles. 'Obviously not.'

'So, Elliot,' I say, moving on swiftly. 'Tell me about your brothers and sisters.'

'I'm the youngest of three; all brothers. They're cool. We get on all right these days, but we took the piss a lot when we were kids. At least my brothers took the piss out of me. I followed them around like a puppy.' He looks sad, then he smiles and takes another swig of beer. 'But I was an annoying little tyke, constantly playing practical jokes, so I can't blame them.' He raises his glass. 'Here's to our siblings, may they never have the satisfaction of knowing how much they screw with our heads.'

'I'm the youngest of three too. We've got something in common.'

'So we do.'

In the pause that follows, I wonder whether Jamie and Bettina have slept together yet. And if I am flirting with Elliot. If so, I admonish myself, I should stop right now. Punters are beginning to leave and every time the door opens I get a blast of cold air. I know that it's time to go, but I'm reluctant. My flat is waiting for me, but after that, what? Once the official goodbyes are over tomorrow morning, the future looms, daunting in its emptiness. My instinct is to go to Mum's and hunker down for a few days, but I'm getting too old for that now; I have to make my life work for me.

'Penny for them?' Elliot says.

I smile. 'Just thinking. It's going to be strange not having a job to go to.'

'Make a plan. That's the best cure for staring into the abyss.'

I look at him, wondering how he knows that's how I'm feeling. Has he been there? Or does he just understand? It's nice that someone does.

'I think I might go and visit Mum. Or maybe my sister in Paris.'

'Paris sounds more fun,' he says.

'*Mais oui. Paris est très amusant.*'

'Don't you go all cultured on me now. Just as I was beginning to think you were normal.'

When we've finished our drinks, I insist on buying a round. I don't want to go home because I have a feeling that once I've closed my door, I won't come out again; I'll retreat from life, from friends. Having Elliot here, joking with me and telling me about his life and his job, gives me hope. We talk until last orders are called, and then we roll out into the night, Elliot supporting me.

'Look at the moon,' I say, stopping and leaning my head back, swaying slightly, one hand on his arm.

Elliot looks up. 'Very nice.'

'It's beautiful. Do you know which stars are which?'

'I know Orion's Belt and the Great Bear. Apart from that . . .'

'Ursa Minor looks more like a mouse, if you ask me.' I trip, and he puts his arm around my waist.

'How's that ankle?'

'Painful,' I whimper.

I like the strength in his arm and the smell of his aftershave. I like his shiny suit because it's true to who he is. I like his voice with its hint of Estuary. He's a bit flash, is Elliot Hill, but there's nothing wrong with that. God, I'm pissed.

We arrive outside the house all too soon and the dread starts to crawl back under my skin. While he pats his pockets, searching for his keys, I lean against his car. He finds them, but they slip through his fingers, falling with a clatter between the kerb and the back wheel.

'Shit.'

Trying to be helpful, I get down on my hands and knees and scrabble in the dirt to find them. I press the button and the locks click as I heave myself back up with the help of the door handle. The interior looks so inviting, and my head feels woozy. I crawl into the back, chucking a couple of brightly coloured plastic toys, along with a digger truck and a fire-engine, into the baby seat.

I curl up and push myself into the corner. It's chilly, the frost already creeping over the windscreen, the moon casting a white glow across it. My head spins slowly. What am I doing?

Elliot pops his head in the door and peers at me, red-nosed, a scarf around his neck. 'You can't sleep in here.'

'Don't see why not.'

'Because you'll get hypothermia for a start.'

I giggle, then stifle it. 'True.' I hold out my hand. 'You get in too.'

His face tenses and I know I've gone too far.

'Laura. Come on.'

He tries to pull me out, but I start crying. He sighs and gets in and pulls his coat around us both. I rest my head on his shoulder and we sit in silence for several minutes. The street is empty, the houses quiet.

'I want to go home now,' I say, as though I'm expecting him to put the key in the ignition and drive me somewhere.

'OK. You're the boss.'

As I limp to the front door, I glance up at my darkened windows and tense every muscle. I'm not sure I want to go in, but Elliot manoeuvres me out of the way so that he can get his key in the lock, and it's too late. At the bottom of the stairs, we pause, eyeing each other awkwardly. I want to laugh out of sheer nervousness. I debate asking him to come up and check the flat for monsters under the bed, but he might think I mean something else. I might mean something else. I remind myself that I do not make good choices when I am drunk.

I reach to give him a goodnight kiss on the cheek, but he catches me round the waist and pulls me against him. He crushes his lips on to mine. I taste beer and a residual hint of GZ. I push him away, but not aggressively. Gently, like I regret it. I don't want to hurt his feelings.

'Better not.'

'Why not?' he says, reaching for me again.

I avoid his hand. 'Cos you're married, and I live here.'

'Phoebe won't know.'

'Not a good idea. Night night, Elliot.'

It's my turn to fumble for my keys and drop them. Elliot picks them up and hands them to me.

'You should be careful what kind of signals you give out,' he says. His face is like stone.

'What?' I'm already halfway up the stairs.

'You know what I'm talking about. If you don't mean

anything by it, don't give men the wrong idea. It makes you a tease.'

A tease? A memory hits me in the solar plexus. Someone accused me of that before. In a letter. *No one likes a tease.* I stare at Elliot and he glares back. I can hear the house, the water in the pipes, the tick of the electric meter, the spiders spinning their webs. I need to get away from him, and I need to do it fast. I'm trembling from my feet to my hair follicles, but the light is dim, and he doesn't appear to notice. Have I made a mistake? After everything that's happened, all that I've done, was I wrong about David Gunner? Has my attacker literally been under my nose all along?

'What did you say?'

'Nothing,' he answers sulkily. 'Never mind. Actually, I think I'll go to my sister-in-law's. I don't fancy being on my own tonight.'

I nod and back away, suddenly sober. I mustn't hurry. I don't want him to know what I'm thinking and feeling, the shock and revulsion. At the top of the stairs, standing outside my door, I hear him go into his flat. My shoulders drop. I let myself in and stand with my back pressed against the door panels.

I think back to every meeting I've had with my neighbour and reassess his behaviour. Sometimes he's been kind, sometimes he's behaved as though I'm an encroaching nuisance. There was that time I overheard him saying, 'Thank God she's gone.' There was the day I met him on the tube. My stomach cramps. Maybe it wasn't the first time. How often have we sat directly opposite each other on the way to and from work? Where was he on the night of the twenty-second of December? Where was Phoebe? Was she home, or had she, like Felicity Gunner, gone on ahead to family? No, it's not possible. I can't demolish my entire argument over one word. It was David. I have no doubt about that.

I crave my bed so badly that I can barely keep my eyes open. Leaning against the wall with a deep sigh, I drop my bag at my feet and feel for the light switch, blinking in the sudden glare.

Something feels strange; some kink in the atmosphere that makes my hair stand on end. I catch the faintest scent of cigarette and breathe deeper, flaring my nostrils. But it's gone.

'Hello?' I reach down and set my shoes quietly against the skirting.

There's no response. My bedroom door is slightly ajar, and I can't remember precisely, but I think I left it wide open. I usually do, otherwise it becomes stuffy while I'm out.

My kitchen is part of the sitting room and there is no other access to it, so I can't arm myself with a knife or a pan. All I have is my new umbrella, hanging on one of the coat hooks, the kind that folds up small. Brandishing it like a truncheon, I tiptoe forward and press the palm of my hand against my bedroom door, push it open and turn the light on. The room is how I left it, with yesterday's clothes still hanging over the back of the chair, my dressing table strewn with make-up. I was in a hurry this morning.

My body is rushing with adrenaline as I step across the corridor into the sitting room. The door to the street closes with a thud, and I run to the windows, watching from behind the fall of the curtains as Elliot crosses the road and walks away.

The glow of the street light casts shadows tinged with orange into the room. There is no one here and nowhere to hide. I breathe a sigh of relief. My sanctuary is still my sanctuary, the place where I nurse my wounds.

I need to think, but I'm so tired and I want to believe that it was nothing, just a word, that I'm being paranoid. It isn't hard to imagine a day when I'll stop going out, stop making the effort, because it's too difficult and I'm too frightened. I'll think about it in the morning. Tomorrow I'll try and talk to Phoebe and find some way of asking where Elliot was the night I was raped. The thought depresses me so much. I feel as though I've rolled the dice and landed on a snake. Back to square one.

I draw the curtains and fall into bed with my party dress on, the zip proving too fiddly for my clumsy fingers to manage, and as soon as my head hits the pillow the room starts to turn in circles. I watch the ceiling making its slow revolutions, until my eyelids grow heavy and sleep drags me into its treacly embrace. In my dream I smell cigarettes again. I dream about a huge white spider, protecting a glistening egg as big as itself, its legs draped over it like pale fingers. The next thing I know, my bed dips as though someone has climbed in beside me, and I'm waking up, struggling for breath, a hand clamped over my mouth and nose.

40

Rebecca

FELICITY KNOWS. THE INFORMATION SITS LIKE A BAD meal at the bottom of her stomach. Rebecca is back at home, curled up like a small child on the white carpet of her bedroom, growing cold. She doesn't know how to react; she is part triumphant, part desolate. Felicity finding out has opened a door to the unknown. When she was younger she would have gone to greet whatever awaited her. She's wiser now, and wary.

She unfurls her body and stretches from the tips of her toes into her fingertips. She lifts her spine and drops her head back. She is trying to clear the fog in her mind, to find a place of rest and safety. She pushes herself up and sits on the edge of her bed, hugging her shins, her face pressed into her knees.

This is what she wanted, but not the way she wanted it to happen. She wanted to control the when and the where. Now David is blaming her. Rebecca has never seen him so angry or so distressed. They had the row behind the stage, with the band providing a sound-screen. His eyes had been practically starting out of their sockets, spittle flying from his mouth. She couldn't find the words she needed, the words she would have planned had she known something like this was going to happen. She should have known, and she should have been prepared.

She glances at her clock. Maybe he'll have calmed down by now.

She picks up her phone and sends him a message. *Can we talk?*

The response is immediate. *Not now. Felicity has thrown me out. I'm with my grandparents tonight. Please do not call me. I will call you.*

Rebecca stares at her mobile. She makes herself think about Felicity, makes herself imagine how she'll be feeling right now. Rebecca owes her an explanation, an apology, an acknowledgement that her behaviour has been unacceptable. Felicity won't want to see her, but if she doesn't go, if she just ignores her friend's anger and misery, then that will be something else that Felicity can hold against her. She must see her, if only this once, and let Felicity tell her she hates her, allow her to say what she wants, to her face. Rebecca is taking her husband, so she's prepared to take the fallout with it. It's not all altruism though; she'll be doing David's job for him, making it easier for him to draw a line under his marriage.

She repairs her make-up, changes into black trousers and a warm shirt and jumper, puts on her coat, tips up her fur collar and strides out into the night.

* * *

The lights are on downstairs, so Felicity is still up. Rebecca imagines her friend, translucent skin mottled with tears, sitting at the kitchen table, surrounded by her perfect walls and carefully chosen possessions and wondering how she missed the fact that she's been living on quicksand, that all this, all the money, the children, the house in France, adds up to nothing.

The raw night air bites Rebecca's cheeks and she holds her coat collar together across her chin. She waits for five more minutes but doesn't get a sight of her, not even a movement behind the vast flower arrangement, that silk monstrosity that shields her friend from nosy passers-by. She crosses the road, walks up to the door and knocks. She doesn't want to ring the bell unless she has to, in case it wakes the kids.

When Felicity sees who it is, she moans and tries to push the door shut. Rebecca slams her palm against it and wedges her booted foot inside.

'Let me in, Felicity. Please.'

'Why the hell should I? I can't believe you've done this to me.'

'I never wanted to hurt you.' Was that true? She was uncertain. Someone was going to get hurt eventually, and she would have avoided being that person at all costs.

Rebecca eases herself inside. Mussy-haired and blotchy-skinned, Felicity is a picture of devastation, her eyes woeful and pink from crying. To Rebecca's surprise, Felicity springs forward, going for her face with her bitten nails and scratching her ear. Rebecca grabs her wrists and thrusts them down, then drags her into the kitchen and closes the door. Pebbles wakes up and stretches, gets out of her bed and comes to see them, pushing her nose under Felicity's hand. Then she sits back on her haunches and growls.

Felicity glares at Rebecca, her chest rising and falling. There is something animal about her, something untamed. There's an open bottle of red wine on the side, two-thirds drunk, and a glass stained with the residue on the table, surrounded by a drift of crumpled hankies.

'I know that I've been duplicitous and underhand,' Rebecca says, 'but I love him.'

'And you think I don't? How could you do this to me? I thought you were my friend.'

'I am.'

'Friends don't make fools of each other. Friends don't screw each other's husbands. I expect you laugh about me behind my back.'

'Of course we don't. We love you and respect you and I've hated lying to you. So has David. But I've loved him for years.'

'Why did you introduce me to him then if you wanted him so badly? Why didn't you take him when you could?'

'I honestly don't know. I didn't take it seriously, I suppose.'

Rebecca squeezes the bridge of her nose. She ought to cry but she can't; even as a child she seldom did. 'I didn't know, not until he asked you to marry him. The finality of it shocked me into recognizing my feelings.'

'How sad and unoriginal. You wanted what you couldn't have. I should have realized something was up when the years passed, and you never committed to anyone. At one point, I even thought you were gay.' She mutters to herself then adds, her eyes scouring Rebecca's face, 'I wish you were.'

Rebecca doesn't know what to say. Felicity is right and wrong at the same time. It was seeing him attaching himself irrevocably to someone else that brought it home. She's never forgotten the awful shifting feeling when Felicity showed her the ring. It had felt like the floor was falling away.

'When did it start? Don't tell me it was before my wedding day.'

She feels a mixture of shame and defiance. 'About a year later. It was when we were setting up Gunner Munro and spending so much time together.'

'Who made the first move?'

She doesn't hesitate. 'I did.'

'I don't believe you.'

Felicity goes to the window, pressing her hands against the frame and her forehead against the cool glass. In her white dressing gown, her blonde hair backlit by the moonlight, she looks like an angel.

Rebecca allows the silence to swell. Eventually, Felicity drops her arms and turns to face her. Her face is a picture of misery. 'When I was pregnant?'

Put so starkly, the betrayal is appalling. 'I'm sorry.'

'Oh Christ.'

Felicity bursts into tears, great heaving sobs that Rebecca fears might bring the children downstairs. She wishes she hadn't come. She wants to leave, but she can't before Felicity tells her to go. She has to give her that at least. After a while Felicity pulls herself together. Her breath is ragged, but she is no longer crying.

'Have you had sex in my bed?'

'No. We wouldn't do that.'

'Oh. So you do have scruples.'

She doesn't answer.

'And you expect me to be grateful?'

'What do you want me to do?'

'I want you to sell your half of the company.' Her eyes lock on to Rebecca's. 'David can afford to buy you out, or he may want to find a new partner. But you have to go. He belongs with his family, and don't you ever forget it.'

Rebecca bends to stroke Pebbles's fringe, then she gets up and leaves.

Felicity doesn't see her to the door and as she crosses the road and looks back, the lights go out. There is an air of finality about it; a line drawn. She has lost a friend, but she won't allow herself to think that she may have lost David too. He will choose her. She hugs herself as she strides through Hampstead. She is over a week late. She is not going to think about that either. She is not going to hope.

41

Laura

MY FIRST THOUGHT IS THAT ELLIOT HAS COME BACK, sneaking silently into the house. I struggle to sink my teeth into his hand, but his grip is too tight, and he has me trapped by his weight, one knee pressed down on my chest, making it difficult to draw breath. My screams are muffled. I pedal against the sheet, to get myself up against the headboard, but he's far stronger than me.

I twist and kick, trying to catch him off guard, but he clasps my wrists in one hand and forces fabric into my mouth, then leans over to pick something up from the floor. He shows it to me, puts it right in front of my face, then holds the tip of it against my neck, pushing it hard enough to dent my skin. Any harder, and he'll break through, maybe nick an artery. Panicking, I strain my neck away, but the knife follows me. And then he hits me and it's so unexpected and violent that I black out. When I come to, I'm gagged, and my hands are bound behind my back.

He pulls me up and manhandles me to the door. I put

up a fight and he hits me again, so hard that my vision fuzzes.

I stagger downstairs, falling and landing at the bottom, trying to reach the door. He rights me and then there's a blank and we're outside, our breath misting in the cold. I don't remember going through the door. I trip over my own feet; a drunk woman supported by her boyfriend.

I pass out and when I wake up I'm lying on the back seat of a car, bruised and sore, speeding along a motorway, the smell of leather in my nose. Lights flash by, so bright that they hurt my eyes, and there's a long rush of air as we cut through the slipstream and overtake a lorry. My jaw and cheekbone throb. The back of his head is blurred. The silence is ominous. I work my wrists to try and loosen my bounds but they're too tight and I only hurt myself. I slowly take in the interior. This isn't Elliot's car. Elliot's car has a baby seat in it.

We veer off the motorway and drive for about fifteen minutes then turn into a lane that zigzags for a mile or so, before crunching over gravel to pull up in front of a house. The air smells of wet grass. The night is clear. The call of an owl, distant and ghostly, makes me shiver. I can see the upstairs windows and three gables in the roof, and above them a dark expanse of sky and a three-quarter moon. The same moon I was looking at with Elliot, only this time it has a weird halo round it.

When he drags me out my feet slide over the seat and hit the ground with a jolt of pain that starts in my bad ankle and flares into my leg and hip. I vomit over his shoes.

'For fuck's sake.'

I recognize that voice. He forces me to stand, then marches me across the gravel, the sharp stones digging into my bare feet, and takes me inside.

'Make one sound and I'll use this,' he says, holding the knife close to my face.

We are in a sitting room, the lights off. I know it's David. I think I have known all the time, only the concussion affected my ability to pin down his name. So, I was right. It was him. Elliot had nothing to do with what happened to me.

Keeping the knife to my throat, he pulls the fabric out of my mouth. It's one of the woolly socks I wear in bed on cold nights.

'I won't tell anyone,' I gasp. 'If you let me go, I won't say a word. I swear.'

'Shut up. I need to think,' he says.

My nose is running and my throat aches, and I hate myself for showing weakness. I look down at my body, at my damaged dress, and hug my arms around my breasts.

'Lie on your front.'

I stifle my panic, shuffle round and press my face into a cushion. The velvety fabric is unpleasant against my cheek.

'How did you get into my flat?' I say to the back of the sofa.

'You left your bag in the dressing room all day. I found your keys and had them copied at the station.'

'What do you want?'

'What the hell do you think I want? I want you to leave me and my family alone. I'm sick of your nasty insinuations and your threats.'

When I speak my voice sounds as though it belongs to someone else. 'I'm the one who's paying for what you did.'

'But it's got nothing to do with you,' he says with frustration. 'I don't understand why you've taken it upon yourself to fight someone else's battle.'

I roll my body round so that I can see him. My head is heavy, but I lift it. He is sitting on an armchair, leaning back, his legs spread, exhausted.

'You raped me. How is that someone else's battle?'

He sits forward abruptly. 'What in Christ's name are you talking about?'

'So, you think it wasn't rape? You think it's all right to conceal your identity to get someone into bed. It *is* rape. Look it up.'

'I don't need to look it up. I didn't rape you, Laura.'

'Yes, you did.'

'When?' he asks.

'After the Christmas party.'

'I don't know why we're even discussing this. It's pure fantasy. If you had been raped, you would have gone to the police.'

I remember something. 'Are you circumcised?'

'Are you off your fucking trolley?'

'Are you circumcised?'

'No, I am not circumcised. What has that got to do with anything? I'm talking about Guy. I didn't rape you. I would never rape anyone.'

'Guy?' I say slowly.

'How did you know it was me? Were you there?'

I'm not brilliant at reading expressions, but his bewilderment is clear.

'I don't understand,' I say. 'Are you saying you didn't get in my cab?'

'No, I didn't.' He grimaces with distaste. 'And I've never been inside your flat before tonight, and as for forcing myself on you, do me a favour. I don't sleep with women who are so paralytically drunk they haven't a clue who they've invited into their bed.'

There's a long pause. Then he rakes his hands through his hair. 'What's going on?'

'You killed Guy.' My mouth drops open and I look at him stupidly. 'Is that what you're saying? You were the driver? You knocked him down and left him to die?'

'It wasn't my fault. He came out of nowhere. I got him on to the pavement.'

'But he was still alive, and you didn't call 999. You were too busy worrying about what would happen to you. You could have saved him.'

'He was under a street light. I assumed someone would see him.'

I can't believe what I'm hearing. 'He worked for you. He respected you, David. How could you have driven away?'

'Do you think I don't feel terrible? I haven't had a decent night's sleep since it happened. He's dead and there is no bringing him back. I have to live with that for the rest of my life.'

I can't bear to speak to him, and what response is

there? Instead I fit the pieces together. He must have gone back to Gunner Munro to pick up his car that night. His ego is big enough for him to think the rules don't apply and to consider himself capable of driving under the influence without mishap. He probably didn't even ask himself the question. When he realized he'd hit someone, I can guess what went through his mind. His career. His reputation. His future. He could lose his business, the respect of his peers; incur the disappointment of his family and Rebecca. No wonder he reacted like he did. I've blundered into another crime.

I can't believe my own stupidity. What was I doing? Trying to punish David was like shoving a fist into a snake pit. He didn't trick me, rape me or come anywhere near me. He couldn't have been in two places at the same time. I got it wrong, there was somebody else in my bed that night. And in that case, was it Elliot after all? Too many weeks have gone by and the trail will be cold. If I live through this, I may never find out who did it. If I live.

I feel a sense of dread and the sudden, crushing stillness between us tells me he's feeling the same thing. That's why I'm here. I am a problem he needs to solve.

42

Rebecca

REBECCA WAVES BETTINA OUT OF THE ROOM, AS THOUGH she's flicking away an annoying insect, the phone pressed to her ear. David hasn't heard the interruption and is still talking. His voice is different. It's a nuanced difference, but she knows him so well that she can sense it in the rhythm and speed of his speech.

'. . . get in later. In a way, it's a good thing that I stayed over, because I've had my head in the sand. They're worse than I thought. Jesus, what a nightmare.'

She pushes her chair back and stands, and immediately feels more in control. 'Have you spoken to Felicity this morning?'

'Not yet. I thought I'd give her a chance to get used to the idea. Otherwise it'll turn into a slanging match.'

She applies pressure to her temples with her thumb and middle fingers. She has a migraine brewing but is too scared to take the pills. Who knows what that sort of medication might do to a developing foetus; if there is one. David is being suspiciously off-hand, cavalier, but he must know that the ground rules have changed; that he doesn't have to stay with Felicity. The hard part is over.

'I don't think it's a matter of her getting used to this,' she says. 'It's going to turn her life upside down. The only thing that is going to help is for you to be clear about what you want.'

Rebecca pauses, giving him a chance to argue, but he's gone silent on her. He has always been an emotional coward. He can close a deal at work, he can work with unreasonable people and wind the most ruthless CEOs around his little finger, but when it comes to women, he's hopeless. He wants them to love him and he can't bear being in trouble. So far, he hasn't told her what decision he's made because he can't face the fallout. She doesn't know why she puts up with it, except that she loves him, has always loved him and always will.

'You're so wise, darling,' David says, but it feels as though he's trying to fob her off, to give himself time.

Behind his voice, and his breathing, she can hear Georgie calling Tony. Then it goes quiet. David must have closed the door.

'You understand, don't you?' he continues, his voice lowered. 'That my priority has to be those two. Their safety and comfort must be guaranteed before I can start thinking about myself. I've been selfish, but all that is going to change. This has to take precedence over my love life for the time being.'

'Meaning?'

'That I can't be in three places at once. It's going to be all right, my love, but I have to acknowledge my responsibilities.'

'And leave Felicity and me hanging. David . . .'

There's a thud in the background, and David swears. 'I've got to go. Honestly, it's like a bad farce here. Sorry.' And he hangs up.

She replaces the phone on its cradle and spins her chair back and forth with her finger, then grips the back, bringing it to a jolting halt. He's left her in limbo. She feels a flutter of panic and focuses on her breathing. In through the nose, out through the mouth. Four beats each way. Better.

Last night, after the confrontation with Felicity, she couldn't sleep. She put her earphones in and listened to Shakespeare's sonnets being read by various household names. This normally works, the words and rhythms spoken by such achingly beautiful voices, wrapping her thoughts in velvet, insulating her nerves and soothing her mind. She lay stretched out under the duvet, her arms by her sides, her spine and neck perfectly aligned by the orthopaedic pillow. It didn't work. She fell asleep sometime before four o'clock and woke to her alarm at seven. Now, even though she knows she shouldn't, she is riding a caffeine wave. No wonder her head is dodgy.

There's a tentative knock on the door.

'Come in.'

Bettina steps into the room. Compared to Rebecca, she's as fresh as a daisy. She noticed her hovering around Jamie Buchanan last night. Before Christmas it was Finn. Bettina has great potential, but Rebecca can't help thinking that she's using this place as her own personal dating pool. She hopes she isn't causing problems.

'What is it, Bettina?'

'Laura hasn't come in. I was wondering whether you had heard from her.'

'No.' She is distracted and doesn't give the girl her full attention. 'I expect she's running late.'

Bettina is still standing there, watching her. She curls a stray tendril of that wonderful hair behind her ears.

'It seems odd, that's all. The last thing she said to me was that she'd see me in the morning.'

'She worked extremely hard yesterday, so I expect she's exhausted. Maybe she's slept through her alarm.'

'Only, I've organized a couple of things for her and she knows something's happening. I've got a cake and a present.'

David had only wanted to contribute ten pounds to the collection, but Rebecca forced him to put in a hundred.

Bettina glances at her phone. 'It's a quarter to eleven now. Do you think I should call her?'

Anxiety is infectious, and Rebecca does feel a twinge, though she's confident it's unwarranted. Laura is fine. The only people not doing so well are Felicity and herself. She hasn't room for any more sympathy. 'If you're worried, then do. I expect you'll find she's on her way.'

Bettina nods. 'Yeah. I'll call her, I think. It'll put my mind at rest.'

Rebecca rubs her head and thinks longingly of her pills and that decides her. She has to know today, preferably within the hour, so that at least she can avoid the migraine if she isn't pregnant.

And truthfully, the need to know is beginning to dominate everything she does, the thoughts dividing like cells, swarming like a virus. It's getting to the point where she can think of nothing else.

She makes a couple of calls, speaks at length to Paige and the director of the commercial, and then dashes to the chemist in Hoxton Street. She buys what she needs and pops it in her bag.

Eddie and Bettina are conferring outside Eddie's office. They turn when they see Rebecca. Eddie is the one to speak, moving towards her, his expression full of concern.

'We've tried Laura's mobile and her home number. She's not picking up. I've messaged her on Facebook too.'

'She's probably on her way. She won't be able to answer her phone if she's cycling. Give it ten minutes and try again.'

She's still pissed off with Laura. It was her who started the gossip that led to Felicity finding out about the affair; that caused the hideous, humiliating row with David backstage. She has no idea how Laura found out, but that doesn't matter. She's been good to her and feels betrayed and, frankly, mortified. She assumes everyone knows. She feels watched, feels eyes following her, people going quiet when she comes out of her office.

Eddie is speaking, and she pulls her attention back.

'We've already done that,' he says. 'It usually takes her less than thirty minutes. If she'd been on her bike when we first rang, she'd be here by now. I'm worried about her. I think someone should go to her house and make sure she's OK.'

'I do think you're overreacting. It's her last day and she's bound to be upset, given the circumstances. She may have decided not to come in.'

He rubs his hand over his beard. 'I knew she wasn't coping. She shouldn't have come back to work; it was much too soon.' His brown eyes meet hers. 'We can't just assume she's OK.'

Frankly, she thinks Laura hasn't come in because she's ashamed and doesn't want to look Rebecca in the eye. Of course she feels bad that Laura's breakdown slipped her mind, but she has a pregnancy test burning a hole in her bag and doesn't have time for other people's melodramas.

She realizes Eddie and Bettina are in earnest and pulls herself together. This isn't about her, it's about an employee, and until Laura has been to Human Resources to collect her P45, that is what she is. They have a procedure to follow if they have concerns about a member of staff's well-being. It would be as well to err on the safe side.

'By all means. If it'll set your minds at rest, someone can go.'

'Better be me,' Eddie says. 'I know where she lives.'

'No, I need you here. Bettina, you look like you're at a loose end. Eddie will give you the address.'

'OK.'

'Don't you think it would be better if I went?' Eddie says.

She shakes her head. 'If you go racing round there, it'll look like we're overreacting.'

He doesn't like it, and she can't blame him for that,

but it would be a poor use of manpower. He borrows a block of Post-it notes from Finn's desk and scribbles on it, pulls off the page and hands it to Bettina.

'It's the bottom bell.'

'What shall I do if she's not there?' Bettina asks. 'Should I call the police?'

Rebecca resists the urge to sigh heavily. Why can't people think for themselves?

'Call Agnes if Laura doesn't open the door. She'll have her emergency contact in the files.'

It'll be a pity if Laura doesn't come in to be thanked and say goodbye properly. Despite personal disasters, the campaign launch was a great success. Simon McAulay put the photos online as soon as he got home last night and, with Finn's involvement, it's all over social media this morning and will hopefully enter public consciousness via the print media as well. The presence of a couple of high-profile models and a soap star should guarantee that.

She shivers, even though she's warm enough. Events are moving rapidly. She goes to the window, parts the blinds with her fingers and scans the road, like a mother waiting for her teenage daughter to come home at night. Once she has got it in her head that there's something wrong, she can't shake the feeling. Seeing Bettina leave the building, Rebecca snatches up her bag and runs, catching up with her before she reaches the end of Percy Row.

'I've changed my mind,' she says. 'I'll go. Laura is my responsibility.'

The pregnancy test will have to wait.

43

Laura

THE VOICE IS QUERULOUS AND DEMANDING AND COMING from somewhere beneath me. I've been watching the dull light filter through the sun-frayed curtains for hours. I'm lying on my side, on a bed, and my wrists are taped together behind my back, my legs at the ankles, and the sock back in my mouth. I try to push it out with my tongue, but I've been gagged with a pair of tights. They aren't mine – mine are still on my legs, the ladders crisped with dried blood. As for the rest of me, I can almost taste the pain; a hangover, my body bruised and aching, a crick in my neck, and blood in my mouth. The house goes quiet. A talkative blackbird repeats its song. It sounds like an enquiry.

Are you there? Is anyone there?

My stomach muscles are strong, and after a couple of tries I manage to get myself into a seated position, my back against the wall. Below me, someone is weeping; it sounds like a woman. I stare hard at the floor, as though I only need willpower to see through to the room beneath. I try to shout, filling my lungs with air, but barely manage a strangled, 'Unh unh!'

I work my wrists, trying to loosen the binding, but he's been liberal with the duct tape, winding it round until it feels as solid as lead. He. David Gunner. The thought of him makes my physical discomfort recede and replaces it with terror. The memory of last night comes flooding back; the feeling that I wasn't alone in my flat; waking with his hand across my mouth and nose; being hit so hard I blacked out.

I attempt to swallow, and gag on fluff. It brings on a wave of claustrophobia and I'm drowning in it, panicking, fibres tickling my throat as I try to drag in air. I stare round the room, my eyes so wide they feel like they might burst. I make myself take a mental step back and try to think about something else, but the only scene my brain offers up is the moment I woke with David's hand over my face. I try harder, picturing instead the family round the table at Christmas, replaying the banter between Mark and Isabel's children. It helps. The panic recedes, my heart rate slows.

I study the window, trying to gauge from the fuzzy silhouette of a tree beyond the curtains how high up I am. I have a memory of three gables beneath a night sky. Maybe there's a drainpipe. If I can free myself, I could get out. He has to go to work some time.

I doze for a while, and when I wake there's a strange man sitting on the floor in the corner of the room, watching me from the shadows. I stare at him, unable to speak, completely disorientated. His hair is brown and tufted, as though he fell asleep while it was still wet. Then it comes back to me in a rush. David.

He gets up and opens the curtains, revealing a clouded sky and the lacy tops of winter-stark trees. He is rumpled and unshaven, and his skin is blotchy. I tear my gaze away and scan the room, taking in the film posters, and the character models organized along the pine shelves amongst the books. This was once a child's bedroom; a boy's room. There's a dark blue dressing gown hanging from a brass hook on the back of the door and next to it a school tie has been draped over its twin. It all looks dusty and forgotten. My fingers start to burn, my skin flaring. I rub them against the sheet, but it gives me little relief.

David seems antsy, unable to be still, pacing the room, peering out of the window, to the right and left, as if he's trying to get a view down the road. Is he expecting someone? The police? His wife? I watch him, pressing myself into the wall whenever he comes near. Eventually, he crouches, and I turn my face away as he reaches for me. He removes the gag and tucks his fingers into my mouth to pull out the sock. Even though I go for him with my teeth, he manages to remove them without being bitten. I scream, and he grabs me, holding the back of my head with one hand, covering my mouth with the other. His palms are damp. I make myself look at his eyes. They're bloodshot and pink-rimmed.

'Shut up,' he says. 'You need to calm down, Laura, or the gag is going back on.'

I nod, and one of my tears dribbles down his fingers. He removes his hand.

'Why did you bring me here?'

'You gave me no choice. What was I supposed to do?' He speaks fast, too fast, the words spilling out, defensive and angry, as though he's the one who's been badly treated. 'You threatened to tell everyone. How the fuck was I supposed to know you had your wires crossed? I thought you meant about Guy. You . . .' He pauses and wipes away the spittle that has gathered at the corner of his mouth. 'You had to push, and push, writing your notes, watching me. And why did you think I raped you? Were you really that pissed?'

'Yes,' I hiss back at him. 'What about it? It was a Christmas party and I wasn't doing anything wrong.'

I look down at my torn dress, at my big toe sticking out of my laddered tights, at my swollen ankle. I look up at his dark hair and his nondescript face, Adam's apple rising and falling.

I narrow my eyes. 'I didn't do anything wrong,' I repeat.

'So why blame me?'

'I worked it out afterwards.' I pause when he gives a grunt of disgust. I know how weak it sounds. 'I didn't know who it was at the time because I'm face-blind.'

'You're what?'

'Get me some water first.' My mouth is so dry I can barely form the words.

I don't scream while he's out of the room. There's little point. He would only get more stressed. There's an unnerving unpredictability about him. He is so close to the edge, it's frightening.

He raises the glass to my lips and I drink. When I've had enough, I turn my head away. He seems less jumpy, but I don't trust him.

'I have a condition called prosopagnosia. It means I can't recognize anyone's face.'

'Big deal. I meet hundreds of people. Half the time I don't have a clue who I'm talking to.'

'It's not the same. It's hard to explain, but everyone is a stranger, even my mother. I don't recognize my own face in the mirror.'

'So, you didn't recognize me when I came in just now?'

'No.' I cough fibres out of my throat, and he tips the glass to my lips again. 'But I knew who you were, because it was obvious. Like I generally know who you are at work. If I saw you somewhere I didn't expect to, like in my flat . . .' I pause to let the reminder of his iniquity sink in, 'I wouldn't recognize you. I rely heavily on people's hair, but it isn't infallible.'

David regards me in silence, his brow furrowing. 'Why didn't I know about this?'

I shrug. The conversation seems to be calming him. His movements are more fluid, less spasmodic. 'I explained it to Rebecca when she offered me the job, because I felt she ought to know, but I asked her to keep it confidential. Apart from that, I don't tell people. It's for my own protection.'

His lip curls as he acknowledges the irony. 'Go on.'

'Someone raped me on the night of the Christmas party and I didn't know who it was, but I knew he was from Gunner Munro. Then I worked out that it must have been you.'

He stiffens. 'Do I look like a fucking rapist?'

'I don't know. I've never met one before.'

'Why didn't you report me, if you were so certain?'

'Because there was no point. It would be my word against the word of someone I can't distinguish from any other man of his height and build. I needed proof. You were the only one who fitted and didn't have an alibi and then when I found out that you and Rebecca were having an affair, I assumed she'd broken her promise and told you about me.'

'And you had to make sure my wife knew about us. Jesus, you stupid, vindictive cow.'

'No,' I protest desperately. 'I didn't mean that to happen.'

The sound of a car turning in through the gate interrupts us. We are as alert as a pair of grazing deer. I shout for help as he forces the sock back into my mouth, covering it with a strip of tape this time. The doorbell chimes. He attaches my wrists to the iron bedstead with the tights. There's no gentleness in his actions.

'Don't make a sound.'

He leaves me and seconds later I hear his muffled greeting, the conversation on the doorstep and those warbling, elderly voices.

'Tell that bitch to get lost,' the old lady suddenly shrieks. 'She's a thief.'

David's reply is inaudible, but the door closes, the footsteps retreat, the car door slams and whoever the visitor was, drives away. I hang my head.

When David comes back, he brings a bowl of cereal. He feeds me, and I eat like a baby, opening my mouth for more. I need my strength if I'm going to get out of here.

'I need to pee,' I say.

He sighs, unties me and heaves me up, but my legs buckle. He tucks his arm beneath mine and supports me out of the room. I catalogue my surroundings, like I do with human attributes; the cobwebby landing with the dirty windows at either end, the two other doors, the threadbare green carpet down to the next floor. The television is on, canned laughter punctuating American voices. He guides me into a bathroom with a pink porcelain bath, basin and loo. The wallpaper has birds on it and a damp patch in the corner. The window is small, and the glass is obscured by a greying net curtain in front of which sits a shallow bowl of potpourri and an air freshener with rust around its base.

David locks the door behind us, shuffles me backwards until the edge of the loo seat bites into my calves. I can feel the heat coming off him and I am so mortified and tense that it takes ages for my muscles to relax.

At the sound of footsteps on the stairs we both go still. Someone rattles the door handle. I roar through the gag, but David yanks the flush, drowning me out. Then he slaps me. My cheek burns, and I want to cool it with my palm, but I can't because my hands are tied, so I rest it against the wall instead.

'Georgie?' David says.

'Who's in there?'

'Christ.' He splays his fingers against the panels. 'Tony. Go back downstairs, I'll be out in a minute.'

'I don't know who you think you are, but I need to use the bathroom. You can't just walk into people's houses and use their facilities. I've a good mind to call the police.'

'It's David, Tony. I'm not done yet. I'll come and find

you.' His voice has risen, and it sounds over-controlled. Fear slams back into me.

'David, dear boy, when did you arrive? I must tell Georgie. She'll be delighted.'

David rocks his head, pounding it slowly and silently against the door; once, twice, a third time, as if he's in despair. I take my chance, though I have no plan. I stand up, forgetting my knickers are round my ankles, and trip. David catches me, his hand like a vice on my arm.

'That's a good idea, Tony,' he says. 'Why don't you do that? Ask her to put the kettle on.' He turns and speaks to me in a whisper. 'By the time he gets downstairs he'll have forgotten what it was he wanted.' He smiles and to my horror I realize that he's pleading with me to see the humour in the situation.

We listen to Tony's slow progress, then David quietly draws the bolt and checks the coast is clear. He rearranges my clothes, and we go back upstairs, locked together like lovers. His body heat is almost feverish, and he reeks of sweat.

'This is unsustainable,' he says, tying my wrists to the bedpost. 'I need to go to work. I'll see that they're settled first and make sure that you're comfortable, but after that, you'll just have to wait.'

He leaves the room and comes back some time later, shaven and dressed in clean clothes, fresh from the shower. He looks almost normal again. There is something white and padded in his hands. I squirm, and he grips my legs to keep me still, then pulls me down the bed. I keep twisting and turning my body until his patience runs out and he forces my shoulders down, his face so close to mine I catch the spray of his spittle on my skin.

'For Christ's sake. Keep still. It's only a pair of incontinence pants, just in case . . . Well, you know.'

That does it for me. I turn my face to the wall and let him do what he wants. The pants are thick and hot. He arranges my dress over them, ties my ankles to the foot of the bed, tugs the eiderdown out from underneath me and covers me with it, then pulls more tape off the roll.

'Wait!' I say as he brings it to my mouth. 'Please. I need you to do something for me.'

'What do you want now? I'm in a hurry.'

'I need you to call Hoxton 101, where we had our Christmas party, and ask them who else hired the bar that night.'

I can't remember the name of Elliot's company, but I think I'll recognize it if I hear it. It's mad, under the circumstances, because it won't help even if it does confirm my suspicions, but I want to know. I need to know.

David is still holding the duct tape, pulling at the threads. 'Why?'

There's no harm in telling the truth. 'I think I may have worked out who it was, and if he was in the upstairs bar that evening, I'm right.' I allow a small sob to escape. 'I need to know who did this to me.'

The sock goes back in my mouth, the tape round my head. He secures me firmly and leaves the room. Minutes later, he comes up again, a screwdriver in his hand, and removes the doorknobs.

Will anyone at Gunner Munro notice that there's something wrong with him? Surely Rebecca will see that he's not right? She must know him inside out. I wonder how long it will take people to realize I'm missing. Thank God I promised Bettina I would be in, otherwise they might assume I've gone to Mum's to lick my wounds. It was what I was intending to do tomorrow. Poor Mum. Will they call her when they don't get an answer from me? She'll be so worried. More than anything else, I hate that I've done this to her.

Time passes, the light changes. Different birds sing different songs. The occasional car goes by and I hear voices, taps running, odd thumps and clatters. But nobody comes.

44

Rebecca

REBECCA PEERS UP AT THE FIRST-FLOOR WINDOW, HER neck craned. She rings the bell again, this time keeping her finger pressed on the buzzer. A woman pushes a pram towards her. She has bouncy, straightened hair and a pretty, heavily made-up face.

'Were you looking for Laura?' she asks. 'She'll be at work.' She unloops her bag from the pram handles and digs out her keys. 'Excuse me.'

'That's why I'm here,' Rebecca says, moving out of her way. 'I work with her. She hasn't turned up this morning, and she isn't answering her phone.'

'Oh. How odd.' The woman pushes the door open. 'Come in. Laura's flat is upstairs. Give me a shout if there's a problem. My name's Phoebe.'

Rebecca hesitates. This must be the neighbour who told Felicity about her and David. The one who Laura gossiped to. But now is not the time to get into an argument with a stranger. 'Rebecca Munro. I'm Laura's boss.'

Phoebe blushes. She knows what she's done.

'What about the bike?' Rebecca says.

'It's Laura's.'

Rebecca goes up, noticing that Phoebe is loitering, flicking through a property magazine. She lifts her eyebrows and turns to knock, calling Laura's name. When nothing happens, she leans over the banister.

'I don't suppose you have a key?'

'No, sorry.'

She chews her bottom lip, then palms her mobile, pulling her hair away from her ear. 'Agnes, it's Rebecca. I'm not getting a response at the flat and her curtains are closed. Her bike's still here.' She glances at Phoebe, cupping her hand over the phone. 'Is that normal?'

'She occasionally goes by tube, but mostly takes her bike.'

'Apparently, it's not that unusual,' she relays to Agnes. 'What number do you have for her emergency contact? OK. Would you call her mum and check she's not there? If she isn't, I'm going to call the police . . . Yes. I'll wait.'

'Why don't you come in.' Phoebe indicates her door. 'I'll make us a cup of tea. It's freezing out here.'

Phoebe deposits her child in his high chair and gives him his lunch, while Rebecca scrolls through her messages and pretends to be amused by the child's babble. She doesn't feel comfortable with all that, although she assumes it will come when she has her own baby. Her baby will be different – but not too different. She touches her stomach as Phoebe bustles around, tidying up and wiping surfaces, and tries to imagine how her life will feel if this happens to her.

'I'm worried about her,' Phoebe says, glancing up at the ceiling. 'She's had some difficulties this year. How much did she drink last night?'

'I don't know. I had other things to think about.' Like the fact that David was livid, because this dopey woman had told his wife about them. She keeps her temper. 'Some of the guests went on to a club after the party ended. Laura may have done, but I doubt it. It wouldn't have been in character. I don't know. This isn't like her.'

'What if she's choked on her own vomit?'

They look at each other. 'I think we should call the police now,' Phoebe says. The baby whinges in her arms, twisting round, eyes wide.

Rebecca is already on it. She calls 999 and tells the operator that she thinks her friend might have collapsed and they need to break into her flat. She runs back upstairs and bangs on the door again.

'What's the lady's name, ma'am?' Logan asks. The police constable's eyes have already dropped once to her chest and he's struggling to avoid it now.

'Laura Maguire.'

They have crowded on to the landing outside Laura's door; two officers, two paramedics and Rebecca, Phoebe and a fascinated, squirming baby. Rebecca backs into the corner, reaching out to pull Phoebe with her.

Logan, who seems young to her, his skin pink and smooth, his brow unlined, thumps the side of his fist against the door and shouts Laura's name, then tells anyone who is listening on the other side that he's going to break in. They wait, pressed back against the wall, holding their breath, as he takes a step back and throws his weight against it. The lock splinters and, after two more tries, gives with a crack.

'No one on the premises.' PC Mughal speaks into her radio. 'There are signs of a struggle in the bedroom and hallway and the owner hasn't turned up for work. Yes. Female, late twenties. Can we have a SOCO here? Thanks.' She turns to Rebecca and Phoebe. 'Have either of you been in the flat before?'

'I have,' Phoebe says.

'Perhaps you could take a look and tell us if anything strikes you as out of place. This is a crime scene, so I'd ask you not to touch anything.'

Phoebe hesitates. 'Do you think something's happened?'

'I don't know.' Mughal moves aside to let both women pass. The baby reaches for her badge.

The lights are on, but they haven't opened the curtains and the flat is gloomy and airless. She and Phoebe tackle the bedroom first. The bed looks like Laura left it in a hurry, the duvet banked up against the wall. Her bedside light has been knocked over. Two of the pillows are on the floor and a glass of water has been spilled, leaving a dark patch on the carpet. The hairs rise on the back of Rebecca's neck.

'This isn't right,' Phoebe says.

'Is she untidy?' Mughal asks.

'Not particularly. She leaves things lying around, in the same way any normal person does; shoes and books, stuff like that.'

They move into the sitting room. Here it all looks as Rebecca would expect, lived in but not chaotic. Her laptop is on the table. Surely that would have gone if there had been a burglary?

'Is anything missing?' Logan asks.

'Not that I can see,' Phoebe says. 'Oh, but . . .' She indicates a bag, collapsed in a hump of floppy brown leather, like a sleeping otter. 'She would have taken that.'

Logan takes a fork out of the drawer and carefully lifts it open, shining his torch inside and nudging the contents.

'Phone's here.'

He speaks into his walkie-talkie and it crackles in response. He breaks off to suggest the women go back downstairs.

The officers decline Phoebe's offer of hot drinks. Logan sits down at the kitchen table, but Mughal moves around the room. She spends a long time peering out into the garden then asks if she can use the toilet.

'When did you last see Ms Maguire?' Logan says.

'Last night,' Rebecca replies. 'We had a work function. She was one of the last to leave.'

'She left with my husband,' Phoebe explains.

Rebecca sends her a swift, questioning glance. 'You didn't . . .'

Phoebe interrupts swiftly. 'Laura invited us both, but I couldn't go because my sister went into labour and I had to spend the night at her place with my nephew. Elliot and Laura came home in a taxi together and then he joined me at Harriet's, rather than stay here on his own.'

Rebecca stares. Does she realize her husband may well have been the last to see Laura? The significance is not lost on the officers, who note it down and then wait a couple of beats before the next question.

'Where does she work?'

'Gunner Munro in Hoxton,' Rebecca replies. 'It's an advertising agency. Today was supposed to be her last.'

'What do you think's happened to her?' Phoebe asks.

'Probably nothing. But we're treating it as possible abduction, given the element of chaos in her bedroom and the fact that her phone is still in the sitting room.'

'Oh God.'

The baby grizzles. Phoebe bounces him on her knee, but it only distracts him for a few seconds before his face crumples and he starts to cry in earnest.

'Laura is face-blind,' Rebecca says.

'Beg your pardon?'

She takes a deep breath, truly understanding, perhaps for the first time, Laura's difficulties. It's a tough concept to explain. She does her best.

'She has a condition called prosopagnosia. Face-blindness, to you and me. She's unable to recognize people. It's common to have it to a lesser degree, apparently, but Laura is profoundly face-blind.'

'Oh yeah, I've heard of that,' Mughal says.

'Oh my God,' Phoebe squeaks, startling the baby. 'Elliot has a cousin who has it. I met her at a wedding. It was weird. We talked for ages, then I went off to have a dance with Elliot and when I sat next to her again, it was like we'd never had a conversation. She was so embarrassed. She said it was because my hair had come out of its clip and I'd wrapped my pashmina round my shoulders, so she didn't recognize me. Apparently, Elliot used to play tricks on her when they were children.'

At the end of this story there's an odd silence, broken only by a sneeze from Noah.

'Do many people know about Laura's face-blindness?' Logan asks.

Rebecca shrugs. 'I can only tell you what she told me. Her immediate family knows, and I'm the only one at Gunner Munro. Sufferers tend to keep quiet about it. It's understandable. If you publicize the fact that you don't recognize anyone, there's a certain type of unpleasant person who might take advantage of that. She told me when she first started. I made it clear that we wouldn't make allowances – any more than we would for dyslexic employees.' She feels bad. She should have been easier on her.

'Do you think her disappearance has something to do with it?' Phoebe asks.

Rebecca tries to catch her eye, but she's focused on her child. Her cheeks are a warm shade of pink.

Mughal glances down at her notes again. 'I have no idea, but it might be worth looking into.'

'From what I understand,' Rebecca says, 'it's entirely possible that she could have gone off with someone, thinking he was someone else.'

'Surely if you think you know somebody well enough to get into their car, there must be something you recognize about them?' Phoebe says. 'Their aftershave, the way they speak . . .'

'Voices don't help much apparently. But you're right,

there are other things; context is incredibly important, as is hair, although that isn't always reliable, and Laura told me gait is useful. But it depends on the situation. If she was drunk, it might be that the same things wouldn't apply.'

Logan shifts his gaze to Phoebe. 'Perhaps Mr Hill could shed some light on her state of mind last night?'

'I'll give you his number.' She needs to raise her voice to be heard above Noah's wailing. 'Sorry about that. He's tired.'

'Not at all. Thank you for your help, young man.'

Noah, surprised at being directly addressed, goes quiet for a full five seconds. Rebecca holds her breath.

Logan takes the scrap of paper from Phoebe and snaps his notebook shut. 'The SOCO team will be here later.' He gives them both one of his cards. 'But call me if she reappears in the meantime. Oh, and,' he adds, 'this is purely routine, nothing to worry about, but we'll need the clothes your husband was wearing.'

Phoebe moves quickly, shaky but smiling, eager to be helpful. 'They're all in here.' She pulls a carrier bag from underneath the pram. It's packed tight and takes a bit of manipulation to dislodge. 'I brought a change of clothes to my sister's place, in case he came over. Good thing I did.'

When they leave, Phoebe takes their mugs to the sink and turns on the taps. Without looking at Rebecca, she says, 'What I said about Elliot's cousin, right? It doesn't mean he had anything to do with this. He was with me.'

45

Rebecca

THERE'S A KNOCK. REBECCA LIFTS HER HEAD, ENQUIRingly, as Agnes walks in. David pushes his chair back and swivels it. Eddie and Jamie pick up their phones, as if they're expecting to be dismissed. They've been talking about the campaign, but the whole meeting has been tinged with worry about Laura. Eddie and Jamie have been tight-lipped and strained, both of them on edge, jumping at the sound of a phone or a door slamming. Once, Jamie leapt up as a taxi slowed in the street.

Rebecca has something else on her mind now. Before she returned to the office, she nipped home and used the pregnancy test in the tranquillity of her bathroom. She sat staring at the test stick, scared to blink, watching for the blue line to appear. When it did, she put her hand to her mouth and cried out. Pregnant. She was pregnant. Her body was on her side after all. She couldn't move; her smile stretched so far it ached. She touched her stomach, placed both hands on it, fingers splayed, and breathed, 'Thank you. Thank you.'

She has decided not to tell David yet. It's far too soon and it would be selfish to celebrate when a woman is missing and possibly in danger. And she's worried about how he'll react.

'Agnes,' Rebecca says now. 'What can we do for you?'

David had pitched up looking terrible, just as she got back from Laura's flat. She cut him some slack, even though he didn't apologize; he rarely does. She's worried. Throughout the morning she's been sensing something; an invisible energy gathering force. He is as concerned as she is about Laura, especially now that she's told him Laura's secret. She feels a twinge of guilt about betraying her trust, but what else could she do under the circumstances? He'd been angry that he hadn't been told before about her condition, but his unsettling mood seems to be about something else. The Laura situation is a distraction, an added stress, not the root of it.

'There are two police officers wanting to speak to you,' Agnes says.

Her voice is level, but there is anxiety in the way her glance flits between the two of them. Rebecca wonders if she knows about them. Rebecca is hyper-sensitive to changes in the atmosphere and is almost certain that news of their affair has leaked into the building, moved through the walls to pool amongst their employees, that the air smells of it. She has intercepted covert glances.

Agnes doesn't listen to office gossip, but when something breaks, when it starts to skip from desk to desk like a flat stone on a still lake, there's no getting away from it. Or maybe she's always known.

Actually, Rebecca realizes with a stab of guilt at her

own selfishness, it's far more likely that she's merely concerned about Laura. She doubts Agnes gives two hoots about what Rebecca and David get up to.

'Ask them to come in. Have you offered them coffee?'

'Yes. They declined.'

Jamie and Eddie get up. She watches them search Logan's face as they pass him in the doorway.

Once alone, she introduces Logan and Mughal to David. David lays on the Gunner charm.

'How can we help? We're naturally very concerned about Laura.'

Logan glances Rebecca's way. 'We've spoken to her mother. Apparently, Laura told her there was someone she was interested in. Someone here. Do you have any idea?'

Rebecca rests her elbows on the table and rubs her forehead. Should she mention Jamie? If his mood this morning is anything to go by, he obviously cares. But then so does Eddie, so do they all. And last night it was definitely Bettina he was interested in. 'I don't think so. But she's a very private person so I don't know anything about her romantic life or her friendships outside work.'

'Eddie might know more,' David says.

'Eddie?' Logan looks down at his notes. 'Edward King?'

'Eddie is . . . was . . . her creative partner. They've worked together for three years; if anyone knows her well, it would be him. He's one of the guys who was in the room with us when you arrived. I can get him back if you like.'

'We'll definitely be talking to him, but there're a few more questions I'd like to put to you two first.'

Logan is respectful, but Rebecca senses a surprising edge of steel for one so fresh-faced. He is immune to David's charm, has probably met his type before, men who think they can get one over on him because they are more successful. She glances at David, but he doesn't catch her eye.

Agnes brings Laura's file in and hands it to Rebecca, then backs out. Her face is marvellously neutral. Rebecca passes it on to Logan, who opens it and quickly scans the information. Everyone they employ, from the two of them down to the cleaners, will have filled out a form detailing any medical issues – allergies, prescriptions, that kind of thing – and listed an emergency contact number. Laura, she notices, reading upside down, has written N/A beside Chronic Health Problems.

'Nothing about her face-blindness in here,' Logan says. He moves it across to Mughal.

'Well, technically, it's a learning difficulty, not a medical condition,' Rebecca says.

Logan drums his fingers on the table. 'You held an event last night.'

'Yes,' David replies. 'We were launching a campaign.'

'Laura organized it,' Rebecca says.

'Did you notice anything odd about her behaviour? Was she upset, or tense?'

'She was upset because she was leaving, but she behaved professionally. She was very busy, but she seemed to be coping well. I left before her. And you did too, didn't you, David?'

David nods. He looks thoughtful. 'I didn't like that guy she invited. Some friend of hers.'

Logan glances at his notes. 'Do you mean Elliot Hill?'

'I don't know what his name was.'

'But you disliked him. Why was that, sir?'

David rotates his head, stretching out the kinks. 'Bit of a tosser. Too pleased with himself.'

And you're not? Rebecca thinks, wincing at his language.

Logan and Mughal watch him in silence, waiting for more.

'What exactly did you base your opinion on?' Logan says. He holds his ballpoint poised over the paper, as if this piece of information is too important not to note down.

David flushes. 'You got me there. Nothing. A gut feeling. For all I know, he's a perfectly decent bloke.'

The atmosphere relaxes somewhat. The two officers signal that they've finished with them for now, pushing back their chairs.

'Thank you both for your time. We'd like to have a chat with everyone at that party, if you could supply us with a list.'

'Agnes can do that,' Rebecca says.

'We'll start with Edward King. Is there a private room we could use?'

Every five to ten minutes, someone passes Rebecca's window on their way to take their turn. Bettina glances in and catches her eye. She doesn't return for twenty minutes, taking much longer than anyone else, and when she does, she knocks on David's door. He's needed again.

Rebecca waits for him to come back, and as soon as she spots him, she walks into his office. He has his phone in his hand, but he puts it down when he sees her.

'What happened?'

He rubs his fingers through his hair and stifles a yawn. A nerve flutters under his right eye.

'You'll know soon enough, so I might as well tell you.'

But he doesn't. He bows his head and she thinks he might have nodded off. She rests her hand on his shoulder then removes it quickly. She made the gesture without thinking. That's not like her.

'What is it?' she asks.

'I had a row with Laura out in the alleyway behind the venue, when we were taking the rubbish out. Bettina witnessed it. She felt she had to tell the police.'

'A row? What about?'

'About the circumstances of her resignation. She accused me of letting her down. Apparently, I should have stuck up for her, not made her feel small.'

'You should have.'

'Whatever. She said she'd had no option but to resign, that I shouldn't have accepted it. She was angry and unreasonable. I went on the defensive and told her a few home truths. Bettina interrupted just as it was getting nasty.'

'And you told them all that?'

'I didn't have an option. But Laura went back inside, and that was the end of it. And we all know she left with Elliot. There's no secret about that.'

'You shouldn't have let it get that far, David. You should have tried to take the heat out of it, even if it meant shouldering some of the blame.'

'I know that now,' he snaps. 'Sorry.' He holds up his hands. 'You're right. And now I feel guilty because we parted on a bad note. I meant to apologize to her today but . . . Well, obviously she's not here.' He sighs. 'I feel like a jerk. Jesus, I don't need this right now . . .'

She waits a moment. 'Are you OK?'

He laughs brusquely. 'I'm not going to lose it again, if that's what you're worried about.'

'Of course I'm worried. Wouldn't you be if it was me? Listen, David, deal with one thing at a time. Get Tony and Georgie settled into a home, so that you can focus again. And for God's sake get some sleep tonight. You look terrible.'

'Yeah, well, living under the same roof as those two has its challenges.'

'You've only been there one night.'

'Long enough. They have my undying devotion, but I'm no good as a carer. I contacted another residential home yesterday and set up a meeting for tomorrow morning. It costs an arm and a leg, but the most important thing is that they remain together.'

'How long are you going to stay with them?'

'If I can move them next week, I'll rent a place in town. If not, I'll have to rethink; maybe try live-in carers again. Either way, I can't stay there; the broadband provision is crap.'

'Can I come and see you?' That was stupid. She shouldn't have asked.

He takes her hand and looks deep into her eyes. 'Not yet, my love. I need some time on my own. You understand, don't you? There's too much going on.'

She says coolly, 'Well, as long as it doesn't affect the business.'

'Of course not. You know me better than that.'

Does she? She is beginning to wonder. There's so much at stake. GZ is going to begin casting for the TV commercial next week and he's said he will be there, as well as at the pre-production meetings and the tech recce. He'll want to show his face at the shoot and at post-production. David is constitutionally incapable of taking a back seat, and now that he's being forced to do so because of circumstances not entirely under his control, it's affecting him. But she can't tell him what to do. All she can do is cross her fingers and hope he keeps it together.

46

Laura

MY BODY JERKS AS I FALL OUT OF MY DREAM. I LIE still, waking properly, allowing the sounds and smells to register, only opening my eyes once I've told myself what to expect. In my dreams, I always know who people are, because I put them there. In this one Elliot Hill was in my flat, holding me in his arms. When I fell, it was because he had dropped me.

The pillow is peculiarly pungent, but trussed up like this, there is no getting away from it. My wrists are chafed from trying to work them loose, my throat sore from the effort to be heard. I'm shivering with cold.

It started to rain while I was sleeping, the drumming amplified because I'm under the roof. For a while, it drowns out the other noises this house makes: the creak of floorboards, the clunk of elderly plumbing and the television's muted hum. I have no idea what time it is, even if it's the same day. I think I only nodded off for a few minutes, but I suppose I could have been asleep for hours. It's dark outside, but then it's dark by around five at this time of year, and the darkness is deeper in the countryside.

David rarely leaves the office till after eight. Sometimes later. I hope he'll make an exception today. My stomach aches from holding on to my bladder, but I refuse to pee into a nappy. It would be like giving up.

I'm alert to the old couple's movements, but as far as I know they haven't come upstairs. I think they would have disturbed my sleep if they had. I doubt they come up here much these days. I close my eyes and try to drift off, but I can hear the old man. Sometimes he doesn't know where she's gone and calls out a mournful, 'Georgie, Georgie. Where are you, dear? Georgie?' He can go on like that for upwards of fifteen minutes, until she reveals herself. Then he gets reproachful and she becomes angry and defensive. Her language is quite something. Even worse than David's.

I go still, holding my breath. They are making their way upstairs. Every step they take is laboured. They stop to argue, Tony wanting to wait until David gets home, Georgie barking at him and calling him wet. They finally reach the landing outside my door, one of them breathing hard. I jolt my body to rock the bed. Every time I move it hurts but I ignore the pain and keep rocking and eventually the metal spoke which normally holds the door handle jiggles.

'Is David here?' Tony says. 'When did he get back?'

'He must have let himself in.'

'Not like him not to say hello.'

'He'll be in one of his moods.'

They confer for a while, even giving the door a

tentative push. Then Georgie says, 'I'll put his supper on. He can come down when he's ready to be pleasant.'

When they leave, I groan in despair. My mouth aches, I'm hungry and thirsty and every so often I get an agonizing cramp in my left calf. Tears make my nose tickle which means rubbing it against the musty pillow.

I hear the owl hoot. It starts to rain again, the wind occasionally turning and flinging it against the window panes in a sharp scatter that makes my nerves leap. The later it becomes the more noises develop, old rafters creaking, pipes knocking. I even think I hear something scurry across the floor. A mouse?

Am I right about Elliot? I met him on the tube that afternoon, and he told me that he worked close by. He also told me that he used to play practical jokes on his brothers. What if, on the night of the twenty-second of December, he was there, on the street, and decided to try his luck? What if the whole thing was a joke gone wrong? Or what if he just wanted to see how much he could push it; how close he could get to me?

Five minutes before David's headlights sweep across the window, I give up the struggle and urinate. The warmth permeates the pad but leaves me feeling wet and uncomfortable. I've lost.

I log all the sounds he makes; his car door locking; his steps on the gravel; the jangle of keys. He lets himself in and the house seems to give a little cough when he closes the door. I hear him clattering around in the kitchen, talking to his grandparents. After what feels like an hour but is probably only half that time, he comes up and fits the doorknob back on, then brings in a tray and sets it down on the bedside cabinet. When he switches on the light it momentarily blinds me. Once I can see, I stare at him, itemizing details about his hair, his separate features, his jawline, his hands. I will never make assumptions again.

'Are you going to scream?'

I shake my head and he ungags me.

'Water!'

'Here.'

His hands tremble as he holds the glass to my lips and I drink my fill, spilling half of it down my chin. There's toast and baked beans on the tray, a feast as far as I'm concerned. He unties my wrists and ankles from the bedposts but not from each other and sits me up so that he can feed me. When he's done, he wipes my mouth with a pale pink fabric napkin with tiny flowers embroidered in one corner.

'What are you going to do with me?'

'I don't want to talk about it.'

He has a tic. It forces me to focus on his features. It's under his right eye and every so often it flickers into life, like there's an insect trapped under the skin.

'Surely it would be better to turn yourself in and be charged with manslaughter than to make things worse by keeping me here.' My chest starts to rise and fall, my breath shortening. 'Are you going to hurt me?'

'I don't want to hurt anyone.' He shrinks into himself, his shoulders hunching and curving forward. He makes a wrenching sound; somewhere between a croak and a sob.

I wonder what we both mean by *hurt*. I'm scared to

think about the options playing through his mind but maintaining the status quo can't be one of them. He can't keep me locked up here for ever. The way I see it, he has drunk-driven himself into a nightmare from which he can see no escape. He is responsible for the death of a young man and he's abducted me, and as far as he is concerned there is no way of undoing the damage. He's desperate, anyone can see that, so, surely, all I need do is show him a way out?

'This is not who you are, David. Let me go, and I promise, if you own up to Guy, I won't mention this.' I know he doesn't believe I'd keep quiet about Guy, so it would be a waste of energy trying to convince him. 'I'll say I went away to get my head together.'

He wipes his forearm across his face and stands up. 'I can't do it. You're asking me to lose everything I've worked for and everyone I love. People will hate and despise me. If I have to go to court, I'd rather kill myself.' The tic flutters again. 'My kids . . . what do you think that would do to them? No, I can make this go away.'

'By making me go away?'

His gaze shifts over my shoulder. He can't look at me. Finally, he says it. 'Yes.'

I lean forward, bowing my head over my knees. My shoulders are aching, my hands have intermittent pins and needles. I cry, and he puts his hand on the back of my head, like he's giving the Benediction. My bladder muscles pick that moment to let me down again.

'I've wet myself.'

When he unties my ankles to change the incontinence pants, I jerk my knees up and kick out, catching him on the jaw. He reels, but rights himself quickly and grasps my neck, forcing me back down on to the pillows. We stare at each other, panting. His free hand is tucked under my armpit, his forearm close to brushing my breast, his knee hard between my legs. Then he abruptly releases me.

'Did you do what I asked you? Did you ring the club?' I mumble. I don't know why I still want to know, it all seems so futile now.

He picks up the damp sock he uses to gag me. 'For Christ's sake. I've got enough on my mind.'

I sink back on to the bed, open my mouth for the sock and close my eyes.

47

Rebecca

Concern is growing for twenty-nine-year-old Laura Maguire. Miss Maguire lives in Kentish Town and was last seen entering her flat at eleven thirty-five p.m. on Thursday the eighth of February, after a night out in Dalston. Miss Maguire works for the advertising agency Gunner Munro, the same company that employed Christmas hit-and-run victim Guy Holt. The police have declined to comment on this connection. If you have any information, please call the number below. Miss Maguire has recently cut her hair short and sometimes wears glasses.

Rebecca perches on the edge of her sofa, repainting her toenails and staring at Laura's face on the screen. She has long hair in the picture, so no one has taken one of her since it was cut. That's odd; everyone documents their lives these days, don't they? She's smiling for the camera, her eyes sparkling. The photo vanishes, and her mother appears, looking tired and anxious, blonde hair tied back, silver-and-jade earrings dangling like dream-catchers. She says the usual things: 'Laura is such a loving person. She's a wonderful aunt to her nieces and nephews.'

To Rebecca that is shorthand for *doesn't have anyone in her life right now*. She feels a pang of sympathy.

'Laura, if you're watching this, please get in touch. We miss you.'

Jenny Maguire stares at the camera, reminding Rebecca of the way Laura would sometimes look at her, as though she was trying to fix her face in her head.

Her imagination starts to work; picturing Laura's body in the woods, half-covered with leaves, or washed up on the banks of the Thames. Everyone is trained by the media to think the worst these days. She shuts down the news page and silence falls. She checks the time on her phone. She is meeting David at half past two for a late lunch because he's visiting the care home this morning. It was a minor victory, getting him to agree, but part of her thinks he seized the excuse to get away from his grandparents for a few hours. No matter. He agreed and that's what counts.

The toenails are possibly over-optimistic, but she believes firmly in the whole-woman approach and she has never yet failed to seduce him. Once her nails are dry she pulls on a pair of black, high-heeled boots, and checks the contents of her bag. While she waits for her car she practises her breathing and tells herself that she is strong and beautiful and wise, and that David needs her now more than ever. She cups her hand over her belly. She'll tell him at twelve weeks, once she knows it's safe. There are seven weeks to go until then, and a lot can happen in that time.

The news comes on as she is being driven past Regent's Park. Laura isn't the first item – the US president has that honour – but she is the second. Rebecca searches the faces of the women she sees hurrying along the pavement. She has never thought about the logistics of looking for someone before; but the sheer number of square acres, the confusing choices, the eliminations and grunt work it must take, is breathtaking. Laura is somewhere; that's all anyone knows. Somewhere.

'It'll be someone she knows,' the driver says. 'It always is. Boyfriend or neighbour.'

'Could you switch that off? I'm trying to think.' She has her MacBook on her knee, open on a casting agency website to which she has paid scant attention.

He glances at her in the mirror, then does as he's asked, adding a quick, 'Ten-to-one they find it's a dodgy uncle.' Like a child determined to have the last word.

That's the downside of having an account. You get the same drivers and they think they know you. Rebecca doesn't respond. She feels a flutter of anxiety and thinks, *Poor Laura. Please let her be found safe and well.*

The cab drops her at the Carlyon Hotel in Kensington. David's car is parked on the street. She flicks her hair back over her shoulders, smooths down her trench coat, takes a deep, calming breath and walks through the minimalist foyer to the restaurant, nodding a friendly greeting at the black-clad receptionists. It's busy but intimate, candles lit even at this time of day, and redolent of luxury and money. She can't help wondering if the fact that this is the first restaurant he took her to after their affair began, is a good omen. Back then he had booked a room for the night.

David is reading a newspaper at a table at the far end. The sight of him gives her an illicit thrill. It's the thought of the challenge. He doesn't see her until she is at his side, but then he glances up, smiles and leaps to his feet. He doesn't look good, she notes as she hands her coat to the greeter and refuses the offer to relieve her of her hefty bag. He has shaved clumsily, his eyes are shadowed, his lips chapped, and the collar of his shirt is dirty. In all the time she has known him, David has never worn the same shirt for more than one day. A chair is pulled out for her, and she sits down.

David has a pale lager in front of him. He starts to fold his newspaper, but she takes it from him. He's been reading about Laura. The photograph is the one used on television, photoshopped to show what she would look like with short hair.

'It's grim, isn't it,' she says. 'And you know what makes me feel bad? I know so little about her. Not much more than the police. I've never asked about her personal life, and she's never told me anything.'

'That's not your fault. Some people like to guard their privacy.'

She hands it back. 'Do you think she had secrets? I mean, beyond her condition, obviously.' And that's no secret any more.

'We all do, don't we?'

Rebecca shrugs. 'I hope to God she's all right. I keep imagining the worst. When someone disappears like that, they're usually dead.'

'Don't be ridiculous. That's just headlines. She might see the news and walk into a police station today. She might be on her way back home now.'

'I hope so.'

She scans the menu, hands damp with perspiration. She wipes them surreptitiously on her napkin. David is preoccupied; as twitchy as she is, his brow knitted as he glances over her shoulder, looking for a waitress.

'How was the home?'

'The what?'

'The care home, David. Didn't you tell me you were going to visit one this morning?'

'Sorry. It was fine. The staff seemed to be genuinely compassionate, which is the main thing as far as I'm concerned. It's an old manor house, surrounded by landscaped gardens. They've got everything: arts and crafts, tea dances and every kind of therapy. I've booked them in on Monday, for a trial fortnight.'

'A trial?'

He grimaces. 'Yes. Clients need to show that they can benefit from being there and won't unsettle the other residents. I'm not stupid. It's shorthand for good behaviour; three strikes and you're out. Pity I can't tell Tony and Georgie that. All I can do is keep my fingers crossed.'

She nods. After the egg incident, they both know how vain a hope that is.

They discuss the problem until their food arrives. Rebecca is having the fish soup with chunky artisan bread drizzled in olive oil and crusted with sea salt, and David, the organic lamb. She declines a glass of wine and asks for fizzy water, expecting him to comment, but the significance of her abstemiousness goes over his head. They don't speak while they eat, and the silence grows until it becomes uncomfortable. Rebecca puts down her spoon and dabs her lips with her napkin. She can't finish it. David glances at her, then looks back at his plate, his focus entirely on his lunch. She watches him chew and swallow.

'I went to see Felicity.'

'What in Christ's name did you do that for?'

She bristles. 'Because I needed to, and I thought she needed to see me. I wanted to give her a chance to say what she had to. We go back a long way. She was my closest friend.'

'You don't have close friends.'

'Right. Thanks, David. That really helps.'

She's all over the place. It's Laura and the baby and her ruined friendship; but mostly the baby. It's astonishing how quickly it has become an entity, a warm-blooded thing whose life she is wholly invested in. She is already awash with emotion.

'Are you feeling sorry for yourself?'

She pauses, watching him. 'No. Are you?'

He looks straight into her eyes. 'No.'

He is, actually. This is all about him; the way he is feeling; the way people are going to perceive him henceforth. His wife has found him out. The man who loves to be loved is going to be an object of hatred to some of his friends, to his adoring in-laws, maybe even to his children, if he isn't careful. The only people who will still love him are fools like her who are prepared to catch him when he falls, and his grandparents. And it looks like they won't know who he is for much longer.

'What are you going to do?' she asks.

'I haven't made a decision yet.'

She feels as though she is picking her way along a path strewn with broken glass. 'You must know what you want.'

'It's what you want that matters, Rebecca.'

She doesn't believe the platitude, but she answers as if she does. 'I want to be with you. I always have.'

He scratches the side of his neck and sits back, but not before popping the last morsel of meat into his mouth. She finds it galling that he can eat at a time like this.

'I owe you honesty,' he says, still chewing. 'So, I'm telling you this. I've worked out what really matters and I'm sorry, but it's my family. You and I will always have a strong bond and I will treasure what we've had together, but that side of things must end. It's taken the shock of being thrown out to show me what I stand to lose. I've taken them for granted for too long.'

That was quite a speech. It takes a moment to process.

'You're dumping me?' She's always known it's a possibility, but still, it isn't an outcome she's ever seriously entertained. She's incredulous.

'Don't say it like that.'

He reaches across the table and takes her hand, tightening his hold when she tries to tug it out of his grip.

This isn't right, she thinks. *This is me: Rebecca Munro. I am extraordinary. He doesn't get to treat me this way.*

'We're here because you don't want a scene,' she says.

He hasn't chosen this place for a romantic meal followed by reconciliation sex in one of the sumptuous bedrooms, he has chosen it because of its reverent and monastic atmosphere. This is not a place to raise your voice.

He doesn't respond. What is there to say? It's so obvious, it's laughable. The man she has loved for so long is a coward. She has been set adrift, and he's putting his coat on and calling the waiter over with an arrogant click of his fingers.

'Bill please. Can I drop you somewhere?' he adds.

It's a punch in the gut. 'No, thank you.' Her voice is stiff and unnatural, as is the way she is sitting, as if she is about to leap up, one hand gripped round the strap of her bag, the other clenched, white-knuckled, on the back of the chair.

'Don't be like that, love. You know how I feel about you. If it hadn't come out, we could have carried on indefinitely, but I've got too much on my plate right now.' His face clouds. 'I'm not dealing with all this particularly well.'

He gazes into her eyes and despite the red rims and the shadows underneath, despite the deepening lines around his mouth, she feels nothing except an abject desire to throw herself at his feet. She is horrified at herself, disgusted. She should be walking away with her head held high.

She remembers the day her father finally had enough and left her mother. She remembers how, as a ten-year-old, she begged him not to go. Literally got down on her knees. She is not doing that again. She'll wait and pick her moment. It isn't over.

He bends and kisses her on the cheek, lingering. 'I'm sorry I can't be the person you want me to be, but it's all I can do to keep the company running and stop myself going insane. I need my marriage and my home, and, much as it pains me, I have to sacrifice us. It doesn't mean I don't care. It doesn't mean I won't miss you desperately.'

God, he still expects her to make him feel better. 'Save it, David.'

She marches up to a waitress and demands her coat. She is not going to beg or humiliate herself further. He is going to regret leaving her. Felicity can't give him what he craves. Does he imagine he'll be content with that? Will he tell his wife he gets off on being punished? She doubts it.

48

Laura

'THE BAR WAS HIRED BY A COMPANY CALLED IDTECH Solutions,' David says. 'Does that tell you what you wanted to know?'

I hang my head. So, there it is. Elliot Hill. It makes perfect sense; why he didn't want Phoebe to get involved with me, his ambivalence towards me; the way he kissed me on the night of the GZ party. How could I have been so stupid? I could kick myself for not realizing the moment he told me where he worked. He's been stalking me, probably for as long as they've lived in the flat. I wonder how it started. Did I fail to acknowledge him once too often? Did he set traps to see if his hunch was right? Does he know someone else who suffers from face-blindness to the degree I do? Did he pay attention to the media coverage a couple of years ago when a celebrity admitted to having the condition?

I look up and nod.

'I'm sorry,' he says. 'I'm sorry that happened to you, and I'm even more sorry that you thought it was me. I don't know what's happened to my life.' He sits down on the edge of the bed and pats my leg, as though I'm a dog. 'I want you to know that if I could do anything to turn the clock back, I would.'

He won't look at me. Do people ever look hard at those they intend to kill? You'd have to be pretty cold to look into the face of your victim, into her eyes and her soul. I am so tired and wretched, so damp and sore. Part of me wishes he'd get it over with; because no one is going to come.

Two more nights pass. By now the room smells of sweat and urine and I don't know what else. Something pungent: a combination of mice and damp perhaps. Whatever; it's revolting. It's still dark but it could be one in the morning or it could be five. The house is quiet, its occupants either asleep or brooding.

Dawn leaches in, grey and murky, cheered only by the competing songs of a robin and a blackbird. My musical ear is better than my ear for voices and I can distinguish birdsong with remarkable accuracy, given the opportunity to concentrate and I've had plenty of that recently.

The morning gropes its way inside. The room has become so familiar that I could describe it with my eyes closed. I know every cobweb, every crack in the ceiling, every forgotten possession.

Downstairs someone is getting up. The tap runs, and the pipes knock.

Voices. Tony and Georgie tentatively embracing the day, not sure which decade of their lives they are in. I imagine them slowly adjusting, coming downstairs to find a thirty-something David instead of their teenage grandson. I hope they never find out what he's done.

Another half hour passes before David comes in. He gives me breakfast, Weetabix again; not much of a last meal. What time does he intend to kill me?

I beg. I say, 'Please, David. Please, please. Let me go. I promise you I won't say a word. Don't do this!'

But his expression is blank, as though he's absented himself, emotionally detached himself from the reality of me; my humanity, my warm body, my mind, my beating heart.

It sounds as though he's dragging cases out to the car and heaving them in. Next time he leaves the house, he's with his grandparents, wheedling and promising, his patience wafer thin.

Hours later he's back. I recognize the engine's hum even before the wheels touch the gravel. I know the sound as it slows to take the corner. I can predict the clean and satisfying thunk of the door thudding shut. I know how many steps it is from car to door and the sound of David's key in the lock. I know the moment of stillness before Georgie and Tony go into a twitter, and how he will soothe and reassure them. But this time, I don't hear them, and I realize he's returned alone. The house is empty but for me and him.

I know his footstep on the bottom stair.

I spit and whip my head from side to side as water and chemicals bubble in my throat. David holds me down with a hand on my shoulder, the other over my mouth, but I'm like a fish, writhing and slippery, unable to think clearly. Some of the pills have gone down, David posting them one at a time, pressing them through my closed lips and clenched teeth, then clamping his hand down again.

He shoves a cloth in my mouth, poking in more and more of it until it's so tightly packed that I gag. Pills that I've kept, hamster-like, in my cheeks are dissolving. I try to get at them with my tongue, to push out the bitter, chalky residue.

Veins pulse at David's temples as he struggles to contain me. He probably imagined a more passive victim. Best-laid plans, as Rebecca once said. Without warning, he drops down on to the floor and folds himself over, and I think that he might be having a stroke, but he clasps his hands behind his neck and rocks. Even in my terror I can guess what he's feeling; the shock at how fast events have moved, the desperation to salvage his life and his good name. If I wasn't so scared, I would feel sorry for him. I think he's realized that, whatever happens today, even if it goes his way, he will never get out of this.

The phone rings and I recognize the ringtone from his mobile. He kneels in the middle of the room, completely still, staring at the door, reminding me of the lemurs in London Zoo. When it stops, the landline starts up and again he doesn't move. It rings on and on, echoing through the house, a lonely sound that captures my desperation in its rhythm.

49

Rebecca

SOMEONE IS SHOUTING OUTSIDE HER OFFICE. REBECCA ignores it. She has been picking her way through the budget proposals that the cost controller sent her. She is not impressed with him – he's little more than an accountant and doesn't always understand the workings of this industry. She makes a note to suggest cutting the build and prep time or possibly hiring a cheaper stage. It'll piss off the producer, but she knows how it works. Maxine Lorimer is a fierce little woman with the instincts of a battle-hardened Viking. Rebecca chews the end of her biro, wondering whether she could argue for one less shoot day. No David this morning. She's thankful for that. After what happened between them, she spent the rest of the weekend in shock, but this morning she forced herself out of it, determined to behave as though nothing has changed. It's a hell of a lot easier without him here.

The voices get louder. In frustration, she slams her hands down on her desk, stands up and marches to the door, throwing it open.

'No, I will not be quiet,' a woman yells.

Rebecca recognizes her but can't immediately place her. Then she realizes that she is Laura's mother. Her face has been on the news. Graham is trying to calm her down. Some of the staff are standing, some swivelled round on their chairs to watch, and some are doing their best to pretend it isn't happening. Rebecca walks forward quickly, puts her hand on Graham's shoulder and moves him out of the way. It's time to take the heat out of the situation.

'It's Jenny Maguire, isn't it?' she says. 'My name is Rebecca Munro and I'm one of the partners here. Why don't you come into my office and tell me what this is all about?'

The woman stares at Rebecca and her chin quivers. Rebecca smiles kindly at her. 'Come on.'

'I want to know who did it,' she says, standing her ground. 'I want to know which one of them raped my daughter.'

Rebecca's mouth hangs open, but she gathers herself quickly and gently guides her into her office. She shuts the door and leans against it.

Jenny paces like an angry cat. She is beyond furious, beyond being reasoned with. Rebecca uses the same tack she uses on David, allowing her anger to wear itself out before intervening. Once she's calm, Rebecca persuades her to sit down. Jenny puts her head in her hands.

'Why don't you start from the beginning?' Rebecca suggests. 'Tell me what it is you think you know.'

She feels she ought to offer her a glass of water at least, but she doesn't want to lose the opportunity. If she's accusing a member of Rebecca's staff of something as appalling as rape she wants to know why and where she got her information.

Jenny's fingers are in her hair, her face hidden by the palms of her hands. Rebecca can barely hear and has to crouch at her side.

'My daughter is involved in research into her condition at Southampton University. She told the professor there that she was raped by a colleague after your Christmas party.' She takes her hands away and presents Rebecca with her tear-stained face. 'It's too much of a coincidence. Whoever did that, he must have taken her. The police found a threatening letter in her flat. Anonymous, of course.'

Rebecca doesn't know what to say. 'And the professor didn't have a name? Laura didn't tell her?'

'No.' The energy has left her voice. 'They'll be here soon.'

'Who?' She imagines the researchers from Southampton.

'The police. I'm surprised they're not here already.'

Right on cue, sirens wail. Rebecca gets to the window in time to see three police cars turn into Percy Row and swoop into the kerb. Car doors slam. She counts nine officers, all in uniform. She peers at the tops of their heads and recognizes Logan's neat side parting as they gather outside the door, then in they barge, like a marauding army.

'Stay here,' she says.

She hurries to the stairwell, where she greets Logan while the rest of his officers cluster behind him. Three of them are carrying hard black cases.

'I have a warrant to search the premises,' Logan says. 'We'll be asking for DNA samples from all the men. This is voluntary, but obviously we'll be interested in anyone who refuses. I'd like a list of every man in the building, as quickly as possible, and a list of who was at the staff Christmas party at Hoxton 101 on the twenty-second of December last year. We also need access to computer passwords.'

'I'm sorry. I'm confused. What's Laura's disappearance got to do with the Christmas party?'

'It's another line of enquiry.'

'Right. Well, whatever you need. Just ask. There may not be a definitive list of who was there, but we'll do what we can.'

This is what it must be like to be hit by a wave. You know instinctively that there is no point querying, that the only way of surviving is to dive in. Agnes prints out the lists and hands them to Logan. He scans them quickly. Rebecca wonders if he's looking for anyone in particular.

'David Gunner around?' he says, glancing up at her.

'No, he's out this morning. Family matters.' Why are they so interested in David? It must be because of the argument Bettina witnessed.

'A man fitting his description was seen getting into a black car with a woman who appeared to be drunk.'

She shakes her head. She can't keep up. 'Are we talking Christmas or last Thursday night?'

'Thursday.'

'Thank you for clearing that up.' She shrugs when he raises an eyebrow at her sarcasm. 'David was at home.'

'You know that for sure?'

'Well, no,' she admits. She had texted him but that proved nothing.

'I see.' Logan walks away, speaking into his phone. From what she can make out of the conversation, he's dispatching someone directly to Constable Lane.

'He won't be there.' She speaks loudly enough so that he can hear her voice above his conversation. 'He's staying with his grandparents. I'll write down the address for you. He may be out though, he told me he was settling them into a care home today.'

She fumbles around the closest desk, trying to lay her hands on something to write with until Finn, helpfully, passes her a scrap of paper and a biro. Bettina is close by, wringing her hands. Rebecca is finding her need to be at the centre of everything increasingly irritating. Laura was a much quieter presence. She appreciates that now.

'I'm sorry,' Jenny says. 'I shouldn't have barged in here like that.'

'Don't apologize. You were only doing what any mother would.'

Rebecca thinks about the child inside her, tiny and fragile, the size of a kidney bean. Her need to protect it is frightening. She tries to think of something to tell Jenny about Laura, something that will make her happy. But Laura wasn't particularly happy herself, so it's hard.

'I didn't want her to go,' she says. 'I was hoping she and David would both change their minds. It was over such a silly thing; a mountain out of a molehill. I'm fond of your daughter. She was a lovely person as well as a great employee.'

'Thank you for saying that.'

Rebecca pauses, feeling oddly inadequate in the face of this woman's anger and fear. 'Do you really believe it was someone from here?'

'It was someone at the party, so yes, I do. Did you see her with anyone?' There is desperation in her voice as well as sorrow.

'I went home early. I had a migraine.'

She should tell the police that Laura and Jamie Buchanan had seemed completely absorbed in each other that night, but it wouldn't be appropriate to share that with her distraught mother.

'Well, they'll find him now. They've been taking DNA samples from her bed and her bathroom. Whoever he was, he'll have left something.'

Rebecca places her hand on Jenny's arm, wanting to help her manage her expectations. 'It's been almost two months. She'll have washed her bedclothes several times since then. You mustn't get your hopes up.'

'What else is there to do?'

'Do you recognize this man?' Logan asks, handing Rebecca a sheet of paper with a photograph on it.

She nods and gives it back. 'I've already been shown this. It's her neighbour's husband. He doesn't work here though, so he wouldn't have been there.'

'Have you ever seen him before last Thursday night?'

'No. I've never seen him before in my life.'

'I have,' Bettina says. 'He's the guy from the taxi.'

'We know that, Bettina.' Honestly. 'The detective wants to know if we've seen him before last Thursday.'

Bettina shoots her a defiant look. 'I'm not daft. I wasn't talking about last week, I meant after the Christmas party. She went off with him.'

'Say that again.' Logan's eyes laser into Bettina's.

She speaks slowly, as if she thinks the lot of them are dim. 'I saw that man' – she taps his image with her forefinger – 'leaving with Laura on the night of the staff Christmas party. He was holding her round her waist, supporting her.'

'Can you swear to that?'

She shrugs. 'Well, I was drunk, but I don't think I'm wrong. I have a good memory for faces.'

'Why haven't you said anything before now?'

'I forgot.'

Logan rolls his eyes as he turns away, his phone to his ear. He strides towards the door, speaking urgently. 'Change of plan. Forget David Gunner. Can you pick up Elliot Hill from his place of work? Get his car impounded as well. I want forensics all over it. I'll meet you back at the station.'

50

Rebecca

NO RESPONSE FROM DAVID. THAT'S ODD AND HIGHLY unsatisfactory. Rebecca hopes he isn't deliberately ignoring her calls but suspects he may be. She needs to at least warn him about what Logan said, even though the detective is more interested in Elliot now.

Bettina brings her a gluten-free wrap, relieved of its packaging and laid on a white plate with a paper napkin, while Rebecca takes a call from the public relations chief at a Norwegian furniture retailer and sets up a meeting in Oslo. She asks Agnes to organize her travel arrangements, and once that's done she sits twiddling her thumbs.

Eddie pops his head in and she nods, signalling him to come in.

'Is it true they're going to arrest Laura's neighbour?'

'If you've been talking to Bettina, then you know as much as I do.'

'What a creep. They'll find her now that they've got him. It's only a matter of time.'

'I'm sure they will.'

He scratches at his beard. 'What the hell's he done with her?'

'Eddie, I don't know.' She understands from the surprised look on his face that the question was rhetorical, but it still winds her up. 'Look, you're worried about her – we all are – but we can't do anything. Now, I need to get on, if you don't mind.'

She is not the type people confide in. She leaves that to the likes of Agnes. She only cares about the baby, and herself. Everyone else is a disappointment. Even David. Most of all David.

Across the way, in the building next to the car park, workmen have been drilling for the last half hour. Rebecca leans back in her chair then gets up and goes to the window, as if she could stop the racket just by glaring at them. She leaves the room. The relative noisiness of the media floor lessens the impact of the drill. For something to do, she wanders over to the coffee machine and selects one of the capsules. She looks at the machine and frowns. She has never used it before – someone usually does it for her – and it's beyond complicated. The water reservoir is full, but she has no idea where to put the capsule, let alone what to do once she's accomplished that.

Jamie wanders over. 'Do you need a hand?'

She smiles and moves aside. 'Do you mind? I'm completely clueless.'

'No problem.'

She tries to concentrate on what he's doing, so that

she can remember for next time. Lift the lid and pop the capsule in without peeling its top off. Press the button at the side.

Jamie's hands are shaking. She watches them then raises her eyes to his face. There are dark shadows under his eyes and his mouth is a thin line, as if he's tensing the muscles around his lips. It strikes her that she was wrong, that he's in love with Laura. But if that was the case, what was he doing messing around with Bettina? Trying to make her jealous?

'They'll find her.'

'Will they?'

'I don't know,' she admits. 'I'm sorry, that was a stupid thing to say. You like her, don't you?'

He shrugs. 'I don't think it's reciprocated.'

'That's tough.'

She'd make a useless agony aunt. Felicity would have known what to say, how to make him feel better. Felicity has that manner about her, something that says, confide in me, let me share your burden, your pain. Rebecca's manner is of the pull-your-socks-up variety.

'I feel so ruddy useless,' he says. 'But I wouldn't know where to start looking. We went on a date and she told me about her condition. She told me you're the only one who knows.'

Rebecca nods.

'That's what's so terrifying. That some bastard—'

'Don't think about it, Jamie. It won't do any good. The police are doing all they can. We've just got to wait and be here in case they need us.'

Jamie pours the frothed milk into her cup and adds a

generous sprinkle of chocolate before she can tell him not to. He hands her the coffee, and she waits while he makes his own. This situation, she realizes, is bringing something new out in them all. She likes Jamie, but he's only ever been an employee. Now things have changed, people she kept at a distance have come closer. She feels more invested in their lives. It could be the baby hormones making her uncharacteristically maternal, or it could be this horrible situation.

'What happened on your date?' she asks. 'I don't mean to pry, but you don't appear to be together. If you were, you'd have told the police, wouldn't you?'

'Of course.' He gives her a rueful smile. 'But I messed up. I rushed things and she bolted.'

'Do the police know about that?'

'Yeah. I told them. They've had a good poke around my flat.'

'Ah.' She sighs. 'Well, hopefully you'll get another chance. Hopefully we all will.'

'Is David not coming in at all today?'

'He doesn't appear to be.' Her manner is quelling. She understands that people are curious and worried, but she wishes they'd stop looking to her for answers.

'He reminds me of my father.'

She sighs. 'I doubt he'd appreciate that.'

'Oh, I didn't mean . . . No, it's just something I've been thinking about recently. He's been a bit off for the last few weeks. Dad was like that before his nervous breakdown.'

'David is your boss,' she reminds him. 'This conversation is inappropriate.' He is annoying her now.

Jamie is undaunted. 'I know, and I'm sorry. But I'm concerned. You may not have noticed, because you . . .' He hesitates. 'Er, work so closely together.'

How dare he allude, even obliquely, to their affair? Her sympathy for him is fast ebbing away.

'David has a lot going on right now; on a personal level. But he'll be fine when everything quietens down.'

Jamie shrugs. 'Still, I wouldn't rule it out. All the signs are there: shorter fuse, high stress levels, anxiety.'

'Yes, all right. Message received.'

'I'm sorry,' Jamie says. 'It's none of my business.'

Perhaps she's been too sharp. She smiles reassuringly at him; she is his boss, after all. It's important everyone here feels that the company is being managed well, that their jobs aren't at risk. 'I don't think there's much wrong with David. He's a little tired perhaps, and has one or two problems at home, but he'll be at work tomorrow.'

Back in her office, she chews at her bottom lip. If David's issues are having an effect on the staff, if they're beginning to talk, then Gunner Munro could be in trouble. Once upon a time she would have said that David's ego was too big to allow him to nosedive, but she knows this is no longer the case. It makes no sense to her; other men have left their wives, other men have had to deal with the deteriorating mental health of their loved ones, other men run successful companies. In fact, they are often the ones who get divorced, who have the financial problems, whose storms are more turbulent and harder to weather than other people's. That is what success means. That's why it's only the ruthless and truly driven who survive. She thought that was who David was.

One problem has already been solved, with Tony and Georgie comfortably settled in a smart care home, for the time-being at least. She'll be at his side, willing to help when the inevitable happens and they're asked to leave. He can't count on Felicity for that. Rebecca doesn't believe he was serious about ending their relationship. He'll be back once he gets bored with domesticity. It'll be OK. It has to be, for their baby's sake.

The drilling suddenly stops, leaving a silence so profound it stuns her. The skies are darkening and there's an ominous yellow tinge to the charcoal clouds. The first drop of rain hits her window. Out of the blue she wonders, what exactly did David do after the Christmas party? No one can vouch for him.

She tries to settle, but it's impossible now. She tries his phone again but gets no answer. She could stay put and wait, but she's not sure she's capable. She has a sixth sense when it comes to David.

A few years ago, he went skiing and broke his leg. He was lucky not to have broken his neck. She had felt something, had been so sure that he was in trouble that she had called him. He didn't pick up, so she had waited for as long as she could bear it, then called Felicity, making some excuse about needing David to answer a question for work. He was being stretchered into the hospital by then and when Felicity told her that it had happened half an hour earlier, Rebecca had tingled all over. She could pinpoint the exact moment.

Apart from that, David never ignores his mobile. The fact that he has done rings alarm bells.

Should she go? He asked her what she would do if she

knew he'd done something bad. This is what is at the root of it, the unknown thing that's playing havoc with his mental stability. Whatever it is, she'll stand by him; she won't let him down. She looks at her watch. The traffic through north London should be relatively light. A taxi could get her there in an hour and a half. Anything is better than sitting here worrying.

51

Laura

I'M FLOATING ON A FLUFFY CLOUD OF DRUGS, SOMEWHERE between fear and oblivion, my vision blurred, my reflexes fuzzy, my mouth as dry as sand. Every so often adrenaline spurts through me, briefly carrying my mind to the surface, and my eyes open wide as I remember what's happening, and then down I swoop again, into the medicinal embrace, the weight of it wrapping around me like a blanket.

'You did this to me,' he hisses. 'This is all your fault.'

I blink open my eyes. My chin is on my chest. I must have slept. How much time has passed?

'I didn't . . .' I slur.

My words are falling back down my throat, my body relaxing again, my head sinking deeper and deeper into the damp pillow. Blackness descends and the next time I open my eyes David is still sitting on the edge of the bed, still watching me. I slide my gaze to the window. It's raining.

* * *

'Why the hell don't you pick up your phone!'

The shouting brings me up again, groggy with drugs, my mind fumbling. Is it his wife? It must be. He wouldn't have let a carer in. I try and picture Felicity Gunner at Guy's funeral. She has fine blonde hair and wears hippy-ish clothes.

Steps on the stairs. Not David's. A door closes. I recognize the sound of the bolt to the bathroom door being driven across its slot. Is there evidence that I've been there? A stray blonde hair on the carpet? Will she see it and frown, pick it up and inspect it, wonder who it belongs to? David calls up to ask if she's all right and she calls back that she's fine. The bathroom door opens on the sound of the flush. I make some noise, rocking back and forth and moaning through the gag, as loud as I can. I hear her footsteps on the stairs. Then the spindle moves, wobbling in its socket before clattering to the floor as the door flies open. She stops in her tracks, her mouth an 'O' of surprise.

'Laura?'

My head is too heavy for my neck, flopping when I try to raise it. I peer at her through my fringe, blink again to sharpen the picture. Blonde hair tied messily back, jeans, brown boots, suede coat.

'Oh my God,' she says.

After her initial shocked hesitation, she runs forward and starts to work at the tape binding my wrists, her hands shaking, her warm breath against my head as she leans over me. She smells of baby lotion and soap. She keeps swearing, a note of panic in her voice.

There is no time though. David is already running upstairs. Felicity makes a whimpering noise – or was that me? But one moment she's tearing at the tape, the next she's flying backwards, her head hitting the wall with a crack before she drops to the floor. There's a weird, almost deathly stillness before she starts moving, dragging herself up by the door frame and out on to the landing. David goes after her and I watch in despair as he catches her round the waist. She struggles, squirming in his arms, clawing at him and screaming that she's calling the police. Then suddenly it's over, he pushes, and she pitches, toppling over the stairs. There is a sickening crack followed by silence, before he charges down after her.

'Lissy! Lissy! Oh fuck, I'm sorry, sweetheart. Jesus Christ.'

I listen to the shuffles and thuds, picturing him pulling her into his arms, weeping into her hair, struggling down the rest of the stairs with her. At least he's forgotten about me for the moment. I pull at my hands; there's more give now that Felicity has made a start. The pain sears like hot pokers through my shoulders, arms and wrists, but I grit my teeth and keep on jerking until the binding round my wrists splits. I sit back, gasping, the room swimming, then free my ankles.

I can see something in the corner, and although it's time I can't afford to spare, I crawl across the carpet and stretch my hands out, my fingers closing round a crumpled ball of cotton. My knickers. I wrestle them on and feel so much better for it. I move my body round and examine the empty spindle, my fingers more reliable than my eyes. I need some sort of lever. David's collection of figurines swims in and out of focus. I drag myself over and choose a warrior brandishing a sword, then stumble with my prize back to the door. The sword fits the hole with a bit of help. I wait for a moment to test the silence, then force it round like I'm fighting with an overtightened stopcock. It works, and I'm out, reeling but free. I clutch the banister and peer down the stairs. It's a long way down and there's blood on the wall, but I have to move.

On the half-landing I pause, listening to David moving around, to my heartbeat, to the rain. Ahead of me is the front door and I debate leaving through it, but decide not to, because he'll hear me and there's no way I'll be able to run in this state. I take the last stairs carefully, hugging the wall to avoid any creaking treads. There's a room to the left. I go in and quietly close the door. A desk sits under the sash window, cluttered with papers and a collection of antique paperweights. There is no phone. I push everything to one side, then climb up and undo the brass fastenings. My shoulder muscles scream in protest but after a couple of shoves the sash window jerks up. I hold my breath, but he doesn't come. I slide out of the window feet first, land in a bed of wet lavender and stand still, listening, trying to detect anything besides the pouring rain. Then I set off at a clumsy trot, and immediately trip over my own feet. I lie in the gravel beside the back wheel of David's car, stunned, then get to my feet and head for the gate. The cold helps to reduce the smothering effect of the drugs, but my gait is slow and ungainly. Torrential rain slicks my fringe to my forehead and splashes up from the tarmac on to my legs. God knows what I look like. Someone's nightmare. I'm torn between leaving Felicity on her own and getting away from this hellhole, but I make up my mind to stagger on. If I go back, neither of us stands a chance.

52

Rebecca

REBECCA MAKES THE DRIVER WAIT ROUND THE BEND from the house. He switches the engine off and the wipers go still. She wrinkles her nose at all the wet green, the heavy clouds, the rain-slicked lane with its muddy verge and hazardous ditch. A miserable-looking bird perches on a bare branch. She finds the countryside profoundly uninviting.

The sight of Felicity's car parked next to David's gave her a shock. Rebecca hadn't expected her to be here, but then, why wouldn't she be? They must have so many things to work out.

This is a mistake. She imagines David opening the door, Felicity behind him, telling her to go away, to leave them alone. Or maybe asking her to come in, putting on the kettle and them all sitting round the table, awkward and not knowing what to say to each other. She came because she thought he needed her and because, even though she dismissed it, what Jamie had said worried her. Now it seems Felicity may have had the same thought.

She sits up straight, drops her shoulders and lifts her chin, opens herself out so that her breathing is unrestricted. She centres herself while the driver stares out at the rain. She is grateful for his silence and apparent lack of interest.

'OK,' she says, more to herself than to him.

He turns to her. 'You're going in?'

'Yes. No. No, take me home.'

'OK, Miss Munro.' He glances at her again. 'You sure?'

'No, I am not sure,' she snaps. 'Stop!'

The car had started moving but he breaks with a jolt that flings her forward against the passenger seat. She ignores his apology and, cradling her bag under her arm, opens the door.

'Go and get yourself a coffee and come back in an hour and a half.'

She walks along the lane, brolly up, feeling like Mary Poppins, waiting on the verge as the car sweeps past. She almost runs after him, and as he disappears, beyond the reach of her voice, she feels a wave of loneliness descend on her.

It's quiet, so they're not having a blistering row. If she interrupts, what will she be interrupting? Still, she can't stand here for the next hour and a half. She has no option but to walk between the two cars, up to the porch.

David wrenches the door open and stares at her in shock. She moves forward, but he pushes her out and pulls the door to behind him.

'What the fuck are you doing here?'

She ignores him. It's just the way he is. 'I need to talk to you and you're not answering your phone.'

'I thought I made it clear that it's over. Get in your car and go back to London.'

'It's too late. I've already sent it away.'

His face clouds. 'For Christ's sake.'

'Are you going to let me in?' What is she? A vampire to be refused entry in case she sucks the life out of him? 'I'm cold.' This is not the outcome she had expected.

'Tell me what you want.'

'Where is Felicity?'

'What do you mean?'

She loses patience and explodes. 'What do you think I mean? Her car's right there.'

He stares at her, that nerve still flickering under the surface of the skin beneath his eye. And then the penny drops. Why Felicity isn't at the door. Why he's blocking her way. She's upstairs. They were in bed together. She's interrupted a reconciliation. She blurts out the first thing that comes into her mind.

'I'm pregnant.'

He rocks. In fact, he rocks so far, that she is forced to brace her hand on his shoulder to stop him collapsing against her. She pushes him away from her and steps into the house.

'Felicity!' she shouts. 'Come downstairs and talk to me. I know you're there.'

'Get out!' David screams.

It's that, more than anything else, that convinces her that Jamie was right. It doesn't sound like David, it sounds insane. And simultaneously she knows that she shouldn't be here, that something bad has happened.

'Felicity!' She wouldn't be hiding; she would confront her. 'What have you done with her?'

And that is when she notices the blood-red smears on his shirt, in the dip between his collarbone and his shoulder, as if a head has rested there, on his hands and even on her own coat. She catches her breath. Felicity's bobble hat is lying on the floor and, behind the kitchen door, there is something covered in clear plastic; a booted foot, cocked to one side at an unnatural angle. There's blood on the door frame too.

'What . . .'

But her reaction isn't swift enough. He swivels her round and rams her against the wall. The back of her head hits a picture, cracking the glass and sending tiny shards down the collar of her coat. She fights back, trying to scratch him, but he's too strong, forcing her down on to her knees. For a second it feels as though they are making love. But only for a second.

53

Laura

I KEEP TELLING MYSELF THAT THE NEXT BEND WILL reveal a farm or an approaching car, but it doesn't. Frustratingly, I can hear a busy road in the distance. I pretend this is Hampstead Heath, and that if I can keep putting one foot in front of the other, sooner or later I will come across someone who can help me.

The rain bounces off the tarmac and batters the hedgerows, making the verge muddy. I skid on the wet grass, land on my bottom, sit in bewildered shock for a second or two, before forcing myself to get up and keep moving. I hear a car somewhere close by, and stop to listen, but it's gone. Sound carries differently in the countryside. I think about Felicity losing her battle for life, and fear refuels me. Help can't be far away. This is Buckinghamshire, not Dartmoor.

I hear the car again and this time I know I'm not mistaken. I lurch into the middle of the lane, my arms stretched out, palms up. Because of the effect of the drugs, I've grossly misjudged, forgotten about wet roads and braking times, and he's driven round a bend and hasn't seen me, and suddenly he's swerving, his wheels locking and sliding, the bonnet hitting my thigh, throwing me into the ditch. I lie face down, my arms splayed, brambles and nettles catching at my skin. The car door opens, and the driver runs over.

'Are you hurt?'

'No, I'm OK,' I lie, as he pulls me out of the ditch. I feel bruised all over. 'Nothing broken,' I add, seeing the colour drain from his face.

'I nearly killed you. Why did you run into the road like that?' His voice booms, his accent possibly Polish.

I pick grass from my mouth, spitting mud. 'Call the police. They need help back there. There's a man and he's already hurt someone. I think he might have killed her. He's mad.'

He takes my arm and supports me to the car, opening the back door. But I refuse and get into the front. He looks round for his phone. I spot it in the footwell where it must have slipped when he braked. The interior is warm, and there is a familiar perfume in the air. I lean forward and wipe the misted windows with my palm while he calls the emergency services.

'What house?' he asks.

'There's only one. I don't know what it's called.'

My knee is bouncing. I press it down with my fist. I wish he would hurry up, but everything this man does is slow and ponderous. He is staring at me, his mouth hanging open.

'What? What's the matter?' I ask.

'But I left my passenger there . . . Hello, yes. Police please.'

'And an ambulance,' I say.

'Yes. Ambulance too. People hurt. One, maybe two. Heron's Brook, Box Lane.'

He drops the phone on to his lap, starts the engine and backs gingerly towards the ditch, then he turns the steering wheel hard round, the windscreen wipers on full speed.

'What do you mean, you left a passenger there?' Something tells me I know the answer, because I recognized that perfume.

'Miss Munro.' He reverses again, and finally makes the turn. 'She is an important account customer.'

I stare at him in disbelief. 'Rebecca Munro? You left Rebecca Munro there?'

'She told me to come back for her later,' he says with a quick, defensive glance in my direction.

'Oh my God. Can't you go any faster?'

'Do you want to be in the ditch again?'

He leans forward, large beringed hands gripping the steering wheel, looking for the gate. I do the same, unbuckling my seat belt as soon as I see it.

'You should wait for the police,' he says.

I ignore him.

Bare tree branches bend against the rain, twigs breaking off and spinning across the road. The tattered remains of my grey chiffon dress cling to my legs, soaked with blood, and I realize I must have cut myself when the car hit me. Bizarrely, I don't feel any pain. The house swims in and out of focus. I concentrate hard, look for a weapon and pick up one of the chalky, rough-cut stones that frame the beds of shrubs to either side of the porch.

The front door isn't closed properly. I push it open a crack and peer through. To my horror, a woman is lying on the floor and David is on top of her, pinning her down, his hands round her throat. Her hands grip his upper arms, white-fingered, before they suddenly go slack and drop to her sides. I move on instinct, adrenaline sharpening my movements as I burst in and slam the stone down. But David must have sensed me because he reacts quicker than lightning, reaching for me and shoving me backwards. I feel like I've been rugby-tackled. He throws his weight on to my body, catching my wrist as I lash out and slamming my hand on to the floor. I release the stone and he throws it out of reach.

'Look what you've done, you stupid bitch. My life is fucked because of you.'

I whip my head to the side when his spittle hits my face. 'You did this to yourself.'

He lets go of me and his hands circle my neck, his thumbs pressing into my larynx. I beat at him with my fists, but he's squeezing the life out of me. A tide of blackness begins to wash away my vision.

'The girl who can't recognize faces,' he mutters. 'Well, you know me now, don't you?'

I can hear the sounds I'm making, the pathetic little creaks from my throat. Then a shadow falls and even though I can't see, the effect is of someone shutting the curtains, or standing in front of the sun. There's a whump noise, and David tips to the left without a word, his hands slackening and falling away. He leans on a little side table, but it slides from under him, and he slumps to the floor.

My vision returns, and I look up to see a fall of dark hair around a sheet-white face.

'Oh God, have I killed him?' Rebecca asks.

54

Laura

AFTER THE POLICE INTERVIEWS, THE MEDICAL EXAMINA-tions and all the fuss, I feel an urgent need to get away, so I spend a week in Paris with my sister. It's term time so Isabel is at work and the boys are at their *Lycée*, but I don't mind at all. I find a way to be at least moderately content while walking city streets that have become as familiar as a friend in the years since Isabel and Eric made it their home. I visit the galleries, check out the Père Lachaise cemetery where Oscar Wilde and Jim Morrison are buried. I visit the Bois de Boulogne, I take a bateau mouche and enjoy being a tourist as it ambles lazily along the river. It's a break from London, a break from my flat and its associations, a way of drawing a line under what happened. David's trial is a long way off. There is the rape trial to go through if the CPS agrees, but that won't be for months either and I can't sit around waiting to be given permission to feel better. And what if he gets off? How will I cope then?

My lawyer says I should brace myself, that it could go either way, and the fact that Phoebe is standing by him, undoubtedly shifts the balance in his favour. It's Elliot's word against that of a woman who cannot recognize faces, who has no evidence, not even a blue shirt, to prove what happened.

The police were excited when they discovered that I'd been in Elliot's car, only to be irritated when I explained. Since then it's been made clear that they would like to close the case; that I haven't got a hope in hell of getting it past the Crown Prosecution Service; that I'm wasting everyone's time, including my own.

They had already found that first letter, the one I hid between my books, the one that made me hack off my hair, but even that didn't impress them. I hate that they've read his words, raised their eyebrows over his description of the night we spent together, his insinuations, maybe even seen his point. But I refuse to back down. I may have been drunk, my condition may make me an unreliable witness, but I know what he did. I only regret that it took me so long to report it.

I've heard that he's moved in with his parents while he waits to find out if he's going to be on trial for rape. I know what happened now. It was coincidence, opportunity and maybe even malice. Elliot knew about my condition, but did he have sex on his mind all along or was it a spur-of-the-moment thing, pure opportunism; an alcohol-fuelled decision that he would never normally have taken, had I not been in the state I was? Of course, according to him, he didn't get into the taxi with me, someone else did. Someone who said he was my boyfriend and told him to get lost. I know he's lying, but the driver of the cab has yet to come forward.

If it was an act of malice, how long had he been playing games with my head before he struck, how many times had he seen me on public transport, passed me in the street, been behind me in the queue at the local grocery? If he admits to having sex with me, he will lie and tell them that I initiated it, that I knew who he was. A knowledge of face-blindness isn't proof.

There is Bettina's statement. She saw me with Elliot and knew how drunk I was and has agreed to testify that in her opinion I was in no condition to make a sound judgement. We both know it's weak, that at best it's moral support. Some people will say I brought it on myself.

I can't think about it for long because it brings back memories that are upsetting and my confidence is at an all-time low as it is. I will have my say, whatever the result. I was raped. He knew what he was doing. He raped me. It was him.

The only niggle I have is my later physical response to Elliot. My body should have reacted, my subconscious should have alerted me. None of that happened, and, in the spirit of full disclosure, I admit that I found him attractive that night after the GZ party. I'm ashamed of it and will never tell Phoebe. She's moving anyway, and soon there'll be someone else living beneath me, someone else who I won't recognize when I meet them in the local supermarket or stand next to them as the train pulls into Kentish Town station.

My nephews keep me distracted. Milo has been practising the three-cup shuffle and is a master of the skill, irritating his brother no end. I sit at the table and stare at the cups as he switches them, his hands moving like lightning, as though he's plaiting hair. Every time I think I've got it, I turn out to be wrong. Somehow, he keeps his eye on the ball. Somehow, he is in control. Eyes, hands, brain. I try it myself, but I don't have the knack.

One nice thing. Jamie rang. We had one of those daft, meaningless conversations where nothing gets said, but there's a smile behind every word, because we just know.

'Hello.'

'Hello.'

'It's me.'

'I know it's you.'

It turns out Bettina wasn't interested in him; she was trying to make Finn jealous. It worked apparently. When I mention it, Jamie says it's news to him, he didn't notice her efforts because he only had eyes for me.

I laugh. 'So you say.'

'I swear it's true.'

I am unsettled when I get back to London and that feeling decides me. I'm going to put the flat on the market and start afresh. The agent gives me a ball-park figure that makes my jaw drop and I sign with a flourish. I'll move south of the river. Cross another line.

I have lunch with Rebecca. Her idea. She's decided on names: Pax for a boy, Aurora for a girl. She tells me she's refused to press charges for David's assault on her, and I'm surprised by how hard she works to find excuses for him. He's in a tricky situation though, having realized that Broadmoor is quite possibly a far worse option than prison. He hasn't been assessed yet, but when he is, he needs to prove that although he wasn't of sound mind when he pushed his wife down the stairs or when he abducted me, he is now. He has admitted to the hit-and-run. His trial will begin in January. A year after Guy's death.

Rebecca blames herself for putting pressure on him, but she expects me to carry some of that blame too. I should have gone straight to the police instead of taking matters into my own hands and blundering around like a blind man in a crowded room. If the police had been involved at an early stage, none of this would have happened.

It's unlikely I'll ever see her again, so I tell her what I think. That if David hadn't decided to get into his car that night, Guy would be alive. That if he hadn't driven away from the scene, Guy would have had a chance and I wouldn't have considered David as a candidate for my rape; that if she hadn't been screwing her boss, his wife wouldn't have chucked him out. She would be alive too.

'So, let's not play the blame game,' I say. 'Can we just put this behind us.'

It's a Saturday afternoon, late March, and it has been raining all day. I've been sorting through drawers and cupboards, throwing things out and filling bags for the local charity shops. It seems to me, that in the three years I've been here, I've managed to accumulate a decade's worth of stuff that I don't need.

Before four the rain stops, the clouds clear and what sun there is left washes the sky in milky blues and pinks.

The streets glisten invitingly. I change into running gear and let myself out of my flat. I'm normally careful to avoid bumping into Phoebe, listening for movement, but today either I'm unlucky, or she has been listening for me.

She appears just as I get to the bottom of the stairs. There's no getting away.

'I don't know how you live with yourself,' she says.

I don't know how to respond, so I just look at her helplessly. She slams back into her flat.

I run to the bus stop and hop on the number 46 to Hampstead Heath. Despite the bad weather earlier, or perhaps because of it, there are still a reassuring number of dog-walkers and runners around, and I set off at a gentle jog, taking the path up to the ponds, crossing them and heading up the hill. I smile when I pass joggers, I smile when I become entangled in a dog lead and I smile when a child on a scooter nearly collides with me. The more I practise, the easier the smiles will come.

I spot a group of teenagers up ahead: all boys, young and sharp with attitude. Two on bikes, circling, one trying to restrain his powerfully built Staffordshire bull terrier, another two messaging on their phones. Even though I don't recognize their faces, I recognize the shape of them and their presence, and I certainly remember the dog and its spiked collar. I will myself to go on. I won't be frightened or intimidated. They're just bored. As I approach, their dynamic changes, their backs straightening as they anticipate me. I'm over-aware of my breasts moving under my stretch-top, the shape of my bottom in my skin-tight running trousers, my pink cheeks and sweating forehead.

As I close in, one of them breaks ranks, looking to his mates for approval. He makes a *tch tch* noise with a quick, upward lift of his chin, that sends a bolt through me. As I put distance between us, my feet eating the track, he calls after me.

'Seen you round here before, yeah?'

'She's too old for you, bruv.'

'Cougar, innit? Hey, don't run away. We won't do nuffink to you.'

Their voices sound threatening as they carry in the twilight, even though they're only posturing, trying to prove something to each other. I tell myself they are harmless, but I am only happy once I'm out of their sight.

I focus on my breathing and settle in, enjoying the rhythm. The air is brisk and clean up here, the sounds of the city muted, though not absent. A rustling noise in the copse startles me, but it turns out to be a blackbird. There are squirrels too, scooting up tree trunks as I approach, and glossy crows fight over a sandwich packet that they have cleverly managed to extricate from the bin. They barely react as I pass close to them, the repetitive thud of my shoes no doubt as familiar and unthreatening as their own cries.

I have been running for fifteen minutes when another runner's steps start to echo mine. The light is fading and it's time I turned back, but I'm stubborn and I don't, I keep going, as if not doing so would be to admit that I am uneasy. This is public land and other people have every right to run here, even to choose the same path as me. It's probably a woman anyway, feeling nervous too and reassured by my presence. A young mum, I tell myself. She's left the baby with her husband, snuggled up in front of the telly, a bottle of formula and a beer between them. I picture it and keep running. I come to a break in the path, one going up to the west – I can see the lights of Primrose Hill – the other to the east. I choose east, hoping to work my way round and back the way I came, but it's the wrong choice because suddenly there are trees on either side of me, and the light has been blotted out. The footsteps keep coming, and I try and count mine to stop myself from focusing on those others. *One Two, buckle my shoe, Three Four, open the door.*

I keep it up, whispering the words in time with my steps, but the runner is getting closer. I try to gauge, from the weight of their tread, whether they are male or female. I pick up speed and branch off to the left, on to another path, but within seconds they have caught up enough for me to hear their breathing. His breathing.

Our breathing.

It's out of sync, like our feet. The sounds overlap as though we are singing a round of 'Kookaburra'. I loved that when I was little. I hum the song, keeping fear at bay. *Kookaburra sits in the old gum tree-ee. Merry Merry King of—*'

'Laura, wait up.'

My mind does its thing, cogs whirring. Who do I know who runs here? I can't think of anyone. Brown hair, medium build, normal. He passes me as if he's intending to keep going, but then he stops and turns, leaning over to splay his hands on his thighs and blocking my path. I wait, my arms crossed protectively round my breasts.

I swallow hard and say it. Because after my difficulties inevitably became public knowledge in the fanfare of publicity surrounding the case, this is what I've told myself I'll do from now on, to avoid misunderstandings.

'I don't know who you are.'

55

Laura

HE LOOKS UP AT ME, COCKING HIS HEAD TO ONE SIDE. 'It's Graham.'

'Oh. Sorry, men in running gear all look the same to me.'

'It's OK. I'm not offended.'

He straightens up and starts walking. Without being rude, there is nothing I can do but fall in with him. I check the time on my phone.

'I was about to head back,' I say, hoping that he hasn't finished his run.

'I'll keep you company. I've had enough. How've you been?'

I resign myself. 'Oh, fine. I'm starting work again in a week, so I'm making the most of my freedom while I can.'

'Good on you. I heard you got a job at S&C.'

'That's right.'

'Lucky girl.'

Something about the way he says it gives me pause. I

am not used to interacting with him anywhere except at work and it feels wrong somehow. He feels wrong. He shouldn't be here. I'm sure he lives in west London; somewhere out beyond Ealing.

'So how is everyone?' I say in desperation. 'I suppose GZ must be in post-production by now.'

'Yeah. It's going well, considering. It isn't the same without David though. Rebecca's doing her best, but she's pregnant, so . . .' He leaves it hanging there, probably expecting me to make understanding noises.

'So what?'

He turns and looks at me like I'm stupid. 'So, her mind's on something else. She's going to be a single mother and the father's going to be locked up. Gunner Munro might not be her first priority.'

'I'm sure she'll cope,' I say, between my teeth.

'Let's hope so.' He pauses. 'You're missed as well. You've been through quite an ordeal, haven't you?'

His glance tells me that he's expecting me to confide in him, to tell him how scared I was, what it was like being trussed to a bed for four days, convinced that every time I heard someone coming upstairs, I was going to die. I don't bother answering.

'So, what have you been doing with yourself?' he says.

If it had been Rebecca or Eddie doing the asking, I'd have replied that I was recovering. Taking one day at a time. Reminding myself to eat. Packing up my life. Speaking to my lawyer. But something about Graham makes the words stick in my throat.

His voice has changed, an element of frustration in there now. He never did like me much, and who can blame him. I didn't exactly put myself out to get to know him.

'Nothing much, just fiddling. You know.'

'I suppose it must be hard to move on from something like that.'

'I don't want to talk about it, Graham.'

'Understood.'

We walk on, then he stops to retie his lace. I wait, conditioned in childhood not to offend.

'So, you really didn't know it was your neighbour that night? That's mind-blowing. How does it work then, the face-blind thing? Do you not recognize anyone at all?'

'No, I don't,' I say, irritated, but prepared to explain, to be patient. 'It isn't that simple. If people are where I expect them to be, like they're at their desk, or in their house, of course I know who they are. But meeting someone unexpectedly in the park, then no. It's difficult. I use other strategies, but these can be compromised if . . .' I attempt a shrug.

'If you're pissed out of your head.' He laughs. 'But you must have remembered something. About his body? I understand it's only faces that give you a problem.'

'I told you, I don't want to talk about it.'

I begin to walk faster. I thought I'd been paying attention to which way we were headed but I now realize we are not going back towards the station, but deeper into the Heath, and it's dark.

'And the way he smelled—'

'So, do you often run up here?' I ask. 'Only I haven't seen you before.'

'Well you wouldn't, would you? I used to feel a bit of an idiot, when I passed you and you didn't acknowledge me. It made me feel invisible. Daft, eh? I should have just waved in your face. But then I happened to catch a radio interview with a celebrity who had written about their face-blindness in their memoir, and he could have been describing you. I was intrigued by the possibilities. I tested it out a couple of times. I wanted to know what it took for you to get to know a person well enough to recognize them.'

He's been following me. How often?

'Why didn't you just say?' I ask, trying to keep the unease out of my voice.

Beside me, he shrugs. 'Because, it was obvious you didn't want anyone to know.'

I shudder. 'Listen, Graham, don't be offended, but I think I'll run the rest of the way. I need the exercise.'

'I'll run with you. You know, now that you're not working at GM, there's no reason why we can't meet for a drink some time.'

I keep my eyes firmly on the path ahead. 'I'm with Jamie now.'

It feels good to say that, even though it isn't precisely true, because all we've done is chat on the phone. But I'm meeting him tomorrow. We have a date.

He keeps pace with me, so close that his arm brushes mine. I edge to the side and he closes in again. He's beginning to scare me. No, that's wrong. I've been scared since I heard him running up behind me.

'Does Jamie like your hair like that?' he asks.

I whip my head round with a gasp. 'What?'

He holds up his hands. 'Nothing. All I mean is, I prefer women with long hair. A lot of men do. It's a primitive thing, hardwired into our DNA.'

My blood freezes; I dart him a quick look and run faster. I can feel a static energy developing between us. I keep my eyes glued to the path ahead, trying to work out where I am, but I've never run on the Heath after dark before, I've always been careful.

'It's spooky, isn't it?' he says, altering his voice to mock-Hollywood shtick. '*Nobody can hear you scream*.'

My legs are beginning to feel weighted down, my ribs to squeeze my lungs. All the things I didn't sense with David or Elliot, I'm sensing now. His proximity, his voice, the smell of his sweat; they are making my nerves prickle, making my thoughts return to that night in a rush, to the dark interior of the cab, to my front hall, to my bed. Clothes being shed piece by piece. My body entangled with his.

'You knew who it was, didn't you?' he says between breaths. 'Don't deny it. You were embarrassed because you'd behaved like a slut.'

Don't react, I tell myself. Focus on getting to the edge of the Heath. Focus on getting somewhere safe.

'I'm not judging you,' he says. 'I'm just trying to get to the bottom of this. I don't believe that you spent the entire night with a man without having a clue who he was. I think you're probably kidding yourself because it's convenient. I hear you passed up on hypnotherapy. That tells its own tale.'

I get a flash of his body looming over mine and this

time I can't help myself. I stop in my tracks. 'You inadequate piece of shit.'

'You've got me wrong, Laura. I didn't say it was me. I was only speculating, trying to help you process it.'

'Get away from me.' My voice shakes.

He smiles, satisfied, as if he's finally got the reaction he wanted. 'We made love.'

'So you're admitting it now.'

He holds his hands up and smirks.

'Are you kidding me?' I say. 'I didn't know what I was doing, or who with. I thought you were Jamie.'

'No, you didn't. You're just trying to justify yourself. You knew it was me, so stop fighting it, Laura. Stop pretending nothing happened.'

'Why did you do it? Why did you think it was OK?' I yell the questions in his face, and he recoils.

My heart is racing, so I take a moment to breathe. I need to calm down, stop riling him and play for time. Someone will come. 'What about your shirt? I checked everyone on Facebook. You were wearing something different.'

'Some idiot spilt GZ all over me. I had a shirt in my bag – I always keep spare gear at work, and I was taking it home to wash. I changed, but then I decided to go. I'd had enough. Jamie was getting on my tits. He wouldn't let anyone else near you. I went upstairs and sat at the bar. No one bothered me. I expect I drank too much, but I was in control; I can hold my beer. I kept out of sight when everyone left the building, and I saw Jamie run back into the club and this other bloke take your hand. I recognized your neighbour and guessed what he was up to.'

'How did you recognize him?'

'Because I'd seen him coming out of your house.'

'You'd been watching my flat? How did you know where I live?'

He shrugs. 'Agnes can be careless. She left the staff files unlocked. Your neighbour's husband had been following you, Laura. I've even seen him sit on the next table to you in Luigi's. You thought that Jamie had come back to claim you, but he was talking to Guy. He'd forgotten all about you. I followed you round the corner to where the cab was waiting.

'I didn't have a plan, I only wanted to save you from doing something stupid. He pushed you in. He literally had to heave you, you were so pissed. I told him that you were my girlfriend and to get lost if he didn't want me to tell everyone what he was up to. You should have seen his face.'

An image pops into my head. My nephew, his hands moving, jumping from cup to cup, weaving them in and out, switching places while my eyes try to keep up, preening in triumph when he manages to outwit me and his brother. Three men, moving in and out of my vision; another weave to trick my mind, another sleight of hand, too drunk to notice until it's too late, and I am trapped.

'Laura, I wouldn't have touched you. I would have been the perfect gentleman, but you leant against me, and our lips met, and you can't, hand-on-heart, say that you didn't respond. It snowballed, didn't it? You wanted me.'

I catch my breath. I remember everything I did. 'No.'

His voice is urgent, self-pitying and wheedling.

'Then in the morning, I felt you get out of bed. I pretended to be asleep. I saw you pick up my shirt. I was going to say something then, but I bottled it. When you locked yourself in the bathroom, I threw on my clothes and made a run for it. It was a stupid thing to do; a big mistake. I should have stayed and talked to you. You would have understood and forgiven me, because we had chemistry. It wasn't rape, Laura. I didn't rape you. At worst, it was a mistake, not a crime. What we did was consensual. You wanted it.'

I stare at him in disbelief. 'I was drunk, and I had no idea who you were. If I had known, none of this would have happened. You're repulsive, Graham. You are a pathetic and insignificant creep who gets off on frightening women and I hope you get raped in prison. I'm calling the police.'

'And tell them what? You were happy enough to point the finger at your innocent neighbour and wreck his life. They're hardly going to look favourably on a complete change of mind. "Sorry, Officer . . . "' he puts on a high-pitched voice. ' "I made a mistake. Silly old me." Come on. Get real. How many times have you got it wrong already? First David, then poor Elliot. Do you think they're going to listen to you?'

He must have seen something in my face because he laughs. 'They aren't listening, are they? They don't give a shit because they know you're a crap witness and they think you're probably lying anyway. And even if you do manage to convince some man-hating policewoman, do you think the CPS is going to allow it to go to trial? Do you even know how hard it is to get a conviction for rape, even with evidence?' He brings his face close to mine. 'Ah ha. You do. I can see it in your eyes.'

I shove him away. 'You are going to face up to what you did.'

'Is that right?' he says.

It's the derision in his voice that makes me do it, the dripping scorn. I kick him so hard that he cries out. Then I jam my fingers in his eyes and run, but he's faster and within seconds he's caught up. He tackles me, catching me round the waist and propelling me off the path, into the trees and down a wooded incline, branches catching at my hair and my top. We fall on wet ground and roll a few feet. He climbs on top of me and pins me down, one hand covering my mouth, the other gripping my wrists above my head. A tree root jabs painfully into my shoulder blade. Graham darts a glance back up the hill, but we are in darkness now, and all I can hear is birdsong and distant traffic. No one in their right mind wanders round here at night. The gloom is impenetrable and there's no one around, no one to help.

He lets go of my wrists and I lash out at him, but he avoids my flailing arms and turns me over, pushing my face down. I only have time to scream 'Don't!' at him, before my mouth hits soil and rotting leaves. He spreads his hand across the back of my head and keeps it there, his fingers clamped hard around my skull.

I struggle frantically but he forces my thighs apart, pulling at my leggings, his hands on my skin. The realization that he's going to rape me gives me the strength to lift my head and scream, before he shoves it down again. I can feel the effect my terror is having on my body as the strength drains from my muscles, as the messages from my brain become muddled. I can't breathe, I can't move, it's as if all the energy has drained out of me, leaving me paralysed. Is this what happens to trapped animals? My struggles become weaker, the pressure harder, my lungs hurt so much. My vision is pin-pricked with stars.

I shut my eyes tight and picture Jamie cycling in front of me, the night clear and crisp, my feet pedalling round and round, my nose and chin stinging from the cold, but not unpleasantly. A smile plastered on to my face. I feel alive and full of joy. He can't hurt me here.

And then there's a new noise that has nothing to do with me or him: a rush of feet, a scrabbling, before something squat and dark launches itself at us. I turn my head as a paw lands on my neck, the nails so sharp they pierce my skin. Graham lets go of me to shield himself and I cover my face with my arm as the Staffie snarls and sinks its teeth into his flesh.

'Get it off me!' He tries to swing the dog away from him, but it won't let go. Its jaw is locked.

I cry out as figures come running out of the gloom. Five boys flinging bicycles to the ground.

'What the fuck are you doing, you perv? Get off her.'

Graham scrambles, tripping and falling on to the earth beside me. Two of them launch themselves at him, restraining him between them, two others help me to my feet, one heaves the dog away by its collar.

'Call the police, man,' someone yells.

56

Laura

ELLIOT IS OFFICIALLY EXONERATED WITH A FORMAL apology from the Metropolitan Police. I write Phoebe an ashamed and heartfelt apology and push it under her door, but she doesn't respond. Yesterday, I watched from my window as she and Elliot filled a U-Drive van with their belongings and drove away.

The authorities are none too pleased with me either. The only person I can bear to spend time with, who doesn't judge, is Jamie. At weekends, we work on my new flat in Streatham. It's exactly the therapy I need. I follow instructions and he's ruthless, forcing me to properly prepare walls and surfaces before I even look at a paintbrush. We snatch breaks, sitting on dust-sheets with mugs of tea and packets of biscuits. I study him when he doesn't know I'm watching, taking mental measurements of his shoulders, his hands, the length of his fingers; I look for particular gestures and listen for verbal cues. When he rings my doorbell, I list things about him that I remember. Even so, he is always a surprise. We've had the odd mishap, like when, on a trip to the theatre, I waited for him outside the Gents and then accompanied the wrong man back to the auditorium. I realized in time, of course, when his girlfriend caught us up. I did a comedy about-turn. It was only a matter of seconds, and luckily, he hadn't noticed his shadow.

There are few absolutes about face-blindness. The only hard fact is that there is no magic pill; this is not a condition I can train my brain out of, despite what people insist on telling me. It is for life, as much a part of a person as touch or taste. Experiences differ, and we each deal with it in the way that suits us best. Some of us believe in telling everyone over and over again until they get it. Some of us never tell anyone but our nearest and dearest and manage to function, but, as I know only too well, that can be a lonely place. It's hard for us to get to know people and, by extension, it's hard for people to get to know us. Some people, when told, refuse to believe that the condition exists, even when pointed towards the research; and that can be incredibly frustrating. They think it's some made-up thing, an excuse for laziness or social inadequacy; or worse, they think it's a mental health issue. These days I tell people when I need to, but I don't keep a list, and that causes as many problems as it solves.

At S&C, life is proving tricky. I thought long and hard about sending a whole-staff email, but when it came to it, I couldn't do it. Some people know, but not everyone. And people quickly forget what they read in the papers. The company is vast, employing over two hundred people; a commercials factory stuffed with creatives and suits. It is confusing, often panic-inducing, and I've already pulled back into myself. Although I try my best, I really do. My copywriting partner is mixed race, which helps, but they are otherwise a homogenous lot. The men are more self-consciously hipster than they were at GM, dressing in tailored suits and sporting tattoos and beards. The women wear quirky frocks and favour glasses over contact lenses. There are so many more desks to mind-map, so many bodies to keep an eye on. It's a job in itself.

When the days become longer, I start running again. Streatham Common isn't Hampstead Heath, but I like the fact that I'm never far from a road. The demographic of Streatham isn't dissimilar from Kentish Town, a diverse mix of class and ethnicity. There's no pressure to be part of things, to find my tribe. I can exist here.

But Jamie is a sociable man and has lots of friends, to whom he is gradually introducing me. Before we go out, he shows me pictures on Facebook, points out what distinguishes one from another and when we get there he addresses everyone by their name, so often that it feels weirdly contrived, but only I appear to notice. It's good to have a wingman, but ultimately this is my problem.

What happened will never leave me. I can't imagine a

time when I won't feel this way. I am still nervous; still worried that I can't distinguish friend from foe. But Professor Robinson said something to me when I called her last week, which put it in perspective: 'None of us can. Not when it comes down to it.'

Acknowledgements

I owe a huge debt of gratitude to the following: Dr Michael Banissy, Director of Research at the Department of Psychology, University of London, for his professional and invaluable insight into face-blindness. Charles Attlee, for talking to me about his personal experience of the condition, and his wife Annie for her perspective on living with a profoundly face-blind spouse, and for showing me the darkly humorous side. Thanks also to my wonderful agent Victoria Hobbs and her assistant Jo Thompson for their patience with me and excellent suggestions, and to the team at Transworld who have been so enthusiastic about the story: Tash Barsby, Rosie Margesson and Hannah Bright. To my first readers, Lulu and Steve, and to Max for his staunch support. Many thanks to the amazing Primewriters, and in particular to Vanessa Lafaye – a woman of remarkable energy, generosity and talent. You are missed. To the bloggers and tweeters who have been so brilliant and whose passion for books helps fire up my writing in the early mornings – I hope you know you are appreciated.

Emma Curtis was born in Brighton and now lives in London with her husband. After raising her two children and working various jobs, her fascination with the darker side of domestic life inspired her to write her acclaimed debut novel, *One Little Mistake*. *When I Find You* is her second thriller.

Find Emma on Twitter: @emmacurtisbooks

WHEN I FIND YOU

Reading Group Guide

- Were you aware of face-blindness as a condition before reading this novel? What do you think *your* defining characteristic would be for someone with face-blindness? What about your family members, your best friend, your partner?
- Apart from their appearance, what is it about a person that defines them? What is the most important element of someone's 'identity'?
- How does Emma Curtis explore the issue of sexual consent in *When I Find You*?
- How does Laura's condition affect her interactions with the other characters in the novel? Is there a difference between her relationship with male and female characters?
- The only people who know about Laura's condition are her family and Rebecca. If you were face-blind, would you choose to tell people? If not, why not?
- Discuss the theme of secrecy and trust in *When I Find You*. Which characters are keeping secrets, and why? Which secrets cause the most damage throughout the course of the novel, and how?

Have you read Emma Curtis's gripping debut novel?

Vicky Seagrave is blessed: three beautiful children, a successful, doting husband, great friends and a job she loves. She should be perfectly happy.

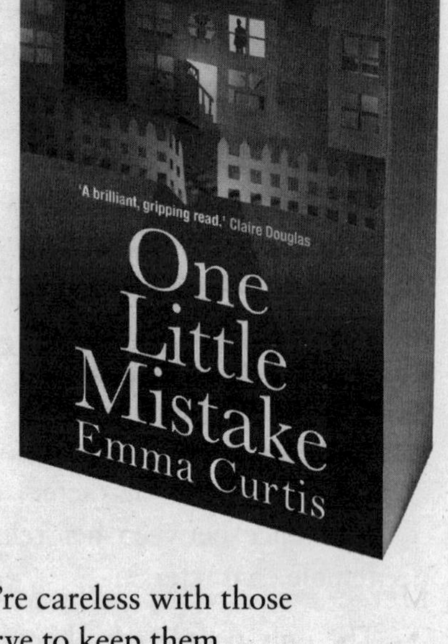

When she makes a split-second decision that risks everything she holds dear, there's only one person she trusts enough to turn to.

But Vicky is about to learn that one mistake is all it takes; that if you're careless with those you love, you don't deserve to keep them . . .

'A compelling page-turner which kept me reading well into the night'
Jane Corry, bestselling author of *My Husband's Wife*

Sixteen years ago, best friends Nancy, Georgia and Lila did something unspeakable. Their crime forged an unbreakable bond between them, a bond of silence. But now, one of them wants to talk.

One wrong word and everything could be ruined: their lives, their careers, their relationships. It's up to Georgia to call a crisis dinner. But things do not go as planned.

Three women walk in to the dinner, but only two will leave.

Murder isn't so difficult the second time around . . .

Available to pre-order now